AN
EMPRESS
OF
EARTH & DARKNESS

By Noelle Rayne

By Noelle Rayne

First Paperback Edition September 2023
First Hardback Edition September 2023
First eBook Edition September 2023

ISBN: 978-1-9196109-6-2 (Paperback)
ISBN: 978-1-9196109-7-9 (Hardback)
ISBN: 978-1-9196109-8-6 (eBook)

www.NoelleRayne.com

A dedication

To my readers—you make every hard night, every sacrifice, every tear, every formatting hell, all worth it. Thank you for returning to this world, you give me light in the darkness.

DISCLAIMER

This book contains words of profanity, adult themes, and scenes of sexual nature.

CALEDORNA

Mountains of the

The Waterfall of Uttara

Helmsdale City

The Fairlands

Huntswood City

Ashdale Forest

The River of Vanadey

The Temple of the Gods

The Lake of Rhiannon

rth

SKYELIR

Tolsah Bay

The Broken Sea of Thorin

en Dimond Mine

Mossgrave

N

W

E

S

THE GODS

 THE MOTHER GOD

 THORIN, GOD OF THE SUN & WAR

 RHIANNON, GOD OF THE MOON & DREAMS

 UTTARA, GOD OF STARS & DAWN

 VANADEY, GOD OF LIFE & BEAUTY

 VELES, GOD OF DARKNESS

THE PRIME

 Chief Commander of the Hunters
Aerrick Stryker

 Alpha of all Shifters
Murk Baxgroll (Wolf)

 King of the Faerie Court
King Oberon

 The Supreme, Queen of all Witches
Unknown

PROLOGUE
TORIN

The smell of blood and stale alcohol was always a prominent feature in the fighting pits. Below the city of Huntswood, where the darkest of souls came to play when the sun went down and forbidden business had to be taken out of sight, ancient tunnels carved their way for miles. It was where the seediest of illegal trades were done in secret passages, and exchanges that couldn't be dealt in the Huntswood Markets would find a sale there. The fighting pits were only a small part of what went on underground, and that's where Torin Blacksteel was tonight.

It had been where he had spent his nights since the last new moon. Since he had finally come to his senses and realised that there were no happy endings for guys like him.

A warrior. A man who had too many scars. A hunter who had to obey his commander above anything else.

It was bloody down here, and brutal. But it was better than being in the Huntswood Tower. That was a fact.

Roars could be heard from men who had just bet their last coin on the losing side of the fight, and the cheers of the bastards who had just won a fortune circled through his ears as he waited in the shadows. Binding the throbbing cuts on his knuckles, he rolled his neck, welcoming the pain from last night's fight. Taking a step from the darkness of the underground pits—a playground for feral beasts —he watched as another fighter geared himself for battle close to the blood-stained ring. There was very little light in the pits, just a few moonbeams that had been trapped in casings hung against the carved-out stone in every corner. Torin could see that the male preparing himself and entering the ring was most definitely Fae— probably around two-hundred years old, since the pompous pricks never aged. His pointed ears peeked through his long braided hair of silver, and his violent eyes were rimmed with something darker.

"Rumour has it that the big bastard worked for the king's court years ago," he overheard a man say as he moved through the crowd.

And given the sheer strength and size of him, it made sense; but since noticing he only had one eye and tallying up the scars on his body, Torin assumed the Fae had been fighting in places like this for a long time. Probably longer than Torin had been alive. The fact that he was still going and hadn't had any injuries that stopped him fighting altogether meant that the big fucker had won most of them.

It was a shame Torin was about to change all that tonight. He might never fight again once he was through with him. Only the hardest bastards fought in the pits. There were no rules, just knock-outs. Sometimes even death was brushed under the rug in the blink of an eye.

Men that fought down here had nothing to lose.

But Torin wasn't in the mood to lose tonight. He wasn't feeling generous, nor was he feeling kind. He was feeling...nothing.

He was empty.

Torin had been emptied of everything the minute his father changed the treaty in his name. The treaty that saw a future with Emara Clearwater as his wife.

The heart-crushing throb that soared through his chest too often these days returned. He shut it down at once. He wouldn't let himself feel anything because when he did, it was soul splitting. He couldn't let himself think of anything other than getting through the day as Emara's guard without talking to her or seeing her. Come nightfall, all he wanted to do was fight like an absolute animal and forget everything about her.

It was the only way.

He stopped himself from moving through the shadows of the crowd as a memory of her face on that dreadful day invaded his mind. Even her name rattled through his bones, shook his heart. He loathed when a memory of her laugh would slip through the iron-clad armour he had built around his mind or when he thought of her soft mouth on his before sleep found him. Or when the recollection of her watching him spar with the glitter of darkness in her eyes overwhelmed his heart.

No one had ever looked at him the way Emara Clearwater did. When she looked at him, she saw every part of who he was.

And fuck, did that hurt like a bitch.

He was still guard to the Empress of Air; there was no getting away from that oath. He supposed that was the true torture of his father's punishment. He still had to be in her life, just not the way his soul longed for. But he and Artem had worked out a pattern to combat encountering her more than his broken heart could handle. Stryker and Coldwell took her training sessions. Torin only really needed to be there to oversee any changes in her schedule and to take the night shift when he wasn't down here spilling blood. Anything that required her to be present as the Empress of House Air, Gideon stood in to meet the *requirement*.

Her betrothed.

Torin pulled back on a flinch, which he knew was an instant mistake. No fucker flinched down here. It was basically the only rule.

The pain in his heart tingled again, reminding him he wasn't numb anymore, but the fact that Torin only took post when there

3

was little to be said sickened him. It gutted him that he couldn't be the one she talked to about her day. He couldn't wipe her tears or comfort her sorrows. He couldn't touch her skin or feel her warmth. He couldn't encourage her not to let the darkness in, and she did, every night. Darkness, like her air, formed around her, circling her like a serpent, only building stronger each day. And Artem was convinced it was because she had a broken heart too. Ever since that ruthless day, he couldn't even look at her without being unable to breathe. His future had been torn to shreds, smashed, and blown into the wind like mere dust.

Viktir would get his day. He just had to pick the right moment. Whether it be tomorrow or in five years' time, his commander would pay for what he had done. His *father* would suffer slowly.

Torin ran a hand over his jaw as it tightened.

Nevertheless, he couldn't think of Emara anymore. Not like that. Not in the way his hands wanted to fight for. Not in the way his very soul sought for. Gideon could make her happy. He could be the man she needed in her role as empress. He had to give her that fighting chance. Someone loyal and reliable, someone balanced.

Someone who wouldn't be ripping apart the world she had just built for herself.

His love for her was forbidden.

So, he had found himself here to somehow take the edge off of the feeling that destroyed his heart. Banishing all the overwhelming feelings, he liked to pretend they were all fully gone.

He made his way over to the dingy bar that had one swinging oil lantern above it, wax seeping out, spilling all over the floor. No one cared to clean it up.

"Rum," he ordered over the shabby den they called a watering hole.

"None," The keeper croaked back at him.

Why was there never any fucking rum down here? It truly was a

An Empress of Earth and Darkness

cesspit. It seemed cheap whiskey or ale that smelled like horse piss was all that was on the menu tonight.

Whiskey it was, then.

He knocked it back faster than the keeper had slid it to him. The man had about three teeth left in his mouth, and hair that had been oiled to his head swept down his dirty, fat, turkey neck. He was pale, as though the sun had never graced his skin, and his eyes were dark, like a nocturnal creature of the pits.

He really was the definition of unsightly.

A ding from the bell sounded, indicating that it was time for the fight to begin, and he welcomed it. He was here to fight until he couldn't fight anymore. To fight until he couldn't feel anything.

Torin turned away from the bar before flicking a coin over his shoulder to the old mole rat, and the crowd parted for him to clear a path to the ring. Swaggering closer to the fighting pit, he could still see the last fight's blood in the ring.

He caught his opponent's gaze, and a cruel grin pulled over Torin's lips.

He would show no mercy. The gambling men of the pits never did like cowards; it was like flinging a broken bird into a nest of hungry wolves. They would be devoured. Savaged.

However, Torin had a feeling this Fae in the ring wouldn't be so cowardly. He watched him move and strike like a trained war snake, practising his hook as he smiled at him. He was fast, he'd give him that, but Torin was faster.

Hearing the roars from the crowd, Torin could no longer make his opponent wait. He ducked under the rope and squared his shoulders, lifting his chin. The sounds of the crowd married with the bell and ignited violence in his veins. It sent an urge for sheer war through his soul. All that was left to do was picture his father's face instead of the Fae's so that each blow could mean something.

It was show time.

5

CHAPTER ONE
GIDEON

The blazing sun warmed the earth enough for Sybil Lockhart to tend to the Tower gardens in her bare feet. Her long jade-green dress blew gently against her creamy skin as she cut back the briar of the rose bushes. Her auburn hair lay curled against her back, shining wildly as the beams of sun hit flecks of fiery reds, vibrant oranges, and strawberry-golds.

As she worked her way along the garden, two hummingbirds swooped down and rested close to her on a tree branch. She smiled at them and dipped her head to acknowledge their presence before she began to include them in her song. Her melody was upbeat but contrastingly soft at the same time. It was wonderful.

Gideon's heart fluttered in a way it shouldn't when one was on duty. He placed a hand on his weapon belt, reminding himself that he was a guard—and only a guard.

He couldn't deny that he liked having Sybil in the Tower. It was easy. She somehow fit into the madness, bringing peace and a comforting energy, especially these past few moons. The Empress of Earth had moved here to help with Emara's recovery after the winter solstice ball, and from that point on, she had just existed within the walls, avoiding a return to her own home.

Gideon assumed it was because of the trauma that had happened to her family there and the murder of her sister by the

Dark Army. Well…the late Supreme, Deleine Orinmore, had been the one to orchestrate the attacks. But he didn't dare give thought to that wretched witch and what she had done to Emara. She was history, her name and legacy all buried in a shallow grave. Torin had made sure of that. Gideon thought that Sybil would need to return to her home at some point, and as her guard, he would travel with her. For as long as she needed the protection, he would be there.

Arlo Stryker was on duty too, and he stood under the safety of a huge willow tree across the grounds, melting into the shade with one hand on the hilt of his short sword. He had been in the Huntswood Markets last night, and Gideon could see the effects of the liquor on his features. The heat didn't seem to be helping his recovery. His russet hair flopped onto his forehead limply, sticking down because of the temperature, and his cheeks were flushed.

Gideon wiped away a bead of his own perspiration that had started to make its way down the side of his temple. The guard tunic really wasn't made for summer months in Caledorna.

"Look, Gideon," he heard Sybil call over to him, and his eyes instantly found her again. "It's a monarch butterfly." She beamed a bright smile that stole his breath, and he walked forward, his eyes fixed on the small creature that fluttered on her index finger. "Isn't she so beautiful?"

He swallowed. "Yes." He smiled back at her. "The colours are remarkable."

"Don't you just love sunny months? Everything blooms." Sybil let out a small giggle and lifted her finger into the air whilst the butterfly took flight. He watched as the small creature circled her, its wings majestically gentle in the summer breeze. The butterfly got so close to Sybil's face, Gideon could have sworn it touched a kiss to the tip of her nose before it floated into the garden again, lost in all of the shrubberies.

"The creatures of the Tower love you." Gideon nodded in her direction.

"And I them." She popped a little shoulder up, and her eyes flickered shut for a second as the sun rays danced across her freckled face. "I love it out here." She craned her neck back and let the beams glow down on her, warmth spreading like a pink ink in her cheeks. "I didn't think I would like to live in a city, but these gardens are beautiful. It makes me feel like I have the best of both worlds."

"Well, it helps that you keep them beautiful," he said softly. "The gardens were always maintained, but with the Empress of Earth here, they seem to have come to life."

Sybil's eyes opened, finding his, and her lips parted to speak, but before she could reply to him, a man's voice shouted, bursting the serene bubble she had created around them.

"Gideon!"

Gideon's head swung to see Marcus Coldwell standing in his grey guard uniform, looking a little flustered. "I have to release you from your post."

Gideon lifted his chin. "You are supposed to be sleeping, Marcus. You took the night shift."

Marcus sighed, his broad chest puffing out. "Yeah, well, warriors don't need sleep, apparently. Commander's orders. He wants to see you in his office. Now." Marcus gave him a wry grin and patted his shoulder.

Gideon sucked in a breath before he nodded to Sybil and bowed. Her lips pushed together into a polite smile, and for a fraction of a second, he wondered if there was a hint of worry in her vast eyes. But she said nothing as Gideon turned his back on her and left for the commander's office, where nothing good was ever discussed.

The knock on his father's office door boomed through the corridor before Gideon slid into the room.

He halted in the threshold as his eyes found Emara Clearwater's. She sat in a leather chair at the opposite side of the wooden desk from his father—his commander. She was dressed in a lilac chiffon dress that complimented her skin tone, and it bared her shoulders to the world elegantly. He took in a breath as her dark eyes met his, tired and swirling with uncertainty. She hadn't been sleeping much, that he knew. Whispers around the Tower had said that she was screaming in the night. And Sybil had told him that she had been letting darkness whirl around her room as nightmares stole her peace. Sybil and his mother had helped her keep the darkness at bay, for now.

Emara lifted her chin in a cold, authoritative way, and Gideon nodded slowly in her direction as he took his place in the other chair across from his father.

Gideon suppressed a shudder.

Viktir cleared his throat. "Thank you both for joining me."

Emara shifted in her seat, causing the leather to creak. She moved her hair from the back of her neck. A rush of air swept in around her, cooling her down, and Gideon was grateful for her gift as he felt the benefit of it too.

Viktir smacked his lips before he began, "It has been a while since our last meeting, and I think it's clear that many moons have passed since I declared my intentions of your alliance to the kingdom. It's true, with the trouble at the palace, I had priorities to take care of before my focus fully set on our *arrangement*. But the majority of my missions are now complete, and this union has my true attention at last."

Gideon's lungs squeezed.

There had been a lot of damage control for Viktir to do, making sure that none of his hunters were involved in the attacks on the witches at the Amethyst Palace or for the kidnapping of Emara Clearwater. Whilst Viktir's eyes had been elsewhere, they had gotten away with their union being at a standstill. Their relationship was...complicated.

"Can I have an update on your status?" Viktir asked as he moved some loose papers around on his desk.

There was a potent silence in the room that lay thicker than the summer air.

"We are still courting." Gideon cleared the lie in this throat. "We will give you an update when we set a date for the engagement to be announced."

"Still courting?" Viktir put his pen onto the table and looked down his long nose that had been broken in more places than one. "What could possibly be left to explore between you?"

Emara's voice was small but stern. "We just need more time. We are still getting to know one another."

"I think I have given you long enough to get whatever was happening between you and my eldest son out of your system. Is that what this is about?" The commander flung a lethal glance towards Emara, and Gideon's mind flashed back to hearing his brother's voice beg his father not to remove the treaty from him. From *them*. "I would have assumed that whilst I was working hard, ensuring your safety within my Tower, that you would have dabbled enough in social experiments with my warriors to last a lifetime. You should be ready to fulfil your duty, Miss Clearwater."

How did Viktir Blacksteel manage to suck the life from every room? He really did have a way with words that could cut into your skin and make you bleed out your own pride.

"And you, Gideon"—his bottle-green gaze landed on him, the wrinkles around his eyes scrunching together—"I assume you have been *courting* Miss Clearwater enough to ensure that this alliance is a successful one?"

His throat dried.

Viktir wanted heirs to the Blacksteel name. It had nothing to do with the success of their marriage. Viktir wanted a strong and powerful alliance, one that could wield elemental value to him. Heirs and magic, that was what this was all about. Power.

A daring, hot anger coursed through Gideon's veins, mixing with guilt and shame. It had been so very clear who Emara's heart had chosen, and this exercise of Viktir's dominance on the clan was truly sickening. He didn't dare take a glance at Emara as he thought of what to say. What lie could he come up with that didn't condemn them both to what "courting" had actually been happening between them?

He opened his mouth to speak, but it was Emara who got there first. "Let me ask you something, Commander Blacksteel."

The tone of her voice was full of unwavering steel, and Gideon's head whipped in her direction.

She remained unfazed by his father as she said, "What professional tone are you setting if you continue to demean me in front of your son, my *proposed* fiancé, by not using my correct title? Is that proper etiquette for an important meeting such as this, Commander Blacksteel? Should I just call you Viktir?"

Gideon's windpipe closed entirely as he whisked his head back to his father.

Viktir's mouth pulled into a taut grin that could have been confused for both anger and respect for her.

Emara continued, "My title is no longer *Miss Clearwater,*

Commander Blacksteel. It is Empress, and I should be addressed as such."

Gideon's heart didn't know whether to jump from his chest and dance or crawl into his stomach and die.

Since the moons had passed on from the winter solstice, Emara Clearwater's heart had hardened. She was one of them now, a valued member of the magical society, Empress of House Air, and a warrior in her own right. In such a short space of time, not only had she won over the hearts of her coven, but she had also earned the respect of the other witches in her efforts to defeat any threats that her faction faced.

Gideon was in awe of her progress, and as he watched her stare down the commander of the Blacksteel Clan, he could do nothing but respect the challenge too. She was fearless.

Or so it seemed.

Viktir gave a cynical laugh. "Please accept my apologies, *Empress*." He clasped his hands together and rested them on a few scattered papers on his desk. "I meant no disrespect. You see, I look at you like you are one of the members of this Tower, and you have stayed within these walls for so long that sometimes I forget you are not. So please understand when I say I forget sometimes that you are a witch with a crown. You have helped raise the wards on this building and restore our protection whilst we sleep. Your fire heats the rooms of my men, and your gifts allow us to communicate with society easily." He blinked slowly, still eyeing Emara like a hawk. "The Clan does not forget these generosities, even when you are not linked to us in marriage."

The commander reached out for the crystal glass on his desk and held it to his lips before savouring its contents. He must know the silence was uncomfortable, and he bathed in its painful glory. Sadistic bastard.

He finished his liquor slowly before raising one finger with a menacing grin. "But what I do need to remind you of, Empress, is that you are only a resident of this Tower for as long as I say you are. You are an orphan, a refugee from Mossgrave that we have taken under our wing. Please make no mistake when I say that you are welcome here, but my patience is wearing thin. For both of you." The commander's eyes slid to Gideon and then back to Emara. "You are here because you are to be Gideon's wife. You are to bare Black-steel boys. Warriors. An heir to our legacy. That is your purpose. That is why you still stay in the comfortable quarters that you do, or you would be on your own."

Gideon choked down a breath as heartbeats pulsed in the room.

Or maybe that was just his own.

"I am here because I provide protection for your men, whether you respect it or not." Emara lifted her chin. "I heal their wounds and I give you as much security as you give me. I am well liked within the community, and that position comes with respect from the elders. I liaise with the prime just as much as you do, and with the same relevance as any man. That, Commander, is all without being a wife. No demon can walk through those doors because I keep them out of your failing wards."

"You don't keep all of them out," Viktir snapped, and his eyes sparkled with an unspoken danger.

Gideon heard Emara's breathing hitch.

"Are you forgetting that I know what blood runs in your veins?" he sneered. "The fact that I am taking a chance on your half-murky blood to produce warriors of my calibre shows how much I respect you. Don't you talk to me of respect. You need to remember, girl, that you have demons walking under your skin. I give you all of the respect you deserve."

Shit.

Gideon could have sworn steam was coming from Emara's ears.

He closed his eyes to regather his thoughts. Shit! This could go sideways, especially now that Emara was painfully quiet.

"Father!" he finally said, sitting forward a little. "That's enough. We decided collectively long ago that we don't care what blood runs in her veins. We know she is of the Light Gods' following. She fights with us. She stands with us. And if she is to be my wife, I beg you, do not use that part of who she is against her. She is our alliance." He looked down at his trembling hands as he stood up to his commander. "And a strong one at that."

His commander ignored him, keeping his eyes on Emara's face. "There are only a select few who know of your blood, *Miss Clearwater,* and should you want it to stay that way, you will obey my orders."

Gideon almost hissed as he took a quick glance at the Empress who sat in the chair next to him. Her skin was flushed now, and he could see how much she was trying to control her anger by the way she had clasped her hands tightly together. She must be trying to control a wave of magic that could blow this room apart.

Viktir sat back in his large chair that swept up higher than his head. "If I were you, I would sign this treaty." He slid a piece of white paper towards Emara. "And I would sign it fast, solidifying your union. You never know what alliances you are going to need if word ever breaks of your ties to the underworld...of whom your father is."

Emara's chest was heaving in rage. The air was warming around them like they had just entered a furness. Suddenly, his collar felt strangling around his neck; he tried to loosen it, but nothing helped.

Viktir raised a scarred hand under his chin nonchalantly. "If rumours were ever to circulate of you being a demon *half-breed,* you are going to need more than just an alliance. You are going to need a credible husband who will support you and legitimise your position as an empress. You will need a strong clan to bulk out your protection, and you will need your coven to feel safe with you on its throne. They need to know you are not a wild card, ready to throw them to your demon king for immortality. After all, a woman needs a husband to ensure normal life, a stable life, to ensure reproduction of magical life—"

"I am sick of hearing about what you think I need, Viktir Blacksteel." Her voice cut through the air like an arrow. "I was more than willing to set aside my feelings on an arranged marriage to suit the needs of my coven before you changed your side of the bargain out of spite. But you are right about one thing; I do need to make sure my alliance is strong, and I need to ensure that my witches are safe. But with you in the thick of my arrangements, I don't feel safe, nor do I feel that it is a credible union. Do you think that you are the only one interested in what I have to offer? Do you think you are the only commander in Caledorna with sons? I think it's about time that I remind you that I am the only Empress of Air in this kingdom. Do not fire threats towards me, Commander. As you can see, I have overcome a lot to be sitting here in front of you, and you are only one man. Rumours fade; alliances are forever."

Emara stood and flicked a look towards Gideon, her midnight hair tumbling over her bare shoulders. Her eyes bore hurt, and if Gideon didn't know her like he did, he wouldn't have noticed the fear in them too. She held her mask well. "I am sorry, Gideon; when I talk of the credible union, it is not a reflection of you. You are a credit to this clan." She dipped her chin, and her hard features softened for the briefest of moments. "Please excuse me. An empress has better things to be doing than tolerating the insults of a man."

Emara bowed her head towards Gideon and then stormed from the room.

Gideon bit into his lip as the door slammed shut. His eyes trailed to his father's face—a face of hard stone and relentless callousness. "Blackmail? Really, Father? You would blackmail her into marrying me? Do you know how low that was to talk of her blood?"

"Gideon..." His father released a deep breath and he repositioned the half-full whiskey glass back on his desk. "Fear is the angle I am going for to ensure this alliance. She is defiant. I told her I would make her bend, and so far, she hasn't. It has gone on too long. Something needs to give." His cold eyes explored Gideon's face. "I used the fact that she fears what would happen to her if people knew of her blood. And that, my son, is her weak spot. She has no one if her coven turns their backs on her, and we need to use that. As for you"—he looked up through hooded eyes—"I am not sure what it is that you are doing to make sure you secure a marriage to the Empress of Air, but it is not working. We have all seen her power. I have to give it to her; she is a force to be reckoned with. The girl knows what she is worth, and I need you to ensure she is not looking elsewhere for an alliance. Do you want to fail me like your brother did?"

Gideon's fists tightened. "A force to be reckoned with? You say that and then you go and treat her like—like she is not an empress of a coven, but a low-bred demon from the underworld. Emara Clearwater is not a toy to be played with, Father, as you have so cleverly pointed out. So why are you toying with her emotions?"

Viktir sat back in his chair again and circled the liquor in the glass once more, letting the smoky aroma of the drink filter into the air. "Because when someone is toyed with long enough, they start to believe that they have no other option but to be a part of your game."

Gideon let out a bitter laugh. "And is that where I fit into all of this? Is that all I am to you? A part of your games? Your pawn?" He flinched as he recalled Torin's words.

Viktir cut him off harshly, "You are not my pawn, Gideon; you are my son."

Gideon's heart beat like a war drum at his father's words. He never acknowledged their relationship or gave any sentiment to the fact that they were anything else but commander and hunter.

Viktir leaned forward and pushed the treaty towards Gideon. "Let's not bring our emotions into decisions that need to be made by warriors, son. Your task is simple. Get her to agree to the treaty and set a date for the union. Courting is officially done. That's a command."

Gideon's fingers hovered over the paper before he snatched it and left the room without looking back.

CHAPTER TWO
GIDEON

A s Gideon made his way through the corridors to the east wing of the Tower, his blood was fizzing.

His father had called him *son*. His commander had called him *son,* and it annoyed Gideon that it meant so much to him. It shouldn't. It should have been a normal thing, but it wasn't. That annoyed him because the minute he had left the Commanding Office, he knew he had been played.

Viktir had played his weakness too, not just Emara's.

Somehow, he always felt exploited after leaving the Commanding Office. The paper in his hand felt wrong. The treaty between his clan and House Air burned his hand like he was holding a hot spindle.

It just felt...wrong.

How could it feel so wrong when it was something that he had been willing to fight for not long ago?

Finally standing outside her door, he knocked three times and called her name. "It's Gideon. Can you let me in?"

The Gods only knew how many times over the last few months he had begged outside this very door for her just to talk to him. He had tried so hard. He had tried everything he could. He had to smooth things over between them. It was an order.

The handle turned quickly, and Artem Stryker opened the door.

He shook his newly tattooed head—an inked arrow flew through the shaved part of his hair—and pulled a face that gave a warning. "Tread lightly, my man. Tread lightly."

Gideon nodded and walked past the warrior who deserved more credit than he was getting right now. Artem was practically a one-man-band of protection at this stage. With Magin gone and Torin's absentee nature, Artem was holding the fort together for the Empress of Air.

Gideon's gaze found her instantly. Emara lay curled beside the big bay window, perched against an array of coloured cushions. She didn't take her gaze off the city view as he came into the room.

She was in her favourite thinking place.

She didn't even cast her eyes over him as she said, "If you came here in your father's shadow to coax me into signing that Gods-forsaken treaty, you can see yourself out, Gideon."

Gideon centred himself and placed his hands (and the treaty) behind his back. "I am here to check if you are all right after...after that meeting."

She turned to face him then, rage still burning bright in her eyes. "Do you think you would be all right if the commander threatened to use your weakness against you?"

"He already does." It was out his mouth before he could stop it. "He does it every day."

She stilled, her eyes finding something on her hands. "I am sorry, Gideon. I didn't mean to—"

"It's okay," he insisted, walking a little closer. "I don't like what he did in there either. I don't agree with him using your secrets against you. It's a dirty move. I hate how he does that. I wish I could change it."

Gideon could feel Artem stiffen behind him. He was one of the protectors of Emara's secret. "I know," was all she said before looking out at the city below again, the wetness of her eyes highlighted by the lowering sun. "I hate that he has something over me. Something that I can't change."

Gideon nodded and walked over to where she lay against the backdrop of the Huntswood. She looked so at home. "He told me after you left that courting is over, but I am sure I can push it out for another month or two. We don't need to rush anything. We can make this work. But we need to come up with a plan. Maybe you could fake an illness for a few weeks."

Even if it wasn't what she wanted, even if *he* wasn't what she wanted, he would still do it to protect her. He would do anything to protect her. A dull ache lingered in his chest.

A horrible laugh left her throat; it didn't sound like her. "Gideon, my time of pushing this inevitability back has come to an end." Her eyes met his, and like always, his heart hammered in his chest when she did. "And you know it too. This haunts my every waking moment, and just when I think I am done with the pain of my nightmares, I dream of this too." She splayed out a hand, acknowledging the paper that he thought he had hidden behind his back. "This is my true nightmare. It's not my choice. Torin gave me that choice back, and your father has ripped it away. He talks of my blood...he is the monster."

Gideon stood before the stinging in his heart took over and his eyes found his boots. "I wish I was him. I wish I could be my brother for you, but I am not. I am so sorry for that."

Emara's head turned so quickly to face him. "Please don't say that. You shouldn't be sorry. You don't want this either." She stood, the sadness overwhelming her eyes. "I can see it on your face, Gideon. It is killing us all, not making us stronger. You don't want this. None of us do."

Shit, only Thorin knew what he wanted. His heart was being pulled in every direction possible.

"All I want is for you to be happy and safe," he whispered, more than aware that Artem Stryker's eyes were on his own boots now too.

Emara's throat bobbed. "Maybe if I—we could just get through to Torin, maybe if you told me—"

"No, Emara." The voice belonged to Artem, and he began to walk forward to stand near Gideon. "We are not telling you where he is. He'd kill us. He doesn't want you to know. You need to stop asking us."

Hurt splashed across her face, and it was so painful to see her heart continuously break.

"We made a promise to him, Emara." Gideon's voice was so small he didn't recognise it. "We promised him that if he left the Tower, we wouldn't tell you where he was. It's not safe for you to go after him."

Emara bit her lip and folded her arms around herself. She seemed to ponder over thoughts, and Gideon wasn't sure if he liked it when she was quiet. He shot a glance at Stryker; his expression was puzzled, confirming that he was in the same boat.

Seconds later, she had moved to her bathing chamber and come back out fully cloaked. She brushed past Gideon's shoulder, and Artem began to move after her.

"Excuse me." Artem pulled on her cloak, and she turned to him with fire lighting in her eyes. "Where do you think you are going?"

"I need to see him, Artem. If I am signing any treaty, I need to speak to him first. I need to see it in his eyes that he has truly given up the fight."

The fight for them.

Gideon moved then too. "You won't find him." He managed to put himself in between the door and the Empress. She walked towards Gideon anyway. "Emara, listen to me. You won't find him."

She halted. "And why is that, Gideon?" She looked around. "Because you all hide secrets from me?"

"Because you have no idea where you are looking." Artem grinned dangerously.

That didn't faze her. "Then I guess I will start with the taverns in the markets. Surely, I will hit a bullseye at one point."

"You won't," Gideon interjected. "It's not safe in the markets for an empress. Not alone."

"Then come with me."

"No," both hunters said, unified.

She let out a frustrated breath. "I am done pretending that I am some unskilled witch who can't defend herself and that he is not out there hurting, possibly drinking too much, and on the route to self-destruction after having declared a civil war against his father. I have sat here for months and played the role of the self-controlled empress, and I have been nothing short of miserable. As I was reminded tonight, I am a half-breed, not a full-blooded witch, which means I need to fight a little bit harder than everyone else here for what I want. And I will put up a fight a little bit longer because Torin did that for me when I needed him to." Her voice broke, as did Gideon's heart. "I must fight for him. I can't pretend that he didn't make promises to me, Gideon; I am sorry, but I can't. Your father is putting you in the crossfire of that and it is not fair." She paused. "And if Torin no longer wants to hold up those promises, then my heart will break, but at least I will know for sure and I can *fulfil my duty*. I need to hear it from his own mouth. If what we had wasn't real, he will let me go. And if it wasn't real, then I will let him go too. But you need to let me try and get through to him. Please."

Artem shook his head and then gave Gideon the eye.

And maybe she was right. She had a huge point. How could *he* go through with a marriage if Emara loved his brother, chose his brother? How could he sleep next to her at night and give her everything a marriage had to offer if her heart was spoken for? If her heart would never be his? He would have no other way of finding out if Torin just lurked in the shadows of his union. If his brother would always be the other person in his marriage, could he really go through with it? Would that really be the best alliance for his clan?

But what other option did Gideon have?

If the Gods had willed Emara and Torin struck by fate, Gideon had to know too. He had to test it properly.

Maybe he should tell her.

"He's not in the taverns, Emara." Gideon hung his head.

"Whoa, whoa, whoa." Artem placed a hand on his shoulder and patted him down. "Hold on there, buddy, we are not giving in to her that easily. That's what she wants. I've put up a fight for months. I am not going to let you ruin that because she has batted a few eyelashes."

"Giving in to her?" Emara reeled. "Batted a few eyelashes?"

Artem spun. "Yes, giving in to you. Luckily, my heart doesn't lie with you and therefore I can think straight and not with *little* Arty." He threw a look at Gideon, and Emara pulled a disgusted face. If it weren't such a serious conversation, Gideon might have laughed. Artem glanced back to Emara. "That's what Gideon is about to do here, give in to you, because the Blacksteels seem incapable of standing up to you. But I won't falter. My brain is stronger than little Arty is—which isn't so little, by the way."

"You really are revolting," Emara scoffed.

Artem turned back to Gideon, unfazed by her repulsion. "Torin will fucking kill us if we tell her where he is, never mind allow Little Miss '*I Want To Wander About Without My Guards Because I Am A Big Strong Empress*' to head into the underground alone."

Gideon straightened as Artem stiffened.

"The underground?" Emara exclaimed.

"Fuck." Artem ran a hand down his face that was covered with a detailed skull as he turned ghostly white.

"Well done on containing that top secret information, Stryker."

24

Gideon clapped his hands. "You did such a marvellous job. Maybe you should worry about yourself next time and not about me since you and *little Arty* are absolutely shit at keeping secret information *secret!*"

Artem threw him a rude gesture and looked down at his pants. "He didn't mean that. He's just an angry Blacksteel."

Emara's hands flew out from under her cloak. "Are we talking about the same underground that runs below the city?" Her eyes bulged from her face. "Where trade dealings the markets won't even allow take place?"

"Shit, shit, shit." Artem inhaled and then exhaled, scratching his head. "Can you not just forget I said that?"

"Artem, this isn't funny. Why is Torin underground in the tunnels? What is down there for him?" She looked from Artem to Gideon, who both stood quiet. "Answer me."

Wind blew through the room, hot and heavy, bristling Gideon's hair and touching his skin.

"Emara, you don't want to know what Torin is doing down there. It's not important," Artem tried to reason with her.

"It's not important? Are you joking right now? Of course it's important; nothing that happens down there is legal and everything that happens is dangerous, so I think you will find it is extremely important to me. If he is making some kind of dark deal—"

"Look"—Gideon stepped towards her—"how about Artem and I go and give him a message from you?"

"Over my dead body are you going to see him without me. This is my fight." She placed her hands on her hips.

"It might be your dead body if you get caught in a brawl in the fighting pits."

Gideon let out a sigh and pinched his nose. "For fuck's sake, Artem!"

"I've done it again, haven't I?" Artem sighed, cringing.

"Yup." Gideon let out a long breath.

"This is witchcraft," Artem challenged and pointed at Emara, who had gone scarily quiet. "She is doing this to me. I am normally good at keeping secrets but Little Miss *I Need to Know Everything* just has a knack for ripping the secrets from my tongue."

Gideon rolled his eyes. "She's hardly *ripped the secrets from your tongue,* Stryker."

"The fighting pits?" Emara had paled. "The fighting pits?"

"Emara, let me explain." Artem tried to block her exit to the door now too.

She batted one hand and Artem's monstrous body was moved aside like a feather in the wind. He slammed against the wall, and her eyes pinned on Gideon. "Move out of my way, Gideon Black-steel, or you are next."

Gideon cursed under his breath and moved to the side as Emara blew the door open with one flick of the wrist. She peered over her shoulder and stopped as she left the threshold of her chambers. "You are either with me or you are not. And if Torin finds out you have let me go to the pits of the underground myself, I don't fancy your chances. He is still my lead guard."

Gideon cursed again, and Artem mirrored him as he pulled himself upright. They both gave each other a look that said the same thing—this was going to be a disaster—and followed her out the door.

CHAPTER THREE
EMARA

The midnight black cloak was too heavy for this kind of heat, but as she required the hood to hide behind, it was non-negotiable, especially for where she was headed. The weight of the material pressed into her sweltering skin as threads of hair began sticking to her neck, weighing down her shoulders.

She took a breath—and wished she hadn't.

The smell was repugnant, and this was only the opening to the underground tunnels. What would it be like under there?

Artem Stryker—her only working guard—walked towards the opening, where protectors stood in armour, strapped head to toe in weaponry. They were not Hunters, but guards of the Minister of Coin.

Of course he facilitated this place.

As Artem spoke in hushed tones to them, Gideon nudged her gently. "Are you sure you want to do this?" He moved to stand in front of her, and she was secretly glad that they had both decided to join her on her mission to speak with Torin. "An empress should not be seen in a place like this. We can turn back."

Emara finally lowered her hood, and a dry breeze kissed her skin, but it wasn't enough to take the edge of the stifling night air. "As the Empress of Air, I will decide where I should be seen and where I shouldn't."

Gideon's lips clamped together, and he took a moment before he answered her. "I don't know if it's a good idea for you to see him like this. He's not in a good way, Emara. He is *different* when he's down here."

For a second, she wondered when Gideon had last seen him down here, and maybe that had been why Torin had been sporting all sorts of cuts and bruises yesterday when she had seen him heading to his chambers.

Emara lifted her chin, like Naya had taught her. "Then all the more reason for us to get him out of here."

The silence was broken between them when the protectors opened the doors to the underground and Artem let out a whistle for them to move forward. Whatever he had said to get them in, Emara would never know.

"Keep your hood up," Artem advised as he pulled at her hood, taking the first steps to descend into the darkness. "There could be creatures down here that would sell you to the Dark King for a shot of whiskey."

A crash of nervous waves hit into Emara's stomach, churning like an emptying bath.

Exactly how terrible was the underground?

Surely, it couldn't be more tortuous than her own mind at this point.

Viktir Blacksteel wasn't only punishing Torin by announcing Gideon as her suitor, but her too. It had been six full moons since that horrendous moment when Torin declared war against his father, and it had taken four full moons to stop the tears from falling down her cheeks every time she thought of it.

The thought of marrying Gideon should feel right, but it didn't.

He was understanding and patient. Of course, that made her feel worse. He was a good man. He had his flaws, but overall, anyone would be lucky to have him. He had tried so terribly hard with her after Viktir made the announcement to the prime that his second son would marry for the alliance. And just to be a total bastard, the commander had sent out the news by fireletter to every hunting family in the kingdom.

Poor Gideon had done everything he could to help mend the relationship they had once had. Strawberries in the morning with a note to wake up to,. gifts of flowers and dinners of courtship. He was...

Not Torin Blacksteel.

Just before she was taken by Silas and Ethan, the Supreme's guards at winter solstice, she had given everything to Torin. Her heart, her virtue, her soul. She had chosen him and he had chosen her and would always choose her. He had vowed to protect her with his life. He had vowed to worship her until the sun overtook the moon every morning. Her heart had chosen, no longer conflicted by how she felt about the Blacksteel brothers, one fire and one ice. The heart wanted what the soul truly craved, and after shedding her emotional barrier at the Waterfall of Uttara, she knew in her gut that she craved Torin Blacksteel. His crystal-blue eyes, his golden skin, his inky black hair. The way his soft lips curved into a wicked grin every time he taunted her. His lethal darkness. Her soul knew his. Her darkness knew his, too.

She had seen the pain in his face for weeks after his father's announcement, the longing in his eyes and the yearning to have her. He wanted to be close to her any time he was on duty or they were in the same room. Fear broke through her heart for him when she started to notice his pain turn to anger and then into nothing.

She knew that was why he had been disappearing so often. It had been too much. Too much to see her every day, knowing they could never be together.

She had understood for some time that he was taking it hard, but after a few moons passed and his behaviour morphed into something so destructive, she'd felt enraged. They had built something together. He had vowed to protect her. He had taken an oath to be her guard and she was supposed to trust him with her life. And here she was, going down into some seedy fighting pit to pull him out of it before someone from the prime noticed that he was avoiding her and he was exiled altogether.

Being an empress, she had to make political moves, and fast. She was running out of time to choose another guard for her trio after Magin's death, and she didn't want to have to replace Torin too.

She had been so lucky to have her friend, Sybil, stay within the Huntswood Tower because at this rate, they were practically sharing guards. Artem and Marcus had been taking turns in Torin's absence to train her with almost every weapon possible. However, the weapon that still called to her was her spear—*the Agnes.* Funnily enough, the present that Torin had gotten her for winter solstice was currently strapped to the outside of her leg. Unknown to the prime, she had used it a few times on demons in Huntswood or the Ashdale forest when she joined in on the hunting from the shadows.

"Can you see all right?" Gideon asked from behind her, his voice wafer thin as they made their way through a dark, damp tunnel. Both guards having hunter blood meant they could see in the dark much clearer than she could. However, Artem seemed to know the way a little too well.

Emara sparked a flame on one finger and then rolled her hand to make a ball of light, her own beacon. "I can now."

The flame burned bright in the middle of her hand, steady and composed. It was easy for her now. Natural. But she wasn't anywhere near discovering half of what she could do, a fact that Naya Blacksteel liked to remind her of every day.

After a while of walking down a tiny path that looked like it could crumble at any given minute, a rowdy crowd could be heard in the distance. It sounded too animalistic for any of them to be human.

"We're close." Artem turned to face her and stilled for a second. The light from the small beacon of fire danced up to reach his under eye. "Whatever you do, don't get involved in any gambling or fighting. Leave that to us. But if you must use your weapon to protect yourself, don't falter. I mean it, take them out. The men down here are foul. Do. Not. Hesitate." He looked at Gideon too, and he nodded. "Okay, let's move."

Emara snuffed out the flame in her palm and followed Artem Stryker until a murky light could be seen at the end of the tunnel.

The boisterous roars of the crowd were like nothing Emara had ever heard before—and she had been in La Luna on a full moon with the Baxgroll wolves. They could be rather savage in the tavern, but this place did not have the security of the wolves she now called friends. Emara couldn't see the fighting pit yet due to her oversized hood and lack of height, but she could hear where the noise— grunts of pain and the thuds of punches and kicks—was coming from.

The noise of two men destroying each other for a crowd. For coin. For sport.

A spiral of utter dread worked its way into the pit of her stomach.

As much as she didn't want to look, she had to know if it was *him* fighting. Why else would he be here?

Making her way through the crowd, pushing past the heavy muscle and stale ale, Emara saw a space in the thronged crowd, a table littered with glasses but unoccupied. They claimed it before anyone else could.

The crowd erupted as a punch landed properly, forcing her attention to the fight in the pit.

Her heart stopped.

It *was* him.

The warrior who owned her heart.

Torin Blacksteel.

An overwhelming urge to run to him pushed into her legs, almost taking over, but she rooted her feet to the floor. Almost instantly, she noticed how badly he was hurt. Her heart rate doubled. Tripled. Her stomach hit rock bottom. There was a cut above his left eye that was now swelling in size, shoving down upon his eyelid. Crimson blood poured from his open wound, and instead of wiping it away, he corrected his stance, unfazed by the amount of gore. He was slick with sweat, and his skin looked darker under the gloomy moon lamps that hung overhead in a dark orange glass casing. They swung back and forth like a pendulum as the vibrations from the fight and atmosphere caused the whole place to quiver. He was in nothing but fighting leathers on the bottom. His feet were as bare as his torso, and the only thing that could be spotted on his top half was the tape that bound his hands. His inky black hair was soaking with sweat and possibly blood. As he lunged for his opponent, Emara saw the bruising on his ribs, his back, his arms...

Sick crept up her throat.

"Kill him," one man roared from nearby, banging a heavy fist on a rickety table that threatened to break.

"Finish him, Blacksteel," another bellowed, spit spraying from his mouth.

Gideon shifted uncomfortably beside her, and it was then she placed a hand on his arm. It was his brother in the ring, after all. She knew he would be feeling this too. This thunder would be in his heart like it was in hers now.

Torin moved like a winter wind, cold and deadly, and hit the silver-haired male right on the chin. His jaw snapped, his head wrenching to one side, and the crowd flared up like a toxic flame as he spat out blood and possibly teeth.

"He's Fae," Artem shouted to Gideon across the standing table as Emara noticed the slight point in his ears. "And a big bastard. But he doesn't have the skills Blacksteel does. He's slower. Tired. And the guy has one eye, for Gods' sake. Torin should win."

"Let's hope." Gideon watched on again as he cracked his neck. "The Fae, he's probably an ex-guard of the king's court. Probably committed a crime against the king and found himself here."

The Fae landed a punch on Torin's cheek and then a knee smashed against his ribs.

Emara flinched as shouts and terrible taunts were hurled from the crowd that was hungry for blood.

"Try not to do that down here," Artem told her.

"Do what?" she quizzed, finally peeling her eyes away from Torin.

"Flinch." He looked around, scouting for trouble. "It makes you an easy target."

She swallowed any fear that started to creep in and looked back to where Torin was standing in the ring with a smile full of sin, his hands up, ready to punch. Even as blood gushed from his lip and his eyes were dark with monstrous danger, she couldn't help but feel her heart swell and threaten to burst for him.

He was glorified violence. Her heart should not connect with that.

But maybe that was her darkness.

It had been coming to the surface a little more. It was harder to control than all her other elements. Even now, it buzzed around her fingertips for release. Ever since the chains broke from her neck in the Amethyst Palace, and the black tendrils of smoke emerged from her hands, she had been desperate to use her darkness. She shouldn't think like that; she couldn't think of the very element that

grew in her blood from the underworld. The more she acknowledged it, the more it came alive, and she had a meeting with the
prime just around the corner. She had to focus on getting Torin back
in some form of order. She wouldn't let this place destroy him. He
was her lead guard, and if he was taken from that post...

She wasn't going to let that happen.

The crowd roared as Torin struck again, and this time, he kept
striking, like a starving snake who had found its prey. Blood and
teeth flew across the room before the Fae went tumbling down to
the mat.

"Get up, you lousy Fae prick, and end that Blacksteel bastard," a
man beside Gideon roared. "Kill the Hunter. Make him bleed out."

Before Emara could even clutch Gideon's uniform, he punched
the man on the nose. Blood burst everywhere. Emara gasped a little
as a fully fledged riot broke out around her.

"Fucking knew this would happen." Artem sighed and rolled his
eyes. "No one talks badly about the Blacksteels but the Blacksteels,"
he said before turning and landing a booted foot in the face of a
man who had come at Gideon with a small sword.

Emara had trained like a true hunter these last few months, and
she was ready to fight anyone who came at her. She braced herself.

"I thought we would be in here a little longer than five minutes
before I had to break noses, G," Artem shouted over the commotion,
pulling another man off Gideon.

Gideon came up for air after landing two punches and turned to
Emara. "Get out of here. We will get you at the entrance. Follow the
tunnel to the stop and wait for us there."

Emara shook her head and dug her nails into her palms. "Absolutely not. I didn't come here for nothing."

It was then she unsheathed her favourite weapon from her leg
and pressed in the beautiful ruby that lay in the middle of it. The
stunning spear turned into something longer and more dangerous

and she felt a rush of adrenaline fill her muscles as it elongated in her hand.

A bald man with an eye patch that looked like it had been dipped in tea made his way towards her. As he bared his teeth that looked like rows of condemned buildings, broken and neglected, a revolting smile pulled his lips apart.

Artem came closer to her as he pushed a man out of his way like he weighed nothing at all. "Don't—"

She pushed out her hand that held *the Agnes*. "I've got this, Artem."

"Oh, I know, I was only coming to say do *not* let anyone harm you, or the Blacksteels will boil my head and bathe in my blood." He winked and leaped to his next victim in the crowd.

It wasn't long before a mob had stopped watching the actual fight in the ring and began wondering what was happening in the hordes of fights breaking out on the floor. If they weren't getting in on the action, they were passing around coin, making another bet on the ongoing brawl.

"Three gold coins on them not making it out here alive," she heard a man roar.

"I'll bet ye four," confirmed another.

The bald man standing in front of Emara was now laughing at her as she held up *Agnes,* showing them how lethal she was.

She would give him something to snigger about.

"Do you know how to work that pole, sugar?" He laughed, and the men standing at his back did too. "Should you not be dancing around that instead of holding it, pretending like you know how to use it?"

Emara gave him an unimpressed glare.

His vile tongue licked his cracked lips as he said, "Are you going to stand there and wave your little stick, or are you going to take off your cloak and show us a good time?" His beady little eyes wormed their way across her body, and the other men all hastily agreed.

Say nothing, she thought. *Keep him thinking that I'm intimidated by him.*

She pouted a little. "You see, I could dance here with this pole for you," she said as the crowd got a little heavier where she stood. "Or I could just knock your disgusting little teeth out with it." She raised an eyebrow as a cruel smile broached her lips, and the corners of his mouth pulled down in confusion.

She moved, finding a weakness in his confusion—always finding a weakness—and struck.

She whacked the spear so hard across his face that stars dazzled in his eyes as his body fell to the floor.

The men around her roared in laughter and shock, some already dipping into their pockets for more coin to wager.

Finally, she looked up, knowing magic was swirling in her eyes. But she knew she wouldn't gain any respect down here if she fought with magic. No. She had to fight the old-fashioned way. She looked at all the men who were standing ogling her. She found that terrible smile on her lips again. "Anyone else wanna see me *dance* with my *pole?* I'm pretty good."

CHAPTER FOUR
TORIN

His Fae opponent hit the floor of the ring with a smack, and he didn't get back up. He didn't even twitch. That was a good sign—for Torin.

It looked like his night of oblivion was just about to begin, the cheap whiskey of the underground numbing his wounds until he woke the next day, but out of the corner of his eye, he saw a spear cut through the air. It hit its target, knocking a man into a table and shattering the glasses on it.

He stopped dead.

The spear had a reddish glint as it flew through the air.

It couldn't be.

He had kept his whereabouts a secret. Only Gideon and Artem knew of his extracurricular activities.

Wiping the blood from his cut eye and leaving his foe on the floor to sleep off the fight, he moved towards the ropes to get a better view. He noticed his white hand wraps were now tarnished with crimson as he placed a hand over his eyes to see out into the crowd. He realised quickly that no one was watching him anymore, their attention on the messy tornado of limbs and bodies that was causing chaos in the centre of the crowd.

Everyone seemed to be engrossed.

"Hey," he shouted over the brawl to a bystander who was taking coin from a Shifter. "Hey, who are they betting on?" he asked, still watching the crowd to see if his eyes were betraying him. They did that quite a lot in crowds. They imagined her standing amongst the crowd with her stunning tanned skin and midnight hair falling around her shoulders, tumbling down her arms. They imagined her ruby-red lips pulling into a smile, her eyes cosmic and stargazed.

"Some bitch with a spear has taken out a few men. Her two bodyguards started it, though. This lot are placing bets on who will be the first one t' die," the weasley man stated as he took a few more coin, counted them, and placed them into a pouch on his belt. "My bets are on the girl. Apparently, she is a witch who can fight. 'Magine that," he cackled. "Covens coulda been doin' with her a few months ago before the Dark Army started stringin' them up by their necks—"

Before Torin could hear the rest, he leapt over the ropes that encaged him, already swinging punches to make his way through the violent crowd to get to where he needed to be.

The first person he saw was Artem Stryker; with his inked hands and his deadly punches, he was giving it hard to a massive Shifter Torin knew to be were-coyote.

A normal night in the pits, then.

Next, he saw Gideon's nimble frame, ducking glasses, punches, kicks, chairs.

He almost laughed.

A gleam of gold and silver whirled past his face, and then a banner of silken black hair dove past him. She was quicker than expected, but it was her. He would have known her anywhere, even if he were blindfolded. His soul could find her anywhere.

Reaching out, he caught her and clutched her to his chest. Her feisty little elbow was quick to swing into his already bruised ribs, and the power behind it could have caused a serious crack. He blew out a breath, still trying to hold on to her.

She pulled back, ready to attack him, Agnes at his throat. Her eyes had that steely fire in them, burning as bright as he remembered, and it almost undid all the numbing he had accepted into his heart.

One fucking look.

The blade almost pierced his skin, but a flicker in her eyes told him she had been so caught up in the fight to notice it was him. And that was the way it should be. He was proud of her. No distractions.

"Put down the sharp weapon, angel. I like my throat the way it is."

She didn't.

She secretly loved the chaos, thrived in it, and when he saw her like this amidst it all, it did something to him that he couldn't explain. He swallowed down another dose of numbness and hoped it travelled to his icy heart.

Their gazes burned for a minute longer than they should have as she lowered her weapon from his throat.

"Your feet are too close together, distribute your weight," he said finally as the violence still unfolded around him. No one would touch her, though, not while he was there. They wouldn't fucking dare.

Her eyes narrowed, the glittering fading to something dark and cold. It was the mask he had seen her wear around the Tower, the one she struggled to keep intact. He knew she was hurting too, and he had caused a lot of it. He had finally had the courage to pull away from her, thinking that giving her that space would allow her to give Gideon the chance that he deserved. His brother was good, through and through. She was an empress, and as much as it killed him inside, he knew Gideon could take care of her.

"In case you didn't notice, Torin Blacksteel, you are not my trainer anymore. You have no right to critique me." She sneered at him.

Why did he want to kiss her already? It had been two fucking seconds.

"I will always correct you when you are not doing something the way you should. Sloppy foot work never did anyone any favours. Or have you forgotten that?"

"Neither did fighting in the underground pits and drinking yourself into a coma every night, but here we are." She shot him a dangerous glare.

She was pissed. So entirely pissed off with him, but so fucking enticing. That scowl. Those lips...

It was incredible what she could do to him with a scowl.

He kept his mask on, keeping a casual smugness in place. He didn't move his hand from her waist, and she didn't do anything to remove it either. He leaned in, and his voice was rich with danger. "You shouldn't be here, angel. Tell me which one of my brethren I should stab first."

"I can be wherever I please." She glared back at him. "And you won't be touching either of them, you utter ass."

Just then, a large lump of a man flew through the air, almost landing on her back. Torin pulled her out from underneath the fat beast before she could hit the ground. He swept her up over his shoulder like he had in the Amethyst Palace and proceeded through the crowd, no one daring to touch them. He couldn't speak to her out here without being interrupted, and that could make him even more murderous than normal.

"Put me down you big...not nice...prick," she screamed.

He allowed a laugh to hiss past his throat. "Someone needs to rinse their mouth out with soap. Or work on better insults. I can't believe you have spent months with me and *that's* the best insult you can come up with."

She used her spear to beat into his back whilst trying to knee him in the chest. "Fuck you! How about that?"

"Slightly better. A little mundane." He tried his hardest not to let a grin appear on his face.

It was cute. So feisty. And so not his to appreciate.

He frowned.

"Stop struggling," he said as he moved through a dark tunnel. "I will put you down in a second."

She punched his back this time. "I don't have a second, you absolute..."

She went quiet.

"Struggling for another swear word that won't make you feel *dirty?*" he jested.

She never did like profanity much. And it amused him when she used it.

The *big not so nice prick* was entertained.

"Just shut up!" she screamed as he made their way through an opening in the old stone that led to a preparation room. A lot of the fighters used them before a match, but Torin never did like them much. It felt more like a cage before he was unleashed. And he liked to roam before a fight, letting the vicious energy of the crowd soak into his skin.

Walking in, he slammed the door shut and placed her down.

She fixed herself before straightening and pushing the wild hair from her face. His heart crunched as the last moments they had spent together seeped into his memory; he had swept the silky hair from her beautiful face, and she had looked at him like he was the only star in a sky full of darkness.

"Why are you in the fighting pits?" he said with a little more anger this time.

She shouldn't be here; he couldn't get carried away with the fact that she was.

She ignored his question and just stared at him, her lip a little swollen from someone's blow.

White-hot anger poured into Torin's veins. and his fingers flexed before turning into a fist. The amusement of her being here passed quickly and the startling reality of the danger she was in crept in, sobering his buzz. "I will not ask again, Emara. Why are you here? Who told you about this place?"

She swallowed, the truth lying thick in her throat, not willing to come out that easy. "I—"

Just as she began to speak, the door flew open and in bounced Artem Stryker and Gideon.

Not giving another thought, he grabbed Artem by the tunic and growled, "Why is Emara Clearwater down here? Huh? Did we not have a deal?"

Artem pulled at Torin's hands, but he shoved him back against the wall. "Get the fuck off me, Blacksteel."

He heard Emara squeal something, but the buzzing rage drowned her out. Before he could hit Stryker's jaw, Gideon pulled Torin back.

"She's here because of you," his brother spat as Torin turned to face him. "Like you didn't know that. She is here because of you. No one else." A little venom washed over his tongue and then he glanced to where she stood—but only for a moment, because it was all he could bear. Her eyes. The hurt crept into her face as she tried to stand so proudly to mask it all.

He almost crumbled there and then.

But he fought it. He had to.

"Emara, you need to go," was all he said.

"I don't need to do anything I don't want to," she battled back, her voice losing the fight she had in it a few minutes prior. "I need to talk to you."

"There is nothing left to say," his ghost said to her without even looking at her face. "Why the fuck did you bring her here?" he asked his brethren, the yell vibrating off the ancient walls of the underground tunnels.

It wasn't safe. Not for her. Not here. If one of these dodgy bastards got a sniff of who she was, he had no idea what they would do to sell her, kill her, or worse.

"You know how determined she can be," Artem said, straightening his tunic sleeves that were covered in blood.

"I don't care how determined she is. It is not safe for her down here and you both fucking know that." He scowled at them both, and he could feel the veins in his neck pulling through his skin.

Emara took a few steps forward. "Let me tell you what's not safe, Torin. Only having one guard in my unit."

He shot her a cutting stare. "I told you to make the changes. Transfer someone else in."

She blinked a few times and then continued, "*What's not safe* is not having my guard trio in unity. Or a trio at all, in fact."

She hadn't picked another guard since poor Magin had been murdered, and one had not yet been appointed by the prime that had much more pressing matters to deal with. They were up to their balls in investigations due to the traitorous hunters who had chosen the Dark God over their oath.

"What's not safe," she added, that fire igniting in her eyes again, "is for you to be down here, in the underground of Huntswood, whilst my coven suffers the adversities of the Dark Army—"

"That is not my problem anymore." A gust of muggy air swept through the room in a blanket of silence. "Take that up with Gideon."

He shouldn't have said that. He wanted it to be his problem. He wanted her protection to be his to manage. But it wasn't. And it killed him, slowly.

She gathered herself before speaking. "You have made it abundantly clear that you choose to neglect your duty to me and my coven. It is evident that you have forgotten that you took an oath to protect my life. After you rooted your pledge to me in the soil of the Caledorna mountains—"

"I would protect your life with my own and you know it. Why do you think I want you out of here?" he snarled, feeling that horrible monster that swam around in the pools of his broken heart speak.

She bit her lip before something darker than frustration curled her lip back. "If you cut me off one more time, Torin Blacksteel, I will suck the air from your throat and make you choke on your interruption."

Artem blew out a whistle and Emara cut him to death with her stare too. Gideon, his hands behind his back, was pale, looking like he wanted to be anywhere but fucking here.

"I am here," she said, bringing his gaze back to her face, "because there has been a prime meeting called for three days' time and I need you there."

The words hit home.

She needed him.

"I am looking to bargain with the prime to make a few *changes* to my court, and as my lead guard, I need you present for it to work. I need you to support my choices."

He had no idea what *changes* meant; he hadn't been around enough to know. The less detail he knew, the easier it was to get over her. He looked at Stryker, but he offered him nothing.

She walked towards him again, her face a little softer than before. "I know you can't stand to be around me." The words killed him like a stab to the heart. "But I need you to suck it up until the prime meeting is concluded. I need you to remember your oath, even if it is just for a few days. I need you to remember your promises to me even if they weren't real."

He wanted to grab her, smack his lips to hers and show her that everything was real. It was so fucking real it hurt. He wanted to show her what oath he wished to instil in their lives, an oath that meant forever.

Instead, he looked over at Gideon, who had gone rigid, and said, "Take her home. That is an order. I still rank above you and you must do as I say."

Gideon drew his eyes off Torin before turning to guide Emara from the room, but she shrugged him off, trying to catch Torin's gaze. He could tell she wanted to catch a weakness, a sign that told her this was all an act. But he was great in this field. He had to pretend to protect her. He hadn't become one of the best hunters in the kingdom without knowing how to disconnect from his feelings. He could do it with ease. So, he put the final nail in his coffin when he roared, "Get her out of here! Now!"

She gasped a little, her eyes opening wide in shock. That made it all the more difficult not to sink to his knees before her and beg her to forgive him for everything.

He looked over to his longest friend and snarled, "You too. I mean it. I am the top guard in this rank. Go, and don't come back here. Don't bring her back. Ever. Or I will slit your throat myself."

Artem shot him a pitiful look, knowing how much he was going to regret this after they left. He knew him inside and out, and that was a weakness within itself.

"Now!" he roared again, almost bursting a few blood vessels in his eyes.

"Are you really that far gone?" she asked in a whisper, still too stunned to move.

Torin swallowed and gave one nod. "Give up on me. I am not worth your time."

Tears built in Emara's eyes before she shot out a blast of darkness, followed by a scream. He dodged the blast, his hair blowing into his eyes as he moved away from it. The chair that sat behind him wasn't as lucky as the gust slammed it against the wall. The wood splintered, and the broken pieces fell to the ground. She hovered for a second more and then gave him one last look. Everything that he hated was packed into her eyes; hurt, devastation, frustration, guilt, love, and weakness.

As Artem ushered Emara out of the tunnel, Gideon lingered by the door.

"If you have something to say, brother, say it and be done with it," Torin snapped.

"I thought you loved her." His eyes narrowed and his frown turned into a scowl. "I stood back and watched you take her heart into your hands. I watched her walls dissolve around you, I watched her trust you. I knew you would do this...ruin the goodness in her heart."

Torin wanted to scream and tell the whole fucking underground that he wanted what he couldn't have. That it was her and only her. That he had never felt that way about anyone or anything before. That all he wanted was her happiness, and he believed he was doing the right thing by stepping out of her life to let her move on. But instead of voicing all of that, instead of facing the crushing reality of his life, he let the ice of his fractured heart crystallise over the cracks until he couldn't breathe. Until his heart felt like it couldn't even beat. "Are you done now?" he growled.

"She won't marry me, Torin." Gideon shook his head, his emerald eyes not leaving his face. "And that puts her at serious risk. She is holding out hope that you will somehow manage to save her, that you will show up and turn shit around, make everything all right. Like always. She has every hope that, deep down, somewhere in that stubborn heart of yours, there is goodness. Light." He took a breath, and Torin watched as his eyes lost a little light when he said, "She loves you, and it's clear to anyone that takes a glance at her; but it is times like this when I question why. You can be a horrible, selfish bastard."

Torin couldn't pull his eyes from his brother's face until he noticed little drops of blood falling from Gideon's cut hands as he fisted them in anger.

His brother spoke again. "However, like me, she knows that deep down, that there is goodness. Light. Hope. And you shouldn't be stepping away from her because of me. Her heart has chosen, regardless of what fate says. And I have a feeling that fate will not get in the Empress of Air's path should she decide differently. And I used to have a brother who was exactly like that too."

Gideon didn't move his gaze from Torin's.

"Father threatened to reveal her blood, who her father is, if she doesn't sign the treaty to marry me."

Torin's heart almost stopped. His throat closed.

Gideon must have noted the shock in his eyes because he said, "Yeah, that's right. She's not even safe from your commander. But you knew that. And you would rather sit down here and get punched numb than deal with the conflict in your heart." His brother shifted. "If you are going to do anything for her, turn up to that fucking meeting and show your support for her decisions. Father will either kill her or reveal who she really is if she rejects the clan, and you know it. Do you really want the blood of the empress on your hands? Because I don't think you could live with that kind of guilt. Your heart isn't as dark as you want us all to think." Gideon moved back slowly before stopping at the threshold of the door. "Show the fuck up, Torin, or you are going to lose her in more ways than one. And that will be the one thing I will never forgive you for."

CHAPTER FIVE
EMARA

Sleep hadn't come easy after seeing Torin, and every time she tossed and turned, she saw his face. He had been cold. Broken. Brutal. Almost gone. But the thing that had kept Emara awake in those miserable hours wasn't the sadness in his eyes or the bruises on his face, but the glint of softness he had shown before she left. When she had blasted darkness towards him, disbelief had flashed over his face, but his eyes had told a different story to the mask he had strung up for her. The fact that something else other than coldness had lingered there only gave her hope that he —*her* Torin—was still in there somewhere. He still cared whether he wanted to admit it or not.

But that hadn't stopped the feeling of her heart being ripped out as she left those underground tunnels. It was just a terrible coincidence that the more her heart broke, the more her darkness feasted on the pain and grew stronger. Even now, as she looked down at the tips of her fingers, tiny wisps of dark air formed around them. She hid her hand underneath the fabric of her airy, mauve skirt.

"Emara?" A voice calling her name pulled her from her own world and back into the room where she sat. "Is that something you should wish to comment on?"

Her head snapped up from her hands, and her gaze flew to the witches that sat in a circle in front of her. The Empresses of Houses

Water, Earth, Spirit, and Fire were all staring at her, as were their maids. The secret meeting that was taking place in a small cottage in the Fairlands had been Rya's idea, and regardless of how much sleep Emara had gotten the night before, it was a must to attend. With no supreme, every elemental empress took their turn to organise a meeting before every full moon.

Lorta gave her a glare that told Emara they had been talking about something important.

She took a breath, trying to steady herself, and released her hands from the material of her summer skirt. "I am sorry, I am not feeling myself today. Headache." She gave them a small, polite smile. "Can you repeat the question?"

Rya Otterburn of House Fire squared her shoulders, her ruby red dress hanging fashionably from her left shoulder. "We were discussing if we had anything out of the ordinary happening within our magic lately. If anything else in your powers had...emerged?"

Uncontrollable darkness? Emara's dry and wicked sense of humour wanted to comment. But it wasn't the right time or place. The witches here were aiming to establish who should be the next supreme.

The next queen of the witches sat in this very room.

Emara cleared her throat. "Nothing unusual." She gave a glance to Sybil, who gave one small, discreet nod. "My magic is roughly the same. Although my healing magic has come on a lot since the last full moon, thanks to the Empress of Earth."

Rya glared from Sybil back to Emara. "And what of your water magic?"

The Empress of Fire knew that water was the missing link in Emara's powers. She seemed to concern herself with it every meeting just on the off chance the element had suddenly made an appearance. Emara securing strong magic in all five elements would threaten her current lead.

"Still not strong," was all Emara said back.

"We can't all be strong in every element, Rya," the Empress of Spirit shot towards her, a grin lining her dark purple lips. Kerrix lifted her chin and sat back in her chair of red and gold fabric. She threw a thin leg over the other, crossing them. "I only concern myself with my own element."

Rya dragged her eyes from Emara's face, and they landed on Kerrix. "If we are to find a leader of the witches and earn our chair back in the prime seats, we must not only concern ourselves with our *own* element, but with all of the elements we are capable of."

Emara chewed into her cheek. It wasn't like Rya didn't have a point; they needed a leader, someone to sit with the prime of the kingdom.

"Besides, Kerrix, you seem to be the only witch that never discloses any of her strengths and weaknesses. All we know is that you are the Empress of Spirit and nothing more." Rya challenged her, "For all we know, you could be our new supreme and are not telling us."

Kerrix's grin only widened. "Like I have said time and time again, Rya, I am only interested in spirit work. I couldn't give a monkey ass about earth, water, fire, or air." She looked between the other empresses, her glittering smokey eyes burning with an apology. "No offence."

"None taken," Sybil said lightly.

"Well, it has to be one of us." Rya's dominant stare worked its way through everyone. "The late supreme has been gone for many moons. One of us must bear the crown and title."

Crown and title.

Apprehension slid through Emara's veins.

"I must admit, I have no interest in being the leader of our covens." Lillian's soft, melodic voice drifted over the room as she placed a hand on her swelling stomach. The Empress of Water had a martial alliance with Clan Coldwell—Marcus's youngest brother, to be exact. And it seemed that the only thing on her mind was her growing family. Emara had sent her congratulations a few moons ago on both the union and the news of the baby. "If I should emerge as supreme, I would gift my crown to someone who should want it."

Lillian's maids looked down at the floor as the statement fluttered through the room.

Rya huffed at that and so did her maids, scoffing like two little mini versions of their leader. "It doesn't work like that," Rya told her. "You don't get to choose. The Gods do."

"The Gods haven't chosen yet," Lillian reminded her as she took her hand from her belly and held her stare. "So, maybe they are leaving fate up to us."

Emara also understood where Lillian was coming from; taking the witching crown was a lot of weight to bear, and the water empress seemed to like her life just how it was in Tolsah Bay.

A small cough came from where Sybil sat. "I do not feel strong enough in fire magic to be the next supreme. It is practically non-existent," the red-headed witch admitted. "It would take a miracle for my fire to come in as strong as Rya's or Emara's." She looked down at her hands and fiddled with the silver ring on her middle finger. "It's not me, I am sure of it. I am happy to keep my earth crown and be satisfied."

A potent silence lingered in the cottage.

Rya's stare returned to Emara's face. "And you are sure you have not had a breakthrough with water?"

A little flash of annoyance ran up Emara's spine. "Empress of Fire, in our circle of trust, there is nothing for me to lie about." She swallowed the darkness rising from her throat to say otherwise. She may not have had an abundance of water magic, but the demon blood that ran through her veins sang for darkness—another element entirely. "I have already told you I have had nothing out of the ordinary happen. Have you?" she questioned.

A defeated flame lingered in Rya's eyes. "Nothing new."

Emara looked between all the women, wondering how long she would get away with lying about her powers rising. Someone was bound to sense it, especially if the ancestors started talking to Kerrix about her and her darkness. But that was a whole other situation to worry about another time. Right now, she just had to keep it at bay and keep her bloodline a secret.

"I guess that means we have another moon cycle to wait." Kerrix Bellfield stood, her black dress swinging to her knees. Sybil stood and then Emara. Lillian followed, a little slower than normal.

Rya remained seated. "Remember, if anyone senses a difference, even if it is just a little, we must call a meeting between us all and inform the prime." Everyone nodded, and a small snigger came from Kerrix, who seemed to already be halfway out the door with her maids.

Emara turned to leave. "Oh, Emara, I was hoping to have a word with you."

Emara stilled, and Kaydence and Lorta hovered near the threshold of the door.

"Alone," she said.

Emara nodded, and her girls exited the room, leaving the two of them alone.

Rya's dark eyes raked over Emara. She rose from her chair. "I would be stupid not to think that you are my competition in regards to the supreme crown. I can see your power. I can feel it." She raised her hand nonchalantly and brushed a few wiry dark hairs from her brow. "I can't make up my mind if you either don't know how strong your magic feels or if you are hiding something from me. From us."

Emara's spine straightened and her jaw locked.

"But I think it could be hairs that split us in our abilities for the crown. Lillian is lacking in fire and spirit, and Sybil seems to be vocal on not feeling the power of a supreme. Therefore, that leaves us, unless I have underestimated Kerrix. She does seem to keep a tight lid on things, which makes me wonder about House Spirit's abilities." Her gaze found Emara's face again. "But I just wanted to let you know that I want it. I want the crown. And it seems like you are neither here nor there with it."

Emara's lips finally parted as she took a few steps in Rya's direction, trying to keep her composure. "I am going to make one thing clear, Rya. This is not a competition for me. I am not going to compete with my sisters in any coven for a crown." She stood still just shy of the Fire Empress. "If the Gods bless you with the crown, then I shall be ecstatic for you. And if the Gods see me fit enough to take the title, I expect the same respect from you." Her eyes did not falter from her face, although she did see Rya shrink a little. "We know enough of our covens' histories to know that unnecessary competition between one another can be fatal. After all, look what Deleine Orinmore did to my mother in her jealousy for a crown. And their paths are not distant from ours."

Rya's throat bobbed, and Emara took a few steps back.

"Why not support one another? Especially since we are seen in the community as weak and vulnerable, with neither husbands nor leaders, we should be sticking together. A sisterhood. An alliance. There is nothing more powerful than witches that stick together, right?"

Rya nodded once and then for the first time in the meeting, she looked towards her feet. "Right."

"I will see you at the prime meeting, Empress." Emara bowed in respect for the fire crown and left the cottage to find the portal where the others would be waiting for her.

CHAPTER SIX
EMARA

When the summer sun had come up too eagerly the next day, Emara had rolled from her bedchambers and got dressed to train and blow off some steam. It was the only thing keeping her sane. Artem Stryker put her through the wringer all day with cardio, weights, combat, and weaponry. By the time he was finished, she was achy all over and dripping with sweat. And to be fair, so was Artem. Emara wondered to herself how much of the training was for him; she had witnessed how much this business with Torin had affected him too. Artem had been silent on the way back to the Tower that night, and it had been so unlike him.

"Hey, Em." Sybil Lockhart slid her plate of food into the space on the table beside Emara's in the dining room.

"Oh, hey, Sybil." She smiled back at her. It was nice having a friend in the Tower who didn't *belong* to the Tower. The growing party of witches living under the Blacksteel roof made her feel like where she was wasn't...wrong. Between her maids, Lorta and Kaydence, and Sybil with hers, it felt like they had gathered a little community. Naya and Rhea also stayed within the Tower, and it was great to have them around, especially when their duties involved ancient magic and politics.

Sybil was still training in combat from time to time, but having such a gentle nature, she struggled, and most of the time she was just happy to sit back and watch on as Emara battled the hunters.

It was an easy friendship. From the minute Emara had put her hand in Sybil's at the ascension ceremony, they had formed an unexplainable bond. A sisterhood as organic and as natural as the summer flowers that bloomed all over the Tower gardens in soft violets, bright oranges, and baby blues.

The summer solstice seemed to have everyone in a good mood, regardless of the impending army of demons that threatened the kingdom. But it did nothing for Emara. Summer wasn't her thing. Was it wrong to long for gloomy nights and storms that both darkened and lit the sky with the magnificent power of lightning bolts? Was it weird to want to curl up in front of a fireplace with a book whilst the heavy winter rain hit the windowpane from outside and blurred her vision of the city below? Sybil thought it weird. She loved the summer solstice, which was just around the corner. But as Emara liked to remind her, seeds and roots needed rain to grow.

"You seem quiet today." Sybil picked up her half-gnawed carrot and twirled it like a wand. "Distracted."

Emara played with the meat on her plate. "I am. My mind is racing."

It had been a heavy few days.

Sybil scrunched her nose.

"What?" Emara asked, knowing that the earth witch had something to say. She wasn't good at hiding it on her face.

"I can tell you another time. It's okay...it can wait."

Emara dropped her fork. "No, it can't. If you know me by now, Sybil Lockhart, I would rather know."

The red-headed witch hesitated.

"Sybil." Emara's eyes widened.

"Okay, okay. I think I have found something."

"Found something?"

Sybil reached into the satchel strapped around her chest that seemed to have more books in it than the Huntswood library. "Here it is." She brought out a leather-bound grimoire that was hanging together by some sort of miracle. "This is the grimoire that Gideon gave to me for the winter solstice." Her cheeks seemed to beam at the mention of the Blacksteel's name. "What does this look like to you?"

Sybil handed over the old book full of witchcraft.

A gasp stopped in Emara's throat as her heart quickened. "Is that..."

"The Resurrection Stone?" Sybil finished for her. "Yes. And look on this page here." She pointed to another diagram that was old and scribbly. "I think this could be the Protection Stone."

Emara looked up and met Sybil's gaze. "Oh, my Gods."

"I know." She smiled. "It's the first thing I have found in months."

Emara quickly looked around herself, noting that the dining room was rather empty; but still, these walls had ears, and they were all for Viktir. She pushed the grimoire towards Sybil again. "Remember to be careful," she whispered. "The commander has spies everywhere, and we do not need him knowing that we are looking into finding the Gods' ancient Stones."

It wasn't just the Dark Army they were against in finding the stones that bound Veles to the underworld. She was fighting her father, Balan, and Viktir was an enemy too.

"My apologies. I just got too excited to show you." Sybil's moss-green eyes shone brightly, like she had found another purpose in life. "I really think I could be on to something, Emara."

Emara chewed on the inside of her cheek. "Who did you say wrote this stuff?"

Sybil grinned from ear to ear. "This is the best part. The journaling in this grimoire has been passed down through the centuries.

It is predominantly witches from House Earth, but the entries involving the stones are from someone else entirely."

"Who?" Emara leaned forward.

"The Black Widow Witch herself." Sybil almost let out an excited squeal.

"As in the oracle who is half witch, half Fae?" Emara's eyes almost fell from her head. "The woman who is hundreds of years old but never ages?"

"Yes." The earth witch leaned forward. "This is massive, Emara. She has written it all in the ancient language, which I am still to translate, but I am convinced she will know where they are."

Emara took in a breath. "This is amazing, Sybil." She bit into her lip to stop the smile from spreading. "After the prime meeting, we will look into it further. You are an absolute diamond."

Sybil picked up another carrot as she placed the ancient grimoire back into her satchel that probably weighed more than her.

Emara let out a breath in the comfortable silence that settled in between them and picked up her fork again.

"Do you think the prime will question why you haven't sowed your oats to Gideon Blacksteel yet at the meeting tomorrow?" Sybil asked casually.

Emara's lungs collapsed in on themselves, and she dropped her fork. "Sybil, by the Gods."

"What?" She crunched down on the vegetable. "It could come up."

A nervous flutter ignited in her stomach. "I hope they listen to what I want to propose in regard to my trio instead of my treaty."

"With what you have planned, they'll listen for sure." Sybil let out a small giggle. "But I can't help but wonder, are you ever going to get over the fact that you are promised to Gideon?"

"Sybil, for the love of Rhiannon, you are really hitting me with

57

the hard questions today." She laughed uncomfortably and used her fork to toy around with her food. It was much more complicated than that. So much had happened. But when Sybil's innocent laugh died down, Emara shook her head. "I don't think I can."

Sybil gave a small yet encouraging smile. "You will. He will treat you well. He's a good man."

Emara agreed, but it wasn't long before she placed down her fork again, unable to eat anything.

"What's wrong?" Sybil asked. "You have been picking at that stew for ages now and I have yet to see you actually eat anything."

Emara sighed and took a deep breath. They were finally alone in the dining area, so it felt safe to say, "It's just...I don't know."

"Talk to me." Sybil placed her silverware down and moved her empty plate away from her.

Emara rolled her lips before letting a breath fall heavily. "I have a lot of moves to make, and sometimes I just find it hard to get my head around everything. It wasn't too long ago that I found out about who I really am, and everything in this world just moves so fast. What if there is another side to me? A darker side?"

Sybil swallowed. "There is more light in you than anyone I know. You are a good person, Emara. Your darkness? It might be testing you, but you have five other elements that are strong too, and they are all of the light."

Sybil had a point.

She took a moment before she spoke again. "It hurts my heart to know that my mother would ever love someone like him—Balan. I mean, he's not just someone from the Dark Army, he's Vele's favourite disciple. He's got to be a monster."

Sybil's hand reached out and landed on Emara's. "Em, maybe you don't know the whole story. I can't for one minute believe your mother was in love with someone truly evil." She paused. "Do you?"

Emara couldn't answer that question.

Had he tricked her? Had she fallen in love before she knew of the darkness he came from, what he represented?

She raised her shoulders. "Maybe she was just a hopeless fool in love with the wrong person, or maybe it was all part of something bigger. I guess I will never know."

"I suppose you could always try to connect with spirits and ask your mother to come forward," Sybil suggested. "You have told me about all the little things that happen so naturally to you, and your gifts from House Spirit. Maybe you should try connecting."

Emara had considered it. "I don't know if I am fully ready for that." She took a sip of her favourite orange juice. "I mean, I have never even had a conversation with my mother, at least not one that I can remember. I wouldn't even know where to start. And spirits are always so cryptic. Besides, I am still trying to get to grips with all of the empress duties, paperwork, arranging my coven, trying to avoid marriage, and then there is *actually* mastering my own element—"

"You can never fully master the elements, Emara." Sybil smiled and sounded so like Naya in that moment.

Emara scoffed. "I know that to be true. I almost set the Commanding Office on fire yesterday."

"There is nothing like a powerful burst of nature." Sybil winked. "Especially when it is so very deserved." A devious smile grew on her cheeks.

Before Emara could respond to Sybil's charming appreciation for violence, the sound of the hunting siren blasted through the dining hall.

A demon spotting.

Sybil let out a squawk. "I will never get used to that awful sound, Gods above."

It was a good thing Emara was already dressed in hunting gear, because tonight she would help hunt the creatures that threatened their world. Her coven. Even if their blood trickled through her veins, she didn't have any second thoughts on ending them. Maybe it was a way of proving to herself that she was light and not of the darkness. If she fought them, maybe that would be a vindication of how she felt inside about her blood.

But there was just one problem about her joining the hunt tonight.

The hunters didn't know it yet.

CHAPTER SEVEN
EMARA

A nd where in the underworld do you think you are going all weaponed up like that?" Artem Stryker's face was glowing red, and his eyes were bulging from their sockets as he took in Emara's heavy artillery and full leather attire.

She really shouldn't enjoy that kind of reaction, but she did.

"With you." Emara stood at the entrance to the foyer with her weapon belt, made to measure from the markets, strapped to her waist.

"Like Thorin you are," he declared as he pushed a hand out to stop her. "Are you mad?"

She huffed. "I know there is a space on this hunting mission; you rubbed Torin's name off the board in the briefing room this morning. I presume he will not be attending the hunt?"

His eyes narrowed. "Empresses don't belong in the briefing room, Emara. They get terrible, terrible ideas."

The comment angered her more than she let show on her face.

"Witches don't deserve to die at the hand of the Dark Army, Artem. But it's still happening. My coven needs to be protected and you are missing a hunter. I can fill that slot. I demand you take me with you."

He let out that howling laugh of his. "You can't demand that I do anything. This is a partnership, little witchy, and even though we might be best friends—"

"We're not best friends."

He crossed his big arms. "Rude." He let a corner of his mouth turn up. "As I was saying, I, for one, am not going to get into another brawl with the Blacksteels over your safety. You are not going."

"I can handle myself and you know it." She dug in her booted heel. "I think I proved myself in the pits."

He leaned in, and his silver nose ring glinted in the dull lighting. "Let me remind you that Torin Blacksteel won't be there to take you out of the fight if it gets rough."

"I don't need anyone to take me out of anywhere when it gets rough, and I am more than happy to remind you of that. You said yourself you think it's ridiculous that I can't fight in the hunt because I am a woman. You said I am good enough."

He sighed and looked the other way. "You are, but it's not my call to let you fight with us."

Emara stood in his line of vision. "It is not your call to say that I can't either, right?"

Artem's lips snapped shut and his attention was back on her face.

She raised an eyebrow. "It would have been the commander's decision, but since he has gone into the city for a meeting, it would fall to Torin to make the call as second-in-command." She paused. "And guess what? He's not here either."

Artem grinned like a cat that had just found a bowl of clotted cream. "Fuck, you are good. I guess we just found ourselves a loophole then, *little miss, I am the Empress who likes to fight demons.*"

Emara smiled back as her magic thrummed through her whole body, readying her for the mission.

Demon flesh wasn't as easy to cut through as the hunters made it look. It was tough and leathery, and the smell was vile.

The spear in Emara's hand was covered in reddish-black gore, but that didn't stop her. She slinked between the trees on the border that introduced the Ashdale Forest with Huntswood. She had taken down a few demons on the way through the woods, but the band had been separated when a monstrous beast with wings flew out from behind a huge fir tree above to devour them. The wolf moon wasn't full yet, but it provided a distant beam of light down through the branches that were covered in thick green needles. She knew the clan was around here somewhere, keeping out of sight, waiting for the demons to make the first move.

She let out a breath and felt her skin prickle, the eerie silence of the woods too much for her heart to handle. All she could hear was the pulse in her neck and the distant flap of wings.

The demon was close.

She swallowed. Should she make a run for it? Should she try and make it out to the clearing where Marcus had instructed they should meet, or should she wait patiently for the Dark Army to reveal themselves again?

Demons were in the trees too, but she didn't know where.

Holding her weapon, she peered around the trunk to catch a glimpse of the forest. Nothing but broken moonbeams highlighted the forest floor.

A gust of wind that felt hot and wet brushed against her skin. The hairs on her arms stood to attention, as did the hairs at the nape of her neck.

There was no wind. She knew the air. Air was in her blood. The demon was stalking her. She spun around, immediately stabbing her spear outwards. Her weapon caught on thick skin, and she came face to face with crimson eyes, teeth like blades, and a face like something out of a nightmare.

It wasn't a lesser demon; this beast was bred for destruction and carnage. It bared its multiple rows of teeth and its nostrils flared; it was mountains taller than her and as sturdy as a tree.

She wasn't sure she could kill this one on her own, but she wasn't left with much choice either. Her heart lodged itself in her throat as fear tried its best to paralyse her. She was ready for this. She talked down her fear and summoned her air. She needed space; the beast was too close.

Before the creature could snap at her, she shoved out her palm and the element of air tunnelled around her, slamming against the beast. The air caught the demon's wings and it was propelled over the forest floor before crashing against the huge trunk of a tree.

It recovered in a second, hoisting its muscly legs up. It stood like a huge monument, heavy enough for its claw-like feet to be digging into the innocent earth. Its massive wings splayed out, and Emara could see the detail in them as the moonbeams hit its dark veins that spread like a spider web across them.

She rotated the spear in her hands, and the demon watched her, tilting its head to the side like the born predator it was.

Before she could strike it, a piercing noise attacked her skull, sharp and excruciating. Her head throbbed like someone had stabbed her with an arrow. Emara gritted her teeth to work through the pain, and it reminded her of when the demon had attacked her grandmother's home, how it had almost immobilised her with a similar sound.

She had to fight it. The legs of the demon moved in slow motion towards her, its giant wings dragging across the ground. She blinked a few times to steady her vision.

Empresssssssssss.

A hissing in Emara's mind made her shake her head. Was she hearing things now? This was a creature of the underworld, not a knight or a man. How would it be speaking to her?

Empressssssss.

An ancient voice hissed again, sending shivers across her skin. The pain in her head increased, and as the beast stalked towards her, she stumbled back, still trying to keep a reasonable distance between them.

Her spine struck bark, and she knew she had hit a tree. She blinked a few times to regain focus, but the pain in her head blurred her vision again.

"Block it out," Torin had coached her. *"Anything I say you must learn to block it out. Do not listen. The more you tune in to what a demon is saying, the higher the chance of it capturing your mind. Do not let it in. Fight it. It's trying to distract you long enough to kill you."*

But this thing didn't seem like it was trying to kill her, not yet. It was trying to communicate with her. She couldn't let it in. Her darkness was tingling. Emara took a breath, and as a roar erupted from her mouth, fire soared from her palm.

Her fire missed and hit a tree, igniting leaves and branches. Smoke began to funnel up the tree as the flames licked higher, but Emara had to shut down the panic stirring up in her heart.

She set her sights back on the demon.

You have daaark blood, it taunted her, looking at her through ruby-red eyes. *You are one of ussssss.* It stalked towards her. *I can smell that you have darkness in your veinssss, yet an undeniable sweetnessss of Light. I know who you arrrre. Don't fight me, pretty one of Balan's seeeeed. Join me. Join ussssss. Come back to the underwooorld.*

Emara's heart almost stopped.

Join us.

Underworld.

Why could she hear it speaking to her? Why could she hear its thoughts? This hadn't happened any other time that she had slain a member of the Dark Army.Her darkness urged at her fingertips for release.

I can smell the darkness in your veins.

Balan's seed.

Balan. King of the Underworld, Protector of the Dark God. She wouldn't be recognised as having anything to do with that evil bastard. Not now. Not ever!

"My name is Emara Clearwater, Empress of Air and grand-daughter to Theodora of House Air. You cannot brand me with your dark filth. I am of the Light. I worship the Goddess of the Moon and Dreams. And I will smile as I cleanse this earth from the evil that you spread."

Emara blasted out fire again, and this time it caught a wing as the creature tried to take flight. Even with its skin ablaze, the creature managed to get into the air, its powerful wings batting around the smoke from the burning trees and turning her vision murky.

Out of the smoke, the demon swooped down.

Emara ducked, falling to the ground. As she rolled onto her back, she saw the creature coming down again and readied her spear to strike. Agnes stabbed into a leg, and, pulling as hard as she could, she brought the creature to the ground. The earth shook beneath her. She scrambled to her feet, leaving her spear sticking in its leg. Quickly, she pulled a small sword from her weapon belt and jumped atop the beast with the full intention of piercing it through its heart. But the creature had moved, its claws drawing up and ensnaring her hands. The demon pushed its full weight over, pinning Emara underneath, and its claws dug into her wrists.

She let out a scream, one that she knew reached the stars in the sky, and she let go of her weapon.

The creature bowed down close to her face, and the weight

threatened to stop her from breathing altogether. Her lungs clutched to the thin air they had left.

The king issssss coming for youuuuuu.

The winged creature let out a shriek of pleasure, and wet drool hit Emara's face just as the smell of sulphur did.

She could have passed out for a moment, her vision blurry and her head numb from the lack of oxygen, but then she heard a growl.

And it hadn't come from the beast.

CHAPTER EIGHT
EMARA

An ash-coloured wolf stood between two trees, its long legs heavy with fur, its huge paws integrated into the mossy banking. Somewhere in between blurred vision and thick smoke, Emara could just make out that the wolf had its teeth bared and its feral face was covered in dark blood.

A growl ripped from its throat, and then the wolf crashed into the demon on top of her. Her lungs burned as the smoke-filled air rushed into them. Rolling onto her front, she pushed up, trying to get to her feet. The woods were brighter with the light of the flames, but Emara couldn't put the fire out yet. Water wasn't her strong point, and the wolf was struggling for dominance with the winged beast. Teeth snapped and animalistic sounds broke through the night as Emara found her spear lying on the ground.

Picking up her weapon of choice, she nervously leaned back on her right leg and put every ounce of strength she had behind her throw. The spear travelled through the air at an impressive rate and broke through the skull of the demon.

The beast's skull cracked open and the contents of the head spilled onto the ashen wolf. Before Emara could catch her breath, fur and legs became skin and limbs.

Breighly Baxgroll rolled to the side before the winged beast fell on top of her.

"Fuck me," Breighly said as she stood, panting outrageously. "He was a big one."

Emara blinked a few times, wiping the sweat from her brow. "That he was." She looked over at Breighly, who was naked as she puffed out a breath. "I had no idea you were hunting tonight."

"I could say the same for you." The wolf grinned. "I didn't think empresses were allowed to hunt."

"And I didn't think the princess of the alpha was allowed to join either."

"What he doesn't know doesn't hurt him." Breighly winked and pulled Emara's spear from the skull of the creature that lay dead on the ground. "This"—she tossed the spear and Emara caught it— "belongs to you."

She held in the ruby and the spear reduced in size. "Thank you," she said to the wolf she called a friend. "Thank you for saving me there. It was bold of you to take on that demon."

A sly grin slashed across Breighly's face. "Don't mention it. The bigger they are, the harder they fall. I would do it again given the opportunity."

The wolf gave a small bow, and before Emara could say anything else, Breighly had turned and started running in the opposite direction from which she came. These were her woods, after all, and she knew them better than most.

Emara heard footsteps before a few figures broke through the smoke. Members of the Blacksteel Clan had found her.

A whistle came from Marcus Coldwell. "Well, well, well..." His smile glowed against his beautifully dark skin. "It looks like you are no longer an amateur fighter, taking out a beast that size."

"She's been training with the best." Artem swaggered through the clouded area, his tattoos a prominent feature coming from behind the smoke. "It's me. I am the best. Just in case you were thinking it was you, Coldwell."

Marcus let out a boyish laugh. "I got that you meant you, Stryker."

"I had help," Emara puffed out. "But she's gone now."

"She?" Artem asked as if he knew the possibilities of it being anyone but Breighly were slim.

"You missed her." Emara smiled in his direction. And his head snapped around, trying to look for a route she could have disappeared down.

Marcus ignored them. "Are you hurt? We heard screaming."

Emara peeled back her fighting gear on her wrists to reveal two wounds. She hissed as the material pulled skin along with it, and the pain seared up her arm from where the demon had held her.

"Oh, great! The Blacksteels are going to order my death." Artem groaned as he walked over to inspect it. "I bet you didn't feel that until we asked about it."

"No, I didn't," Emara said, now feeling sick with the pain.

"It's always the same," Marcus confirmed. "When the dust of the hunt settles, that's when the pain will kick in. The adrenaline of staying alive will always keep you moving."

It was also like that in her heart. The pain often kicked in when the adrenaline died down from a prime meeting or a training session. And when the dust settled down and she was left alone in the darkness of night, that was when thoughts of who she was, what she was, plagued her.

"Come on, let's get you back to the Tower with all your little wounds so I can prepare to die," Artem huffed and placed his arm around her.

Emara laughed at Artem's dramatics. She did always appreciate them when the mood could take a sombre turn. But she would never tell him just how much she appreciated having him around; she didn't need to live in the misery of him bragging for decades.

Marcus roared through the trees, "I will try and round up the clan." He then turned to them. "It's not the same without Torin's big, loud voice commanding where we should be."

A pain struck through her heart instead of her wrists. Marcus threw her a sympathetic smile and dashed off through the trees to where she assumed the other hunters would be waiting.

"Do you think he will show up at the prime meeting?" Artem asked as he helped Emara along a path away from the burning trees and dead demons.

Emara bit the side of her cheek. "I have no idea anymore, Artem. I am starting to wonder if everything I have done is a lost cause."

He patted her shoulder and held her a little tighter. "Don't give up on him just yet."

Silence filled the space between them as they walked back to where the wagons were stationed. If she had mastered the portal by now, she could have completed their return to the Tower in seconds, but it was something she was still working on.

She halted. "I have something I need you to do for me, Artem."

He sighed. "I am not going to the seamstresses again for your dresses. I would soon rather train Kaydence in combat."

Emara laughed, and a pain in her wrists reminded her of how she needed a healer. "Well, actually, it involves going to a tavern." She looked over at him, and his eyes had lit up under the restricted moonlight. "And I am in no state to go to a tavern like this. Naya would scorn me for not getting healed."

Artem moved in front of her, and his golden eyes lit like sparkling gold. "Tavern, you say? Now we are talking. Spill."

CHAPTER NINE
BREIGHLY

The heart-racing beat thrummed through La Luna as all sorts of creatures found pleasure in song, dance, and liquor—perhaps in each other too. A hazy smoke passed through sparkling, coloured lights as it washed away the crowd's troubles, adding a layer of mystery and privacy to the tavern. Bodies moved, writhed, and pulsed to the music as drinks were downed, and laughter could be heard as a second harmony to the music.

It was home. And she was glad to be back from the hunt in one piece. She had known about the hunt tonight because of Roman, and only Roman knew of her escapade in the Ashdale Forest to join them. Waylen didn't know, which was why she'd had to remain in the shadows. But La Luna was packed tonight, and it was time to get to work.

This tavern was her favourite place to be. Lately, she would rather work until exhaustion claimed her than listen to the silence in her own head. Ever since losing Eli in the battle of the blood moon, it seemed too quiet around her cottage, a little lacklustre. But here? There wasn't room for silence or anything dull. That was the good thing about a crowded tavern—no one seemed to be missing, sad, or gone forever. Most people in here meant nothing to each other but a good time and fond memories. La Luna represented the present, not the past. Everyone lived in the moment.

It had been a while since she'd gotten to fight the Dark Army, and every demon she got to slay with her own fangs was another point to the Baxgroll pack for every life they'd claimed of her blood. When she had heard a girl scream in the forest, she had assumed that a villager was being attacked. She'd been shocked to find it was no ordinary girl, but the Empress of Air.

They had hung out a few times. Emara came here when her world got too much and she wanted to let her hair down. She felt comfortable around the wolves, and she should, because they would always have her back after what she'd done for her brother in his last moments. The Baxgroll pack would always be fond of Emara Clearwater for taking Eli's pain before he passed.

And Breighly had been at the Tower when Emara had unexpectedly wanted advice on how to deal with men in politics and the newest fashions.

She liked the empress, respected her. She was a breath of fresh air in a stuffy world full of traditions.

As Breighly stood behind the bar, a dark-haired gentleman in a black velour suit moved, sleek and smooth, towards her. His skin was deathly white and his eyes looked like stars had congregated to form a new galaxy. His lips pulled into a cruel smile that rendered him dark and dangerous, and it accentuated his jawline that could cut through marble. Even though the magic of her blood ignited to tell her that he was threatening and savage, his charismatic charm pulled her in and lured her to watch him.

Vampire.

He placed his elbow on the bar and his enticing eyes wandered around the bottles displayed behind her. She could tell by the power radiating from him that he was a very old vampire despite looking to be her age. It seemed he was an extremely rich vampire, too, given the way he dressed. There was no weapon belt around his waist, nor was anything malfitting on his form. He was immaculate.

"I will take a glass of red, please," he said, finally pinning her where she stood with his black irises sparkling.

Foe or not, he was strikingly handsome. An animal dressed as a gentleman; a dangerous predator with a smile so wicked it could stop hearts.

Exactly her type.

Breighly leaned forward, making sure her neck was on show. She had just escaped danger tonight, but she was happy to find herself dancing on the edge of it again. "Are you looking for *fresh* red or bottled?"

A dangerous glint made his eyes a little darker. "You serve fresh?"

Breighly combed her hair to one side, exposing even more of her skin to him. She was a natural at flirting, and she didn't even want to consider where that trait came from. "At La Luna, we cater for all of the Gods' creatures."

The vampire's alluring face was so inviting yet so very feral, and as he smiled a true grin, his long fangs glistened under the lights and rested on his full lips. "I am ecstatic to hear that." His melodic voice drifted over the bar like a hand stroking her face, and the animal in her purred.

The wolf was awake. And heated.

Breighly smiled back. "I am happy to help."

She liked this guy. even though he was a *vampire*. Fuck it. She didn't care if they kept themselves to themselves and everyone knew little about them. It didn't matter that the prime were reluctant to involve themselves with this faction, shunning one of Vanadey's creatures.

He was cool, calm, and collected. He was mature—he probably was eight hundred years old—but he had a sophistication about him that a wolf didn't normally have.

Neither did hunters.

"On ice or heated?" she said, dropping her voice low, knowing he would hear the change over the music with his talented ears.

He leaned in a little closer as a corner of his mouth turned up. "Body temperature."

She laughed out loud.

She was a sucker for a funny guy.

No pun intended.

But she needed something tonight—a distraction. It had been a while. What was a lot of fun and a little danger mixed into one evening?

A fucking good time, that's what.

She leaned in too. "If you go out the back exit and wait"—she bit into her lip seductively—"I would be happy for you to take a sip of my room temperature."

"Even though you are a wolf?" His brow danced up.

Breighly had heard sex with a vampire was incredible, and the bite a rush of pure stardust. Exhilaration. She didn't care if *prime law* thought it immoral.

"I have no mate, and I am not spoken for," she reassured him. "You won't have any trouble from the wolves in here. I run this place."

The vampire took a step back from the bar, a keen smile on his lips, before getting lost in the crowd.

"Hey, Jett," she shouted over the crowd, signalling to one of the wolves who was standing guard of the door. If anyone caused a scene, Jett was one of their biggest wolves and he'd sort them right out. "Cover for me; I will be back soon. I have an errand to run. If my brothers come looking for me, I have a meeting with a syrup supplier."

Jett's black curls made their way through the crowd, and he leapt over the bar.

She rolled her eyes. "Did you really have to do that?"

He smiled a boyish grin. "Of course. I will keep guard of your castle until you're back, princess."

"Thank you." She kissed him on the cheek. "You are my knight in shining armour."

He laughed, his amber eyes shining like two coins. "I don't think you will ever have a knight in shining armour, Bry."

She laughed back at him, looking over her shoulder as she moved from the bar. "You know me so well."

Before taking the back exit into the alley, Breighly made sure her lips were painted dark pink and her neckline was more plunging than before. Pulling open the door, she felt the hot thickness of the air smack her face and she pulled in a husky breath. It was already hot in La Luna, but by the Gods, it needed to thunder over Huntswood and break this air. It was unbearable, and it had been building for weeks. When she was in wolf form earlier, she couldn't wait to get out of her fur, and that wasn't like her. She loved the summer solstice, but the temperature could ease up just a little.

Taking a few steps out into the night to look for *lover vampire*, Breighly halted when she heard the sounds of a heated argument and a possible struggle. Her feet pounded the dirt track of the market alley until she reached where they kept the empty bottles and trash.

Artem Stryker stood against the backdrop of the market tents, every pound of sheer muscle tense, threatening. He had his large hand around a blade that was directly pointed at the vampire's throat. His gold-flecked gaze met hers, and for a second, a crackling in her heart sent butterflies into her stomach. But she grabbed control of herself before she let anyone see her surprise. Before she could go spiralling down that road where thoughts often led to him.

"Oh, there she is." His stupid, upbeat, sarcastic voice knocked the air from her lungs, and as he turned to face her directly, she could see all of the smug grin that was pulling at his mouth.

"What the fuck do you think you are doing?" she asked in a higher pitch than what she would have liked. The vampire watched her from behind the blade that was still pointed at his throat, his teeth bared. "Put that weapon down. Now! Artem, now!"

"Indeed, I will not." Artem lifted a perfect brow. "This creature said he was waiting here for you." His eyes glittered as he watched her. "This vamp"—he pointed the silver blade closer to the vampire's neck, and he hissed.—"claims that he is waiting here to drink from you."

How dare this big fucker just show up here, waving blades at her new friend? Silver blades could seriously harm a vampire. Who did he think he was? Her boyfriend?

Breighly held her chin up. "His claims are correct. You can put down your blade."

"What?" It was then that Artem lowered his blade, his eyes narrow. "You were going to let him drink from you?" The warrior's voice was low and rough, and it stirred that wolf inside her to life in a different way.

"You heard me." She squinted at him. "I can let him drink from anywhere I want."

It had been a while since they had been together, almost a whole moon cycle since the last *moment of weakness* that she'd had with Artem Stryker. Sometimes he just appeared randomly, or if they saw each other at an event, it always led to them taking off their clothes and getting lost in each other. It was always feral, and pure need. Sort of magnetic.

But it wasn't going to happen this time. It was never going to happen again. After the last time, they had sworn to each other after three rounds of blissful, passionate fucking that they were drawing a line in the sand.

It was for the best.

She didn't need any more mess. Her life was a mess.

Fuck, she barely even liked him. He was smug and prideful and always the one to say the wrong thing. Plus, he was the chief commander's son, second-in-command of his stupid clan, which meant he soon had to find a nice witch to make more stupid hunters with.

But damn, was he not as handsome as Thorin himself—if the God had a nose ring and was covered head to toe in ink. Standing in the alleyway covered in blood from the hunt, he looked murderous. Ugh, why did that give her forbidden tingles?

She had smelt his scent coming after she had helped Emara kill the demon, and to avoid her hands finding themselves in his leathers, Breighly had avoided him.

So why was it that he'd ended up here? He lowered the weapon and stalked towards her in his black hunting gear as violence streaked through his eyes. Although you couldn't normally wipe the stupid grin off his face, he did take his oath seriously, and there was no mistake about that when you saw him in action. The vampire took a breath, still reeling from his encounter with Artem, but his eyes found Breighly, probably for some sort of explanation. She had promised him no trouble, after all.

Artem's lips parted as he came to a halt. "Oh, I know you can do what you want, princess, but if you wanted someone to bite you, all you had to do was ask. You don't need a vampire when you have me."

What an arrogant son of a bitch.

"Are you here for a reason, Stryker? Or are you just a fan of hanging around my garbage?" She looked down at her nails, giving him the impression that she was unfazed.

He sniggered. "Had I not been hanging around your garbage, *lover boy* here would have had you as a midnight snack." He pointed the lethal blade back at the vampire. "I can't let that happen, can I?"

"I swear to the Gods," the vampire said with a little frustration, "I am not conducting anything illegal. You are out of line, hunter."

Artem turned, his teeth bared. "And what god is it exactly that you swear on, vampire?"

The vampire curled his lip over his teeth, exposing those deadly fangs. "I am over five hundred years old and I have never let a hunter talk down to me just because they have a direct god to worship. I have worshipped the Light Gods for my entire existence, and I'm older than that metal you point at my face like I am your enemy."

Feeling the tension rise, Breighly took a few steps closer to them.

"Anyone that drinks the blood of women is my enemy." Artem squared up to him. "No Light God wants that for their kingdom. You know the boundaries set by the prime."

"I drink men who are willing too," his articulate tongue hissed. "I don't discriminate."

"I am sure you don't, night stalker," Artem barked.

"It is not illegal if I have their consent and you know it." The vampire moved forward as if to strike, and Artem moved into a battle stance. "You cannot bend the rules to suit yourself. I may not be bound to a clan or a member of a Fae court, but that doesn't mean I do not worship your gods."

"That doesn't mean I don't find it revolting," Artem spat, bringing out another weapon—a silver stake. "You are just a cut above a demon. I am sure Vanadey's skin crawled when she made you by accident."

"Hunters..." The vampire spat as he squared up to him, going nose to nose. "Always thinking they are the fucking Gods themselves."

"Enough! Enough!" Breighly roared, finally getting in between them and pulling them apart. She imagined it would be easier to split two mountains. "Not outside my bar. Not here. This is my business." She looked at the vampire, who was still looking like he could rip out Artem's throat with his fangs. "I am really sorry, and it kills me to say this, but you need to leave," she said to the creature of night. As she looked at Artem's smug face, a vessel almost popped in her neck. "And you," she roared at him. "You too. Did you think I was keeping you?"

It was then his eyes dragged from the vampire's face to hers. "Unfortunately, I am here on official business. I require a moment with you, alone."

The vampire finally pulled back, straightening out his expensive jacket that probably cost more than her bar. "I am sorry to have caused you any trouble here. Maybe I will come back some other time."

Before Breighly could agree, Artem jumped in, "And maybe I will *still* be here, lurking in the garbage."

Breighly turned to face Artem. "Do you realise how creepy that sounds?"

"Yeah, and I hope that he has nightmares of my creepy face, lurking in your garbage."

"You are fucking insane," she said through her teeth. "Do you realise how much I wanna punch you right now?"

"Do you realise how much I would like that?" Artem's eyebrows rose like he was now interested in where the conversation was going.

"You are ill."

"And you like my kinks."

That was true no matter how much she tried to fight it.

"I am going to take my leave," a voice said from beside her, but she couldn't pull her gaze from the hunter. "Will you be all right with this brute?"

She nodded.

The vampire speedily disappeared into the shadows.

After she'd growled at him for a few seconds, she asked, "Artem, what the fuck was that?"

"What?" he asked as he placed his weapons back on his belt.

"Showing up here and going all *hunter* crazy on my new boyfriend."

"He...is not your new boyfriend." He placed his large hands on his hips. "I would know if you had a boyfriend. You've already played this trick on me."

Oh shit, she had forgotten about that.

"If I wanted him as my boyfriend, I could have him." She pursed her lips.

"You could have anyone you wanted." His golden eyes softened to a warm liquid, and his hard features relaxed.

He was the kind of handsome that made your heart swim up your throat and your lungs punch into your chest.

He was the summer rain she so desperately needed right now.

Her heart stuttered, and she took a breath in.

"I am not doing this shit with you." She turned before she could feel anything else and began running from what made her coldness melt. This wasn't good for her.

"Wait, stop," he commanded from behind her.

"Fuck off, Artem." She flipped him off.

Before she knew it, his massive form was in front of her.

Well, she did have heels on. That was the only explanation for him being quicker.

"You need to hear me out," he said, all jests gone from his face.

She halted with a sigh. "What part of *off you fuck* does your brain does not comprehend?"

He fought a small smile before collecting himself. "I am here on official business for the Empress of Air."

She straightened.

"Emara?"

He nodded.

"But I just saw her."

"Well maybe if you hadn't been avoiding me, she could have told you the news herself."

Breighly swallowed down a smile as she bit her lip. Maybe she wasn't as sneaky as she thought. "She could have sent whatever she needed to me by fireletter. That's what she normally does. Are you just making up excuses to see me now?"

He grinned a little. "She didn't want to write to you, not for this." His eyes dazzled in amusement.

Why would Emara not want to fireletter her?

"I am listening." She folded her arms across her chest. "You have one minute to impress me before I shove my foot into your favourite area."

"Your mouth?" His cheeky smile rode across his face like a wave.

She bit back a laugh. "Shut up. What is this official business, then?"

He crossed his arms too. "Excuse me, but I have had less than a minute to impress you before and succeed." His nostrils flared as he grinned, and his tiny silver nose ring glinted under the moonlight. He quickly placed his hands over his crotch, knowing she was three seconds away from kicking him.

"And that lasted thirty seconds until I was disappointed again. So you better be quick...like you always are." She winked.

"So cruel." Finally, Artem's expression turned serious. "Emara wants you to be at the prime meeting tomorrow."

Air whooshed from her lungs.

Breighly, for once, was stunned. "But why? I want to avoid those meetings where I can."

"Maybe she is looking out for her favourite guard and letting him bring a date to the summit."

Breighly rolled her eyes so hard it hurt her skull. "Artem, you know I can break bones really easily. Why do you test my restraint? We all know it's already weak."

He laughed his barking chuckle before he settled back down for business. "The air witch has her reasons for why she wants you there."

"I want you to tell me why." Worry curled in her stomach. "You have that weird glint in your eye like you know something that I don't, and it is making me want to kick in your balls."

"Because the Empress of Air has been thinking of ways she can change the world, as usual." Artem's brow rose, and his fondness for the empress shone bright in his eyes. "She is making big moves tomorrow, and I think you will want to see this."

Breighly shifted her weight in her heels and searched his face for answers. "Why? Am I in trouble? Did I do something wrong?"

He considered something before he spoke. "The fact that you have to ask that probably alludes to the fact that you have done something illegal. But no. It's not because you have done something wrong. It's because she is going to campaign to the prime for you to be her official third guard." He began to move, but before he left, he threw her a look over his shoulder. "If she's successful tomorrow, you are going to be the first female guard in the history of the kingdom, should you want it. Why would you want to miss history being made?"

Breighly Baxgroll had never been stunned speechless, but she was now. And as she watched Artem Stryker walk away, she couldn't help but feel a shit-eating grin flex in her jaw.

CHAPTER TEN
EMARA

Don't worry, he'll come," Artem reassured her as his broad shoulder bumped her own. "I know he will."

Members of the prime and magical factions had begun pouring through the old-fashioned mansion doors into the room that was holding the summit. This was one of the stately homes of the Minister of Coin, and you could tell that old wealth had decorated the room. White stone columns stood in four corners, intertwined with gold ribbon, and a glass chandelier glittered in the middle of the room, hanging like a diamond earring. The wooden floors shone like a pretty coin, and paintings of elder elite members were hanging on the walls, framed by gold plates. A humongous oak desk sat at the top of the room, five chairs stationed around it. It was always five chairs, no matter that there were no longer five prime members. Benches had been set out for the other attendees of today's summit, and in true elite style, they had maids bringing everyone refreshments.

The room was noisy, full of chatter and footsteps, making Emara even more nervous that she would need to stand in front of these people and ask for something that had never been done in the history of Caledorna. Her stomach increased its churning dramatically.

Noting the Empress from House Fire walking through the doors first, Emara gave a nod in her direction, followed by a smile. Rya Otterburn returned the polite gesture, her face still set harshly as always. Emara had been thinking about her encounter with the fire empress since the gathering in the Fairlands, and she disliked how she didn't know where she stood with her. She was so incredibly hard to read. Rya didn't trust her fully, that was clear, but Emara supposed that might always be the case. The scorched black bone of her crown sat jagged on Rya's head. The crown sparkled with black and red rubies that looked like they contained tiny embers. She did look regal. Maybe she would bloom into the supreme soon and this unwanted rivalry could end between them.

Kerrix Bellfield was the next witch to stroll through the room with her guards. She took a seat down from Rya and her house, a few members from her coven appearing to support her. Kerrix's enchanting crown was wedged into her moonlight-coloured hair. When Emara looked at the crown of spirit, she could see that it was the thinnest of them all, held together with fragments of coin, gold chain, and crystals. Although it didn't sit like a crown, high in her hair, it fell over her forehead beautifully, glistening under the light. Her eyes were alert, like the ancient spirits of this room were telling her a few tales.

The Empress of Water floated into the room just after House Spirit, her beautiful sandy hair weighed down by the crown of coral, seaweed, shells, and pearls that sat gracefully on her head. She was aloof as always, and beside her sat her husband, the only member of Clan Coldwell to have attended.

Just as Emara was about to flex her skills in spirit magic, hoping to find an energy she knew, Breighly Baxgroll strolled through the door, wide-eyed and flanked by her pack.

Emara stood.

Her pack was menacing, full of muscle and fangs, and the wolves always came to these events like a unit of force. Breighly wasn't always in tow with them, but her brothers were. There was a sharpness in their eyes and an edge about how they looked, especially in a place as pretentious as this one. The Baxgroll wolves were more frightening visually than in real life. They had always been nothing but kind and welcoming to her. But she knew that could change in a heartbeat if she was considered a threat.

Casting her golden eyes over the crowd, Breighly spotted Emara and smiled. She winked one of her dangerous winks and bowed her head full of golden hair in a sign of respect for the empress. She took a last scan of the crowd before taking a seat with her brothers, Roman and Waylen, who looked intrigued. She wondered if Breighly had told them her reasons for being here or if it would come as a complete surprise to them. Her father, the alpha of every Shifter in the kingdom, took his place at the end of the room in one of the five faction chairs.

More hunters, Fae, witches and elite piled into the room, and Emara had to almost drown out the chatter with the buzz of her own nerves to concentrate on her task. It reminded her of being under trial for the events of the Amethyst Palace.

It had been a gruelling few days when the hearing had taken place, and sometimes she had seen a different outcome in her nightmares. One where they had found her guilty of treason for killing her supreme, or one where the prime found out about her blood and deemed her a threat to the kingdom. In the same dreams, Viktir Blacksteel had arranged her execution, and she had always awoken drenched in her sweat before he brought down the almighty sword on her head.

But none of that had happened, and the prime had found Emara nothing but innocent. Having the Blacksteels' influence in the magical society had helped a lot, and the fact that the other empresses had sympathised and praised her also went in her favour.

Emara shuddered thinking about it.

As she readjusted her focus, she caught a glimpse of sapphire eyes filled with agony and black hair that shone like a bottomless well of ink.

Her breath caught at the sight of him. He was here.

He had come to the summit.

Torin Blacksteel stood in the threshold of the door, aloof but powerful, his body stealing the light that tried to come through the door.

The happiness in her heart was short lived as she noted the bruises on his face and the cuts on his lip and above his eye. His cheeks were swollen and his eyes were distant, vacant, his thoughts gone to someplace she dreaded to even conjure in her own mind. He looked tortured.

He had clearly refused a healer, and Naya would be furious with him.

But he had come like she had asked.

A swell of hope formed in her heart as she took in his silvery-grey guard uniform, and her gaze travelled where he did as Torin walked across the centre of the room, reaching a seat a few feet in front of Emara at the opposite side of the hall. At the opposite side of Viktir.

It was a telling tale that he did not sit with his clan, with this commander, but on his own.

Torin was in direct view of her but not too close either.

She swallowed the thickness in her throat as their eyes met for a few seconds, her heart screaming in her chest, then he clasped his busted hands in his lap and looked towards the prime.

Oberon, King of Fae, had taken his seat, as had the Chief Commander, Aerrick Stryker, and Emara had to admit it was strange for the supreme to not be sitting amongst them.

Suddenly, the room was too warm and sticky sweat began beading on her skin. Her heart started pounding, and it felt like the ceiling of this huge mansion was falling. The supreme wasn't sitting on her throne because Emara had been the beginning of her end. Her death.

Rumours had circulated around Huntswood about Emara being the next supreme, which was entirely ridiculous. No wonder Rya had pulled her aside at the previous meeting to warn her about the fire witch's intentions for the crown. Emara was struggling to keep above water as it was, never mind adding the title of supreme onto her shoulders. It was just rumours. No jolt of instant power had happened, no awakening, no Rhiannon, Goddess of the Moon and Dreams, had appointed her to the Five Covenal Throne. Nothing...

Nothing but a growing darkness.

If Emara had to take a bet on who the next supreme would be, it was Rya Otterburn; she had already mastered every element, strong in every single one. Maybe a witch with dark blood in her veins couldn't be the supreme. *The king issss coming for youuuuu.* The demon from the Ashdale Forest flashed into her mind.

Balan of The Underworld.

Her father.

Emara would do anything to keep him in his cage, exactly where her mother had put him, but she needed the stones that her mother had worked with to guarantee that he stayed put. However, the problem was, she didn't even know which ones her mother had used.

Suddenly, her chest felt too heavy—heavy with her blood, her secrets, her grief, her guilt...

Emara needed air. The prime could wait—or start without her. There would be other people to voice their requests today, not just her. Before she could rise, Artem Stryker placed a hand on her arm.

"Take a deep breath. Everything is going to be okay." His golden eyes found hers, and he gave her a friendly smile. "You've got this."

She did as she was told, breathing in through her nose and out through her mouth.

"Sybil," was all Artem said before the earth witch's calming hands were on hers, wiping away the distress.

Her friend whispered as she squeezed her hand, "Stay calm, I am here. You have so much support today."

Emara nodded, acknowledging the steel in her heart and the truth of knowing her support was there.

"You are powerful and in control." Sybil's soothing voice sent vibrations of calm through her.

Artem, Naya, Gideon, Marcus, Sybil, Breighly

They wouldn't let her fail.

She looked up to see Torin's icy gaze across the room, studying her face.

She could tell he knew something was wrong, something in his eyes giving that away. It was like he was fighting with himself to go to her or stay seated.

He wouldn't want to highlight her panic or cause for concern, so he stayed in his seat, his eyes burning through her soul. His lips parted, and Emara caught a glimpse of his straight white teeth under his full lips. He gave a wink that had less swagger in it than normal. He was there too. From a distance.

Her heart squeezed. It wasn't enough. She wanted more from him. But she knew for certain that right here, in this setting, she wouldn't get it.

Torin had always painted her in a light that was strong and courageous, always pushing her to make bold decisions and own who she was. She had been trying to be that person these last few months.

If only he could truly see how she was doing.

Without his wicked grin, his guardianship, his friendship, her heart was hurting. Without his hands, his kiss, his heart...everything was flat.

"You need to centre your thoughts, Emara," Sybil warned. "I can feel your energy shifting. Not here. We can both freak out together after the summit. Not here. Not before you get what you came for. Not in front of them."

She knew who *they* were. The elite. In fact, anyone who thought that women shouldn't have the same rights as men. The men who viewed women as weak, lesser than them. They thought they were too emotional to make decisions and too tolerable to fight the Dark Army. They were too weak to wield a sword and too maternal to put a dagger through an enemy's heart.

She had to get it together.

Today wasn't about her broken heart; today, Emara Clearwater was going to change life for every young girl and woman in the kingdom. Emara hoped with all her heart that she could make everyone equal.

"Good day to you all." The chief commander nodded as he rose from his chair before placing his hands behind his back. He was so official. He never took a step out of turn. It was times like this that it was hard to imagine Artem and his father coming from the same clan. "If I could have your cooperation for silence, that would be much obliged. There are a few decisions to be made between factions today involving marriages, guards, and territory." He walked to a table with documents stacked rather high and began his first assignment.

The chief commander talked through territory, stations of men, and where the Fae would like their army placed or pulled back. He covered Shifter business with Murk and touched upon finances with the Minister of Coin, whose appearance made Emara's skin crawl. It always reminded her of the self-indulgent, greedy, ostentatious faction he represented, and she wondered if she would ever see the good in what he embodied.

Once the chief commander had sent his congratulations to

House Water and Clan Coldwell on the news of their growing family, his eyes landed on Emara. "Can the Empress of Air please rise and take to the centre of the room?"

As the leader of the hunters, it was also his duty to read from a letter that had been sent to the prime, and it was clear he was shocked by Emara's request. As he looked at her over the paper in his hands, his eyes narrowed. Emara took a deep breath but held herself the way Naya had taught her as she walked onto the floor that would be her stage. All eyes from the factions were on her now, and the silence of the room was staggering.

Finally, the time had come for her to appoint a new guard, and she was ready to advise who she wanted.

The chief commander's eyebrows scrunched again, and his mouth moved from side to side like he was deep in thought, possibly trying to process his surprise at the contents of her request.

He ran a large hand over his chin. "I hold a very interesting letter here, Empress Clearwater." He finally put the letter on the table in front of him and looked at her. His skin was the same colour as Arlo's, and she could see some resemblance in his tall frame, thick arms, and russet hair. But the hunt had aged him before his time. Creases around his eyes showed wisdom, and the lines around his mouth demonstrated experience. He wasn't as handsome as Artem or Arlo, but he did have a charming quality about him.

She adjusted herself, pushing her shoulders back and raising her chin. "I hope it caught your attention in the best of ways, Chief Commander Stryker."

The full room was so silent you could hear a pin drop, but she tried to focus on the reason for being here. Determination ran through her veins.

"It has absolutely caught my attention, Empress of House Air." Chief Stryker's voice was deep with meaning. "Call me highly intrigued."

Emara paused, halting the conversation; he held the power in this discussion, and so it should be him to ask the next question. She had to remain poised and look like none of the pressure was getting to her. She allowed one eyebrow to rise.

He observed her silence. "For the members of the summit here today who have not read the letter from the Empress of House Air, she is in need of a replacement for her late guard, Magin Oxhound."

The Minister of Coin spoke in the same way all elite men did, looking down their nose. "I don't see what needs the attention of the prime; surely that would be arranged with her closest clan."

"You will see why it requires our attention," The chief commander mused as he gestured his hand for Emara to give insight to her letter.

She blew out a short breath. "As the court knows, my guard was murdered in cold blood by his own brethren—who turned dark—at the Amethyst Palace during the winter solstice." Emara kept her gaze on the commander, feeling like if she placed it anywhere else, she would lose her nerve. "We are six moons on and yet I haven't replaced him—"

"Down to your choice, Empress Clearwater," the chief commander commented. "I have offered plenty of hunters for the position of your third. Yet, you refuse them."

"I do...I have," she cut in sharply, not allowing him to dominate from an early point in the negation.

Nip them enough to bleed so they know you want blood, Torin would have said.

Dominance.

"Please do not take my refusal of your hunters as a means to wound your offer," Emara continued. "I am very grateful that you have presented such fine hunters for my counsel, but from my letter of request, you now know why I cannot accept them."

The chief commander rolled his lips, and the rest of the prime sat with intrigued looks plastered on their faces.

"Whilst reevaluating my situation and that of my coven, I have found that my trio of guards requires something more diverse," she disclosed, finally finding her feet in the flow of her political stance. "Something that looks more inclusive. Something that works for me."

A few murmurs broke from the court.

"I believe that my next guard shouldn't be of hunting blood, but of wolf's blood." Emara pulled in her cheeks and lifted her gaze to every man who sat on the prime panel, before saying, "I believe that the third person in my trio of guards should be a woman."

Gasps came from the crowd. She didn't dare move until the commander broke the stare first. When he did, turning to see the reactions of those on the panel, Emara finally let her gaze float over to Torin for the briefest second. She found no smile, but there was a twinkle of sly amusement in his eyes.

"A woman?" The Minister of Coin snorted, finally sitting back in his chair. "Why are you wasting our time today?"

She ignored him, turning her head to the alpha. "In fact, I have asked for you to hear me speak at this meeting to honour your daughter for the position, Alpha Baxgroll. I wish to appoint Breighly Baxgroll as one of my guards. She is bright, fierce, and brilliant, and I believe that she is the perfect fit for my cluster."

The large wolf stood, and another unified gasp made its way through the room.

Emara sucked in a secret breath too.

"Let me get this straight, Empress." His inability to wrap his head around the conversation showed on his face. "You are asking for my daughter, a wolf, to be a member of your guards?"

"That is what I want, yes." Emara's gaze did not falter from his face. Her posture did not change even though her muscles ached from tension.

It was then the Minister of Coin let out a chuckle so vile even Murk looked towards him.

"You cannot be serious." His hacking laugh spread nothing but anger over Emara's skin. She pulled on the reins of her magic as it burned to be released to smother him. Air was building in her blood, and it wouldn't be long before fire did the same. "The House of Air would be disgraced if you let a wolf in amongst the hen house, let alone have a woman as a guard."

A slight growl came from some of the wolves in the crowd, and she could see the bulking muscles that Murk held on his frame flexing in distaste of that comment.

"I disagree, Your Grace." She used the term lightly on a man so filled with secrets and atrocities. "I believe a woman could make a difference for the greater good in my trio. It could widen the horizons for us all, giving us more choice and less pressure on the current men on post, who are spread thin across every coven. We must open our eyes to the possibility of women guarding for our kingdom just as well as a man. We have just as much to fight for. This move would certainly allow room for some of your exhausted men to be relieved from posts. And since you still require the clans' protection, it could open up doorways for everyone, including you and the protection your faction requires."

The minister sat up straight in his chair, his eyes already dazzling with the idea of conflict. "Then I suppose your coven should bear more sons in aid of your cause, *Miss* Clearwater, so that women do not need to fight. If the clans are spread so thinly, then why do you not see it as your duty to produce more warriors?"

"My coven," she punched back, feeling that fire in her belly, "have protected and given magical aid to your faction for longer than the gold on your fingers has shined." She knew her eyes glistened with darkness, but she didn't care. "Therefore, I think you should leave the decisions of childbearing to the sex who know something about it. Even the magic of a witch cannot determine the gender of the child, therefore, we cannot guarantee the birth of any sons. I think we should be making more strategic and progressive moves than leaving it up to fate, Your Grace."

Witches in the crowd agreed, and she heard a few male voices too, including Artem's.

The Minister of Coin scoffed as he twirled a diamond ring on his pinkie finger. "I have never witnessed a decent-bred female wolf fight. How can we be sure that she is up to par with the hunters? Are you sure she will want to get her claws dirty?"

Just as Emara expected a comment from the alpha, a voice came from behind her.

"I am not the kind of woman that you normally deal with in your world, Minister of Coin."

Emara's head turned to witness Breighly standing tall just behind her shoulder. Emara had to control the smirk on her face as she turned back to the panel, who were still staring at her, wide-eyed.

"I am not the kind of girl from *your* world that is wrapped in silk and told when she can and cannot speak, Your Grace." She walked forward and took her place next to Emara. "I am skilled in many ways; I am as destructive as my pack when in wolven form and I can fight just as well as the hunters in human form. I am the kind of woman our enemies should fear. If you want to see me in battle form, all you need to do is ask."

"Yes!" A booming clap came after a shout from the crowd. Emara didn't have to turn to know that it was Artem Stryker. They evidently had his support—or at least Breighly did.

A few muffled voices could be heard agreeing.

Breighly lifted her chin to Aerrick Stryker. "Chief Commander, I would be honoured to stand beside Emara, the Empress of Air, as her guard, and would take the oath in the same way the hunters do to prove my loyalty and devotion to the role. I have thought about this thoroughly, and I am prepared to make that choice for myself. I have my pack's agreement. I just need my father's blessing in front of the prime."

Emara glanced over to where the Baxgrolls were sitting. Waylen certainly wasn't happy about what was unfolding, but it wasn't like he could stop his sister. Roman had a protective glare in his eyes that posed danger to anyone who spoke out against her. All the others looked on edge.

Emara had taken a risk even asking Breighly to entertain the thought of being a member of her guardianship, let alone vow to take an oath, but it was a strong step for Breighly to play that card. It showed her tenacity to the cause.

"You are a wolf." Murk's deep voice hit off the back wall of the room. "And a wolf does not take the same oaths as a hunter. You do not vow anything under the God of War, but only to our God of Life and Beauty."

Breighly shifted her weight. "I worship the same Gods as everyone else in this room. We all worship the Light. And if you can think of an occasion when the Dark Army has stopped to ask us about what Gods we worship on the battlefield before slaughtering anyone, then I will step away from this honour and never look back."

A positive acknowledgement came from the crowd, and Emara swallowed.

Breighly seemed to be a popular choice.

"Vanadey may be Breighly's factional god, but in the light, she stands like I do. Therefore, we should show no distinction when we speak of the Light Gods and how our factions come together to unite as one." Emara held the commander's gaze. "The Baxgrolls have shown time and time again that they defend these lands fiercer and prouder than any other, so why would it be so unnatural to have a wolf as my guard? Have you not fought with the Blacksteels before to come together to protect your territory?"

Another stir from the crowd proved that Emara's seeds were taking root. However, she did hear some grunts of disapproval, but she couldn't focus on that. Not now.

Murk took a step forward to join Commander Stryker. "Then why can I not give you one of my sons as a substitute for your guardianship request? Waylen or Roman would be honoured to take the opportunity."

Emara was sharp and unrelenting as she said, "Because I have made it clear I do not wish to have any of your sons in my trio. I have pledged for your daughter if the prime would grant it."

The alpha looked tense, but he hadn't yet said *no,* and Emara wondered if Breighly had spoken to her father beforehand. She did come under his jurisdiction; she was his princess.

Emara took a step forward. "I have seen her fight the Dark Army under the grace of this kingdom's moons, and I know she is worthy of the position, as do you, Alpha Baxgroll. She is fierce and loyal and has never faltered when sending the Dark Army back where they belong. I know it is hard for you to consider that your daughter be anything but your delicate little girl, but she is powerful and a grand fighter. I wish to have her by my side to ensure my magic's safety. To ensure this kingdom has an Empress of Air. It would mean that the pack also has my protection and anything I have to offer. She has shown more than once that she is capable of my protection, Alpha."

Murk took a few seconds before a small, wry smile appeared on his face. "Oh, I know she is anything but delicate. She is a wolf. My wolf." His eyes softened as he looked over his princess, and it was the only time Emara had ever seen his dark eyes turn a golden brown. "Do you want this, Bry?"

Breighly smiled at her father as she looked him in the eye and said, "I am ready, Papa."

CHAPTER ELEVEN
EMARA

For the first time in all of the meetings and summits Emara had attended, the Faerie king rose from his seat and looked over the crowd. His stunning silver hair hung loosely at the sides of his face, his ears sticking out from underneath. His eyes were shining like amethysts as he drank in the sight of her standing there.

Emara's heart skipped a few beats, and even Breighly tensed beside her.

Although he was a slender man, you could still see the strength in his stance as he stood like stone. His cobalt dress jacket swept the floor behind him as he slowly walked over to her, his fancy shoes clicking on the wooden floor.

Emara didn't know if air had entered her lungs or if it had hidden away as the king stood before her. His ancient-looking hand took hold of hers and she couldn't hold back the audible gasp that left her throat. She had never seen him do anything of the likes before. He normally sat unmoving, listening and making cordial nods in agreement or disagreement. He wasn't interested in being involved in any political business that did not directly affect his court. Never before had she seen him move or make an effort to speak to someone standing at a summit.

She bowed lower than she had ever before, hoping that she

hadn't offended him. Had she disrespected him in some way? Did Fae views differ from her own? Had she lost his vote?

As she straightened her spine, her gaze met his, and an amused smile tantalised his thin, pale lips.

"Empress of House Air," he said in a voice so elderly she would have thought him a relic older than the Resurrection Stone. "It is my pleasure to greet you fully."

She had met him a handful of times before, but she thought it rude to correct a king, so she nodded her head gracefully and said, "The honour is mine, King Oberon."

The room that had gathered momentum just moments before fell into a stunned silence, and she felt like everyone was holding their breath.

"My enchantments are of ancient practice, and very different to how you wield your own." He spoke quietly, but his pointed features were full of meaning, his gaze locked on hers. "I can feel the power of your wind and flame beckoning to my own sorcery, as I stand before you. When I dream, I can see your abilities in spirit reaching out to connect the stars in our universe, touching on galaxies untold. And when I hold the bones of your hand now, I can feel the magic of earth in the tips of your fingers; I can feel the need to heal the broken parts of this world. If you can find the connection to water, witchling, you will be unstoppable."

Emara's head dizzied, her hand that was still in the grasp of the king beginning to shake.

"There is a gap in our history that dates back to when the ancients left this world and the Gods found sanctuary somewhere more magical than Caledorna, and I believe you are going to fill that gap, Emara Clearwater. Your power is infinite." He leaned in and whispered to her only, "Even if I can feel a terrible darkness brewing in you. You must search for the Light, always."

Before Emara could even register the compliment or take in

what the king had just said about the darkness of her blood, King Oberon turned to the crowd. Dropping her hand, he said, "All in favour of granting the Empress of Air, an heir of royal witching blood and defender of the Light Gods, the right for her choice of guard, please make it known. Stand." His galaxy-filled eyes looked around and then back to her.

Emara's mouth fell open slightly as people began rising from their seats in her favour. Rows and rows of the magical factions stood. The king nodded in her direction with a wise smile that was almost too coy to see and began making his way back to his chair on the panel.

"What the fuck did you just do?" Breighly whispered in her ear, laughing a little.

"I have no idea," Emara whispered back as she took in the crowd, her own heart beating like an enchanted drum.

A few still sat in their chairs, but that was okay because it was clear she had the majority vote. Her empress sister stood, watching her in amazement. Kerrix Bellfield of House Spirit smiled, and Emara knew she had changed the game for her too. Rya's face gave nothing away. Emara could have choked on her own heart as she took in all the eyes and faces watching her change the course of history.

"Then it shall be done," the king said, showing no hint of surprise like the others from the prime. "Can the faction leaders make their vote known even though there is an overwhelming majority in the empress's favour?"

A crash back down to reality had Emara's eyes back on the prime. Regardless of if the people had made themselves known, the prime still had the final say.

It took a moment, but Murk nodded, and a smile as radiant as the moon lit Breighly's face.

"Commander Stryker?" the king urged.

Aerrick seemed to toy with the decision in his mind, drawing out a long silence. "I will agree to her terms on a temporary basis," the chief hunter said as he placed a hand to his mouth, rubbing his lower lip. "The empress makes a valid point about my men, but because the wolf will be working alongside my clans directly, I will need to clear Miss Baxgroll before I allow her into my formations. I will need to assess her skill, tenacity, and mind."

"Of course, Chief Commander." Emara nodded her head.

As she stole a glance at the Minister of Coin, who remained seated, she could feel his blood boiling under his expensive attire. She flashed him a victorious smile.

He flashed her one of his own back, surprising her. "It seems congratulations are in order."

"There is no need to congratulate something that should already stand." Emara placed her chin in the air again.

He smiled a terrible grin, one that rattled her core. It was like she had just fallen prey to one of his hideous traps.

"Talking of things that should already stand," he began. She took a breath and prayed to Rhiannon as a darkness spread in his smile. "Shouldn't your second name have been altered by now, under the treaty of marriage?"

"I wasn't aware there was a time constraint on my engagement," Emara quickly batted back, feeling the thunder in her heart.

"Engagement?" He huffed a laugh. "I see no promise ring on your finger."

The crowd dropped silent again as they took their seats.

Emara opened her mouth to speak when the minister cut her off, "Given the fact that it is an alliance that you require as an empress."

Oh Gods, where in the underworld was this headed?

"The fact still remains that none of the Blacksteel hunters have owned up to their part of the deal between your house and their clan. It seems that they cannot provide you with an offer that you cannot resist." He ground his teeth and then stood slowly. "But I think that's about to change. I will make you an offer that should be irresistible to a woman who needs an alliance."

An uneasiness had spread through the crowd, and whispers like an eerie song had begun to flutter, but the pounding of her heart seemed to drown everything else out.

"Instead of marrying for a hunter alliance, I could offer you much more than protection for your coven, Miss Clearwater. And since you are all about paving new paths for the women of your world, why not come to an agreement with someone who offers just that? Someone like me."

Emara blinked a few times before she concluded that she was not in the middle of a nightmare. Before she could respond, the chief commander, who had made his way back to his chair, said, "That won't be necessary, Minister of Coin. The empress is not a trade deal. She is set to wed Gideon Blacksteel when they both see fit."

The statement hit her worse than a punch in the gut.

The truth of her so-called fate.

She was running on borrowed time, that she knew, but she hadn't expected the topic of her marriage to appear in today's meeting. She thought the shock of her request would have at least bought her a few more moons.

"I understand that there is a treaty in place for her to be promised to the Blacksteels, whichever one it is this month." The Minister of Coin finally took his eyes from Emara's face and looked to Viktir Blacksteel, who was wearing a dangerous scowl. "But I am looking to put forth my offer to the Empress of Air for her consideration to take my hand in marriage. With no true leader in Emara's corner, with no seat on the prime, every witching coven is at risk, and I can provide the wealth that the air coven needs."

Emara watched the spineless man who led the human faction try to create fear amongst her witches. He wanted them to feel vulnerable. He wanted her to need him. He wanted to see the temptation in her eyes when he laid out his offer. That was what men like him did. They abused all the power they had, they manipulated, and they took advantage.

His slimy voice brought her attention back to his face.

"If you were to be my bride, I would offer you a limitless pocket of coin for your coven to use as they see fit. We could pay guards handsomely. You wouldn't need a wolfpack or a clan. You would have me and my wealth. With your potential and my influence in the kingdom, we would be the ultimate pairing."

Trickles of panic could be heard from her coven whispering in the front row. Emara glanced at Lorta, who was holding hands with Kaydence, and their terrified faces were not the only reason that she had fire pulsing in her fingertips.

This was not how marriage offers were supposed to be presented to an empress, and he knew it. He was not only insulting her, but her coven too. He was trying to make her look inferior to him. Weak.

"I am not interested in how much coin you are willing to hand over to my coven for my hand in a treaty," Emara assured him. "What we require is more than a small piece of metal that is heavy in your pocket, especially when I can have a warrior of Thorin that would provide ten times the artillery that you can."

"Why would an empress only be interested in artillery when she could be the bride of someone wealthy enough to buy every army in the kingdom?" He twirled that pinkie ring again, and she had visions of cutting it off his hand with a dagger.

However, Emara was still in a formal setting, with the eyes of the kingdom on her, and she couldn't let this man goad her into something terrible when she had just been victorious.

She swallowed down what she really wanted to say and plastered the mask of an empress back onto her face. "I am flattered by your offer, Your Grace, but I can't accept it."

An arrogant shine beaded in his eye, and cruelty pulled at his lip. Something had switched. "Today, you may have won over the alpha in your little game of equality, and you may have enamoured the Fae king with whatever elemental enchantment you hold over him..." He came out from behind the table and strolled a little closer. "And the Gods only know how you have managed to keep the most powerful hunting clans at your back." He paused, looking over her. "But you don't have me fooled, girl. I know all it takes to persuade a woman in a powerful position is the right settlement figure and a husband whose life is not on the line every night they step out into a hunt." He threw a glance over his shoulder. "Chief Commander, if you dissolve the alliance between Clan Blacksteel and House Air, I can make you an offer that could make you one of the wealthiest men in the kingdom. Name your price. You know I can pay it."

Emara couldn't help but scoff, even if it were unprofessional of her. All he could offer was coin. But that didn't haunt Emara as much as why he wanted her as a bride. That part was frightening.

"This is a direct insult to my can." Viktir Blacksteel stood, his chest puffing out.

The chief commander raised a single finger as a command to stand down.

For once, Emara agreed with Viktir. The Blacksteel Clan was wealthy enough in their station and powerfully respected in their duty.

But this was Emara's fight, and she would not back down.

"I reject your offer." She looked the Minister of Coin in the eye as she said, "A Supreme may not sit on the witching throne for now, but that does not make us vulnerable." She looked over her empresses, and the magic in their eyes shone back at her. "I will not be a slave to your coin and neither will any other coven be, especially not when I can melt your gold with flames. Tell me, Your Grace, what would your coin be worth then?"

He gave a smug laugh. "A hell of a lot more than your treaty with the Blacksteels, and you would be wise to consider that. What is your price then, Empress? We can even look at negotiations." His eyes sparked. "Everyone has a price."

"She is not a diamond that has been plucked from one of your mines to be shined for auction and sold."

A deep, husky voice came from where Torin Blacksteel had been sitting.

Emara turned in a whirlwind spin to see him leaning forward in his chair, his uniform straining around his physique. Torin's glare was deadly as he stood, his chest puffing out and his features murderous. "She is priceless. She cannot be purchased. The empress has stated a few times now that she wishes to refuse your offer, so that will be the end of that discussion. Doesn't no mean no to the elite faction?"

Something turned over in the minister's dark eyes as his head snapped to Torin. "And who are you to speak out against me, boy?"

Torin grinned so wickedly before rolling his lips. "Boy? You know exactly who I am. And you know fine well I am no boy." He rolled up one sleeve of his tunic to reveal that pulsing blue vein that always caught Emara's attention. Damn that blue vein. "The work my clan has done for you does not require boys, but men skilled enough to kill without blinking an eye."

The minister's snobbish laugh broke his lips. "You are of Blacksteel blood, I presume? I find it interesting that you are the one who steps forward for the Empress of Air's honour, yet your brother, the one promised to her, has yet to say a word."

Emara didn't turn around to look at Gideon, but she knew he

would be reeling with anger, probably standing now too. She hoped Naya was there to keep him in check.

"What I also find interesting is the letters that you have sent to the prime, Torin Blacksteel, pleading for your courtship to wed the empress that stands before me. They were some very good reading, I must say. But hold on a second, does that not go against your commander's orders?"

A hiss came from the crowd.

Emara's legs almost came out from underneath her, but a steady hand caught her. She had forgotten that Breighly Baxgroll stood at her side.

He had written letters to the prime?

Torin Blacksteel had written to them, pleading for them to be wed instead of her and Gideon?

Her heart shattered all over again, breaking and breaking until her breath left her. She'd thought he had given up on them, on their future.

"I am aware of what my commander asked of me." Torin walked forward, and Emara didn't know if his closeness was a comfort or torture. "If you deem Emara Clearwater so worthy to put forth a quest to her hand in marriage, you will need to understand how she works." Torin breathed in. "This is just a heads up, she doesn't like it when men don't take no for an answer. Now let her return to her seat with no further questions. She has stood up here long enough, and this matter is uncalled for."

He finally looked at her, his eyes blue enough to crush souls. He gave her a nod. Emara fought the tears in her eyes as she watched Torin turn and head back to his seat.

"I think we ought to call it a day, Chief Commander, and pick up where need be at the next summit," Murk advised, and the crowd released more breaths than Emara could count. "Everyone is tired."

Tired wasn't the word.

The King of the Fae nodded in agreement, and the chief commander nodded as he pinched his nose.

As the room broke up, Emara turned to try to reach Torin, but a crowd swarmed her. Some had tears in their eyes at what she had done for them. Some kissed her hand and swore they would never forget this moment. All had so many questions. Lorta and Kaydence rushed in to save her, moving her through the crowd that felt like they were clawing at her for attention.

Even though it didn't feel like it, she had just broken the chains of conformities in Caledorna and changed the path for women all over the kingdom. One of her guards was going to be a wolf. A woman.

Perhaps she should feel more victorious than she did, but a heavy shadow thickened in her heart, and she just wanted the ground to open up and swallow her whole.

CHAPTER TWELVE
EMARA

Emara sat at the oversized window in her bedroom, looking out at the city below her. The lights of homes and workplaces twinkled in the orangey-red glow, and as the sunset fell behind the buildings, Emara noted that she had never really gone exploring in the city, just the markets. And from this view, the city looked so beautiful. She made a promise to herself that she would go wandering once everything settled down. She would experience the city she so often stared at from the windows of the Tower.

She had been in her room ever since coming back from the minister's mansion, the day's events rolling over in her mind tirelessly.

Her new guardianship, her encounter with the Fae king, her stand-off with the Minister of Coin. The slight glimmer of hope that had welled in her heart when Torin defended her...

It was all too much. Her mind just needed a rest.

Maybe she needed some air; being with her natural element always calmed her, but there was nowhere for her to go downstairs without being seen. The Tower was heaving full of magical factions since her achievements, and the gardens would be well used on a summer night like tonight.

A promising thought had Emara standing in a second.

She knew of a place that would give her a view of the city and air on her skin as she worked through all the thoughts in her mind.

Heading to the door, she met Artem at his post, as always.

"I want to release you from your post for the night," she announced, meeting his eye, knowing full well that she was about to find herself in another showdown. "You should go and enjoy the celebrations."

"You know I can't do that." He crossed his arms over his chest, leaving the wall behind. "Why are you trying to entice me with celebrations? What tricks do you have up your witchy little sleeves tonight?"

She closed her eyes on an outward breath. "Artem, I just want to be alone for an hour. I am going to the rooftop of the Tower, not the fighting pits."

Artem lifted his brow. "You never know with you these days."

Spending so much time with one person meant that you got to know a lot about them, their mind, their strengths, their weaknesses...

Emara put her hand on the door frame. "I will be fine. I just need to feel...free. I need some time alone. Plus, I need you to find Breighly Baxgroll. She should be back at the Tower soon. Your father should be clearing her now for the position and is keen for her to take the night post. It will give her time to think if she wants to take the oath or not and it will give you time to rest. Plus, she might come looking for me...here."

His eyes sparkled. "Oh. Okay. Do you think she will come to your quarters? She knows where they are, right? Do you want me to wait here in case you miss her or aren't back on time?"

"Yes, Artem." Emara bit back a grin. "Do you think you can give me a little space? Just for a teeny tiny hour."

He nodded quickly, running a hand through his russet hair. "Okay, sure. I can wait here. Okay, yeah. I will wait here. Makes sense," he said, his forehead wrinkling as his eyes narrowed. "No rush. Take your time. I will be right here."

She placed a hand on his huge bicep. "Thanks, champ."

He leaned in, a stern look on his face. "Do not leave this Tower. I mean it, *Empress of Wandering into Trouble.*"

Emara offered her guard a smile and then disappeared into the corridor to hide her amusement at a very flustered Artem Stryker waiting for a certain wolf.

Climbing the stairs so quickly burned her thighs in a way that validated her strength instead of her old weakness. Before, she would have been out of breath, but her training recently had increased not only her speed but her endurance too. When she could feel her lungs burn, she called on her element as a remedy. Reaching the old door that looked extremely out of place, she burst through the threshold and was smacked by a strong summer breeze. It was muggy, but it was enough to soothe her skin after her climb.

Closing her eyes, she let the breeze cool her face, neck and mind, letting the summer air whirl around her body. Her element had found her like she had called to it, and it gave her what she required, wrapping her in a delicate, comforting embrace.

The sounds of punching leather and throaty grunts interrupted her, and she opened her eyes before taking a few steps out onto the rooftop properly.

A brown leather punching bag stood like an enemy of the Blacksteel Clan at the furthest side of the roof.

Emara's heart fluttered into her throat as she witnessed Torin Blacksteel's bare knuckles battering against its weight. His strong back muscles moved under his slick skin, demonstrating how powerful his body was as he made blow after blow. Emara sometimes forgot how lethal he was, but seeing him like this was always a reminder of how much of a powerhouse he truly was. His feet moved just as quickly as his hands, always surprising her with how graceful his movements were for the sheer size of him. His torso rotated, showing his carved abdomen as he punched and punched and punched, obliterating the punching bag.

His breathing was heavy, his chest convulsing more than she had ever seen. He had been up here a while, she guessed. She could see evidence of the leather starting to burst at one side of the bag.

How many times had he punched that thing?

"We've got to stop meeting up here, Torin," she called as the gentle breeze blew at a few loose strands of her braid and carried his name out towards the city below.

He halted, his back more tense than before.

"I didn't realise you trained up here," she said, and she took a sharp inhale when he didn't respond to her. "Or that you were still at the Tower."

She had wondered if he had gone back to the pits to fight himself to death or drink himself into an oblivion again.

But he hadn't. He was here.

Torin didn't look around as he started punching again. "I am not training."

He was self-destructing.

What was worse, he could barely even look at her, and it had been that way since his father had told the prime of his amendments to the marriage treaty. However, today, for the first time in many moons, she had seen a little glimmer of hope as he defended her at the summit. A sliver of how he felt about her. His eyes had locked with hers and he'd held his breath when he looked at her.

In that moment, she'd vowed to herself that she would find him again, find his soul, and fight for him. She would take it upon herself to tell him her stance in all of this. He was lost right now, but she would always find him. It wasn't over for them.

Viktir Blacksteel was not a god, and he did not decide her fate.

"Thank you for showing up today—and for being in my corner," she called out, hoping it would reach his heart. "You didn't have to—"

"I did have to." He punched into the bag with full force, the impact shuddering through the air. "You were being preyed on by the vultures of the prime. The Minister of Coin is a squirming. Piece. Of. Shit." He struck the bag like it was the elite man's face.

"At least we agree on something," she tried to joke, but her voice fell flat. "You always seem to come to my aid when I need you most."

She felt like her heart was open, bare for all to see, and when he didn't respond, a spike of shame turned into anger.

Torin punched until the noise began to burn in her ears. "I wasn't going to let him hound you like that in front of everyone," he said finally, surprising her. "Oh, and by the way, you need to stop being cordial to people who don't respect you."

"What would you have wanted me to do? Light the Minister of Coin's mansion on fire?"

"Exactly that."

He punched and hammered and beat the leather. With every second that passed, Emara's blood boiled hotter.

"Stop!" she roared, an overwhelming sensation pouring over her. "Stop punching."

He halted again, stopping the weighty bag from moving. She took a breath, hearing the blissful silence, but she was soon swarmed by everything that had been left unsaid between them.

"Please, just stop punching," she whispered.

He looked over his broad shoulder at her, his dark hair spilling over his brow that dripped with perspiration. For one desperate moment, she wanted to be the only thing in the universe to fill his shattered eyes with hope. She wanted them to fill with desire and admiration for her like they used to, to fill with jest and wicked taunts meant only for her ears.

He turned to face the punching bag again and his head fell

towards his chest, his strong neck straining as he looked at the ground.

"Maybe we should talk about this." A small voice that didn't sound like her own passed her lips.

"There is nothing to say, Emara." He whispered her name back like a plea to end his torment.

Her throat bobbed, shutting in all the emotion that she could feel escaping. "Why won't you look at me anymore?"

"Emara—"

"Why?" she cried, finally breaking the tension in the air. "You are acting like I mean nothing to you."

"You know that's not true." He glanced back at her.

"Stop shutting me out, Torin. I know you care about me. I know you do, so why can't you show me your heart?"

He lifted his gaze to the sky that had begun to absorb the summer pastels and turn them into night. The wolf moon had not yet entered the sky fully, but a slow glow set over the city like a dampened oil lamp.

He shook his head and let out a huge exhale. "Do you think that is fair of you to ask me that?"

Her heart cracked open. No, no it wasn't. But she couldn't stand this any longer.

She wasn't about to let some things go unanswered.

"Why didn't you tell me that you had sent letters to the prime requesting our union be favoured?" A single tear tracked down her face in frustration and hurt. "Do you not think that I have a right to know of such requests?"

He placed his hands on his hips and turned to face her. Overhead, Emara could see a dark cloud forming, and it blocked out the glow that illuminated his skin and striking features. Instead, it carved them out, sending darker shadows across his face and a coldness into his eyes.

"There was no point in telling you that I had written to them if it were not to come to fruition."

Emara's heart had never hurt more as she looked at him, tortured by what she knew was his hope for a different future too. He had shared that intimate thought with her, the deepest parts of him. He had shared with her everything that he was. And she had shared it all with him too. Her heart had chosen him.

She gritted her teeth. "The point is that I would have known about it. I would have known that there was hope in all of this, known how your heart felt. Instead of this...nothingness. This ice. You have done nothing but avoid me, Torin."

He took a short breath and then glanced out at the city.

"Will you look at me?" Emara's voice grated against her throat.

Her magic was stirring. The air thickened and somehow managed to get clammier than it already was. Her flames threatened to lick her palms and her wind gathered around them, blowing at their hair.

"Look at me!" she finally screamed.

"I can't!" he roared back, finally turning. He no longer looked hurt, but devastated. "I can't look at you because every time I do, I see everything that I ever wanted. I see everything I can't have. Why don't you fucking understand that? Yes, I have been avoiding you—because my heart cannot bear to see you."

He might as well have punched her in the face. She took a stumble back.

But he took a step forward. "My heart bleeds every time I see you. My heart shatters every time your name is mentioned," Torin seethed, his hair rustling in the newly formed wind. "And I can't stand the thought of you being married to someone else. It fucking kills me! Is that what you wanted to hear?"

"Of course not." She shook her head as tears blinded her vision.

Emara tried to take a few steps towards him, but her stupid legs wouldn't listen. "Maybe we can go to the prime—"

"And what then?" His hand flew out. "Have your way in court for another time this month? That's not how politics works in this world, Emara. I think you might have reached the limits of favours from the prime."

"I have overcome things that people didn't believe in before. We just have to make them see another way."

He scoffed. "Another way? And what would that be?"

Anger built in her heart, and she scrunched her fists as tears rolled from her eyes. "This...defeatist attitude is so very *un-Blacksteel* of you," she spat.

"Oh?" He turned to face her again. "Are you now an expert in Blacksteels just because you are set to wed my brother? How are the wedding plans coming along, by the way?"

The sting of his comment pierced her heart. "Maybe if I were an *expert* in Blacksteels I would know how to deal with how pathetic you are being right now."

"Pathetic?" Irritation finally reached his eyes, screwing them tight. "Is that what you think of me?"

"Are you doing anything to prove otherwise? At least I am acknowledging that we could do something about this. I am trying to think of ways we are not eternally miserable. But you have just accepted that fate, and that is so weak of you."

He walked towards her slightly, his knuckles strained white. "What would you have me do, Emara? Stand before the prime and beg for them to release me of my commander, of my oath? Because I was going to do that and you stopped me. You told me that I couldn't. I was going to throw in this whole fucking life because all I wanted was you." He paused, the pain in his heart reaching the features of his face. "You are all that mattered. I would have run. I would have packed a bag and we could have disappeared. But you couldn't. And I understand that. I do. I get that you had a lot more to give up. You are the Empress of Air." He rolled his bottom lip between his teeth. "Gods, Emara, I even stuck around when my father was announcing your engagement to my brother. I watched as Gideon tried his best to court you in front of me. But I couldn't do it anymore. I couldn't watch it happen. So what would you have me do?"

Torin had come to her a few days after the winter solstice ball, when she had been cleared by the healers, and he had asked her to go with him—go anywhere in the kingdom—and she had refused him. She had asked for more time. That was all she had seemed to be doing lately, working off borrowed time.

She took a moment before answering him, the stinging in her chest finally reaching her eyes. "All I am asking from you is to..." She stopped herself from speaking and found another way around saying what she really wanted to. "Have patience. Have faith that this will work out. I will find a way."

He shook his head, his hands falling down by his sides. "You can't ask me to be patient for something that I will never have."

Emara could feel the word vomit climb in her throat. "You used to look at me and stop the world with the passion in your eyes." Her hands and voice shook. "And then when you found out about my blood—about who I really am—my world spun so violently because I couldn't even fathom a world where you didn't look at me like that. And now my only option is to believe that you can't look at me the same because you know who my father is. Is that the reason you won't fight for this?"

The air around them dampened like a storm was imminent, and the sky turned a darker shade of black-blue.

"Emara, all I do is look at you." His lips pulled over his teeth, his gaze holding hers in a fiery frustration. "All I do is see you, even when I pray to Thorin to stop such cruelty in my dreams. I dream of you with my brother, having the life that I envisioned for myself. For us. You shouldn't want me to feel this way for you anymore. You shouldn't want me to look at you like I used to." He moved forward and then halted. "I don't give a fuck about your demon blood, and I certainly don't care that Balan is your father." An icy mist passed through his eyes. "I meant what I said to the Supreme at the winter solstice ball. I know your heart, and that's what kills me, because I know how it feels about me too. I am being punished because I disobeyed my commander and put my heart before my duty. And I am enraged that the punishment involves you too. I will be forever sorry for that. I hate myself for it."

She pulled a few strands of hair from her face. "I don't care if I am punished anymore, Torin, because it feels like torture without you anyway. I can't do it. I can't marry Gideon. I just can't. And you need to hear that. I won't marry him."

"Don't say that. You need to." He swallowed then, possibly a bit of his pride or his heart. "I am not scared of what would happen to me if we defied my father, but for you. It would make sense for you to marry him over me. He can make sure you are safe. What we have...it's forbidden."

She let him see a tear fall. "How the heart truly feels is never forbidden. The heart rules over everything."

He looked at her with those piercing blue eyes, and she swore that a thunder cloud had merged just behind him, creating a menacing backdrop.

Finally, his lips parted, and he shook his head. "If I were a better man, a good man, I would let you be with Gideon. I would let you be with my brother and find happiness. I should walk away. You don't need me to interfere with that."

Emara shook her head as the lump formed in her throat again. "You have no idea what you are even saying." Her voice rose. "That is not your decision. You can't make that decision for me."

"Yes, yes I can." His chest rose sharply and then fell. "Especially when it comes to putting you first—"

"You are not putting me first, Torin." A horrible laugh bellowed from her throat. "So don't you dare say that pushing me away is a choice that you made for me, because it's not. You may be protecting me, but I don't want it. Don't dare say you are stepping away because of my happiness, because you are doing the opposite of what I want."

"I have no other choice." His frustrated brow pulled in. "Why would I put you in the firing line of my father, Emara? Tell me why. You don't know what you are dealing with when it comes to the levels of cruelty that Viktir Blacksteel will stoop to. Nothing would be a stretch. Nothing is out of bounds."

"I know that already," she roared back, her muscles beginning to shake. "He has already threatened to reveal my blood if I don't set a date to wed Gideon." A boom thundered across the sky, followed by a flash. "I know the levels to which he will go to ensure that I am ensnared in his trap. And I still won't break under his pressure. I refuse to let him break me."

Rage poured over Torin's face. "I could fucking kill him for doing that to you." He took a breath in, and she saw a trace of fear flare in his eyes.

She let her tears run, and the saltiness hit her mouth. "My soul knew how I felt about you before my heart would give in and admit it, Torin. Don't give up on us."

He looked at her through his lashes, through his own broken dreams, and his lips parted, but he stilled as the wind of a storm picked up his dark hair, making it unruly.

"Those scars on your hands and body are proof that you have gone into every battle and come out alive," she said to him. "We should treat this—how we feel about each other—no differently. We should fight for what we have. I know that I am ready to." She paused, heart beating horrendously fast. "I am just earning my scars, and I want you with me as I do. I am the Empress of Air and I do not accept a treaty that I do not want for myself or my coven. And you should not accept this fate if you don't want it. Fight for something else. Fight for what is in your heart."

He ran a hand over his face, and his nose wrinkled. The scar that lay between his dark brows pulled together. "Until my father is gone, I am just a pawn in his games with the Gods. He decides my fate, not the Gods, and his stupid little sport with our hearts is proof of that."

Emara stepped forward as another flash lit up the sky. "That's where you are wrong, Torin; you decide your fate, and I need you to realise that before it's too late. We have an impending war brewing in the underworld, and fate is telling me that you and I need to stick together." She paused before allowing a fraction of a smile to grace her lips. "Even if the notorious warrior of the Blacksteel Hunting Clan is acting a *little* pathetic right now."

He scoffed a laugh, and as his ocean-blue eyes found hers, she saw the storming waves in them.

He walked over to the railing and held it tight as he looked out at the city below him. Seconds that felt like years passed between them before he turned to her and said, "Has anyone ever told you how stunning you are when you are pissed off, *angel?* You are truly breathtaking when you fight for what you want."

She finally managed a real smile, and it spread across her face like the summer sun. "Yes. Someone who once promised to stand by my side through more than just an oath, through something more than an alliance. Someone who promised me that his soul would find mine even when his bones were nothing but dust and stars."

"That oath still stands." His face was serious and deep with thought as he looked over her.

She lifted her chin as dark strands of hair battered into her face. "Then I need you to prove that to me, Torin Blacksteel. I want you by my side, no matter what it takes. Not your brother, not anyone else in this kingdom, you. I will not accept a fate that tells me otherwise and neither should you." She did not let her gaze falter. "I have shown you all of my cards. Now you must decide where yours lay."

He let go of the railing and turned to her fully, and with the way a lightning bolt hit through the sky behind him, he could have been a masterpiece, art to be hung in the temple of the Gods. A thick black cloud rolled over the Tower, swallowing the light and devouring the sky. A thunder crash boomed through the city, rocking the railings.

Concern threatened his brow as he finally opened his mouth to speak. "Are you not afraid of the mess in my heart, Empress?"

Yes. She was terrified that if she let go of the final string that her heart clung to, she would be lost in Torin Blacksteel forever. But this was fated, and she would rather go tumbling into fate with Torin than without him. She could feel her magic acknowledging her decision as it stroked her face, her lips, her skin, her heart...

"Are you not afraid of the darkness that runs in my blood?" she battled back, the question meaning way more than the words that formed the sentence.

"I am not afraid of anything except losing you." There was another flash followed by a tremendous crack of thunder just over their heads, and its full echo vibrated through her. But Torin spoke again, unfazed by the approaching storm as his smouldering eyes devoured her. "It's a good thing that I am not the same kind of man as my brother, Emara Clearwater, because I can't let him marry you. Thorin himself is going to have to kill me first."

Emara's heart kissed the inside of her mouth as Torin Blacksteel strode towards her in nothing but leathers as another thunderous crack broke through the sky. He stopped mere inches from her face as bolts of lightning dazzled the clouds. Her favourite scent of pine and frozen berries hugged her even in the season of summer. Her breathing stopped as their gazes connected, her desire for him setting fire to her soul.

This was right.

They were fated.

A few heavy droplets of rain hit her face. Torin took a heavy breath, as if breathing her in, and his hands flew out. His fingers found themselves tangled in her hair in seconds, and she let a soft moan leave her lips at his touch.

His touch. Only his.

He pulled her closer, and the Gods poured rain—warm and inviting—from the black clouds. "I had convinced myself that I had lost you, that I was doing the right thing by you, and I will spend the rest of my life begging for your forgiveness. I was wrong. You were made for me, Emara Clearwater." Placing the top of his brow to hers, Torin murmured against her mouth, "I don't want anyone else to have you, and I don't care if that is selfish. I want you. Only you, angel." He paused as the rain pelted their skin, and she laughed as her tears mixed with the sweetness of the summer rainfall. A fire ignited in Emara's core as he looked down at her, pulling her body close to his, the collision thrilling and harsh. One sinful dimple appeared when he finally growled, "You're mine, always."

That was all it took for something celestial to shift the world's sphere before his mouth came down on hers, hard and fierce, like he had never kissed anyone else in the world.

CHAPTER THIRTEEN
TORIN

Pounding rain pelted Torin's bare back as he took Emara's head in one hand and the small of her back in the other and dragged her into him. His lips hit hers with a thunder louder than what was in the sky. Her chest collided with his, and the feeling of her curves softening against him was everything. His tongue opened her mouth further, deepening the kiss as her hands grabbed his neck and hair.

Pulling.

Needing him.

He had kissed her hard and wild, but how she was kissing him back was matching every part of what he had offered her.

His equal.

His superior.

His thrill.

Trailing his hand from her hair round to her throat, he reluctantly pulled back and whispered into her mouth, "I am so unworthy of you. I see that every time I look at you, especially when I see how you fight for a better world. What I have done makes me so undeserving of you."

"Torin..." She panted against his mouth, clutching at his neck.

"No, you have to hear this." He opened his eyes to find hers watching him, droplets of rain clinging to her lashes. "Don't think for one second that I never wanted this—us. I wanted all of it. I swear to Thorin, I wanted it all. I just didn't know how without putting you in danger. I wanted to give you the best chance at being an empress."

Her midnight hair was soaking, hanging heavy and straight around her shoulders. Her lips were swollen from his kiss and slightly parted, unable to speak. Her skin, drenched in raindrops, was darker, and it was evident that it had been bathed by the sun's light. But even in this storm, she finally had a glow around her again. That steely gaze was back in her eyes, that fire and magic swirling endlessly. Her grey summer dress lay against her curves, highlighting where she rounded beautifully, all places he had worshipped before and wanted to worship now.

She was the most exquisite creature he had ever laid eyes on. Their chests heaved as they looked at one another. The energy charged around them, and he could have sworn that the lightning that split the sky in half was all for her. For them. She was the storm. She was the stars. She was the moon.

And she was right. She was always right. They couldn't go down without fighting for this. How could he not fight for this?

That was very un-Blacksteel of him.

He pushed her dark, wet hair back from her face and leaned in further, his fingers splayed on her cheek. "I never thought I would find someone like you, Emara. The first time you ever scolded me for being a dick was the second I knew I was in trouble, and I was addicted to you from that moment on. I had to know every inch of you, your heart, your soul. I had to be the reason for your tremendous smile, and I had to know that the dangerous glint in your eyes was for me. Only for me." He kissed her again; he needed to feel her lips on his, it had been too long. He pulled back, leaving them both breathless. "I have darkness too, Emara. And you have been so very patient with that. I was not afraid to see your darkness. I'm still not.

And I do not care what blood you have running through your veins. I am so madly in love with you and nothing can change that."

He noticed her eyes widen and change colour as shock hit her heart. As her lips parted to speak, he kissed her again, this time with a little more poise than last. Emara pulled his head to hers again, not settling for anything less than hard passion as she pressed her body against him, drinking in every inch of his mouth. She wanted more of him, and he wanted all of her.

Maybe a moment of madness slipped past them both, but they laughed against each other's mouths, and when she pulled back to look at him, he couldn't for one second more believe that this was not the path the Gods had set for him.

It was her.

She was magical.

She was rainstorms and beauty. She was fire and steel. She was chaos and harmony. She was darkness and light. She was...

She was everything.

She was *his* everything.

"I love you too." She smiled up at him as if she could feel what he was thinking and then she said, "Kiss me, Torin Blacksteel, and don't stop."

His grin must have been wider than the broken sea as he took in the memory of the first time he had begged her to say those little words. Words that meant more to him than she would ever know. Words that had changed the course of their path.

His hand found its way behind her ear. "I will never stop kissing you, Emara Clearwater. Not for anything. Not even for the Gods."

He picked her up like the Goddess she was, and she wrapped her body around him before his mouth was on hers again and he was striding towards a place where he could have every inch of her glorious bare skin against his.

EMARA

Emara was unsure how she'd made it down the stairs or through the corridors without as much as opening her eyes or taking a breath.

Torin had just burst through a door and slammed Emara against the wall. His hard body pressed into hers, and she let out a moan of want—of need.

What he had said to her on the roof, how he had looked at her, how he had kissed her...

She would take some time alone to process it all, but right now, with her back against the cool stone and Torin Blacksteel at her neck with this wicked mouth—and tongue and teeth—she wanted to let the worries of everything slip away, leaving only them.

"You have no idea how much I have wanted this." He nibbled into her skin, and her body moved against him the way the moon commanded the ocean's tide. "What I have thought about every time I saw you."

Her mind tried to conjure up words, but nothing but pleasure and fire rode through her veins, silencing her speech entirely.

How could he do such things with one press of his mouth against her skin?

She couldn't even take in the surroundings of his room as her head fell back against the cool stone and all of his hardness pressed against the heat of her body. Still dripping wet from the rain, he licked up her neck all the way to her ear, and a primal moan earthed from his throat just as one left hers too.

"It has been too long since I heard those moans from your lips," he said as he pulled at her ear with his teeth.

"Has it?" she managed to say through wavering breaths.

"You know it has, angel. Don't you agree?" His free hand started to roam over her skin.

It made her toes curl. "I have also thought about this, I can't lie to you."

He pulled back slightly at that, a cheeky grin curling in the left corner of his mouth. "You have?"

She swallowed and nodded.

"Now you need to tell me what you thought of," he demanded in a voice so low and raspy that it sent a tingle straight to her core.

Unhooking her legs from his waist, she slid down him slowly, and it sent a shiver through his whole body. Reaching out for the button to his leathers, she said, "I thought of doing this." She undid the catch, and the opening to his leathers gaped open, revealing a little trail of dark hair.

Emara could feel the flames of dominance that burned in his muscles to take over, but surprisingly, he let her lead.

For now.

Once she had unclipped the fastening, she kneeled, taking his leathers to the ground, revealing every inch of him. She kissed up his thigh, and his head fell back as a hiss left his throat.

His eyes clenched shut. "You thought about teasing me, did you?"

"I thought about doing everything with you."

He curled a finger under her chin, and she met his gaze. "Stand up, angel, and I will tell you what I thought of." His eyes glistened with wickedness that made her heart leap.

She stood, meeting his gaze again.

"I thought about you, on my bed, with nothing but that little winter solstice present on." He looked down to take in her body and then back up to her face. "But since we don't have that intriguing garment tonight, it doesn't seem right to keep this one on." He pulled at the thin strap of the dress and tugged it off her shoulder.

Her heart squeezed in her chest as his grin widened and turned wicked. He turned her so that she faced the wall, her hands slamming into the brick with how quick he had moved her. He quickly unhooked the fastenings of her dress, and she could feel her exposed skin greeted by his lips.

Why did he have to tease her to the brink of extinction every time?

A tightening ran up her core and into her stomach. But by the Gods, did she love it.

Torin ran his hands down her back, taking the dress with it, grabbing her underwear as he went. He moved it over her ass and then her thighs, and she felt the warmth of his hands on her skin.

He leaned into her as the material of her soaking dress hit her toes, and she could feel every rock-hard muscle press against her spine. She gasped a little, her fingernails scratching into the cool stone as the hardness of his shaft pressed against her opening.

"The last time we went *exploring,* I was very careful with you," he announced as he swept her hair over her shoulder so that it was hanging down past her face, covering her nipple.

She was exposed to him, her hands still on the wall, and he must feel how ready she was for him.

Oh Gods, she was ready.

"Mmm," she hummed back as a dangerous pleasure rode through her, his cock almost entering her as he ground against her ass, his strong thighs moving her to where he wanted.

"I don't think I can be as careful this time, angel. Not when I see you like this."

"Then don't be," she rasped.

He grabbed her, moving her from the position she was in and spinning her to face him.

A thrill ran through every single part of who she was. Even her darkness beckoned to him for a taste.

Pulling her against his chest and forcing her to wrap her legs around him, Emara didn't have time to breathe before his mouth landed on hers again, hot and searing. He moved gracefully towards the bed, and before she could find time to kiss him back, he had her on her back.

Torin was over her then, moving her hair from her face as he placed himself between her legs and let one lazy thrust roll his hips. "Tell me you are mine."

"You know I am."

He moved back, placing a finger on the bundle of nerves between her thighs. Already, she was about to cave under his touch. "Tell me."

"I am yours."

"Say it again when I am inside you." He slid one finger inside her and then two, wasting no time. Sparkling orbs formed in her vision as he stretched her.

Through staggered breaths and a moan, she managed to say, "I am yours."

"You are so ready for me." He withdrew his fingers and placed all of his hardness against her centre. He moved his hips, circling and rubbing, driving her wild.

Always teasing.

"You are going to tell me you are mine when my cock is inside you, and I am going to hear only my name from your lips when you release. Do you understand, angel?"

"Yes," she pleaded, not knowing if she had whispered it, shouted it, or even sang it.

He pushed himself into her, and she took a breath, finding his neck and broad shoulders to grab onto. Every solid, thick, long inch of him filled her, and a gasp left her mouth. Both delight and an unusual stretching mixed together beautifully, causing a moan to slip past her lips.

He moved slowly enough at first as she got used to him, but as his mouth landed on hers, the pace of his thrusts picked up.

Emara couldn't think of anything else as he moved inside her. Nothing else mattered. Only this. Them.

"Say it."

"Torin, I am yours."

"And I am yours," he said as the love between them became wild and untamed.

He grabbed the back of her head, pulling her hair back, and a moan escaped her throat as he pounded inside her. Her eyes closed as he slammed his mouth to her neck and sucked. In that moment, Emara could have sworn she saw a whole other galaxy above her as the pleasure morphed into something more, something unexplainable.

She could have cursed, could have prayed, could have roared, as the pleasure of Torin Blacksteel's strokes hit her core endlessly. She lifted her hips to roll into his movements, and a groan from his throat made it clear that he liked it. Loved it. The way he bit into his lip also suggested that he was fighting the pleasure of release.

His fingers untangled from her hair for a sweet moment and made their way across her skin to her peaked flesh. He took one of her nipples into his mouth, still not missing a stride. Her head fell back against the pillows as she continued to meet his thrusts, each one building to something momentous.

As she dragged her nails across his skin, he hissed, but that only seemed to encourage his wicked tongue to flick her nipple quicker.

They were on the verge of ecstasy. It was dark and it was raw and it was invigorating.

He lifted her other leg, wrapping it around his back, lifting her ass from the mattress as he rolled his hips against her.

A swirling, coiling tension rose from her body, and Emara felt it from her neck all the way to her toes. She had felt this sensation before, but she could feel the power in this climax. So much more power. So much more pleasure.

As Torin slammed into her again, her release broke, fluttering all the way through every morsel of her being, pushing her senses out of her body and her heart out of her chest. She cried out his name again, and as she did, a tingling spread over her spine. Arching her back, she called out something intangible and her muscles went weak. Emara heard a change in Torin's breathing, his movements altering as he chased his release, finding the pleasure of hers all too much.

A moan ripped from his throat and his body ceased, every Gods-carved muscle tightening and then releasing. He only just stopped himself from collapsing on top of her. They both took a deep breath before their gazes met once again.

He leaned down, placing his strong nose to hers, and kissed her lips, making her heart flutter in a different way. Her stomach rolled and flipped.

How could he be so strong and wild in one moment and so careful and gentle in the next?

For a few moments, they both lay together as he curled up beside her, their hands and legs intertwining.

"I promise, Emara"—his voice came out broken and low—"I will protect you and your heart until this world dissolves into nothing and we are not anything more than lost stars in the universe. I can't lose you again. Not for any man or any oath."

At that, she rolled onto her belly and pulled up the covers so that her body was covered a little. "And I will stand by your side until the sun falls from the sky."

His eyebrows pulled down as he found a strand of her hair to play with. "Not even after that?" he jested.

Emara rolled her eyes. "Okay, even after that."

The back of Torin's hand brushed all the untamed hair from her face, and she took a moment to just look at him in all his beautiful glory. His angled jaw, his striking eyes, his full lips, swollen from how hard he had kissed her. His body relaxed on his bed like he was meant to be in this moment with her. Like this was where the Gods wanted them to be.

And then a thought occurred to her.

She sat up abruptly, taking the covers with her. "Oh my Gods, I am in your room."

He rolled onto his side, still stark naked, and said, "And is that a problem?"

Emara laughed as she took in her surroundings for the first time. She blinked a few times before swallowing.

She had never been in Torin Blacksteel's bedroom before.

His bed was massive, twice the size of the one she had in Moss-grave, and absolutely bigger than her one down the corridor. Surrounding them on the bed were four posters of dark oak, and light charcoal fabric hung in ties at each corner. His sheets were crisp and as white as snow, decorated with furs at the bottom. Plenty of pillows lay scattered around, and she let out a giggle at how messy they were from what they had just done.

His walls were white, but the art that hung there was complete with forest landscapes and midnight skies full of stars. Weaponry dotted all over the room too, of course, like some sort of mini training room. Axes and swords hung on the walls, and by the door that they had broken through in passion hung a tiny archery set, like the one a baby Torin would have first practised with.

She had no idea why her heart reacted the way it did when she thought of a small hunter, dressed in training gear, with a little mane of inky hair and baby-blue eyes. The menacing scowl, she imagined, would still be the same.

She banished the thought and the emotions it conjured up and cast her eyes around the rest of the room. He had a dark oak wardrobe placed next to the large window like her own, and she assumed it was stacked to the brim of nothing but black garments and hunting attire. A light grey oil lamp sat on top of the same black-oak drawers as the bed, and one sat at either side of them. A few royal-blue rugs lined the floors, and she noted a bathing chamber off to the right that seemed to be carved in white marble.

His room was nothing like the Tower outside of this room, cold and meaningless.

Torin's room was cosy and, surprisingly, rather stylish.

"Should I be worried that you haven't said anything as your eyes have investigated my entire bed chambers?" He laughed slightly as he still twirled the strand of her hair in between his fingers.

"You shouldn't be worried." She turned back to him and smiled. "It's just I have never been here before. I think...it's not what I expected."

"Not many people have," he said back coolly. "I don't let people in here. It's mine."

And that surprised her too.

"No *friends?*"

It was then that he rolled his eyes and let go of her hair, his back finding the mattress once more. "No *friends.* Just you." He pulled on her elbow gently, and she fell back onto the soft mattress to feel his warmth again. "It's only ever going to be you that's allowed in here. In my own little part of this Tower I am supposed to call home."

"I could get used to that," she said, holding back her smile as she blinked at him. "I like it."

"Just smile." He grinned as he looked at her. "I know you want to. I bet you had all sorts of little sordid fantasies about what my room would look like."

She wanted to laugh so hard because it was true. But she couldn't, not yet. She couldn't let him know that he was right.

She hit him with a soft fist on the chest. "Shut up. I will smile when I want to smile, not when you tell me to." It was then she couldn't trap the smile that graced her lips. "And I can't tell you about the kind of fantasies that I had about this room because I don't think you would class them as fantasies."

"I bet a gold coin you thought I would have ruby-red silk sheets and a sex swing in the corner?"

She could feel her eyes bulge out from her skull. "A sex swing? Torin Blacksteel! I did not for one moment think you would have a sex swing." A flustered laugh escaped her. "I don't even think my mind could conjure up a thing."

He chuckled. "Give yourself some time," he said, his smooth voice coasting through the small distance between them as they lay together on the bed. "You haven't been to the markets on a full moon. You would be surprised to see what they sell on those nights."

She bit her lip. "Oh Gods, is it bad that I am now curious about what a sex swing would look like?"

A deep laugh rumbled from his belly, and it was the first she had seen him laugh properly in Rhiannon knows how long. "There is always the next winter solstice."

She gasped. "You wouldn't."

"Wouldn't I?" His eyebrow rose, and the glittering in his eyes sent her heart into a frenzy.

She clamped her lips shut, because the fact was she couldn't tell if he would or not. Heat coated her cheeks at the thought.

"Who needs a spear when you can have a sex swing?" He nudged her gently.

"Shut up, I like my spear." She smiled too.

A lovely, lulling silence filled the room for a few moments as she continued to look around herself.

"I was right about the red silk sheets though, wasn't I?" A sinful smirk pulled his lips apart.

"I will never confirm or deny anything." She pouted.

Without saying a word, he pulled her into his chest as a little laugh broke through his grin. "I've missed you." He let out a breath. "Even your fists. In fact, especially your fists, and I can't believe I've already been hit with a right hook."

Emara let out a giggle of her own. "You know that wasn't a right hook, Torin Blacksteel."

He hummed in agreement, and she felt it go through his chest. "The only thing missing in all of this was that sensual little leg strap holding your spear. Don't tell me you stopped wearing it?"

"Oh, I still wear it. I wore it in the pits.," she said as she placed her head to his heart.

"Let's not talk about the pits tonight."

She tried to laugh, but the intoxicating warmth of Torin Black-steel's chest had lulled her eyes to shut. "Oh, and by the way, I have missed you more," she whispered.

"Impossible," was all she heard him say back before the constant beating of Torin's heart sent her spent body into a calming sleep.

CHAPTER FOURTEEN
EMARA

S tirring awake, Emara was no longer pressed against the warm chest of a warrior, but against a soft, feathery pillow. She blinked a few times and stretched out her hands, a yawn on her mouth.

Sitting up, still pulling the sheets around her naked curves, she searched for Torin. Her heart began thudding in her chest, but she quickly found him, and the wave of concern wore off. Torin sat over in a chair by his window, the glow of dawn crystallising his eyes. But it also revealed the dark circles underneath his eyes. He sat with his hair askew, in nothing but loose black pants. His hand was hovering over his mouth, and his face was filled with thoughts too deep for Emara to understand upon first glance.

"Did you not sleep?" she croaked, feeling the soft cotton on the palms of her hands as she pulled the sheets around her again.

Although he appeared to be casually lounging at first glance, she could see that his full body was ridged. Something about his whole demeanour alarmed her enough to feel a wave of fear jolt through her spine. Gone were the laughs, gone were the lust-filled looks and the light in his eyes. All that goodness that had been between them last night had clearly been washed away with the stars as dawn approached.

"No, I couldn't sleep, so I didn't want to wake you." He attempted a half smile, but his mask was well and truly off.

Something horrid swam in her gut. "You could have moved me if you weren't comfortable."

He finally looked at her properly, a sharp concern knotting his brow. "The reason for my unrest isn't having you against my chest. Thorin knows that's the only thing that kept me in this room all night."

She toyed with the idea of going to him, but she stayed put just a little longer. "Torin, tell me what is going on in your head."

He tilted his head towards the window, and a ray of soft light highlighted the fullness of his lips, the curve of his cheeks, and his strong, masculine chin. "It's okay; it's not for you to worry about." He faced her again and tried to wear one of the masks he wore often. For the first time ever, he failed. "It's early. You can still get a few hours of sleep in yet."

A string pulled through her heart, telling her gut that something was torturing him. Why had he stayed up all night? Was it because of her? Was it because of what they had done?

"Torin..." She moved, bringing the sheets with her as she stood close to the last poster that framed his bed. "You need to learn to open up to me. If we are going to be in this together, we must share with one another our torments, the things that eat at our souls during the night." She padded a little closer, and he watched every step she took until she had sat against the windowsill casting shadows onto his broad chest. "We need to be a team. I want to know what's going on in there."

She saw his chest rise and then fall before he spoke. He took a long, slow breath before he released it. "I am trying to work out how we can be together without disgracing you and your coven or without me being exiled from the clan." His tormented eyes met hers. "The options are minimal."

She swallowed down her heart that had somehow made its way into her throat.

"We will figure it out." She cuffed her arms around herself. "There is a continuation from the prime meeting taking place yesterday. I could go to the prime beforehand—"

"You're not going to anyone; you've done your part," he said sharply, his jaw flexing. "Now it's time for me to step up."

Step up?

"What do you mean?" she questioned.

When he didn't respond and only looked at the city once more, dread coiled in her stomach.

She rose from where she perched. "Torin—"

"You don't need to worry about it," he repeated, and his thick throat bobbed once.

"I don't need to worry about it?" she repeated, her voice a little higher than expected. "Of course I need to worry about it, especially if it kept you from sleeping all night. The thoughts running through your mind were unattended, and that's never good, especially when you are dangerously quick to react."

He sat forward in his chair, his muscles moving in a way that distracted Emara enough to watch him in silence as he moved with that effortless agility she always admired and strode towards a small cabinet by his wardrobe. He ran one hand through his hair, sweeping it back before he uncorked one of the glass bottles that sat on display, full of rust-coloured liquid. He poured it into the finest crystal glass he had, amounting to a finger or two, and began his stroll back across the room to sit in his dark blue chair again.

He relaxed, letting his bare shoulders reach the outer cuffs of the chair. "Emara, I told you last night that I am going to do what I need to for us to be together without anything standing in the way. I have run over multiple scenarios and thousands of options and I can only think of one way that I am going to be able to achieve that."

He placed the glass to his lips and swallowed the whole lot.

Why did fear engulf her soul?

"And that is?"

When he didn't speak again, his gaze turning icy as he watched a small vein of rum drag down his empty glass, Emara wondered what could be swallowing up his sanity.

An awful, terrible realisation clicked in her heart.

She gasped and one hand reached out to steady her against the sill. "Torin, no. Tell me you are not—"

"There is no other way." His tongue rolled over his lips, and his head hit against the back of the chair. His dark lashes swept down as he looked at the ground instead of her.

She took a step towards him. "Please, please, tell me you are not thinking of killing your father?"

When silence answered her question, Torin got up and reached for the bottle again, pouring himself another glass of rum before dawn. Horror filled her bones and she had to lock in her knees to keep herself standing.

"Torin, you can't be serious!"

He looked at her through icy darkness as he sat again and said, "I would do much worse to make sure that you are safe."

She went to him then, perching on the arm of his chair. Her hand reached him and coasted softly over his cheek. "We can go to the prime, you said yourself that I can be convincing."

"Emara—"

"We can speak to the chief commander, and we can surely encourage Murk to see our side."

"Emara—"

"We could show King Oberon what we mean to each other. If we speak from the heart and with passion, like I have done before, we can persuade the prime to overrule your father. The king has never—"

"Emara, stop," he said, now leaning forward to hold her. "You need to stop. I can see no other way."

She sank into him. "There must be another way."

"There is not. For us to have any sort of happiness or future, I must challenge the commander of the Blacksteel Hunting Clan for his commandership." He grabbed a hold of her face, his large hands engulfing her cheeks. "I have got to challenge him, and win, so that I can become commander of the clan. Only then will he not be in a position to have such interference in my life, and only then I will be free of him. I could make decisions that better my clan, strengthen them. And I could make decisions that keep you from danger or a miserable existence. With him still in any role of power, that will never happen." He looked at her, his face as grave as stone. "Today, I will express my intentions with you at the summit, and if my father does not agree to the terms to change the treaty, then I will formally challenge him to a duel of commandership. There is no other way, angel."

Emara's hands shook and her stomach convulsed, but she swallowed back the tears of her panic for Torin. She knew what that meant. She had been around hunters long enough to pick up their traditions and customs, and one custom meant that challenging the commander of a clan was a battle that would leave only one of them standing.

Viktir or Torin.

Thou shalt not challenge thy commander of any clan, unless warranted for overthrow. If challenged, the two clan members must fight to the death until the victor is announced, thus succeeding the new or current commander.

A fight to the death.

"No, Torin, please. I can buy us time."

"It is too late." He held onto her hand, and his sapphire eyes bore through her soul. "You cannot change my mind. It's done. I promised my father a war a long time ago. It was always inevitable."

Emara let out a cry of fear and frustration. This couldn't happen. Viktir would not change his mind in front of so many people, making him look remotely soft or yielding. And it was too late for Emara to change Torin's mind—she could see that in his eyes.

It was done.

Torin had decided. If Viktir did not agree to change the terms of the Blacksteel alliance with the House of Air, Torin would challenge his right to the commandership.

He would not back down. He would not surrender and give in to his commander's orders. He would fight to the death for his cause.

Today, Torin Blacksteel would either stand victorious or he would fall.

CHAPTER FIFTEEN
EMARA

Leaving Torin's room alone was like someone else had taken over her body and was somehow controlling her, like a wayward spirit had possessed her mind and was pushing everything into slow motion.

She was a puppet in the strings of fear.

Emara felt numb. Sick. Frantic.

But she couldn't let the detachment of her mind cloud her next steps.

It was inevitable. His mind was made up. She could see there was no changing that.

A coldness spread across her skin, and she wasn't sure if it was her clothes, still damp from last night's rain, or the fact that she had left Torin to prepare himself for battle. She couldn't even use her fire to heat her bones right now as she walked back to her room, too numb to summon anything.

As she entered her chambers, the light from the dawn was lazily pouring through the windowsill, sending a glow up her walls. Specks of dust shone through the beams. She focused on that for Gods knew how long and then she let out a breath as the door to her room closed behind her. Emara placed her head against the wood, shutting her eyes for a moment.

The Gods had a plan for her. Rhiannon had a path for her.

And it couldn't only be sorrow and heartbreak.

They had a plan for everyone.

She placed her palms together and whispered endless prayers up to the Light Gods. She asked Rhiannon, Goddess of the Moon and Dreams, to make her dreams come true. She begged Uttara of the Stars and Dawn to let Torin see another sunrise. She prayed to Vanadey of Life and Beauty to let Torin stay by her side. And she pleaded with Thorin, God of the Sun and War, that there would be no more deaths. Please. Not him.

Of course, there would be more deaths; that was also an inevitability. But, please, not Torin. He was her protector. He was who she was truly meant to meet in this life. He was her best friend. Her heart. He was the person her soul sang for.

Just as the walls of her room heard the end of her prayers, a rustling came from the direction of her bed, followed by a few curse words.

Emara's head swung up from the door, her hands now parted. But she wasn't armed, so magic would need to be her aid. She supposed that was a good thing about being a witch; she was almost always armed.

Just as she gathered a ball of air in her hand, ready to strike the intruder, Artem Stryker appeared from around the wall panelling that kept her bed hidden from the small hallway she had taken a moment to pray in. He had a guard tunic on his top half, but it seemed that he had lost his leathers, only sporting his undergarments. His russet hair was pulled in every direction, and it was the first time she had ever seen it untidy.

"For the love of Rhiannon," Emara breathed, dissolving the element that was ready to strike. "I almost blasted you with air." Her eyes roamed over him again. "Do I even want to know why you are half naked in my room?"

He grinned bashfully and covered his private area with his large tattooed hands. "Er...I..."

Emara heard another hiss, and a curse came from behind the wall.

Emara took one more look at Artem Stryker and curled her lip. "You didn't."

"I can explain—"

Emara walked forward, summoning that ball of air that she had banished as she sucked in the air of the room. "Is this the part where you tell me you didn't just have sex in my room?" she roared. "My bed?"

"I—"

Wind blew into a ball, ready to blast from her hands. "Tell me I am wrong, Stryker! Today is not the day to lie to me."

"Oh fuck." Artem's eyes lit up a flare of worry as she released the air ball and it flew towards his face. He dodged it. "I am sorry. I truly am. If you could keep your balls of air to yourself and let me explain—"

"If I could keep my balls of air to myself?" she screamed. "How about you keep your balls to yourself, you absolute animal!"

"Can you calm down?" he yelled back, still trying to cover his manhood. "Let's talk it through like the good friends we are—"

"You really think that we are good friends?" Emara hissed. "You have just defiled my space. My room. I could kill you right now."

"Please don't do that." Breighly Baxgroll, sporting the same bedhead as Artem, trailed out from behind the wall with an embarrassed look on her face. "Please don't blame him. It was my...fault." She squared her shoulders and held a tunic against her body. She threw Artem his leathers, and he caught them with one hand. Artem looked at her like she had said something in the tongue of the underworld as he speedily jumped into them.

Oh, for the love of Rhiannon, she didn't need this right now.

"I can see you have finally made it into your uniform." Emara glanced at Breighly, and uncharacteristically, the wolf's lips slammed shut. Her eyes darted to Artem. "When I asked you to wait outside for Breighly to show her the ropes of the Tower, I didn't mean in my bed."

Emara probably shouldn't have said that. But maybe her crippling anxiety was coming out in ways that she didn't understand.

"Please..." Artem turned to Emara. "Please accept my sincerest apologies; it wasn't Breighly's fault. It was mine. I cannot help myself when I am around her." A small moment of silence calmed the tension in the room. "Breighly arrived just after you left for the rooftop. I came to look for you to let you know that she was here, but you weren't there." He shrugged. "I saw a beaten-up punching bag and a trail of rain that led down the steps, so I put two and two together. I went to Torin's room. And that's when I heard—"

"Stop. Stop!" Emara lowered her hand. "There is no need for you to report what you heard."

A mutual understanding of what Artem had heard coming from Torin's room, set Emara's cheeks on fire. He nodded, his head bowing low, his golden glare looking anywhere but her face.

Breighly's shimmering brown eyes met her own. "Emara, I give you my word that this will never happen again."

She saw a bob in Artem's throat, and some of that golden flare diminished in his eyes.

Breighly walked towards her. "I am a fool for getting distracted whilst you were gone, and I have discredited my position and everything you fought for yesterday. Please, I will never make that mistake again. We got carried away."

Artem straightened behind the wolf, shoulders back and raising his chin like he had taken a hit to the gut with her words.

Emara looked at their shameful faces. Had she not had the heaviness of what today would bring resting on her shoulders, she would have probably laughed it off.

It's not every day you find a wolf and a warrior of Thorin in your bed.

She sighed, releasing some of the pent-up energy she had been holding in. "I am not as high as the Gods to judge when desire for one person takes over." She nodded towards Breighly. "Perhaps I understand it a little too well." She met Artem's gaze for a solitary second before finding Breighly's again. "I will not mention this again, as I am sure you will both forget it happened."

"Absolutely." Breighly nodded. And it was peculiar to see something like her position as a guard mean more to her than her pride. "You have my word, my oath. Anything."

"You can count on it," Artem said dryly. "It won't happen again."

She walked over and placed her hand against the mantle of the fireplace. Letting out a curse, she ran a hand through her hair and dipped her chin low. "I need you both ready as soon as you can be."

"Are you okay? Emara, what is going on?"

As she listened to the magic of the embers burning gold and vibrant below her, she tried not to think about how her whole world could fall apart again. She swallowed her fear that the Gods might not have put Torin in her path for happiness, but heartbreak.

Breighly shuffled forward. "Emara, you don't look so good. Are you okay?"

A tear tracked down Emara's cheeks, and a broken sob left her throat.

"Shit." Artem moved towards her. "Do you need me to call on your empress maids? Do you need anything?" He placed a hand on her shoulder and lowered himself so that he could look at her fully.

She raised her chin and said, "You better get ready for today." They both paled. "Because there is going to be an uprooting of everything you know about the current Blacksteel Clan."

Artem's concerned features pulled in tight, making him look murderous. "What do you mean? What happened this morning?"

She placed a hand to her mouth and another to her stomach as she said, "If Viktir doesn't agree to change the treaty by revoking my marriage to Gideon"—her voice wavered, but she fought through her emotion—"Torin is going to challenge the commander today. He is finally bringing the war he promised his father."

"He's what?" Breighly's mouth fell open, her eyes clouding.

"And I am fighting the sickness in my stomach at the thought of it because this is all because of his affections for me." Emara grabbed the damp material around her stomach and clutched hard, almost tearing the material. "It's my fault." She took another breath that didn't quite reach her lungs. "I wanted him to fight for me, but not to the death. I thought we would have found another way."

Artem ran a hand over his face. "Torin was never going to be diplomatic, Emara. It was a matter of time," he said lowly, a huff of air coming from his chest. "It was a matter of time before this happened. It is not your fault. Torin Blacksteel wasn't born into this world to be second-in-command to anyone." Artem ran an inked hand over his head and cursed.

Emara turned to him, acknowledging that Artem knew Torin better than anyone. "I asked him to speak to the prime; I said that we could plead our case. All we need is a little more time." Emara's breath caught in her throat. "When I asked him to fight for us, I didn't mean *literally*. I didn't mean his father. This is all my fault—oh my Gods." She found her legs betraying her, and she almost ended up on the ground.

Artem caught her. "Look at me," he said in the way a commander would. "This isn't just because of you. Yes, he is using your relationship as a catalyst for the event, but that's not the only reason he wants to fight for commandership. He wants to fight for you, for him, his brothers, freedom, and for Naya." Artem made sure

Emara was listening by moving into her eyeline again. "Torin has been keeping notes on Viktir for a long time. He doesn't agree with how some things have been handled. He doesn't trust him." His grip on Emara's arms grew lighter, and her leg muscles locked in strong. "This has been coming since Torin was born. You don't name your son after the God of War and not expect him to rise to the challenge."

Emara let out a breath.

"But that doesn't mean you should just challenge your commander. You of all people should know that," Breighly pointed out, and Emara noted the concern in her eyes. She had grown up with the Blacksteels, she knew what it meant to challenge the commander.

"Oh, I know more ins and outs of commandership than you both can imagine. My father is the chief. There was no pissing about when it came to commandership in my home." He looked back at Emara. "What I mean to say is when a good hunter sees something wrong in his clan, he has every right to voice his opinion. Call it out."

"Voicing his opinion and challenging his commander are two different things," Breighly batted back.

"And challenging your alpha isn't the same?" He folded his arms over his chest in a way that indicated he knew he had the winning blow. "Are you not now shaping different paths for female wolves because you went against your alpha at one point?"

Breighly's lips shut tight, the first time Emara had ever seen Breighly lose in an argument. It was kind of staggering.

She jumped in before it got hostile. "I fear that I have pushed him to this," Emara announced, placing a hand on her forehead. "I just know what my heart wants, and it's him."

"Push Torin Blacksteel to do anything?" Artem let out a loud laugh. "There is no such thing. It's a *miracle of Thorin* that the guy made it this long without challenging any of the commanders in rank. He has come close to it before, I know that for certain. And I think you forget that I spent years with him in the Selection; I have seen his hatred for obedience on a different scale. I have seen how much he has challenged the system before and how much they had to break him into who he is. Blacksteel is a natural-born leader. He may make a few mistakes from time to time, but he's a man. That doesn't make him unworthy." He turned his gaze to Breighly, who was now looking at the embers in the fireplace. "What can you do when you are born to be at the front of the pack?"

Breighly glanced towards the inked warrior.

Artem stepped forward again and reached out for Emara's hand. "If he was going to challenge Viktir on any of the stupid calls he has made before, why shouldn't it be the one that means most? Why wouldn't it be the one thing that actually means something to him? Why shouldn't he fight for this?"

Emara looked up into the golden gaze of the guard she now called a friend. "I am so terrified for him."

Artem rolled his lips before he said, "Don't be. Torin Blacksteel doesn't lose."

Emara couldn't help it when she wrapped her arms around her guard's neck. "Who knew you could be the voice of reason?"

Artem let out a snigger. "I have many talents, witchy. Just call me Artem of all trades. Man of the Gods. Voice of the people."

"Okay, that's enough." Emara pulled back, and Artem offered her a boyish grin.

Artem looked to Breighly and then back to Emara as he crossed his arms over his huge chest. "We've got you, *Empress of Unfortunate Luck*. Now go and get your battle paint on. We have a summit to attend."

CHAPTER SIXTEEN
GIDEON

Something was wrong; Gideon could feel it in the air.

Just a few moments ago, he had taken a seat beside Sybil, who seemed to be the only one acting normally, as she sat making a chain out of daisies. She had already looped a few through braids in her hair, but apparently this one was for her wrist.

Artem Stryker was unusually quiet, his head down and his hands clasped together. Emara looked ghostly pale and not her usually primed self. Gideon noticed that she was holding Sybil's arm like she was in some sort of pain, squeezing it. He had tried to smile at her, like he always did, but she had rejected his gesture. Her wonderful eyes alert and sharp as she stared at a blank space on the floor.

Breighly Baxgroll sat behind her. Her leg jumped nervously, like she had received bad news or was fighting sick trailing from her stomach up her throat. If she hadn't passed the tests with Aerrick, then she wouldn't be sitting here, so it wasn't that.

And then there was Torin, who was not dramatically late like he always was. He sat beside the wolf, behind Emara, geared up in fighting attire instead of his uniform.

And as Gideon looked back at his brother, he could see in the plains of his face that something was well and truly off. There was no exaggerated hunter mask or cocky smirk. Something tortured his eyes, and his hands looked a little shaky.

Gideon couldn't help but feel like he'd missed something over the last twenty-four hours, and he needed to get to the bottom of it. Torin Blacksteel was never shaky.

He looked around to find his father and Marcus, who all seemed to be making normal conversation and speaking with the elder hunters around them. Naya was reading a book, *The Herb of Helmsbrook,* and she seemed to be passing time before the meeting began. Kellen was trying to smooth out his hair, and Arlo was talking to a witch in the earth coven.

Normal.

Everyone was acting normally except for Emara's cluster.

Had someone tried to attack her and they were keeping it under wraps? Had there been a disagreement? Surely, Breighly and Artem hadn't knocked heads already. They had been nothing but friendly towards each other.

That wasn't it. But there was definitely something. And the more Gideon studied them all, the more it irritated him that he couldn't pinpoint it.

He leaned into Sybil, whispering low so only she could hear. "I need to ask you something." Her vast green eyes found his face. "Can you sense something right now? Like something's not right?"

She huffed a laugh, brushing a fiery curl from her face and putting down her flower chain. She leaned in. "I am an earth witch, Gideon, not the Empress of House Spirit," she whispered back. "You would need to be more specific."

One of her loose curls bounced back into her face a second later, and Gideon's eyes followed it. Why did he have the urge to push it back from her face and tuck it behind her ear? That would be very unprofessional of him. He coughed, tightening his grip around his weapon belt. "I am being serious," he said. "Something is wrong. Do you not feel it?"

He nodded discreetly to Emara's hand interlinked with hers.

"She does that when she's nervous," Sybil whispered back. "It's not exactly a new thing."

"My point exactly. Emara had her case heard yesterday, surely nothing must come of it today, right? Did she say anything to you?"

A small smile pulled at her lip. "Gideon, you're being paranoid," she said, giving her hand over to him. "Must I soothe your paranoia?" Her creamy hand lay softly over his. It was tiny in comparison to his hand, and a small emerald ring sat on her middle finger, twinkling.

Her sister's ring.

On their walks around the garden, she had told him many stories of her sister, how they were when they had grown up, close in age and even closer in bond. She missed her dearly and often looked to the emerald on her hand when she was thinking. It was like she was asking it, "*What would Meryl have done?*"

He smiled back at her as the soothing magic entered his body. "You need to teach me how to do that."

Her delicate cheeks turned a pretty shade of pink. "You can't learn someone's sheer talent, Gideon Blacksteel. You either have it or you don't."

His grin was wide on his face as she removed her hand from over his. He whispered in her direction, "That's very true."

Before she could respond, the chief commander announced something that Gideon couldn't hear as his gaze caught Sybil's. For a second longer than it should have, something burned between them, bright and powerful. Something unexplored.

But she must have not been as ignorant in their moment together as he was; she must have understood what was happening around them as her head snapped to the commander and then to

Torin. Shock brushed over her face. Gideon turned his head, looking around, finally coming back into the room. He watched as Torin rose from his chair, a whole court of people gasping like he had just wielded the element of fire or something.

What had the chief commander said? What did he miss and why did it involve Torin?

When Sybil's mouth fell open wide and Emara's knuckles tightened around the earth witch's hand, he knew he had missed something unmissable.

"No, Chief Commander Stryker, I did not write to the prime prior to today for you to hear my case," his brother said as he produced a letter from under his attire. "Because I feel that I cannot wait a moment longer to say what I have to say. I have sent you all endless letters and they have never been heard. But you need to read this one."

Gideon looked from Torin's face to Emara's, and he could feel something uncomfortable coil in his gut. The chief commander took a few steps forward and removed the letter from Torin's grip. After a few moments of terrible silence, Aerrick looked to Viktir Blacksteel, who was sitting rigidly in his chair. Gideon peeked at his mother to see that concern had found its way into her eyes. Utter panic pulled Naya's shoulders up close to her ears.

"What I have here, Commander Blacksteel," the chief said, "is a letter in plea from your son for me to command you to entirely dissolve your current treaty with the House of Air."

Viktir rose, chest puffing. "How dare you, girl—"

"Are you not listening, Father?" Torin bit in that nonchalant way he did to get under Viktir's skin. Gideon had always envied how he could do it. "The chief commander said that I wrote the plea, not her. So you can take that poisonous stare off her face."

Gideon's heart launched itself across his chest a few times.

Fuck!

Viktir growled, "I forbade this."

"You did," Torin said, and if Gideon wasn't mistaken, there was a small, sly grin on his mouth. But Gideon knew Torin too well; that look was for show, for the audience. Gideon knew deep down the depths of how hard this had been for him. "And that is why I am going above you."

Gideon's throat squeezed shut, and he looked towards his poor mother again. Thank the Gods Rhea was by her side.

"You see, Chief Commander Stryker, my father has been the leader of our clan since my grandfather died at the hands of the Dark Army. And he has made many decisions, ones that I have not seen eye to eye with, yet I have taken instruction. I agreed to follow him obediently."

A fierce hiss of disagreement came from Viktir.

Torin ignored him. "I stood by him when he chose to ignore the fact that our wards had been failing for many moons, rendering us unprotected as my clan slept. I was silenced then, commanded not to speak a word of it. I stood by him when he sent our men out, unprepared to fight the horde of Dark Ones that were ransacking our kingdom. He had the men in our clan be his spies in the markets and city for his personal gain as we lost lives. I stood by him when he made decisions on wives for the clan. I have been second-in-command to his barbaric training techniques and backwards coaching. I have watched him punish not only me, but my brothers, my mother—" His voice cracked a little then, and Gideon felt the urge to stand. "I have kept my tongue unmoved in my mouth when I have witnessed him take sides with people who have wronged his own clan for coin, and as his second-in-command, I was silenced. But I will not and cannot obey him when he orders my silence on the matters involving Emara Clearwater, Empress of House Air."

An unholy stillness smothered the room.

Gideon's heart stopped, and Sybil let out a gasp beside him.

Torin finally spoke again. "Chief Commander, King Oberon, Alpha Baxgroll, and Minister of Coin, I stand before you today asking for support to pardon the treaty my father has forced upon Gideon Blacksteel and Emara Clearwater. I'm asking for a different verdict from what my father has granted us time after time." He looked at the other prime members and then into the crowd. "You see, as a hunter, I have been selfish and arrogant. I have drunk in every tavern after spilling the guts of Dark Army every night since I could swallow hard liquor. I have been blinded in thinking that my path was already laid out for me, numbing myself to the fact that I didn't appreciate a marriage or an alliance with anyone that I couldn't choose for myself. I considered my fate to be all but marriage for convenience, a life of fighting and bleak work until my eventual death." He paused. "But that all changed when Emara Clearwater came through the Tower doors and entered our world." Torin's gaze found Emara. "My world was turned on its axis, for the better."

Gideon looked to Emara, who sat a few seats down, her stare unfaltering from Torin's face as she watched him lay down his heart before the factions. He had always known there was something between them, but Torin was so utterly in love with the Empress of Air.

A strange beating thrummed in his heart, but he couldn't place what it meant.

"You see," Torin played out to the crowd again, showing his usual confidence, but with a vulnerability he had never displayed before, "I was under the impression that the first-born son of a clan's commander had to marry for nothing but an alliance. Emara, she changed my prospects on that. She showed me light in a dark future that I cannot even bear to think of. And she has time and time again shown me that she is worthy of a better man to stand by her side."

His eyes finally found Gideon in the crowd, and a moment passed between them that made Gideon's heart hurt.

Emara stood, causing the crowd to suddenly look her way. She gave Torin one final nod, and there was a fire in her eyes that was deeper than desire, deeper than friendship, deeper than respect for her guard. Gideon had never seen that fire when she looked at him.

It was then he understood that she and Torin were destined for each other. No one could change that course. Even if he had been holding on to some foolish hope that there might be a chance for them to find happiness in their forced alliance, he realised now that there was no way for them to find their way back to how it had once been. They couldn't pave something new.

As Torin stood in front of his commander, challenging his decision, Gideon knew it felt right.

Strangely, his chest felt a little lighter.

He took a deep breath as he looked at his brother, standing in front of the crowd, his sapphire gaze on Emara's face, his longing for her unhidden, open for everyone to see.

"She has given me something"—Torin turned back to the prime, who all had straightened in their chairs, their eyes wide with astonishment—"that I never thought I could have. A future that is ours to build. And that is why I stand before you and ask that you overturn your decision to marry my brother to the Empress of Air. It should be Emara's choice."

Viktir's face was red with rage, probably horrified that his son had chosen emotion over obedience.

Gideon quickly surveyed his clan, all of them in shock. Marcus Coldwell looked like he could fall from his chair at any moment. Kellen's eyes were soft with tears. Gideon found his mother, her face portraying a thousand emotions at once.

Commander Stryker moved forward and put down the letter.

"Commander Blacksteel, speak on the matter presented. I would like to hear your thoughts."

The room was deathly silent.

Gideon could feel his throat bobbing, his shoulders tense, every muscle coiled.

Viktir's lips thinned as he scowled. "My decision is final."

Gideon knew this was all in an effort to punish Torin for something that felt like it had happened years ago. Gideon wished for one silly second that Torin had just told his father of the Resurrection Stone and maybe then he wouldn't still be trying to torture him.

But that was the difference between Gideon and Torin. Torin was brave enough to challenge his commander for the girl he loved.

The prime gave Viktir a moment, but as everyone looked at him, it was clear he would not change his mind. Gideon wouldn't have expected anything else, and maybe Torin hadn't either. Maybe he had been clever to show everyone how ruthless and callous his father was. Would that swing in his favour?

For one Blacksteel to win, one must back down, and they were both as stubborn as the mountains of the north.

The Minister of Coin rose from his seat, and his eyes found Torin's. "It sounds like temptations of the flesh to me." He walked to stand over by the chief commander. "Couldn't you just continue your relationship after your brother marries her?" He sent a vile smile in Torin's direction. "Everyone has a mistress."

Did he have a death wish?

Gideon prayed to Thorin that Torin stayed calm. He had done such a good job to show a different side of himself today. The chief commander's eyes found Emara's. "Empress of Air, do you agree with Torin Blacksteel in his claims that you should be allowed the choice of whom to marry?"

Why did Gideon's heart rate suddenly speed up?

She swallowed before raising her chin. "It shakes every part of who I am to believe there should be a piece of paper that determines whom I should marry, especially when it was not my hand that signed the treaty." She paused, letting that statement filter down to the community around her. "However, I do not shun the respectable alliance to Clan Blacksteel. I, as an empress of this kingdom, would only like a say in whom it should be to." Some of the spectators who had not been in her corner yesterday seemed to have softened towards her, their glances sympathetic. "What I will say on the matter of the current alliance is that it is unfair to toy with the emotions of one's sons to punish them for no good reason. An alliance now hangs by a thread due to such harsh behaviours. It is self-indulgent and an abuse of power."

Viktir scoffed. "There is no one more self-indulgent than Torin Blacksteel, Empress Clearwater, and you better believe that as the truth before you challenge my decision."

"That is where you are wrong, Commander Blacksteel." Emara's eyes turned a steely grey as she walked forward from her chair. "I can see your sons' hearts, and all of them are a credit to your clan. There is only one person who lets the Blacksteel name down."

Fuck, fuck, fuck! What was she doing? Did she want him to tell the world about her blood? Gideon realised that would condemn Viktir too; keeping a secret like that from the prime was unacceptable.

"Your son has declared what he thinks is best for the clan's interest, and you are too stubborn and selfish to right your wrongs." She finally lifted her gaze. "And I hope the prime can see that today. It is unfair for you to drag us through this process just for your own vengeance." Her gaze found Gideon. "And I hope they recognise that it is not just Torin's heart that Viktir does not respect, but Gideon Blacksteel's too."

A hot flush took over him as she looked at him. He didn't know what he was doing as he rose from the chair; he even felt Sybil tug on his arm, but something had taken over him.

"Members of the prime..." His voice did not sound like his own, it was higher and somehow louder than usual. He cleared his throat. "Since my name has been mentioned, I would like a say in how this treaty should go too."

"Sit down, boy." He heard Viktir speak, but Gideon didn't glance in his direction. He couldn't lose his nerve; this was the first time he'd ever disobeyed his commander.

The Fae King moved in his chair, reminding Gideon he was in the room, and he caught his wise, violet gaze. The king gave him a nod to continue. "I believe the warrior should be allowed his voice in court." His glittering eyes cast over the chief. "After all, his name has been mentioned a few times now, has it not?"

His voice was earthy and ancient.

Murk nodded in agreement, as did the Minister of Coin. He seemed to be enjoying the hunters being in the hot seat for once.

Gideon lifted his gaze to his chief commander. "I would agree with my brother on his stance regarding the alliance." Emara looked over at him with tears in her eyes. This was not only final for Gideon, but Emara too. Every moment together had led them here, led him to save her from the treaty. "The reasons my father suggested to the prime that I replace my brother was not due to the stability of my character like he said." He placed his hands behind his back. "It was for punishment for Torin's well-intentioned actions. Therefore, I am unable to say that I could go into the alliance with the House of Air. I can assure you all that there is no stronger alliance than that of Torin Blacksteel and Emara Clearwater. I would be doing my clan a disservice if I married the Empress of Air." He found Emara's face once more, and the tears in her eyes humbled him. "She deserves someone like my brother. I am in full support of their alliance, should she choose him. Torin and Emara are right, an empress should have a choice in the matters of her heart."

Torin's jaw flexed before his throat shoved down a swallow, and Emara let out a half sob.

"Chief Commander," Viktir cut in as he stood, "I will not overturn my decision here today. If one of my hunters will not obey my rules, they know the consequences. An oath is an oath. A treaty is a treaty. They will be exiled."

The chief commander threw a look at Torin, and a concern rose in Gideon's stomach that Aerrick agreed with Viktir.

Viktir's word was final.

"And you are not even going to attempt to persuade my father?" Torin asked, disgust lingering on his lips as he took in the reaction of Commander Stryker. "You are the chief; you could command him to do that without it going to a deliberation."

A small rumble went through the crowd, showing support for Torin's challenge. Gideon even heard a few sighs and curses.

The chief placed his hands behind his back. "I can see he is a man that is not willing to budge. If I ask my prime members here today to take a vote, it may be overstepping their jurisdiction when it comes to the oath of a warrior of Thorin."

"Even if it's wrong? Even if the decision is unjust? Even if you have the power here in court to make him budge?" Emara let her voice be heard.

The chief commander said lowly, "What kind of chief would I be if I overturned every man's quandary with their commander? Where would the authority lie in the clans?" His dark gaze found Torin again. "If you were commander and your word was final, would you expect it to be challenged over something as political as a marriage?"

"But—"

"It's done, Emara." Torin looked over his shoulder at her, and she wobbled on her feet so marginally that it would have taken a hunter to notice it. "We tried."

Gideon fell back into his chair, and he heard his mother let out a small cry.

"I had the smallest sliver of hope that it wouldn't come to this," his brother said before turning and finding Gideon in the crowd. He lowered his lashes with a darkness in his eyes, almost saying sorry as he looked to Kellen and his mother. He turned back to Viktir, who looked smug. "But you have left me no other choice."

Gideon tore his hand from Sybil's grip and stood once more. "Torin, wait—"

"I have no other choice, brother." Torin lifted his blue eyes from the floor to his face.

The crowd gasped as Naya Blacksteel shot from her seat too, but Marcus Coldwell was faster than a cobra to grab her and pull her back. Gideon swore he could hear her trying to negotiate with Torin over something, but there was a lively buzz in Gideon's head. Torin was going to challenge his father.

A final challenge.

The crowd was now moving and whispering, and all Gideon could see was the Blacksteel War happening before his eyes.

"My relationship with Emara is not a rejection of my oath to my Gods," Torin shouted, and it brought Gideon back to the room.

"It is a direct rejection of your commander's orders. Do you think your Gods would want you to do that?" the chief challenged.

Gideon halted as Torin roared, "Maybe I don't believe in your fucking Gods anymore! If they are saying that Emara and I are not meant for the same path, then I don't want their guidance."

Every member of the court flinched.

"Torin—" Naya tried to go to him, but Marcus held her firmly. "My love—"

Torin's fists curled as he heard his mother's pleas, her cries. But like the unyielding warrior he was, he stood tall and faced his audience. "On this day, as we stand here together, you all hear my declaration. I, Torin Blacksteel, second-in-command of the Blacksteel Hunting Clan, challenge the commander of the Blacksteel Hunting Clan to a duel of commandership."

The chief commander walked forward as Murk stood. The King of the Fae sat forward in his chair, his brow showing a hint of irritation towards the chief. The Minister of Coin snickered, and Gideon wanted to punch the life from his body.

Aerrick was the first to speak. "I suggest you think about what you are doing, warrior."

But Torin ignored every single person in the room as he glared at his father. "It's done, Viktir. It's either me or you."

CHAPTER SEVENTEEN
TORIN

People moved from the room quicker than Naya Blacksteel ushered them out, leaving only the prime, Emara, and his brothers. Torin stood in the centre of the room, watching his father's face turn from bright burgundy to a ghastly colour of grey.

The summit was over.

Torin seethed as he looked upon the face of his punisher.

His father was an arrogant prick who beat his children into submission and often raised a hand to his wife. He was sly, devious, and the biggest hypocrite Torin had ever known. He was an ill-tempered hunter and still a threat to Emara.

Torin had taken a gamble on challenging him in front of everyone. His father could have told the world about Emara's blood just to spite him. But in the early hours of the morning, he had realised that Viktir didn't want to reveal Emara's blood or who her father was to anyone. He wanted her alliance. He wanted her power, her status. And he knew that he hadn't informed the chief commander of her heritage, which was a punishable offence. Why hadn't he made that move?

He was keeping it up his sleeve for something bigger. And Torin had to make sure that Viktir's influence in the clan was minimal. They had come to blows many times before now, but this...

This was it.

This was the war he had declared six moons ago.

As the final person left the room, silence fell over them like a hot blanket, and it threatened to suffocate the life in the space. Naya closed the door and Torin could hear her walking back to the centre of the chaos.

"Well, there we have it." Viktir's lip pulled back over his teeth. "I was wondering when this would happen. I thought over it many times, thinking it would be over something of meaning. But over a girl?" Viktir sneered and his mother flinched. "You are challenging my commandership over a witch? You are certainly no son of mine. Pathetic doesn't run in our blood."

Torin only let out a snarl.

"Torin, I urge you to think this through," the chief hunter announced, leaning over the prime's table in disbelief. "What you are saying cannot be undone."

"My decision is final," Torin said in the same way Viktir had spoken to him. "If the commander of the Blacksteel Hunting Clan does not wish to amend the treaty, then I challenge him to a duel. Whoever survives will be commander. It solves the dispute."

"No," his mother cried. He heard Kellan trying to calm her. "Torin, please, my love."

"Dispute." Viktir sneered, a growling laugh radiating from his chest.

"This is not Shifter's business, nor is it any other faction's," Murk Baxgroll said, rising from his chair. "We will take leave and you can sort this out between your clan. We will not be involved in hunter politics if it does not involve us."

"I second that motion," Oberon agreed. "I have no appropriate input for a case like this. After all, it comes down to the oath of Thorin."

The King of the Fae and Murk moved to take their leave, but the Minister of Coin still stood by his chair.

"I did not realise you'd taken the Oath of Huntership under Thorin." Torin glared at the elite, his fist clenching tight. "I don't think your nose fits into this jurisdiction either."

The minister grinned, every bit of him enjoying the turmoil of this. He stopped just before Torin, fixing his white undershirt before he looked up into his eyes. "Enjoy bleeding out at your duel. I will make sure your father has the best odds to win. Death always makes so much coin."

The pretentious dick was lucky Torin was saving all his energy for Viktir. He wanted to lash out and show him who could *really* bleed out. Oh, how many ways he could make that elite bastard suffer.

A small hand found its way into his, and he calmed as Emara sent waves of energy through him. Her earth magic had certainly improved since he had been gone, and a soothing vibration settled almost every violent thought. Almost.

"Have a great day, minister." Emara smiled at the elite faction member as she gestured to the door. He took his leave, dragging his beady little eyes from her face before walking as slowly as he could.

"Torin," the chief commander almost pleaded when the door closed again. "This is your last chance to back out of the challenge. Tensions always boil over in clans, but we work it out. Are you absolutely positive that you are unable to bend the knee to your father, your commander?"

Torin swallowed and looked down at the woman leaning into his arm. Her eyes were black with concern and her face was scrunched with fear. When neither of the Blacksteel men even flinched and no words came to evade the duel, the chief said, "Okay, Blacksteels, should you require a duel with weapons or bare fists?"

Torin wasn't surprised when both he and his father served the same answer, "Weapons."

It was easier to kill with a weapon. If they chose fists, it could mean hours of fighting, and he wasn't in the pits anymore. He wanted this over with as soon as he could make the killing blow.

The chief commander stood in between both Viktir and Torin, taking a glance at them both. "So it shall be done. The prime will see you both tomorrow at the first light of dawn. The duel for commandership in the Blacksteel Clan shall be fought for. May the best warrior win."

CHAPTER EIGHTEEN
GIDEON

Gideon found Torin on the rooftop of the Tower, his inky black hair shining in the sunset, his face high-lighted by the lowering sun. Torin was leaning against the railing, a glass in one hand and the other firmly around the barricade.

Gideon was surprised he was still in the Tower at all.

"Bourbon?" Gideon asked as he walked slowly towards him. "No rum? That's not like you."

He looked over his shoulder, and it was then that Gideon saw the raw torment of today's decision in his eyes. But he answered in true Torin fashion. "Finished the rum."

A laugh scraped against his throat as he held on to the railing and looked out to the city below. "I suppose that's more like you."

Torin let out a small huff and swallowed the remainder of his bourbon.

Gideon took a moment letting the silence settle between them. Growing up, it had always been the two of them fighting, playing, and arguing. Torin had always been there for him in his weird Torin ways. He had never let Gideon fear anything or anyone because he had always been at his side. Even when they were going head-to-head, he knew that his brother still loved him. And it was the same for Kellen even though he had come into their world a little later.

"I can't let you go down to the duel tomorrow without saying something." Gideon surprised himself with how much emotion had already swelled in his throat. Torin's eyes narrowed. "I am proud of you, big brother. I am proud of you for standing up for what you believe in, and I am in awe of you for finally admitting what is in your heart. You said today that Emara doesn't deserve a man like you, but that's exactly what she deserves. You."

Torin swivelled, his attention now on Gideon's face. "Gideon—"

"Hear me out," Gideon said as a gentle breeze coasted between them. "It took everything for you to stand up there today and do what you did, and I should have done the same a long time ago."

Torin swallowed and looked down at his glass, his huge hand surrounding it.

"But I didn't. I have watched Father take our happiness for a long time. Mother tried to protect us all from it, as did you." Gideon's tongue rolled into his cheek as he took an unsteady breath. "I remember it, Torin. I remember, even as a child, you would stand up for us all and he would beat you. He would beat you just for standing in front of us as his fists came down. Even when you were young, you stood as though you were eight feet tall, unafraid, and I have always admired that."

Torin turned away from him, his glittering sapphire eyes on the view.

"But you would always pay the price," Gideon choked out. "And tomorrow, I will be praying to the Gods that you win, because you are the kind of commander I want leading this clan. There is no one braver, and there is no one that I trust more. You will be a marvellous commander."

Torin stood up, his spine straightening. "I would rather die than let Emara down, and that is just how it is. I couldn't have gone on and lived my life the way it was headed—the pits, the taverns, the misery...And she reminded me why it was all worth it. She has saved me time and time again, although she will never truly know it. I need to fight for commandership. And if I don't win, then I will know at least that I have fought for something worthy and I can die an honourable death. I can die knowing that I tried to protect you and your honour too. You don't deserve to be pushed into my punishment and have your heart messed with too. I stood up there today to pledge my allegiance to House Air and its empress, but I have never not thought of you in that process. You are my brother, my blood. And I will not allow him to terrorise us any longer."

A few moments passed before Gideon said, "Seeing what I see now, I couldn't have gone through with the marriage. But I should have said something sooner. I should have fought harder."

Guilt ran through his body, causing him to shake again.

Torin lowered his head for a second, looking at the half-empty crystal bottle on the ground before pouring a splash of bourbon into his glass and passing it to him. "It's okay to do what your commander asks of you. That's what has been drilled into us since birth."

"Not if it's not right," Gideon replied. "Not if it ruins people's hearts. You have shown me that."

Torin gave a silent acknowledgement. "I suppose that's the fucked-up thing about being a hunter. You are expected to blindly follow someone with no questions asked."

Gideon let him work through his thoughts for a few moments as he took a sip of his drink.

"You heard what Emara said today," Torin said finally. "She doesn't want a treaty that tells her who she should marry. She doesn't want anything in place that tells her where her heart should lie." He turned to Gideon, and he nodded at his brother. "That's why I am fighting for my life tomorrow; I want to be able to give her that choice back. It's not so that she can marry me by the order of the original treaty. I will burn that piece of paper if I ever make it into his office. It is so that her heart can be free to choose who she wants, when she wants."

Torin's selflessness hit him harder than his fists ever had. He wasn't fighting the commander of the Blacksteel Hunting Clan out of his own want for Emara, but so he could hand her back every drop of power she had lost when the first empress had signed the treaty for their coven.

Gideon had never been more in awe of an act in all his life. "You are a better man than I will ever be, brother," he announced, his heart squeezing. He took a swing of bourbon.

"I wouldn't go that far," Torin scoffed, sounding a little more like himself. "Are you forgetting that I must try to kill our father in the morning? Surely, you must resent me in some way."

They both laughed awkwardly.

"You are going to win. My faith is in you, big brother."

Torin said nothing. It was another silent acknowledgement of his appreciation. Gideon had always tried to remain in the middle when it came to the fight for dominance between his brother and father, but with what was coming tomorrow, he had to pick a side. He had to choose. "I will stand by your side, Torin." Gideon placed a hand on his shoulder and leaned in. "And when you are victorious tomorrow, we will face this together. You are not alone in this. I will not let you face commandership alone. The Blacksteel boys always stick together."

A muscle under Torin's eye twitched. "Thank you," he said, his voice strained and strangled with emotion.

The side of Gideon's head rested against Torin's. "You are going to win." His hand cuffed the back of his neck. "And then we are going to get blindingly drunk and talk about all the silly things that I will need to stop you from doing as commander of this clan."

Torin's hand came up and tapped his brother's a few times, and he nodded with his eyes closed.

The door to the rooftop opened, and both brothers turned to find the Empress of Air standing in the threshold. Her midnight black hair fell around her shoulders like a sheet of silk, and her silver strappy dress hugged body as the gentle summer breeze caught the fabric, blowing it against her skin. Her eyes were full of that steel and fire, but her face still remained so full of grace and beauty. They contrasted so brilliantly.

Gideon smiled before looking at his brother, who was staring at her like she was the Goddess Rhiannon herself. "I will leave you two alone."

"Actually"—her hands dropped to her sides and her gaze lingered on Gideon—"it was you I was looking to speak with."

"Me?" He couldn't hide the surprise in his voice.

"Yes, if that's okay," she said gently.

"Of course." He threw a glance at Torin, who nodded once.

"Come and find me when you are done," Torin said to Emara as he walked towards her. His hands found their way into her hair, and she softened, closing her eyes. He pressed one small kiss to her forehead, and Gideon had never seen such a gentle gesture from his brother. It crippled his heart. He had seen him with her on many occasions, but now that his love for her was out in the world, they both seemed more comfortable showing their affection in front of others.

Gideon swallowed down a feeling he didn't quite understand as Torin left the two of them on the rooftop.

There had been a time before Emara's ascension, before the Amethyst Palace, when Gideon had sworn that he would fight for her. And he still would, until his last breath, but not in the way he once vowed. He wasn't going to fight for her heart anymore; they had said goodbye to each other, standing in the foyer that day, yet somehow it had not felt like the end. But as they stood on the rooftop of the highest tower in Huntswood with the breathtaking sun falling into the earth behind them, whatever had happened between them felt like history.

She moved forward, her strides precise, before stopping a few feet away from him. "I tried to find you before today's meeting." She paused, searching his face. "I wanted to tell you about what angle Torin was going to take with the prime to see if you could do anything to persuade him to change his mind, but I couldn't seem to reach you."

"I was in the gardens with Sybil just before," he said quietly. "The ones around the back, near the stables."

"I know." Emara nodded. "Lorta told me."

Gideon felt his shoulders relax. "I help her plant flowers and herbs before mid-morning."

Emara smiled, and true endearment shone in her eyes. "I can't believe Sybil has turned you into a seedsman."

"I find myself in the gardens more often than not now," he said in return. "I mean, I am Sybil's guard, so I am required to be there, but I enjoy it. Friendship is a funny thing."

"Yes, isn't it just?" She clasped her hands together.

A moment passed between them, causing them both to look out at the city. A few candles or oil lamps had lit the windows of homes, and the smoke from the chimneys began to look less powdery in the darkened light. The trees in the distance looked full and green, contrasting with the colours of the streets and buildings.

"I am sorry that you found out the way you did," Emara said, so gently, "about Torin and I and the decision that my heart had made. So much has happened. There were probably so many moments I could have said something or told you, but—"

"But you weren't ready then," he finished, understanding completely.

The tension in her shoulders fell. "I don't think I was ready for any of this."

Gideon raised his chin. "You were. You were ready for all of it. You just didn't see it coming." He allowed a smile to turn up one corner of his mouth. "I mean, how can you predict falling for my brother?"

She let out a snort, and it was the first time her smile had reached her eyes today. "Trust me when I say I am still in disbelief."

He laughed too. "I am not."

She looked at him funny, but she didn't say anything as her lashes swept down and then up again.

He had seen both of them from the beginning. This wasn't a shock. The looks, the small gestures, the tension in their arguments that weren't really arguments. Time after time, she had opened up to Torin, allowing him further into her heart. She brought out the best in Torin. It was what the Gods called balance.

"I am sorry that I didn't challenge my father more on the arranged marriage," he found the courage to say. "You deserved better than that."

"It's all right, Gideon. I understand that your traditions are special to you." She sighed as she found the railings too.

"I wouldn't say special," he said, trying to find some sort of humour in this mess. "It's just not how I wanted things to be, you know? For things to turn out this way."

She nodded politely. "I know you didn't."

Another moment passed, her gaze still on him. And she must have known that he was working up to asking her something significant because she seemed to be waiting for him to say something.

"Answer me one thing," he finally said, not waiting any longer for his final piece of closure. "Truthfully, after all of this is said and done, if my brother wins tomorrow, it is his path to become the commander of the clan. If he tears up the treaty that chains you to the Blacksteel Clan and states that your heart is free to choose whoever it wants, will your heart still choose him?"

She took a moment, and as she thought it over, a long strand of hair worked its way out like a silken banner, blowing across her face.

"Yes. Gideon, my heart would choose Torin." Her throat bobbed. "My head, if it were sensible, would tell me to choose you. It would tell me that we would have had a good life together, a great friendship. But my heart cannot allow me to do that. My heart belongs to him. Our souls are attached." A pool of tears swam in her eyes, and guilt etched into her features. "I know you wanted to fight for us, for something that your father wanted. But he inflicted that pressure on you, and that wasn't fair to you, your brother, or me." She stepped forward, and Gideon could see a small tear glitter down her cheek. "Thank you for offering to fight for me, but I will not allow you to sacrifice your happiness anymore. It would be cruel of me to give you any kind of hope that my heart is undecided on where it lies. Whether I realised it or not, it's been settled for a long time."

"I know," he said, looking at his boots. "I realise that now. But please don't cry." He quickly closed the distance between them so that he could wipe away her tears. "You should be happy that your heart finally found its unwavering, core-rattling, soul-on-fire kind of love."

She laughed as another tear fell. "With us, it was like trying to fit a key into a lock that just didn't quite fit."

"Oh, the key did fit," he said back, his hunter charm lingering in the air. "It just doesn't unlock the door."

Emara laughed again and rolled her eyes. "Right," she said. She stood back with a smile and wiped her own tears.

"I said to you long ago that it would be an absolute travesty if someone won your heart that wasn't worthy of it. But my brother is. I am happy for you both." Gideon tucked one hand into his pocket.

Emara rolled her lips, another tear falling as she mouthed, "Thank you."

He threw her a cheeky grin. "So," Gideon teased, feeling the energy between them shift, "what was it about him? His downright bad attitude? His swaggering arrogance? The rebellion in his eyes?"

Emara's laugh travelled into the dusky pink sky. Gideon laughed with her, feeling a little lighter.

But when she settled back down, she had that beautiful magic in her eyes. "Torin is formidable, and when he looks at me, he makes me feel that way too," she replied. Her eyes softened, and her heart burst open wide for the world to see. "He makes me feel like I could conquer anything."

Gideon smirked. "You should see him when he gears us up before a hunt. That might really tip you over the edge. Some say he's the most formidable warrior in the clan, but don't tell him that. We don't need his ego getting any bigger."

They laughed again, and as the amusement settled into silence, Emara spoke. "Whatever happens, I don't want us to lose this, our friendship. We almost have before, and I don't want that to happen again."

"It won't," he promised her. "We are on the same team."

"Good."

He let out an over-dramatic sigh. "Well, I suppose you should go and find *the formidable, Torin Blacksteel*."

"I liked you better when you were sulking," Emara jested, sticking her tongue out at him.

"No," he laughed. "But you should go. He needs you tonight."

A softness found its way into Emara's eyes again, and her features relaxed. She nodded once. "I am glad I caught you."

"Me too." He smiled politely back at her.

Emara turned to walk away, but just as she reached the door, she swirled around, her dark hair swinging over her shoulder. "Take her freesia." Gideon's brow must have pulled down because Emara laughed. "Freesia is Sybil's favourite flower. There is some growing in your mother's garden, you will know by the smell. They are beautiful. Pick her a bunch and take them to her. The white ones are her favourite."

With a smile, the Empress of Air disappeared down the steps.

Freesia was Sybil's favourite flower.

Interesting.

Feeling like a huge weight had been lifted from his shoulders, Gideon quickly moved from the rooftop, leaving his past behind, and found himself heading to the corner of his mother's garden.

CHAPTER NINETEEN
EMARA

Emara knocked on the oak door in front of her, her knuckles rattling the old wood. She let out a bated breath, having held in so much anxiety before speaking with Gideon. She took in another firm breath and wiped her brow. Although the Tower was normally cool and breezy, the warmth of summer still felt sticky on her skin. She was exhausted. But she couldn't think of that, not as she was doing her rounds of the Blacksteels tonight.

The door opened on Kellen wearing a loose white shirt that was unbuttoned at the collar and a silver chain around his neck. His dark Blacksteel hair was swept over to one side, and his unusual eyes searched her face in surprise. "Emara?"

"Can I come in?" she asked, wasting no time.

"Would it not be rude to refuse an empress?" His eyebrow went up, and in that moment he looked so like Torin.

"Yes," she said as she made her way into the room and ran a hand through her hair.

Kellen closed the door behind her, and there was a casualness about how they were together now that made it a lot easier to communicate with him than before. "What brings you to my room after dusk?"

"I saw you today, during the meeting." Emara clasped her hands together. "Out of the corner of my eye, I saw that glow as we were leaving the summit. Did you have a vision?"

He let the side of his cheek sink in so that his teeth could grab it. "I took an elixir; you weren't supposed to be able to see that."

"My magic is getting stronger," Emara said. "Why didn't you tell me you had another dream? What happened?"

Kellen had been telling Emara all about his *dreams* recently as a way to help him destress and get them off his chest. Sometimes they were about battles that happened the next day. He wouldn't always share the details with her, though, the pictures and memories too disturbing for him to revisit.

He pushed his hair back, shifting his eyes from hers. "Emara, I cannot change anything that is about to happen between my father and Torin, even if I tell you about my dreams. You know that. There are some that just need to be kept to myself."

Emara's voice was small when she asked, "What did you see, Kellen?"

He looked away from her. "Nothing that will change the course of tomorrow."

"Did you see who won?"

Kellen shook his head. "No, I didn't. I'm sorry."

"But you did *see* something?" She took a step towards him.

Kellen nodded. "You know they have been happening more frequently, but that doesn't mean my visions are any clearer."

She took a moment before she asked, "Was it anything tangible?"

"Not really." He shrugged, making his way over to his burnt orange sofa, which was stacked with creamy pillows. "You know they never make any sense until whatever I'm dreaming about actually happens."

"If there is anything you can tell me—"

"Whatever I saw was in regard to the Temple of the Gods. Whatever happens tomorrow will lead us there," he began, probably knowing she wouldn't rest until he told her something. "But I am unsure why it is all connected. There was a pond, but the water was red. It didn't make any sense. There was a scent of sulphur in the air, and it was darker, murky. Eerie. It could have been stormy, but I am honestly not sure. There were vines that climbed so very high, but I couldn't see where they led. It most definitely had something to do with the Dark Army, so I am assuming that it has nothing to do with tomorrow."

Emara took a seat with him for a moment and let her spine sink into the comfiest chair he had. Her stinging eyes closed for just one moment. "So you couldn't see any faces?"

"No faces. Just feelings this time."

Emara chewed her lip again, shocked that she hadn't yet made it bleed with her growing anxiety. "I hope the feelings aren't too strong and you can sleep tonight."

"Me too." Kellen relaxed again and looked out the window. The window looked out over the forest, a refreshing difference from the view in her room. "You should get some rest too. No offence, but you look exhausted."

"None taken." She laughed a little because she knew what Kellen was saying was the truth. "Have you decided which side you will stand on tomorrow?" she asked him softly.

"I always stand on my own," he whispered.

Emara reached out and took his hand in her own. "That's not true anymore; you have me."

"Come in," Torin said.

When Emara opened the door and made way through the

entrance, she saw him on his chair, freshly showered and sporting only a towel. "You did not need to knock on the door. You can just come in," he said, his piercing blue eyes on her face.

She halted, taking in his glistening skin under the light of the moon that beamed in gloriously from the window. The moon knew exactly how to spotlight him and stop everything else in the world from mattering as she shone her light on his ridiculously carved body. He rose from the chair, the towel lying perilously low at his hips. The small trail of hair that paved a path from his stomach got lost under the towel.

"My eyes are up here," he said as he reached her. A finger curled under her chin and lifted her gaze to his. With a gentle smile, he took her hand and dotted a kiss to her knuckles. She sighed as the touch of his lips made its way to her fingers, unravelling the tension in her neck, her fears, and the distractions in her mind. Torin said, "I've missed you."

"I would have found you sooner but—" Her words were cut off as Torin's hand trailed a path from her neck down her arm. "I needed to...to...take care of a few things before—" Torin caught her wrist with his teeth and gently scored along it.

Holy Gods.

"You had things to take care of, did you?" he said against her wrist, his voice low and dangerous. "How very empress-y of you."

It amazed her how a single kiss could spark a burning desire in her core that spread all over her skin.

"Yes," she breathed. "Empress business."

"That sounds so official." He kissed the crease in her arm where her skin folded and continued upwards.

"It was." She almost let out a moan as he worked his way to her shoulder.

He paused. "Your body is so tense."

"Can you blame me?"

As he reached her neck, Torin stopped his lips from worshipping her. "If I could take this burden of tomorrow from your shoulders, I would. It would take it all."

"I know you would. But I would never let you carry that burden alone. We are a team, remember? I just can't think of something happening to you."

He pulled away from her neck and caught her stare. "Emara, something terrible could happen any day of our lives. But we can't think like that, not tonight. Not in these moments just between us two. We need to live just for us."

She knew what he wanted to say: Not when tonight could be their last night together; not when it could be the last time he touched her. She pulled back, taking a few deep breaths, and her hand went up to hold in her sobs. She had held it together all day and night, but she could show her true self around him, and the tears burst from her eyes.

"Come on," he said, reaching for her. "Don't do that."

"What?" she said, turning from him.

"Don't let the panic and fear win. You're stronger than that." His hands were on her hips, travelling up to her waist and past her curves. They landed on her face, cupping her jaw. "Let's not talk about tomorrow or what the fate of the Gods has in store for me. For us." He nodded, looking deeply into her soul. Emara couldn't breathe. "Let's just take this moment as the stars come out in the sky and the moon shines down on us to get lost in one another. Just us. Just tonight."

She gripped his hands and squeezed her eyes shut, trying to push out the trepidation of tomorrow. The dizziness almost won, but her heart blocked out everything else in the world but him. The sky could be falling down around her and all it would take would be for Torin Blacksteel to wink at her and she would forget about everything.

"I am sorry. I just feel a little overwhelmed. Can you pour me a drink?" she asked him. "Anything you have."

His eyebrow went up, but he moved over to where his crystal glass sat, untouched, by his chair. Walking back over, Emara felt the temperature of the room intensify as if the sun herself had come up from her slumber underground to fill the room with warmth. Maybe it was Torin in nothing but a fluffy white towel, but heat swarmed her.

"Would you like a sip?" He held up the glass, and something wicked glinted in his stunning eyes.

She nodded, swallowing a breath. "Yes."

His eyes dazzled like polished sapphires as he held up the glass close to her mouth. "I will give you a sip, angel." He paused, his grin turning devious as his lips fought to hide his pearl-white teeth. "But only if you promise that we can share."

After she nodded, his lips turned up at the corner, finally revealing one of those sensual grins that dimpled in his cheek. Those unholy dimples sent fire through her heart and flutters into her stomach. He put the glass to his mouth, all eyes on her, and let the liquid slide into his mouth.

He moved fast, grabbing her neck with one hand and opening her mouth with his own.

Delightful shock knocked the breath from her as he let the bourbon flow from his mouth to hers, sending tastes of spice, notes of vanilla, and grains of caramel onto her tongue. The alcohol burned a track down to her stomach and his kiss came down hard on her lips. He broke away all too quickly, leaving her chest heaving.

"More?" His husky voice told her that he had something more than bourbon on his mind.

"Always," she said, nipping his lip with her teeth.

He groaned as his hand slid around her waist. He pulled her flush with his chest, and she could feel the hardness of her nipples pushing into him. "You cannot waltz in here wearing that dress, drink the bourdon from my own lips, bite me, and then expect me not to want to fuck you so hard that we both forget our names."

"What is it about me waltzing around in a dress that gets you so hot and bothered?" She met his stare.

"I would prefer it if you didn't have one on," he challenged.

Emara's hands nipped down to the hem, and she pulled her dress over her head, revealing her undergarments. "Like this?"

He took a step back, studying her with a burning flame of chaos in his eyes. He finished the rest of what was in his glass before placing it on the dark oak drawers. "Why do you continue to surprise the fuck out of me?"

He collided with her, and his large hand wrapped around the back of her neck this time, angling her exactly where he wanted her head to be. His lips separated hers, and he groaned against her mouth as if she tasted sweeter than the bourbon.

Emara drove her hands up, pushing through his thick, silken hair, and kissed him like it was the last time she was going to. And he kissed her back like he couldn't guarantee her another. She reached down, pulling the towel from his waist just as he unhooked her bralette, exposing her flesh. He slid the fabric of her underwear past her ass with two strong hands and gripped her thighs, bringing her effortlessly into his arms. Her legs wrapped around his rock-hard torso as teeth and lips devoured each other.

Torin swivelled and fell back into his chair with her on top of him, unfaltering from her mouth. His tongue pushed against hers, desperate and consuming, greedy and powerful. Running his hands up her stomach to her breasts, he grabbed and palmed at her skin, making her breath halt in her lungs. He sat up, taking one of her nipples into his mouth sucking and nipping at her tender skin. A flood of heat rushed to her core and she called out, not knowing— not caring—if anyone else in the world could hear her saying his name. As her eyes fluttered open, she found that his gleaming ocean eyes were on her too, enjoying every minute of the pleasure that he was making her feel.

Heat blushed her cheeks. "I want you," she said, trying not to close her eyes again. As his wet tongue whirled around that same nipple, the sensation brought her eyes shut. Her back arched in total submission to his touch.

"Where do you want me?" he rasped against her skin, knowing exactly where she wanted him.

"You know where."

"Say it."

"Inside me," she breathed.

"Is that what you want, angel?" he teased as he grazed his teeth over her breast.

"Yes." Her head tilted back as he kissed between her breasts. "Wait," she said through laboured breaths. She rested a hand on his chest to steady herself. Her eyes opened again, finding him.

"What's wrong?" He stopped moving instantly.

Her cheeks burst into flames. "I've never been...I've never done anything *this* way before."

His shoulders relaxed, and he fell back a little in the chair. "Emara, with you on top of me, looking like that, I feel like a king. Please do not worry. There is nothing you can do that would be wrong. There is no way that you could move that wouldn't send me wild." He grabbed her face, bringing it down to his. "You are mine. You are an empress, and you are in control. And I don't want you to forget this as you ride me—you are a goddess."

His lips were on hers quick and fast, and she returned it. She pushed through the confidence that he had just given her and seared it into their kiss. He was right. She was an empress, and he made her Gods-damned feel like one.

Torin moved his hand down past her stomach, and a finger

found the bundle of nerves that had Emara's back arching and a moan escaping her mouth. He moved in slow circles with his fingers as he found that soft spot on her neck and sucked in hard. She bucked again, but his other hand held her hip in place, unwilling to let her shy away from the pleasure.

He circled faster, building up that beautiful tension that could break any moment. Just at the right moment, he slid one finger into her, feeling how truly ready she was for him. He added another finger instantly, and she cried out, her head falling back. Her spine arched even more and she secretly prayed for the sweetest release to bring shivers down her bones.

Those sweet, intoxicating little shivers.

"You are so fucking beautiful as you take my fingers," he said lowly.

"Torin," she gasped as his thumb found her clit again.

Her hips found a stunning rhythm as he pumped two fingers inside of her, and the rush of euphoria was building high. Just as he drove his fingers in her for the last time, he stroked her with his thumb, and the feeling was too perfect for her body to bear. She screamed, her climax crashing down on her like an avalanche. There was nothing but bliss as she came for him, nothing but pure, untouched pleasure. She clung to his body, her hands in his hair until she regained her vision.

He shifted her, moving her to his cock. Emara gave a soft whimper as the tip of him grazed along her swollen apex, and he waited until she looked at him. Emara licked her lips, her vision finally clear of all the glittering spots and speckles of ecstasy. She glanced down at him waiting for her to take every inch of him.

He moved his hand down to help her guide where he was supposed to go, and she slowly lowered herself.

"Take your time, angel. We don't have to rush this."

A gasp left her lips as the tip of him edged into her entrance, and he moved to place a kiss into her collarbone. She relaxed and moved again, rolling her hips a little, taking him deeper. An exhale from Torin had her eyes wide open. To her surprise, he was struggling to hold his release already. Something about a warrior like him below her, at her mercy, sent a craze of power through her body. Her magic ignited. Her darkness coiled around her spine. Her air blew through the room.

She moved again, this time circling her hips like what his wicked fingers had done to her. He hissed, biting his lips so hard. The veins in his neck started to appear.

"You have never been more magnificent than you are now, taking me all the way into you," he rasped.

She lowered herself again, gliding down him further, placing her hands into his solid chest. She dug her nails in as she rolled again, taking him deeper and a little quicker. But this wasn't the pace that she was used to with Torin.

She plunged down, finally taking everything he had to give. All of him.

"Fuck," he breathed, his hands slipping to her hips. "You feel so fucking good."

That was all she needed to hear as she began rocking against him. She never knew how fierce it could feel to be on top of a man like Torin Blacksteel and watch as he lost all control. He gripped her hips as the two of them moved together, grinding into ultimate satisfaction. Torin quickened his thrusts to meet hers, and the pounding of their skin could be heard over their gasps.

A second release built up in Emara's stomach, travelling all the way to her toes and right back up her spine. The final thrust he gave before his release came sent a wave of undiluted exhilaration into every part of who she was. She moaned his name, and he called out hers too. When she opened her eyes, she found the same slick expression on his face as he lay back watching her. Both covered in perspiration, they embraced each other, panting.

Existing.

Together.

Torin pulled back again and pushed the untamed hair from her face. After a few minutes of laboured breaths, he said, "If the Gods are not in my corner tomorrow, I want you to know..." He took her face in his large hands once more. "I will die free." He placed his head to hers and wiped away the tears that were now blinding her. "You freed me, Emara Clearwater. You allowed my heart to be free."

A cry broke from her lips, but he silenced her with a kiss. Before she could break down entirely, he swept her up in his arms and walked towards his bed, promising to kiss her until the sun broke through the kingdom.

CHAPTER TWENTY
EMARA

No hunter spoke as Emara made her way through the gardens to an old sparring room that lay open on the outskirts of the Tower. The stonework had crumbled and the old ruins were used as a training facility, often where archery or axe-throwing would take place instead of the sparring room.

But not today.

The morning dew had just descended across the shrubberies, and in the sky, clouds of orange, yellow, and gold began drifting their way across the kingdom to wake her. The setting was a contradiction to what was about to take place here, a history that should be etched in a palette of storms and chaos. This would be a battle that should be fought in harsher conditions—something more fitting than a calm sunrise and pretty songbirds.

It felt wrong. It all felt wrong, and Emara's stomach hadn't stopped rolling. But the sun's presence was mere moments away, and maybe the Gods would rise with it and protect Torin. Her heart was pounding in her chest as she kept her eyes on the ground. One foot in front of the other; that was all she needed to do. Breighly Baxgroll trailed behind her, quiet and pale and so very unlike herself as she blended in with her empress maids. Artem was nowhere to be seen, but the possibility of him being with Torin was high. She wasn't sure if she was unsettled not to see Torin beforehand or if she was secretly relieved to have a few moments to gather herself.

There was nowhere to sit, but it was evident that a marker had been etched into the gravel, a marker of where the challengers where to stay until one of them had taken their last gasp.

Emara's darkness tugged at the strings of her magic, and as she walked through the space, she could feel the dark magic push through her veins, urging for release. Air was swirling inside her like a possessed spirit, her stomach matching the motion. Fire was heating her palms, but she pulled it back too before it ignited all through the gardens. Emara felt a Light presence with her, not from Lorta or Kaydence who walked beside her, but from something more regal, more ancient. Spirit was here, the ancestors also coming to this momentous occasion. And the minute this fight began, she knew the element of earth would urge her to heal, to help.

But there would be nothing she could do.

If Torin was hurt, or worse, she wouldn't be able to go to him. He would bleed out on the ground. The darkness, like a spider, crept in through the cracks of her walls and began forcing its way out. She pulled it back, knowing how busy the clearing was. If she had an outburst of darkness right here, she would reveal her blood.

She halted, noticing everyone looking in her direction. She couldn't go down this route. The darkness was taking her mind to a place of defeat. She couldn't be there. She had to stop herself from getting lost down that rabbit hole of despair. She had to have faith in the Gods to protect him and faith in her ancestors on the Otherside to treat him well. Even if she was drowning in fear on the inside, she would never show that on the outside. She would prove today why she was Torin's equal.

She was strong, unyielding, and powerful.

Her coven would expect nothing less, and neither would the other witches who would hear of this day. The clans would expect nothing less. By now, this event would be the talk of the kingdom, and all eyes would be on her to see if she crumbled.

A hand on her shoulder sent an unnecessary shiver down her spine as she turned to see Marcus Coldwell's dark eyes gazing upon her face. He bowed quickly. "Empress of Air."

She nodded, separating herself from the girls. "Marcus, you know to call me Emara."

"I know, but I still like the sound of *Empress of Air*." He smiled kindly.

She couldn't even falsify a smile as she stood watching him.

He held out his arm for her to take, and Lorta and Kaydence moved into step behind her. Breighly walked off to the left, giving them a little space to talk. Marcus gave her arm a quick rub. "I thought you would need someone to hold onto as the Blacksteels are preoccupied."

She gripped his arm tighter. A few more hunters arriving had her stomach somersaulting. "How do you hunters always remain calm in the face of death?"

They took a few more steps past the can. "You're going to be okay," Marcus said on a low breath. "He is going to be okay. I know it."

She closed her eyes for the briefest moment. "The Gods know I have prayed for it enough."

Marcus took a breath. "Me too." There was a silence between them, and a bird's song could be heard from the trees that surrounded them. "When they come out"—Marcus's eyes were hit by the first light of the sun, and it was like Emara could see his lovely soul behind the darkness in them—"we must choose a side. We all must choose a side to stand at so that when the victor wins, he can see all who did not stand with him."

Emara's heart slammed up her throat as her fingers tightened around Marcus's grey tunic. "Why are hunters always trying to discover a problem with each other? I thought they were supposed to be the peacemakers of this kingdom."

A small chuckle left Marcus. "We do not worship the God of Sun and War to always keep the peace. That is where our role is often contradictory, Emara."

Emara thought over his statement before asking, "So the clan will be divided entirely today?"

Marcus finally reached his stop, where the edges of the decaying brick lay, and he looked around himself before he spoke. "'When the successor to the commandership is announced and the clan stands apart, he can see who stood with him and who stood against him.' It is the first rule of commandership to set a precedent in their punishment. It defines his leadership. He needs to demonstrate how harsh he can be by punishment, exile, or intense labour. It's the way of the warrior."

"It seems all so pointless." Emara's head shook, and she could feel the ends of her hair brush along her lower back in her thin gown. "If Torin is victorious, he must ask anyone who stands on his father's side to bend the knee to him and then he will punish them? How does that make sense? Surely, that will make him unpopular among the clan."

"The clan understands the consequences of what side they choose. How we endure the punishment is our way of honouring and respecting our commander. It's tradition. The men would never respect him if he didn't punish the ones who choose the opposite side. And the clan needs to respect their leader. The first thing a commander must do is crack the whip. And anyone who stands on the opposite side from Torin will receive his wrath should he win."

Emara flinched at the thought. "Then that means you must choose a side too."

"It does."

Emara's brow pulled tight as she remembered the details of how

Viktir Blacksteel had taken in a young Marcus who had just failed the Selection process in his father's eyes because he hadn't made the top one percent. He had been a relation of Viktir's, and Emara wondered if the current commander had once had a heart. Viktir had trained him, given him a home, and Marcus had willingly pledged an oath to serve Clan Blacksteel instead of his own.

The Coldwells had always been clan rivals to the Strykers, who were by far the biggest clan in the Helmsbrook area, and they often fought over territory and hunting jurisdiction.

For a brief second, Emara wondered who Marcus would choose.

A whistle sounded, startling Emara from her thoughts, and she glanced around to see Aerrick Stryker move into a space in the ruined threshold. All heads turned to witness Viktir Blacksteel stride through the garden as the clan parted for him. His wrists were bound, his boots laced tight, and his face was unreadable and stern. A knot tightened in Emara's stomach as she noticed that he had taken no chances on the vital killing spots. A thick leather gilet lay over his torso, the collar coming around his neck like a guard's uniform, protecting one of the main arteries in the body.

A second later, the crowd that had gathered parted again to reveal Torin Blacksteel.

Emara couldn't look at him, not when his eyes had wandered all over her face last night in a way that told her his soul knew hers. Not when his lips had told her own that he would rather die than stop kissing her. Not when his hands had roamed every inch of her body like he may never worship it again. She couldn't look at his face because if she saw fear, she would burn the entire Tower to the ground with Viktir Blacksteel in it.

Kellen came just behind Torin, then Artem and Gideon, their arms linked with Naya's. Her face was so horrifyingly pale it sent shock waves through Emara's bones. Her lavender-ringed eyes confirmed that she, too, had not slept at all, and the puffiness of her cheeks suggested that she had cried all night.

Emara suddenly felt like she was looking at Callyn's grave again, numb and disbelieving of what her senses told her. This felt similar, only Torin had not been slaughtered in front of her. This wouldn't be the same. It couldn't be.

She gripped Marcus tighter as the sickness rose from her stomach.

Her heart was still so sore about Callyn. And when she thought of her, which was every day, a sharp ache reminded her of the emptiness that her death caused. That dizzying grief that almost flattened her and took control of everything.

Marcus patted a hand over hers.

When she looked up from the floor of the gardens, the two men fighting for the Blacksteel honour stood at either side of the marked-out battle ground. It was then that Emara could see Torin, also clothed in full black leather that was harsher than the regalia he hunted in. It was thicker, more resilient to weather the weapons he might face today. The two swords strapped across his back formed a deadly X at the back of his strong neck, and just as the new sun began peeking from the earth, beams of light hit them, and they glistened.

In that moment, Torin and Viktir were a mirror of destruction, and they had never looked more alike.

The chief commander made his way to the middle of the markings and spoke to the crowd. "As the sun rises in the east, we must choose between north and south." The chief looked at the crowd, his strong features twisted into something that Emara hadn't witnessed before. "As chief commander of the clans, I am the only person here who has the validation to remain impartial in this challenge. Everyone else must choose to stand in the south with Viktir Blacksteel or in the north with Torin Blacksteel. And you must choose before the sunlight hits above the trees behind us."

A few people moved quickly; it was clear they had made their decision overnight.

Emara didn't even have to question where she would stand.

She let go of Marcus's arm, who looked at her with a void in his eyes. He had an impossible choice today. Viktir had once saved his life and Torin was like his brother. It wasn't going to be easy for him at all. Emara gripped his hand and whispered, "Choose what future commander you want to stand behind when the Dark Army comes for us in full force."

He nodded once, his dark eyes pained, and she left him behind to choose his side.

As she walked across the clearing, she noted that Gideon and Kellen were already standing at Torin's back, as was Artem. Naya Blacksteel moved too, her head down and eyes on the ground. Kellen put out his arm, wrapping it around his mother; she was so petite against his frame. The youngest Blacksteel stood like the rest, his chin in the air and his shoulders back.

Turning away, she noted Sybil and Rhea in the crowd that backed Torin. In fact, most of the earth witches that resided in the Tower stood in support of the second-in-command.

The Tower's guests split evenly until there were only a few left standing. Breighly moved and joined Lorta and Kaydence by Emara's side, and Emara noticed Roman Baxgroll, the only other wolf present, drifting through the crowd to stand beside his twin.

Emara's eyes fell to Marcus, who was now one of three men still left to choose.

With his head bowed under the pressure of his decision, Marcus Coldwell shifted his weight between his feet. He ran a hand over his face, his dark skin glowing with the sun's reflection. He blew out a breath and looked up at the Gods' sky.

"Come on," Gideon Blacksteel whispered beside her, his eyes on his friend. "Come on, Marcus."

Gideon's leg shook impatiently as they all awaited his verdict.

Marcus Coldwell's dark eyes found Torin, and a sympathetic frown pulled around his mouth. "I am sorry," he mouthed. "If you are victorious, I will follow you through any battle. But the Gods do not allow me to choose you today."

Torin didn't react, the mask of a warrior cemented to his face. He watched Marcus move to stand by his father's side, and Viktir gave a taunting grin.

Gideon hung his head and let out a breath through his teeth, his fists balling.

Everyone had chosen their camp.

"When I sound my horn, both challengers who have laid claims to Commander of the Blacksteel Hunting Clan must step forth. All others must not interfere by hand or by magic until one submits or is killed, rendering the other triumphant. The opponents must only have two weapons on their person, and if their weapon falls out of the designated zone, that weapon is disqualified. The person who is announced successor at the end of the duel is immediately instated as the commander of the clan. Are the rules clear?"

In unison, both Blacksteel men announced, "Yes, Chief."

As the commander stepped out of the battlegrounds, his eyes drifted over both men and said, "May the God Thorin wield you best at war. May Rhiannon bless you with dreams in the afterlife. May the God Uttara bless you if your soul reaches the stars or if you make it to a new dawn, and may the God Vanadey bless the soil your body will rest in."

Hearing those traditional words sent a shiver skating over Emara's skin.

The horn broke through the air, startling Emara, and her heart broke free into her mouth. Naya Blacksteel slid her hand into

Emara's, and she could feel the shake of her body as her husband and first-born son drew their weapons.

They were in perfect synchronisation, and Emara wondered how many times they had fought each other. Torin had been trained by Viktir, and you could see it now as both men assessed the other, their movements almost identical.

Torin was the first to attack; he advanced on the commander and took a few swipes at him. Viktir blocked every blow, his footwork precise and his sword work meticulous. Clashing metal rang through the air, and Emara wished that this was only a lesson in weaponry like the one she had first witnessed between the Black-steel brothers before the Blood Moon.

Torin pulled back, having failed to hit his target, but in the same breath, Viktir took a stab at Torin's chest.

His heart. The most vital killing point.

Emara gasped, and Naya pressed her hand to her mouth, stifling a cry.

Torin dove, narrowly escaping steel on his skin. As Torin ducked to the side, he brought his sword up, aiming to make a mark of his own, but Viktir blocked the hit with both of his weapons, twisting them up to create a shield. Torin advanced again, giving no time for Viktir to regain his balance properly. He was relentless as he forced his father back, swinging one sword right and then left. Sheer muscle and force swung forward in a skilful battle, but Viktir blocked the blows until he had reached the end of the fighting space. Torin had backed his father into the corner of the space. Emara's heart squeezed, and her throat dried up.

Rapidly, Viktir swung up his sword, clattering off Torin's hand, and it sent Torin's left sword through the air. As soon as the weapon hit the ground, Emara closed her eyes, hearing the gasps that broke through the crowd.

Viktir was going to strike like a caged viper.

"Don't lose focus," she heard Gideon whisper. "Don't let it rattle you."

Torin took a step back, rolling the only sword he had left in the palm of his hand before his fingers flexed around the hilt, bringing it back up to his eyeline.

Viktir gave off a triumphant smirk as he lazily swung both swords before taking up another fighting stance. He lunged like an animal at Torin, ready to stab him with not only one sharp point, but two. Steel clashed on stee as the weapons collided.

Torin moved like the wind, and as quick as Emara could see, he had pivoted, rolled to the ground, and came up behind his father. Emara held in a breath as Torin lunged forward to aim for his spine. Viktir must have sensed his move as he veered to the side, but it wasn't enough to escape Torin's blade. A tear in the leather gilet was all Emara could see before she noted the commander was bleeding. She heard a hiss from Viktir's support, some people now shifting nervously in the crowd.

Gideon shifted his weight, his eyes on the battle. His hands never left his weapon belt; it was like he wanted to be in there, helping his brother.

Viktir stumbled slightly as Torin powered a blow in his direction, and the clash of steel rang through the kingdom. A shout of pain came from Viktir as he stretched to block his son's sword, his wound now gaping even more. Two more swipes came from Viktir, trying to injure Torin, but he was unsuccessful.

Torin darted forward, spying a weakness in his father's stance, but Viktir met his one sword with two, locking him in.

It was a trap.

Emara's breathing hitched as both Blacksteels stood eye to eye.

Torin kneed his father in the gut and then delivered an elbow to Viktir's jaw. It bought him enough time to free his sword and disarm one of Viktir's. The weapon fell to the ground with a heavy thump and Torin kicked it aside, then corrected his stance.

Naya gasped behind her hand, and Breighly let out a sharp curse.

"Evenly matched again." Viktir sneered.

"This isn't an even match, old man." Torin's cocky grin pulled across mouth as both men circled each other. "It hasn't been an even match since I returned from the Selection, bigger and better than you, and you know it."

"Always talking yourself up, Torin." Viktir sniggered as his fingers gripped the hilt of his only sword. "But do I need to remind you in front of everyone that I was always the one who beat that stupid smirk from your face?"

Viktir lunged forward, going for Torin's throat. Leaning back as his father's sword almost severed his head, Torin twisted and kicked out into Viktir's stomach. The commander stumbled back, losing his balance. Torin was on him again, and he swung his sword with a roar, every muscle in his body engaged as he propelled Viktir's final weapon from his hands.

Viktir wasted no time, and stuck his boot in Torin's knee. He wobbled, hissing as his body tensed in pain. Viktir seized the moment and tackled Torin to the ground.

Emara let out a squeal and covered her eyes. Air lodged in her throat. All she knew was that Viktir had landed on top of Torin. She could feel his brothers both taking a step forward.

It was then that Naya let out a desperate cry, "Not my boy. Please, Rhiannon, not my son."

The scream rolling up Emara's throat was hideous, full of fear, rage, and darkness. But she couldn't scream, not when Torin was fighting. He would know it was her.

Finding courage from deep within, Emara peered at the fight again.

Viktir's harsh hands began pummelling into Torin's face. "Does this bring back any memories?" he spat venomously. "Putting you back in your place."

The only answer Torin gave back was a grunt as the blood spilled from his mouth, his head snapping from side to side by the force of his fists.

"Come on, Torin," Gideon shouted. His entire body was now jolting with anxiety. "Get the fuck up!"

All the hairs rose on Emara's arms and neck as she took another step forward. She had never heard Gideon's tone so brutal, and it added to the fear that was now vibrating up and down her spine. "Get up, Torin," she whispered. "Get up. Please."

Out of nowhere, Torin's huge fist broke through the air, and he took a swing at the man on top of him.

Viktir's head snapped to the side as Torin's fist battered his cheek. Torin was quick to roll onto his side as the commander fell on his back. He straddled his father as the blood ran down his head and into his eyes, and it was then that Emara could see how bloody his face was. His mouth was split open, ruby-red blood running down his chin, and his left eye was almost closing over.

Artem Stryker's booming clap pounded through the space in support of his violent comeback, and Emara considered it to be one of the loudest sounds she had ever heard. "That's it, Tori-boy. On your feet, sunshine. Get up. Come on."

She could feel the nerves waving from Artem too. The inked warrior always wore some sort of cheeky grin, but not right now. In any other circumstances, his nickname for Torin would have made her smile.

Torin forced himself up and onto his feet, but Viktir's arm shot out, grabbing his ankle and pulling. The crowd broke into a frenzy as Torin tumbled back down on top of the commander.

Torin used the extra force of gravity to his advantage and whacked his head into Viktir's face.

There was a horrific crunching sound, and blood burst from Viktir's nose. The crowd sucked in a breath. A rumbling groan broke from Viktir's throat, but Torin had stunned him enough to allow himself to land another punch. And another, and then another. He hit him again and again, his fists bursting skin, beating bones...

Emara could feel the sick in her stomach swirl again, around and around like a portal.

"Finish him, Torin," someone roared from the crowd, and suddenly, Emara felt like she was back in the pits.

Torin leaned over his father's limp body, gripping one of the swords that lay glistening in the morning sun. The twinkle of the blade shone lethally as he got to his feet and pointed the steel at his father's heart.

Everyone who watched took a step forward, even the chief commander.

Emara took a moment to consider that this awful tradition could be over soon if Torin drove the sword through Viktir's heart. But he hadn't moved. Torin's face looked tortured, his brows pulling into a scowl as his burst eyebrow bled all down his face.

Emara wanted to go to him, but she rooted her feet to the ground, her magic urging her to heal him. The sword in Torin's hand began to shake. He roared and jabbed at the man lying in a pool of blood again.

But the blade did not enter flesh or bone.

"Fucking do it, you coward. Stick your sword through my heart." Viktir's cruel voice breached the morning air. "Go on then, do it."

Torin's hair rustled on his brow as he shook his head. "I do not need to see your blood spilled on the ground to know that I have won," he spat in return. "Submit your title to me and this will be over. Forfeit your commandership. You do not need to die."

Viktir spat blood onto Torin's leg. "Push that fucking blade into my flesh, you weak cunt."

Torin hesitated, and Emara could see how torn he was about finally killing his father. "He never hesitates," Kellen whispered to Gideon.

"I know," Gideon replied lowly.

Viktir let out a vicious laugh as crimson blood coated his teeth. "You are unworthy of the Blacksteel name if you cannot finish what you started."

Torin's blade pieced into the commander's chest a little further, pushing him back into the ground. "And you were unworthy of the Gods granting you a wife and sons, but here we are, watching your shameful fall from leadership." Torin regained his stance. "Submit to me."

"Submit, Viktir," came a shout from the crowd.

"Renounce your commandership," another bellowed from his side, and Emara wondered if they wanted him to stay alive.

If Torin didn't kill him now, then Viktir could regain strength and come back for him. Was the darkness in her veins edging her away from compassion?

"Stand," shouted another. "Get on your feet, Commander."

No! This couldn't be happening. Why was Torin not ending his life?

"No life needs to be taken today," a hunter from Torin's corner said. "He is sparing your life, you ungrateful prick. Submit."

"I never asked him to spare it," Viktir growled.

"That's my decision, not yours. I won." Torin let his sword stray away from the commander's heart. "Because if I pierce your heart with my blade today, I am no better man than you. I would be just like you, and I refuse to be that man." Torin's jaw flexed, and his eyes fluttered shut for a second longer than they should have. "So I am going to give you one last opportunity to surrender your commandership over to me and I will let you live out the rest of your miserable life."

Naya stepped forward. "Viktir, by the grace of the Gods, lay down your pride this once. Do you really want your boys to see their father killed by their own brother?" Naya's voice broke. "Your own son? Is that what kind of human you have become? Will you really let your own flesh and blood push that sword through your merciless heart? Because if so, then you are no better than the darkness that breathes in the underworld."

A moment passed between Naya and Viktir, a moment that no one else would understand. A stale silence darkened the air, and a small cloud must have drifted over the sun because the surrounding area dropped in temperature. A cool breeze tugged at the crowd as everyone watched Torin standing over his commander.

"Please surrender, Viktir," Naya pleaded. "Please."

Torin raised his sword to his father's heart once more. "You have five seconds."

Viktir pushed the blade aside. "You are a fucking coward," he roared as he got to his feet, stumbling, his legs not able to support his weight. "A disgrace."

"Four seconds." Torin's back muscles flexed under his armour. "I need to hear the words."

"I concede." A defeated exhale spat more blood onto the ground before Viktir's green gaze found Torin's. "You'd better exile me to the farthest part of the kingdom you can think of, boy, or you and the people who stood in your corner today are not safe."

Torin took a few strides towards his father. "The people that stand in my corner are the safest people here, and do you want to know why? Because under the oath they will take before me and Thorin, they are protected from punishment by anyone other than me." He spat looking down on him. "You underestimate how much I have noted your abuse of power, *Father.* I have observed carefully every single time you pulled rank or pushed your authority around like a dead weight. Don't you forget that I learned from a very cunning and deceitful commander that you do not give a person who defies you any room to negotiate." He pulled back, and Emara watched Viktir wipe the blood from his nose. "You see, my commander taught me to always find someone's weakness. Find something that someone wants so badly, and then when they defy you, you strip that person of what they want." Torin took a few steps back, and the power that radiated from him captured the attention of everyone in the crowd. "You only threaten the ones I love, the ones who stand by my side, so that I'll send you off to some foreign land where you can live the rest of your shameful life in the shadows. But I am not afraid of your threats, and I will not be part of your manipulations anymore. I am the Commander of the Blacksteel Hunting Clan. I command you to stay in the Tower as part of my clan."

A few whispers blew around the crowd.

"You are a laughingstock," Viktir hissed. "First you couldn't slash your blade through my throat, and now you will not exile me? Commandership is going to come down on you like the Gods are throwing bricks on your head."

"No, Father, I will not exile you." Torin squared his shoulders. "Because only then, by not allowing you to disappear into the shadows of the kingdom, will you receive your punishment. I will see it on your face every day. Your hatred to watch me in command. Your utter embarrassment to take instruction from me, to be at my mercy. Why would I allow you a few moments of pain over a lifetime of shame? Why would I grace your body to bleed out before you go over to the Otherside and have no punishment for what you have done to my family? You are mine until the Gods take you. And there you have my first command, *Father*. You are fucking mine."

A warm breeze blew through the crowd, and that was when Emara finally caught a breath.

"The Gods have spoken." The chief commander walked forward and removed the commander's badge from Viktir's chest. "Torin Blacksteel, first of his name, I now pronounce you the Commander of the Blacksteel Hunting Clan." Aerrick moved across to Torin, but his gaze was on the Tower in the distance as the badge was pinned on his chest. The chief's eyes found his crowd. "Bow before your honourable commander."

Tears spilled from Emara's eyes as she dropped to one knee in her gown, and everyone else did the same, bowing their heads before their new commander.

Torin Blacksteel.

CHAPTER
TWENTY-ONE
EMARA

I t was over.

The fight for the Blacksteel Commandership was over, and Torin had been victorious.

Oaths were recited, knees were knelt on, and warriors held their palms to hearts in the sight of Thorin that they would honour and obey their newest leader. Emara witnessed the newest commander stand before his brethren like a god. He stood in front of his men, power radiating from him even as blood dripped from his body. Even the ones who had not chosen his corner now did, knowing that they would receive punishment for not selecting his side.

They now had to bow to Torin.

And that included the former commander. A slight awe crept into her chest to acknowledge that she was proud of Torin for not murdering his father. His heart was so much bigger than anyone could have ever imagined. And now his soul would not be tarred with the memories of killing Viktir.

It was wise of him to know that Viktir's biggest punishment would not be death, but to be ranked under his son and to be dealt the hand that the commander gave him.

And Naya, thank the Gods for Naya. Torin could have been forced to end his father's life had it not been for her.

When it was over, Torin fled from the ruins, avoiding anyone who tried to congratulate him or even speak with him. Healers had run after him, but he had shrugged them off, telling them to attend to Viktir first. Naya had hugged Emara until she couldn't breathe, tears streaming from her eyes, and even Gideon had embraced her.

Artem Stryker, being himself, announced an honorary service for Torin's commandership, which of course meant that he would order wagons full of ale and there would be a few days of revelry for anyone who celebrated the new commander.

As the preparations for the service began at mid-morning, all magical factions that stayed within the Tower pulled together, making pastries, shining glasses, and dressing tables in fine lace that needed a little flair. As letters were sent to clans across the kingdom, as maids polished every oil lamp, as everyone buzzed around prepping the Tower for the commemorations, Emara felt numb.

She couldn't find Torin.

She had searched the Tower all over to find him. His room, the library, the rooftop, the stables, the infirmary, but nothing. No witch had seen him for healing, no cook had seen him for eating, no hunter had seen him for sparring. He was nowhere to be found. Marcus declared he hadn't left the grounds, as he had not passed the foyer doors, so that meant there was only one place left.

The Commanding Office.

A strange feeling passed through Emara as she stood outside the large oak door to the office she had entered a few times to speak on political matters with Viktir. She hated the place. It was cold and dull, and there was nothing pleasant about it.

Her knuckles rattled on the door before entering, wondering how many times Torin had dreaded coming through this very door.

"Enter," Torin commanded in a voice that didn't sound like his own.

She opened the door slowly and halted when she saw him.

A darkness festered in the room. The poor lighting hid Torin's face as he sat in what used to be his father's chair, sprawled out, his feet on the wooden desk in front of him. His hand rubbed along his brow, his knuckles still bruised, but at least he seemed to have had them cleaned up. He tried to smile at her with a weary grin that didn't reach his eyes, and he placed down a paper that he had been reading on the desk.

Emara flicked her wrist in the direction of every candle and, one by one, a flame ignited, adding light to the dim walls and allowing a glow to soften Torin's fierce features.

"Did no one ever tell you that reading in the dark was bad for your eyes?" Emara tried her hardest to find humour in the moment, but an overwhelming sadness took over as she glanced upon his injured face.

"Well then, I guess it's a good thing that I have such a talented witch to light my candles." His smirk was small and almost non-existent.

Defeated.

She took a few more steps into the room. "They are throwing celebrations for you down in the main hall to honour your victory. I have never seen so much liquor." She chewed on her lip. "Breighly even organised for the La Luna sugar spice and rum recipe to be served for you as a toast to your triumph."

"I know," was all he said as his fingertips drummed a short beat on his temple.

She glanced around the room, not knowing what to say to him, and he took his feet from the desk and planted them on the ground.

"Can you come over here?" he asked as he looked at her through dark lashes. "Please," he added, and the weakness to his voice almost made her knees buckle.

Emara strode across the room and flung herself against him. She wrapped her arms around him before he pulled her into his lap, and she nuzzled her face into his neck. All she could feel emerging from her soul was the healing energy of her magic; it took over everything else. She pulled back, placing her hand on his injured brow and allowing her magic to aid his bruised skin. His eyes didn't falter from her face as his skin knitted back together and he twitched slightly in pain.

She could have lost him today, but the Gods had spared him, and for that, she would thank them every night and day. He had been the better fighter. Torin pulled her against his solid frame once he had had enough healing.

It was over. He had lived. He seemed to relax against her, his muscles softening as she stroked the back of his neck. They sat in silence for a moment more. She could feel his fingers intertwining in her midnight locks, threading through the strands as if he took comfort from it somehow.

"You won," she whispered as tears threatened to course down her cheeks.

"I was always going to win because it was going to bring me back to you," he breathed into her cheek, and his lips found her skin as he scattered a few kisses over her face. "I was always going to come back to you." He embraced her a little tighter.

She found his lips, and she didn't care if they were swollen. She pressed a kiss to him, and he swallowed hard. Emara pulled back slightly, curiosity taking over. "How did you come to the decision to let him live?"

His large hand stroked past her face and into her hair once more. "My father might have been a cruel man with awful tendencies, but he is intelligent, and if there is one thing that I have taken from my lessons with him it is that you should always keep your friends close and your enemies closer. I might need him."

She sat up in his lap and ran a hand down his swollen cheek. "I respect what you did, but I could have lost you."

He looked up at her with hope roaming free in his glittering blue eyes. "You won't ever lose me again. I promise."

She kissed him again, bringing her lips to his in a thankful embrace and thanking any of the Gods or ancestors who had listened to her prayers. A well of emotion crashed around her, and she could feel that familiar sting in her eyes as she let out a sob against his mouth.

He pulled back, concern ablaze in his eyes. "What's wrong?" he whispered so gently.

Her hands tightened around his arms, his tunic. "When you were just gone from the battle...I thought...I thought—"

He looked at her with guilt, knowing what she would have gone through today. A long finger curled under her chin as he commanded her to meet his gaze. "Emara, look at me when I say this." His voice was deep and promise lingered there as she raised her tear-filled eyes to his. "I am never leaving your side again unless you order me to as your guard, as your partner, as anything more should you want it. I am not going anywhere." She ran a quick hand over her eyes to wipe the tears that had escaped and took a sharp breath to steady her emotions. "The minute I had been sworn in as commander and the battle was done, I knew that I had moves to make right away. This"—he looked around—"it's Viktir's personal cave of secrecy and knowledge. Anything valuable to him will be in here. Anything that I shouldn't know about, anything that he's been hiding, should be in here. And now the key belongs to me. I had to find it before anything could be destroyed."

"I understand," Emara whispered, her heart feeling a little lighter.

He pushed back her hair, which had managed to stick to her tear-covered face. "I wanted to come to you right away and feel you against me. But I had to see what I could claim in here. What I could use. So please forgive me for just stepping out on you and the celebrations. I had to secure this office."

Emara raised her eyebrow and smirked. "Spoken like a true commander of the Blacksteel legacy."

He finally smiled, truly smiled, and even with a burst lip, it was magnificent. "Don't look at me like that." His hand travelled a little further up Emara's dress as a deep breath huffed out of his chest. "I had no intention of christening my new desk until early next week, but if you keep looking at me like that, these papers that I have so *carefully* sifted through will be a mess once again." One of his eyebrows rose as if he liked the sound of the challenge. He wanted her to challenge him. "I fear I would lose all my hard work."

Emara let out a laugh that finally reached her belly. "It seems you are making such progress already, and I wouldn't want to come between that." She placed her hands over his shoulders and around his neck once more. "I would hate to be the cause of such destruction in your new office."

A wicked, deviant flicker burned in his eyes. "I would love nothing more than for you to be the cause for such destruction."

She laughed again just as his dimples appeared on either side of his mouth and the scar in between his brow smoothed out. He traced little circles up her leg.

She grabbed his hand that had begun travelling to a place of no return. "I will not be the cause of your new office being *mistreated.* You have new responsibilities, Commander."

His full mouth pulled into a grin. "Oh angel, you know that when we go exploring, I never mistreat you." His eyes roamed her face, and those wicked fingers ran all through her hair and over her dress. Emara's skin almost went up in flames. His lashes lowered before he spoke again. "However, Empress, regardless of my unbelievable restraint to not explore every inch of you, I do have something for you."

She rose as he did and his hands rested on her hips, guiding her to sit on the edge of his desk. She watched him in confusion as he limped over to a unit that housed a few things like liquor and glasses. He withdrew an engraved box coated in gold and black paint. As he brought it over, he removed a brass key from his pocket and opened it.

Lying there in a white silk wrapping was the Resurrection Stone.

Emara gasped as she looked at it for the first time since Gideon had stolen it from her. The dim candlelight flickered over the stone's polished edges, and all the brilliant colours flared through it.

She had forgotten the feel of its supremacy, even as it lay untouched. And now that she had tapped into her power, she could feel hints of fire, earth, water, and spirit in the stone, the elements calling to her.

He pushed the box along the desk to where she sat. "This is yours, I believe."

Emara looked at Torin, her mouth open. "The prime said I couldn't protect it properly."

"The prime doesn't see in you what I do." His angled face told her that his decision was final. "Fuck the prime."

Her heart caught in her chest. "That's not very commander-like." She smiled.

And he smiled back. "I am not one to follow the chain of command, am I?"

Heat simmered her blood as he watched her.

He lifted his chin. "I want you to do what you wish. Keep it, destroy it, throw it in the Broken Sea." He sat in his chair again and managed to push one of his legs in between hers. "I can keep it for you or I can hand it over. What do you want to do?"

The choice was a shock to her. He was mere hours into his commandership and he had already given her back the power that had been taken from her on one of the worst nights of her life. The

Resurrection Stone was more powerful than anything she had ever known. Her mother or grandmother had hidden it in her possession; there must have been a reason for that.

But the stone was sought after. It was a relic that people would kill for, yet he trusted her with it. She didn't even know what kind of magic it wielded. She didn't know the depth of its power or how she could use it.

"I don't know what to do with it," she admitted.

"Well, it is here for you when you decide what you want to do. I can keep it in the Blacksteel vault. It was where my father kept it after Gideon took it from you."

She nodded and bit into her cheek before asking, "Are there any other stones in the Blacksteel vault?"

She had been so busy she hadn't been able to catch up with Sybil to see if she had made any progress with the ancient grimoire. Maybe she had already unlocked something within the text. Maybe she had worked out where the other stones were.

Torin let out a little laugh. "No. Not until you showed up. We haven't tended to be successful in finding anything worthwhile."

She rolled her lip in her teeth. "Well, I do need to let you in on a little secret of mine."

His brows pulled together in a sort of amusement. "Oh, you know your secrets are my favourite kind of secrets."

"Sybil and I," she announced, ignoring the grin on his face, "have been looking into the Gods' stones. We have been researching where they might possibly be. Well, Sybil has been doing most of the research; she has more education on ancient languages and runes."

His lips pursed. "And have you found anything valuable?"

"Actually, we think we might have found something. But it could entirely be old witches' tales."

"Do tell." He let his knee rub against her leg.

She gripped the desk to stop herself from flushing with desire for him at this inappropriate time. "I mean, it might be nothing, but—"

"It's not nothing if you think it's important," he said as he leaned back in his chair.

"Sybil has a grimoire."

"Yeah, the one Gideon gave to her for the winter solstice?"

"Yes, exactly. And she has been obsessed with the ancient magic in it ever since. There are lots of spells and magic long lost to us. But there is a section on enchanted stones unlike anything she has ever studied before. She said something about it being a mixture of Fae and Witch magic, possibly citing an old oracle who could still be living."

Torin's eyes raked over Emara's face as he sat forward a little.

Emara continued, "She also said something about how she still had to translate most of it, but there were drawings of stones, and we believe one is the Protection Stone."

"Did it say where the stone was?" he asked.

"We haven't gotten that far yet." She chewed her cheek. Emara placed her hands on his strong legs and leaned forward. "If we find the two remaining stones, it will mean that the Dark Army can't. It would put us in a position of power. I believe that my mother only used two of the stones to banish Balan into the underworld, so that would mean that it would only take those two stones to get him out."

Torin looked to be mulling over her words. "If we have them, it would keep you safe from him."

"It would keep everyone safe," Emara reminded him. "Torin, I am not naive to think that it wouldn't also put a target on our backs. No one can found out about us trying to locate these stones. Only the Empress of Earth and I know about this."

"You know your secrets are always safe with me."

Look at us...we have our own dirty little secret.

As the memory of Torin teasing her many moons ago appeared in her mind, she punched his leg. "I am serious. No one else knows I am even looking into this."

"So am I. We have had plenty of secrets together, and I like it that way." Torin ran the back of his hand over her arm and her skin prickled, reacting to his touch.

She shook off her body's reaction to him and tried her best to focus. "We already have the Resurrection Stone. So all we need to locate is the Protection Stone, which is invisible in any of the stories except for what we have found in the grimoire. We'll need the Dark Crystal too, but there is a whole lot of folklore on that. The one that Thorin slammed into the land in battle to save his men, breaking apart the continent, is said to be lost to the Broken Sea. If we have the majority of the stones, it means that no one can free him." She looked down at her hands on Torin's legs for a second before meeting his gaze again. He was patiently waiting for her to continue. "My mother locked him up for a reason, Torin. He is a monster. But having the stones also means Veles will never get free and we can control the Dark Army. Is that not the clan's true goal, to either stop them or destroy them?"

He leaned forward in his chair. "You, Emara Clearwater, are fucking incredible."

Her breathing hitched as she fought a smile. "What do you mean?"

"I just love how your brain works." He grinned a little. "But you are right. It would certainly put us in a position of strength should we have more than one of the Gods' Stones," he agreed. "But we cannot go on the quest alone; it is too dangerous to have only a few men on a mission like that. It could take us years to find anything. Should we find any information or one of the stones, we would need something far greater than just myself and two empresses to protect it. And I have just gained more responsibility than I've ever had. I can't go wandering off on a quest. The clan would look for answers."

She tucked a stray hair behind her ear, and he followed it with his ocean eyes. "Then we take them with us. Think about it, with more men, we can cover more ground. It can be a secret mission for the Blacksteel Clan, the first that you will command to demonstrate the kind of moves you will be making as a commander." She reached out to touch his arm. "It also confirms your authority. It's a power play, and a respectable one." She let him think on that for a second. "It is in the clan's best interests just as much as it is in ours to seek out the stones. More and more humans are finding out about the Dark Army, and what is protecting them from the shadows? Nothing. Yet the Minister of Coin can only think about greed and gold instead of the protection of his faction. It is only a matter of time before the Dark Army uses humans to find the stones too, granting them immortality. You saw what he did with Taymir, and he was a member of a powerful elite family. If Balan can convert the magic community to become darkened, then think what a human with nothing to lose would do for immortality." She sat back a little, and Torin looked like he didn't want the distance to come between them. "We know they have the Immortality Stone, let's not give them any more power than they already have. Let's be the ones to protect the kingdom and secure the keys to the cage of the underworlds."

Torin sat in silence once more, likely pondering over what she had just said. "Let me think it over. I will speak with Gideon and Artem and see what they think of it. I will seek out my first counsel, since I will need to appoint my second-in-command soon."

She nodded. "Should it not be Gideon? Is it not his birthright?"

"Actually, it would be *my* son's birthright." He looked over at her, and she felt her throat thicken. "It is only Gideon's name until the Gods grant me a son. And as commander, I need to write a decree that announces who it is until I have a successor. But even then, clans have fought over less." His lip pulled at the corner.

Emara snorted. "I think you hunters just make excuses to fight."

Torin chuckled. "It's how our world works. It's competitive."

She rolled her eyes. "I hope there isn't a queue of people lining up outside your door this very minute to be your second-in-command. How would you choose?"

He rested back into his chair with a cocky smile on his face, and he looked like an oil painting in one of the Minister of Coin's rooms, powerful and strong. "Whoever it is must be as good-looking as me and able to swing a sword just as easily. But I guess it's not fair to set such high standards."

"You are honestly the most arrogant asshole I have ever met." She lightly hit his leg with her hand, and before she knew it, she was laughing as Torin Blacksteel caught her hand and pulled her in.

His eyes narrowed. "Are you insinuating that someone is more handsome than me? Because if you are, I am going to have to kill him." He tickled her side, and her laugh and scream could have been heard around the Tower, but she didn't care. It was a welcome reprieve.

He paused and ran a hand over the back of her head, sending shivers of her body. Torin looked into her eyes and said, "See, it's not only your flaming candles that light up the room. It's your laugh too." He tilted his head to the side, displaying the angles of his face. "Maybe this room won't be filled with endless misery after all."

A long silence waded in on them as they looked at one another, not willing to look at anything else in the world. It was just them and the light of a flame, the unseen magic that burned between them the magic of a thousand universes. "Marry me," he uttered, and Emara's heart stopped. "Marry me here. Marry me now. Marry me tomorrow. Marry me anytime you want." He took her hand in his. "But just be mine forever."

Unable to stop the hand moving to her heart to clutch anything she could touch, Emara sucked in a breath. Shock must have taken hold of her tongue. She was sure she wasn't speaking, or maybe her heart was not beating. Or maybe she had imagined the whole thing.

But Torin spoke again. "I was going to ask you at a different time, at some stupid ball or at some monotonous formal event, where everyone in the kingdom could have talked about how I got down on one knee and asked for the hand of the Empress of Air. But I cannot believe in my heart that it would be more perfect than asking you here, now...especially when you are smiling at me like that." He slid her off his knee for the second time, and as he stood her upright, her legs shook, almost leaving her body to drop to the floor. But he held on to her hips as he moved from the chair and onto one knee.

Torin removed a small box from the breast of his leather tunic and clutched it in his hand. "For years, I was terrified of this little box, more terrified than I was of anything that moved between the shadows or that could have been discovered in the lakes of the underworld. I have been terrified to give this box to anyone but you." He opened it to reveal a stunning gold ring holding a black diamond in the shape of a teardrop. Emara's breath faltered again as he spoke. "I tried giving this to you at winter solstice as a second present—not to rush you or make you feel that I was igniting pressure for a formal treaty, but as a promise that I was all in with you. As a promise that there would be no one else but you." His eyes glittered with darkness, and Emara's lungs squeezed in her chest, starved of air. "It was a symbol that I didn't want to search for anyone else to be by my side." Tears began flowing from her eyes, and Emara found her stomach contracting as she forced herself not to cry. "But we were interrupted and I gave this ring to Magin to give to you should anything ever happen to me. After you were taken, I couldn't believe how foolish I had been, and I promised myself that I would be the one to give it to you. And now that the Gods have willed me to live another battle, I still want you to have it. It was my mother's, and I know she would be honoured to see you wear it. But there is one more thing I need to show you before you answer."

One more thing.

Was he trying to kill her?

She tried gasping for air, but her element was just as shocked as she was. It was failing her, stunned into silence.

"Open the bottom of the box." He pressed his full lips together as he placed it in her hands.

There was a small compartment that slid open as Emara pulled it open with trembling fingers.

In the candlelight, it looked like a strange powder, and Emara looked down at Torin, still kneeling before her, not understanding.

"It's ash," he said.

"Ash?"

He nodded. "The ashes of your treaty to the Blacksteels."

Emara's heart punched against her ribs, not knowing whether to stop altogether or to burst.

"So if you choose to marry me, you would be marrying me because you want to and not for a treaty or an alliance, but because you choose me and I choose you. Just like I said last night, meeting you has set me free from so many boundaries, and I will do everything I can to ensure the same freedom for you." He took hold of her hand again. "So, will you do me the honour, Emara Clearwater, and marry me?"

CHAPTER TWENTY-TWO
BREIGHLY

The announcement of Torin Blacksteel challenging his father for commandership had made its way through Huntswood, and more and more people were turning up at the Tower. Gossip and whispers always did seem to end up all over the city faster than the feathers of a plucked chicken in a winter wind. But as the midnight chime came from the grandfather clock, Breighly Baxgroll noticed that Emara had still not returned from the commander's office where she had disappeared hours ago.

Breighly had been standing since dawn, unwilling to leave Emara's side, and her feet were burning in her new boots, rubbing in ways she'd thought only fashionable shoes did. Her back was aching, her legs were stiff, and she was kind of pissed that she was missing all the food that had been cooked in Torin's honour.

Her stomach betrayed her and let out an awful grumble.

It was a great start to being a guard of one of the most powerful witches in the kingdom, an honour that her body should fucking acknowledge instead of fighting against. How ungrateful did her human form need to be?

She had only just gotten over the embarrassment of Emara finding her in the bed of her own room with Artem Stryker, so she wasn't ready to let her guard down again, not when Emara had put her neck on the line for her to be here.

She would wait on post, even if her stomach was eating itself inside out.

A wolf and hunger never did any favours for humanity.

Maybe she should knock on the door? Check in? Make sure everything was okay?

If she wasn't going to leave this post until she knew Emara was okay, she should check in. Her boot kicked off the wall, springing her up and into action as she started her way down the corridor.

"I wouldn't do that if I were you," a deep, silken voice said from the hallway that connected to hers.

Breighly swivelled, and a scent of baked oranges and summer rain hit her face.

An inked warrior of Thorin stood at the other side of the corridor.

Artem Stryker.

She folded her arms, too grouchy to be interrupted. "And why would I listen to you?"

The last time he had whispered instructions to her, he had been ripping her clothes off. After that, his skin had been on hers, pounding and relentless. The biting, the licking, the feral kissing...

A heat flashed deep in her core at the images of his body on hers.

Shit!

She had to forget all of that. It was normally easy to forget the relations she had, but for whatever reasons the Gods had, her thoughts seemed to linger of Artem Stryker.

Fuck, he'd absolutely love that if he knew.

Artem sauntered down the corridor, his large presence invading the dim lighting. "You should listen to me because I have more than enough knowledge of what is likely to be happening in that room, and Torin wouldn't be happy if he was interrupted whilst *making love*."

Breighly scoffed. "What have I told you about making ridiculous remarks? *Making love* is a horrendous term. You need to behave yourself."

He grinned wider than before. "You need to stop pretending you hate the words *making love*."

She gave off a fake shiver. "Revolting."

He ran his teeth over his lip, trying to keep his smile tamed. His dark golden eyes glanced at the floor before finding her eyes again. "I brought you this." He handed her a bread roll with chocolate spread that she hadn't noticed was in his hand. How did she miss that? "I could hear your stomach rumbling over the music downstairs and it got annoying after a while."

She laughed and swiped it from his hand. "Hunters don't have that good of hearing, don't kid yourself."

Her teeth ripped into the warm bread, and a moan almost escaped her lips as the chocolate melted in her mouth.

Artem bit back a grin. "You are welcome, cranky pants."

Her eyes darted to his face. "You do realise that I have my own weapon belt now, right? And I would be a total liar to say that my palm isn't twitching to try some of my new steel on your flesh." She gave off a small growl laced with a smile. "Don't mock a hungry wolf, idiot."

His eyes flashed full of dangerous desire as if her words only excited him instead of warding him off. But the casual grin spread across his mouth faded. "I wanted to find you before the celebrations started so that I could say I was sorry, but I kind of got caught up in it." His thin nose flared, allowing the fiery torches in the corridor to flicker down on the dainty silver circle in his nose. It glinted like a star, and she cursed herself at how much distraction a little silver hoop caused her.

Breighly cleared her throat, swallowing down the last of her bread. "What for?"

He placed his hands behind his back and his lashes swept down. "For putting you in a position where you could have lost your guardianship before it even fully began."

Something punched in her chest.

Okay, this conversation was actually happening.

Instead of showing that she was surprised, she rolled her eyes. "It takes two to dance in the bedroom, Artem. I am as much to blame as you."

"I know." He closed in again, and she could feel the heat between them already. The thick, warm, magnetic heat. "But I wanted to let you know I respect you more than that."

Her heart banged in her chest.

She shut it down.

Why was that little shit doing that?

He spoke again. "I just wanted to let you know that I am sorry for that."

"You don't need to say you're sorry for having sex with me—unless you are." She looked at the door Emara had disappeared behind, wishing she could do the same right now.

She wanted to hide from this conversation. Maybe Torin's reaction wouldn't be as bad as Artem said.

"Of course I am not sorry—"

Breighly snapped her head back towards him. "Then let's leave it there."

Artem pressed a shoulder to the wall. "You don't have to cut me off."

"And you don't have to give me a limp-ass apology because you feel guilty that I get looked at differently for having sex because I am a woman."

Emara hadn't really cared about the two of them giving in to temptation, but if someone else had found her in that compromising position, everything could have been different.

"Men get away with giving into their desires all the time, but if a woman does it, she is unprofessional. Not fit for the role. A whore."

"I—"

"Don't even try to defend that," Breighly snapped, feeling the hunger in her belly turn into fire.

He uncrossed his arms. "If you would let me speak for one second, you would understand that I just wanted to make sure you were okay."

A little laugh huffed out from the most broken part of her. "So now you want to empathise with me? You feel guilty because I was caught with you like I am some kind of victim. Like I didn't choose that for myself. You didn't put me in that position, Artem. I put myself there. I allowed myself to be under you to distract myself from how numb I feel."

The words were out her mouth like vomit, and there was no way that she could take them back. She bit back a flinch.

Hurt darkened Artem's eyes, and it was the first time she had seen a vulnerable reaction loiter over his face. He had always been the joker, the jester, and now he was a warrior, standing in front of her with hurt turning into rage in his eyes.

"I am a distraction?" He let out a callous laugh.

She hadn't meant it like that. She knew she had crossed the line the minute her stupid mouth had spilled her guts, but it was too late to put her unkind words back inside the terrible box in her mind.

"I am just a distraction to you?" he repeated when she said nothing.

This was what always happened when Breighly felt insecure; she would push people out. Maybe she hadn't realised how insecure she felt standing next to the warriors of Thorin, but she had a lot to live up to. She wasn't a hunter, she was a wolf; Aerrick Stryker had made that *very* clear in his examination of her.

"I didn't mean it like that," she tried to claw back her words.

"You did." Artem's chin rose and his full lips parted. "And that's okay. I get that you are a woman in control of your own destiny, a wolf who is fiercer than any warrior I have come across a guard who is the first of her kind. I understand that you have a lot at stake and this is your chance to prove how worthy you are, not just for yourself but for all women. But you need to understand that I am not trying to change any of that for you."

She had no answer.

She always had an answer. His calming energy was incredible to balance out her rage, and she wondered if that was a little hunter tactic to get her back on side. After all, it was part of their training.

Artem's lips parted. "I get it. You are emotionally unavailable. You don't want a relationship."

"Relationship?" Breighly snorted as her eyes widened. "This is not a relationship, by the Gods."

"You know what I mean." Artem's voice was a little deeper than before, darker. The warrior in his eyes killed out the witticism and let the danger shine through.

It stirred something in her.

"We have to work together," he said, his hip rising from the wall. "Professionally. Whether we like it or not."

"Professionally," she repeated. "Even if it could be torturous."

He grinned, finally chasing the shadows in his eyes away. "That's not what I said."

"I know." She gave a feral grin back. "That's what I said."

Artem huffed a little. "If you can't handle what lies between us, sassy pants, that's on you."

She almost choked. "You know as well as I do that I can handle anything you throw at me." She crossed the distance between them and looked up into his eyes.

His jaw clenched as she pressed her chest against his. "That's a little hard to believe when you can't even handle how you feel when you're around me."

Her throat tightened at his truth. "One-night stands are not meant to follow you into a new moon."

His eyes narrowed as he stepped towards her. "We've had more than one night of fun, you and I."

She always underestimated the size of him. His huge body made her feel safe in this moment. She swallowed the thoughts of them both writhing together, feeling pleasure that she had never felt before, and dismissed thoughts of his mouth around the sensitive nerves between her legs.

He stuck out his hand, and it saved her from giving in to the sweet memories of their past. Again.

"What are you doing?" she asked, screwing up her face.

"Striking a truce...in the *love making*." His hand remained out, a boyish grin on his lips. "That's what you want, right?"

"Are you not embarrassed by your choice of words? Like...ever?" She grinned back.

"Nope."

"A truce?" She lifted an eyebrow.

He nodded, his lips thinning. "Shake my hand and we call it over."

She swallowed and placed her hand into his, his skin covered by a red rose of winter. Suddenly feeling like she was doing something the Gods didn't approve of, her heart dropped. "This thing between us...it's over. No more fucking."

"Over. No more *loving*," he repeated, gripping her hand and shaking slowly. "Strictly professional. We are just two normal guards. Two very sexy, normal guards."

If it were over, why did his touch feel like a warm charge of energy brushing over her skin?

She hid a grin of her own.

"It's done," she agreed.

And just as a spark of something she didn't understand ignited in her heart, the door to the commander's office opened, revealing the new commander and the Empress of Air.

CHAPTER TWENTY-THREE
KELLEN

Kellen Blacksteel sipped on a white wine as he stood in a corner, watching the celebrations in the Tower. The partygoers were nearly overflowing from the room set aside for weddings and birthdays. It wasn't the largest room in the Tower by any means, but it had character with mismatched chairs and artwork colouring the walls. Rugs of different origins and fibres littered the floor, making it more homey than any other part of the Tower. The tables were all different heights and makes, some oak and others marble. There were game boards, music, and a bar set up in the corner.. It was a travesty that this room wasn't used more.

What was even more of a travesty was the amount of lager and ale that Artem had had suppliers bring in. Kellen had a more refined palate for liquor, but he didn't turn his nose up at the roasted pork skewers that the cooks were bringing around on serving dishes.

Merriment from a fiddle and accordion could be heard from the front of the room near the doors, and witches joined the clan in a dance. Feet were tapping, arms were linked, and everyone was laughing as the alcohol seeped into their blood, the severity of today disappearing into the night like some kind of daydream.

But he was happy to stay away from the fuss of it all.

Kellen supposed he was like Gideon that way. He would rather be on a chair or in a dark corner than be on a dancefloor. But, to his surprise, even his brother was dancing. The Earth Empress seemed to be the one leading their movements. It wasn't about the actual rhythm or the steps for Kellen, it was more that he didn't feel comfortable enough in his own skin to be in the middle of a crowd. He had known for as long as he could remember that he was different from most of his clan. He was different from his brothers, his own blood, and he had been different from a lot of the boys in the Selection too.

All but one.

Arlo Stryker.

And as Kellen stood in the shadows of the room, he could see Arlo standing in the limelight, working the crowd. Very much like his elder brother Artem, Arlo knew how to command a room and the attention of the factions. He had been in the same selection year as Kellen, and Arlo's willingness to present himself had sucked Kellen in. He had such presence, and a charming wit that everyone around seemed to enjoy. Girl after girl, woman after woman, Arlo worked his way around them all, laughing, chatting, and caressing.

It was a stunning performance. An enviable one.

Why couldn't he do the same? Why couldn't his blood heat when he saw a girl dance or smile at him? Why couldn't he even act like it did? Why couldn't he feel...*normal?*

Kellen swirled the wine in his glass before inhaling its fruity aroma. He pressed the glass to his mouth, letting the tastes of crisp citrus devour his taste buds. Moments like these were when his heart reminded him that he and Torin had a common trait too; they numbed themselves if they began to feel things they shouldn't.

He took another sip of wine, not bothering to taste it; he just wanted to stop feeling.

Out of the corner of his eye, he noticed Torin enter the room, followed by Emara, finally joining the revelry. The crowd moved towards them, and drinks were already being passed around to offer them. He hadn't seen his eldest brother since he'd spared his father's life, and he was still stunned at Torin's move to keep his father alive and not exile him.

Their father, he reminded himself.

There weren't many examples of mercy in the clan's history. Torin's decision hadn't been the first like it, but it had been a bold move to keep his opponent alive.

Kellen had been happy to stand on Torin's side when the clan had been split between the two Blacksteels. Ever since Kellen hadn't made the highest ranking in the Selection, Viktir had pretended like he was just another member of the clan instead of his son. It hadn't been a difficult decision.

Kellen suspected Gideon would have been more torn on who to choose, but in the end, he had chosen Torin too. It had been a day full of surprises, mixed emotions, and endless torment.

His mother had picked Torin—that had been a given. She despised the ground her husband walked on. A strange feeling urged Kellen to go and see his father in the cells of the Tower. It was probably the darker part of his soul that wanted to see Viktir sitting behind the iron bars, stripped of his commandership, his ability to bully and shame stuck within a cell. His power to lay a finger on his wife and never be reprimanded for it was caged for good. But Viktir played mind games, and Kellen wasn't sure that it would be the best move for him to go.

"You look lost in thought." A familiar accent pulled Kellen from the abyss of his own thoughts.

He looked up and saw Arlo, his grey tunic unbuttoned at the top and his reddish-brown hair askew from all the dancing.

"You don't seem to be lost at all," Kellen said back, knowing his tone was sharp and cutting.

Arlo took a stance beside him so that his shoulder brushed his own. Kellen's heart sprung into his mouth and he finally felt the heat of the room. Arlo watched the dancing for a few moments before saying, "I am sorry that I haven't written you back or been around much. I have, um...been extremely busy."

After them being seen together, Arlo had ignored him and dismissed him privately. Yes, they chatted in public, making everything seem okay, but when Kellen had sent fireletter after fireletter, no response ever came.

Coward.

Arlo was a respected guard to the Empress of Earth, but he had many opportunities to write him back.

Kellen took a drink of wine that he hardly even tasted. "Hunters do not need to hear apologies or excuses."

He couldn't believe he had just quoted his father. The irony.

Arlo lowered his hand and let his knuckles brush against Kellen's. "Hunters tend to say things...do things that they do not believe in because of who they are. I still think about you."

Kellen pulled his hand away even though it took all he had as a warrior to fight the urges flowing through his body. "You cannot just ignore that I exist and then find me for comfort."

Kellen stepped out to take his leave, but a warm hand caught his wrist.

"It is not for comfort that I seek you out, but because I want to." Arlo's chocolate eyes bore through his soul.

Kellen's heart stopped altogether before speeding up in his chest. "Is there not a woman in the crowd waiting for your next dance?"

Arlo's soft grin found his lips. "You know if I could pick without consequence, I would choose you to dance."

And there it was—pain sharper than any lashing his father ever gave, deeper than any cut he had ever gained in weaponry, harder to deal with than any training in the Selection.

The pain of his hidden truth.

Kellen Blacksteel had a lot of secrets, and he tried too hard to pretend that they didn't exist when he was on duty.

Life made him resent ever being born at times. He would never fully fit in.

Arlo rubbed his thumb into Kellen's wrist before letting go. "I don't like it when you are silent. I always know you are torturing yourself in your mind."

"It's hard to watch you do it so easily," Kellen finally said, meeting his gaze.

"What?"

"Pretend."

Arlo took a breath, stepping forward. "It's not as easy as it looks. If my blood has a talent at anything, it's fighting and pretending to be something they are not. I need to be this way."

What killed Kellen was that he understood that more than most.

Arlo took a step too close, especially in public. "But what would you have me do, Kellen? I am the chief commander's son; putting on a show, pretending, is in my blood."

"You know you don't need to put on a show. You are not the first-born son. The commander's responsibility does not lie on the second son." He finally turned to meet his gaze. "Or the third. You don't see me flashing a grin at every girl who wants my affections. I don't need to do that. That is my brother's job."

Arlo's cheeks turned crimson. "You are being unfair and you know it."

"And you are being untrue to yourself."

"And you are not?" Arlo scoffed. His voice lowered so that no one could hear the conversation. "I don't see you standing hand in hand with a man. I don't see your lips on his in front of the factions. I don't see you in the middle of the room, letting them know anything about who you truly are. What I see is someone standing in the shadows of the room as always." Kellen flinched, and the air in his lungs escaped him. Arlo inhaled and then exhaled deeply. "If you want to live in the dark corners of society, that is fine, Kellen. But I don't have to. I know your day has been awful, so I wanted to come over here and see if I could offer you support, but I can see it is unwanted. This was a mistake."

Just as Arlo took off to get away from him, a wash of something dreadful filled Kellen's bones. Darkness unfolded around his vision, blurring everything out completely. Instantly, his skin prickled and his muscles seized.

It was happening, but it shouldn't be.

He wasn't sleeping. This couldn't happen.

Kellen tried to clutch his head, tried to stumble forward to somehow prevent this from happening here of all places, when the room was swollen with warriors of Thorin.

He felt something shift and lock from within him, letting him know something had altered course. Something in the world had changed. Unbearable stabbing pains shot into his head as darkness invaded his consciousness, rendering him completely blind.

He let out a yelp as his hands found a table and he tried to steady himself. But he was gone. He was not with this world, but another one. A cold sweat took over his body like his skin was seeping, pouring water from him. He felt his knees hit the ground and he heard glasses smash around him, but it wasn't the force of his bones hitting the hard floor that had him screaming.

It was what came to him in the dream.

CHAPTER TWENTY-FOUR
GIDEON

I t was a wonder that Gideon could laugh at all after the day he had had, but it was a nice surprise to know that he still could. Even though she was small, Sybil had swung him around so hard during a dance, almost wiping out the man with the fiddle. The harsh curses that had come from the fiddler as he picked up his instrument had Sybil clinging to his arms, in stitches laughing. He couldn't believe how sore his jaw was from the amusement too, the smile still plastered on his face.

"I cannot dance with you again, Gideon." She finally let go of his tunic to hold her belly from laughing pains. "I fear that you will break the legs of the accordion next, and I will not be responsible for that. I am a healer, not someone who breaks bones."

His laugh broke through the music as it began playing again. "Oh, no you don't. I am not being held responsible for taking out the fiddler. You may be small, but you had the strength of a warrior there. If it weren't for you, that man wouldn't be cursing me out."

She playfully smiled. "Accidents happen." Sybil smoothed a hand over his chest, and her lashes fluttered shut for just one moment before her hand dropped from where it sat.

"Although, if I were going to be strategic," Gideon whispered to her, "I would take out the man with the accordion next time; he seems to be playing a little off beat."

She beamed back at him, and his heart constricted in his chest.

A cough came from beside them, and she turned her head to see who it was.

Gideon reluctantly pulled his eyes from her face and did the same thing to see a member of the Fae Court standing before him. Gideon had no idea that the Fae even cared about what had happened here today, but nevertheless, they were enjoying the merriment. The man had white-gold hair, and his complexion was dark and glowing. He wore the cobalt-blue jacket of King Oberon's men, and Gideon knew that he was probably going to report everything that he saw to the king.

He took a low bow, his twinkling eyes focused on Sybil. "May I cut in and ask the Empress of Earth to dance? They speak of her beauty and skill in Skyelir, and I have come to see it for myself."

Sybil nodded her head, still holding that same smile that had been for Gideon. "I hope the rumours of my beauty have not brought you all this way for nothing, Your Grace."

Why did Gideon's heart twist in his chest as she acknowledged the Fae?

"Your beauty does not disappoint, Empress," he said so smoothly it almost made Gideon's eyes roll.

A blush took up residence in her cheeks, and his stomach flipped.

Gideon stuck out his hand before Sybil could take the Fae's, and she placed her soft fingers in his. He bowed down low and kissed her delicate hand before rising. "Have fun. Come and find me if you want to piss off the fiddler again."

She laughed, and before she could say anything, the Fae stepped in and had her spinning around like a child's toy away from where they stood. As he sauntered back over to the seating, which was full of members of the factions in deep conversation, he was met by Marcus Coldwell with an ale jug.

"Drink this," he said as he pushed the semi-cold jug into his hand. "You must be thirsty from all of that dancing."

Gideon took the drink reluctantly.

Marcus Coldwell had been a member of the Blacksteel Hunting Clan for years after Viktir took him in from a distant cousin's rejection. However, Gideon couldn't place how he had felt as he watched Marcus choose Viktir over Torin. Gideon suspected Marcus could feel the tension of that decision lingering in the air as they stood together.

"To Torin," Marcus said roughly, raising the jug in toast.

"To the Commander of the Blacksteel Hunting Clan." Gideon raised his own, and they both chugged a drink in appreciation of their newest commander.

For the first time today, Gideon wondered how Torin would punish all the members of the clan who stood on Viktir's side. Marcus had always been like a brother to both Torin and Gideon— a shoulder to lean on, a friend to talk to—but he had stood on the opposite side today.

"I would rather cut to it, Marcus." Gideon's words spilled from his mouth before he could stop them. "Why did you stand with my father today?"

Marcus sucked a breath through his teeth, and his eyes widened. "Because I had my choice and you had yours. We both had to make a hard decision."

Gideon took a sip of ale and swallowed down the awkwardness. "That's just stating the facts, Marcus. That's not giving a rationale behind it."

He let out a sigh that finally relaxed his shoulders. "Because I knew Torin would win."

Confusion pulled Gideon's brown down. "Then why would you not stand on his side?"

A dark hollowness glittered in Marcus's eye. "Because I wanted to repay an old debt. I wanted to pay some respect to my former commander who took me in when I needed him most, and it was the only way I knew how."

Gideon understood then. Marcus would always be grateful to have been brought into the Blacksteel clan and to be reared as someone of worth. Sometimes Gideon believed that Marcus was the only person on this earth that Viktir had time for. He saw something in Marcus, and he had always trusted him.

Their moment together was cut short as Rhea ran towards them, eyes filled with a brightness that Gideon had not seen in many moons. She pulled Marcus onto the dancefloor. "You owe me a dance for healing your broken ankle from the last hunt."

Gideon laughed as the hunter was whisked away by someone so gentle that she made a mouse look warlike. But there was a strong side to Rhea, like his mother. They would not suffer fools gladly. Even though they may be earth witches, they were no pushovers. And as Gideon looked at Rhea and Marcus now, he could see that Coldwell was beaming from ear to ear.

"Giving up your dancing shoes so soon?" Breighly Baxgroll bumped her shoulder against his as she smirked.

There was a lightness that he didn't know he needed as he saw her. She stood by his side in the silver guard uniform. He released a breath and his shoulders relaxed. The tension in his body dispersed. "I think my dancing days are over."

She laughed, and it was honest and comfortable. It always was between them. "You did good." She patted his shoulder. "You were extra smooth when you almost took out the musician. Such a catch, Gideon."

He laughed it off. "How is guard life?" he asked her. "I am proud of you, you know. You never give up in your crusade to make it known that women are equal to men."

She laughed again, this time a little flush in her cheeks. "Oh,

Gideon, women are not equal to men. Therefore, my efforts have been in vain. I was never trying to show the world that women are equal, but that we are superior." Her chin tilted proudly as a zestful smile brightened her face. She was beautiful in a feral way that men didn't know how to handle. Even the hunters in the clan felt intimidated by her.

"Yes," Gideon agreed. "Yes, you are superior." He stood beside her, taking a drink of his ale and letting it wash down old memories of them being together. "Not drinking tonight?"

"Nope," was all she said. And in the way that she held herself, he knew it was because of her newest responsibilities. Gods, she even had her hands behind her back.

He leaned in, bumping his shoulder to hers. "You know you have nights off, don't you? This being one of them."

Her eyes were immediately on his face. "You forget I am not a warrior of Thorin, but a wolf of Vanadey," she said in that wild way she always had to bite back. "I don't follow the same rules as you. Plus, I don't want to mess up again."

Again?

Gideon made the wise choice not to question her on that.

Breighly's brow pulled together, and her features twisted. Gideon knew the look. She was young when he last saw it lingering on her face. Breighly felt guilty. She blamed herself for her mother never returning. She blamed herself for being too much, even as a cub. It wasn't true, but there was no way of getting through her armour. And she was blaming herself for something now.

He placed a hand on her shoulder. "You are not going to mess up," he reassured her. "You were born to fight, to be in the position you are."

Her teeth gnawed at her lip. "I am glad you think so, Giddy." She smiled, and her hand came up to touch his.

Gideon couldn't help the eyeroll if he tried. "What have I told you about calling me that?"

She bumped her hip into him. "What have I told you about telling me not to call you that? Not going to happen."

He did his best not to chuckle, but it happened.

Giddy. He laughed to himself as he watched the dance floor, his eyes constantly trying to find the auburn banner that was gracefully whirling around.

"Do you like *like* her?" Breighly asked, leaning in closer.

Gideon's gaze snapped to her face. "Who?"

The wolf tutted. "The earth witch you are keeping an eye on as she dances with that strapping Fae."

He didn't like the way Breighly said that. Was the Fae that attractive?

Unable to answer, he watched as Sybil spun underneath the Fae's arm. As he caught her, his hands landed on her waist and he pulled her closer, bringing her into his chest. A spark ran between them as their gaze locked.

A twinge tightened in Gideon's heart, and a streak of something unfamiliar rose from the depths of who he was.

Breighly laughed beside him. "Looks like you better hurry up and make up your mind if you do. Look at the brawny muscle on that Fae guard. Oaaaffff." She let out a dramatic sigh as she fanned herself. "And he's just touched the small of her back. How could a girl resist him?"

Gideon drank the full jug of ale in one go, his heart thumping against his ribs.

"Give me that, you idiot." Breighly snatched the jug from his hand. "If you don't go and rescue her, smack your lips to hers, and show her the best night of her life, I will, dumpling head." She paused, sizing him up before she looked back to the dancefloor. "But you never know, Fae-boy might get there before me, considering the size of his thighs and the fact that he is holding her like he might—"

Gideon threw a hand up. "By the Gods! Don't finish that sentence. Okay, okay, I am going."

A victorious smile slashed across her berry-coloured lips. "Good boy." She reached up and patted his forehead with her palm. Hard. "It's about Gods-damned time."

Just as Gideon geared up to head over and interrupt Sybil's dance, a terrible scream broke through the room. He didn't have to guess who it was; a Blacksteel knew the screams of another Blacksteel. A rush of hunting adrenaline coursed through Gideon's body, like it always did when he was about to slay a demon. He turned and ran toward the screams.

Yet, he saw no members of the Dark Army. He saw Arlo Stryker on the floor, holding Kellen in his arms, who looked painted white, and his eyes were glazed with a bleached coating.

"Kellen," Arlo cried in panic. "Wake up, Kellen. Please."

Gideon, being trained to feel demonic presences, scanned the room again, fearing that he had missed something. Torin was also in a battle stance, still hovering over his brother, a small sword unsheathed at his side.

As Arlo held his head, Kellen began twisting in his arms, writhing as he spoke in an ancient tongue. A crowd began to gather around them, and screams of panic and whispers began circling.

Gideon had slain things that the normal person couldn't even bear to conjure up in a nightmare, but this was the most sinister thing he had ever witnessed.

"Who's doing this to him?" Gideon shouted at Torin.

"If I knew, would I be standing here instead of ripping out their fucking hearts?" Torin spat back, and that's when Gideon saw fear in Torin's eyes. He had no idea what was happening.

"Is it magic?" he heard someone whisper.

"Let me through," his mother said, parting the crowd. "Let me through."

"Stand back," Torin commanded. "All of you. Move back."

Everyone obeyed instantly, and for the first time, Gideon witnessed his brother's power as the commander. A shiver crept over his body. Not out of fear, but out of respect for him. The same blood that ran in Gideon's veins ran in Torin's, yet at times they couldn't be more different. He was a leader, his superior, and Gideon had no issue with stepping into line for him.

Naya broke through the crowd, closely followed by Rhea, and they both hurried to Kellen's side.

"Cover him," Naya hollered as she rested a hand on his head.

Torin moved first and then Gideon, blocking the crowd's view of the youngest Blacksteel and what was happening. Unexpectedly, Emara cast a rush of air around them, whirling like a pool, giving them a hint of privacy.

Emara knelt too, all three women talking and whispering. They could have been chanting for all he knew; Gideon couldn't make it out for the buzzing in his ears and the pumping of his blood. Arlo rose to stand beside the brothers, unable to help the witches aid Kellen. Arlo's normally cheerful face was frozen with worry, his body ridged.

"He will be okay," he threw the comment to the Stryker Clan member. "I know he will be."

"Is he dying?" Gideon heard one person from the crowd ask. Torin clearly heard it too as he swivelled to face the swirling wind.

"No one is dying here tonight," he growled, and the crowd that stood behind the protective element pressed back, feeling his wrath.

"We need to move him to the infirmary," Naya called out, pulling the brothers' attention back to where the witches knelt on the floor. Kellen was still unresponsive, but no longer screaming. Although he was no longer talking in an ancient tongue, he was panting, his face screwed up like pain had taken hold of his body.

Arlo moved first to help the witches lift him, but Emara placed out a hand, stopping him. "I will move him if Naya can help keep her hand on him to steady his heart rate. If I wrap my element of air around him, he cannot hurt himself or anyone else. We don't know what is going on in his mind."

Everyone looked at Torin for approval. "Do as she says."

Gideon watched as Emara stood, raising her palms and chanting softly. The wind around them all dispersed and moved into the shape of a ribbon to hug around Kellen's body. Her magic was so controlled now, especially her air, and it swelled around them like a blanket.

Kellen's body hovered from the ground, and Emara's gentle magic started weaving around his body like silk, ensuring no harm would come to him in his cocoon of air. A soft breeze lifted him higher as she moved her wrist, and Naya joined hands with Rhea whilst they both kept one on Kellen.

Whatever they were doing was working. Kellen began to soften and calm.

But none of that explained what had just happened to his brother, and Gideon needed answers.

CHAPTER
TWENTY-FIVE
EMARA

Emara sat in the infirmary on one of the only chairs in the room whilst she watched Naya bathe a cold cloth over Kellen's forehead. Her healing magic urged to help, but she knew he was in good hands with his mother and her sister. So, Emara focused on keeping everyone else balanced in the room, reaching out to them all and soothing their worries.

Gideon stood against the unlit fireplace on the right in silence, and to her left stood Torin, his arms folded across his chest, an uneasy expression still screwed into his features. She knew Artem and Breighly stood outside with Arlo, guarding.

No one knew what had happened to Kellen, and that was the way they wanted it to remain until they worked out what to do. She hoped that the whispers that would surely spread of Kellen's condition only claimed that he was intoxicated or that he hadn't eaten enough and the trauma of the day had taken over his body.

But she knew the truth.

Kellen had had a vision without sleep, and it had wiped him out, the vision so powerful, so destructive, that it had taken Kellen to his knees and rendered him unconscious. It had forced him into a nightmare.

Naya knew it too, and Emara hoped that the glances they exchanged were discreet enough for no one else to pick up on.

Emara now understood why the hunters deemed it bad luck to have a True Dreamer fighting for them; if Kellen had been hunting when the vision occurred, he would have been helpless, unable to fight. It was terrifying to watch him squirm on the floor, lost in the horrors of his own head. And if that had been on a battlefield, he might not have made it out of there alive.

Emara only wished that the clan would see Kellen's visions as a blessing if they could stabilise them. They could be a tool, a skill and talent that could be honed to make the Blacksteels and their unit unbeatable. If Kellen learned how to control his visions, he would be an incredible asset and powerful weapon. He would not be bad luck or a hindrance. He could only make them stronger, but she had no idea what questions he would get when he awoke from his slumber.

"His temperature is coming down," Naya confirmed as she removed the muslin cloth from his head. "Once Rhea comes back with the elixirs and I know he is okay, I will head down and tell everyone that it was a seizure caused by the stress of today."

Emara nodded. "Is there anything I can do?"

Naya smiled woefully, her hair an unbound heap all around her shoulders. "You have done everything you can, my love. He will be okay, thanks to your protection."

"And is that what it was, Mother?" Torin's voice croaked out. "A seizure? Because there was an awful lot of whispering. If there is anything else going on, I should know."

Emara twirled the ring on her left hand around and around, hoping it would take the edge off the frosty air even as the heat of the summer night swelled her hands.

Naya rose from the bed. "To the Gods above."

Emara lifted her gaze to find Naya's eyes planted on her hand.

She looked from Torin to Emara, her mouth open, eyes filling with tears.

Emara pulled her hand into a fist and immediately tried to hide it, but it was too late.

She hadn't even thought to remove it until a better time.

"We didn't have a chance to tell anyone." Torin's voice was rough. "We were going to announce it earlier, but there was a change of plan." His ocean eyes went to his brother and then back to his mother.

Gideon sucked in a breath, his chest puffing out, and a warmth twinkled in his pine eyes. He pulled himself from the fireplace mantle and walked towards his brother before wrapping his arms around him in an embrace. "Congratulations, brother."

Torin's eyes widened and shock set into his features as his arms came up to return the embrace. Naya let out a cry of happiness, her hands coming up to cover her mouth and her cheeks flush with surprise.

The door opened sharply. "Is he awake?" Artem Stryker asked, but his face fell as his eyes took in Kellen, still unconscious. Arlo and Breighly peered in from behind him.

Naya whirled to face the inked warrior. "No, but the Gods have given us a gift of good news whilst we wait for a miracle."

Artem's gaze explored the room and he squinted like he always did when he was trying to put a puzzle together. Breighly moved into the room, and Arlo hovered by the door.

Naya cut across the space to where Emara was now standing and took her into her arms. As she clung to her, she whispered, "I saw this in the stars for you, my girl, many moons ago. I am utterly thrilled. Thank the Gods it's you. Gods bless Rhiannon."

Emara fought back an emotion that almost choked her as the small earth witch pulled back. Her motherly energy was always so comforting and it smoothed out all the worry in Emara's heart, even if it was just for a few seconds.

"Are you happy?" she asked as tears pooled in her glittering blue eyes.

"Yes," Emara breathed as her chin dipped. "I am."

"Happy about what?" Artem called out, still confused. "What is happening here? Someone fill a guard in."

"Seriously," Breighly scoffed, rolling her eyes before they set on Emara and then Torin. "Congratulations." Her smile was genuine.

"Congratulations?" Artem looked for a sign of something to celebrate.

Emara's cheeks flushed as she flashed up the hand that bore the engagement ring, and Artem's grin instantly beamed across his face. "You have got to be fucking kidding me." He ran at her, lifting her into the air and squeezing her. "Apologies for cursing, Mrs Black-steel." He fired a look at Naya before he turned his attention to Emara once more. "I knew it! I knew it! I knew it!"

"Put me down." She elbowed his ribs the only way she could, squished by his huge embrace.

"I knew Tori-boy had it in him," he said as he let her drop back to her feet. Torin coughed, and Artem flashed him a grin. "I mean, congratulations to you both. Seriously." His golden gaze was back on Emara's face, ablaze with so much genuine happiness. "He doesn't deserve you, and don't let him forget it." He winked before making his way over to Torin. "Come here, big man."

Torin tried to put his hands out to stop him, but his big inked arms reached out and got him in a headlock. "Engaged, eh?" He rubbed his head with this knuckle. "No longer a free man! Who would have thought Torin Blacksteel would ever be in love?"

Torin stuck his leg behind Artem's and swept him to the ground, letting him out of his hold. The massive warrior hit the ground in a loud dump.

"Boys," Naya barked. "Really, here?"

Artem bounced up from the ground and swung an arm around

Gideon. "So, who is it going to be, T? Your best man at the wedding. Come on, let us know. Me or him? May as well put Gideon out of his misery now."

Gideon rolled his eyes, shoving him off, and Torin gave his friend a rude gesture that earned another scolding from Naya. "Boys, do I need to remind you that we are in an infirmary? For Rhiannon's sake."

Artem bowed his head and whispered, "Sorry." He nodded in Torin's direction with a cheeky grin. "So, when did you ask her? I need all the details."

Torin didn't look fazed at all by his questions. "I am giving you no details, Stryker."

Emara giggled, and Naya rolled her eyes as she wandered over to look out the window. Arlo tried to smile as he gave them his congratulations too, but his eyes were on his friend.

Artem strolled over and tapped Torin's shoulder. "Come on, man, just one little detail. That's all I ask. I am in this now. I am invested. I am president of the *Tormara* fan club."

Emara scoffed.

Torin gave a cheeky grin of his own. Trust Artem to be the only person in his own club. "I asked her when she found me in the office."

"The commander's office?" he gasped like a wife of the elite. "You asked the Empress of Air to marry you in the commander's office?"

"It was perfect," Emara cut in, and she could feel Torin's gaze on her. "It didn't need to be anywhere else or anything else. It was perfect for us."

"So, let me get this straight, this happened *before* we walked you back down to the entertainment hall?" Artem's voice was high in disbelief as he looked from Breighly back to Torin.

"Yes. Not everyone needed to know until we were ready to

announce it. And if I had told you, the full kingdom would have heard about it by now."

"Damn right they would have," Artem agreed, scowling at Gideon, who just sighed. "That's what a best man would do."

Emara let out a giggle, and Torin gave her a quick wink before his gaze set back on his friend. "I asked her to be my wife because I can't go another day without her."

"Awwww," Artem cooed. "You honestly surprise me every day, Blacksteel. I knew there was a nice bastard in there somewhere." His eyes flew to Naya. "Again, apologies for my language."

Everyone in the room laughed, including Gideon. Even Naya smirked.

Emara played with the ring on her hand again, looking down as it sparkled. "We were going to tell everyone at the celebration, but everything moved so quickly..."

"It's okay." Naya's kind azure eyes blinked a few times before she stepped towards Torin, her emerald gown sweeping the floor. "I am so proud of you, my boy." She reached up on her tiptoes and ran a hand over his face. "I have never been prouder of you than I am today."

When Torin hugged her, dwarfing his mother, Emara's heart found itself in her mouth and tears stung her eyes.

"Rhiannon has blessed us when we needed it most," she said as her heels found the floor again.

"Yes, she has, Mrs Blacksteel," Artem said. "And I am sure she will bless us again and send health to Kellen too."

Arlo looked up with concern then, his eyes went to his brother as his words echoed around the room.

"She will," was all Naya said.

As Artem begged for more details from Torin and Naya went back over to Kellen, Emara found her feet travelling over to Gideon.

"Congratulations," he said with a nod. "I am happy for you and Torin."

"Thank you." She flashed a nervous smile at him. "You have no idea how much that means to hear that from you."

Gideon nodded before letting out a small laugh. "There is never a dull moment in the Blacksteel Tower, is there?"

"No," Emara said back, a little note of endearment in her voice. "There really isn't."

Her head turned to the door when Rhea came through it holding a tray full of elixirs. Gideon moved quickly to hold the door open for her and then Torin moved to take the heavy tray from her hands.

"Did you find the witch-hazel and the leaf of a mandrake?" Naya asked.

"I found everything we need," Rhea confirmed. Her hair was a mess, hinting that her search for the plants had been frantic.

Once everything had been crushed, mixed, and brewed, Naya placed the vial of potion to Kellen's lips and poured the liquid down his throat.

Before long, Emara saw the greyness of Kellen's skin start to take on the golden Blacksteel colouring again. Relief washed over her as his fingers relaxed. As the potion worked through his arms, legs, and spine, the tension in his body eased. Naya took a seat on the edge of his bed and brushed his hair back from his face. "Come on, my baby. Come back to us."

His chest began rising and falling normally, and his lips parted from the thin tight line they had morphed into. His eyes flickered open, and Rhea handed Naya some water for him to drink right away.

A gasp left his mouth, and Naya caught the back of his head, encouraging him to drink.

"My baby," Naya cried out. She hugged him tightly. Gideon let out a heavy breath, and Torin ran a hand over his face and through his inky hair.

"Welcome back, baby Blacksteel," Artem announced. He nodded in Emara's direction, taking his leave. "I will leave you guys alone."

"Actually..." Kellen's voice was scratchy like his screaming had done some damage, and everyone froze. "I need as many of you to hear this as possible."

CHAPTER
TWENTY-SIX
TORIN

Naya placed her forehead to her son's as she gripped his hands. "Kellen, you don't have to say anything in front of anyone. We can talk about this later."

Torin watched his mother brush his brother's hair with her hand again. Arlo moved to stand beside Rhea, and Breighly and Artem took a step back, giving the family space.

Kellen's rare eyes flashed with something that Torin knew all too well before he said, "I fear that if I don't say something now, I will be responsible for the bloodshed that is going to happen in this kingdom. I cannot bear that alone, Mother. You must understand that."

His mother's face turned pale before she lowered her hand from his hair. "Please, baby, I know you are scared—"

"What are you talking about? What happened in the entertainment hall, Kellen? I thought you had been attacked by the Dark Army or some sort of underworld magic." Torin's skin prickled as he found himself walking a few steps forward. "But there was nothing to be seen. Why do I get the feeling that I am the only one who doesn't know what is going on here?"

Kellen's eyes, one blue and one green, looked up at him from where he lay soaked in his own sweat. He drew in a breath, his eyes shutting briefly. "I need to tell you something, not only as my brother, but as my commander."

"You don't," Naya cut in. "You don't need to say a word, Kellen."

Emara nervously shifted near the fireplace, and Gideon also took a step forward.

Rhea lingered respectfully at the end of his bed. "Kellen, listen to your mother's words carefully."

Torin shifted and placed a hand to his head. "What in the underworld is going on?"

"Kellen, give it some thought," his mother whispered desperately. "Please give it more thought."

He reached out for her hand as he lay back on the pillow. "I have had years to think it through, Mother. I stood on Torin's side at dawn because he is not our father. I trust him and so should you."

The words hit Torin like a boulder, sweeping away his breath and crushing his heart.

I trust him.

With what?

"I do, my love," his mother whispered back, unable to look Torin's way.

"Then there should be no fear."

"I will protect you, Kellen," Emara's lyrical voice said. "I support your choice."

Torin turned to see her standing with hands clasped nervously together, her eyes a dark shimmer under the dim light of night. Torin glanced across to Gideon, whose face was wholly blank. His brother's emerald eyes met his own and he frowned a little. It told Torin all he needed to know.

He wasn't in on this secret either.

Fucking secrets.

"You need to answer me, and quickly," Torin said firmly. "What do I need to hear?"

Was it so bad that the room had flooded with silence to prepare him for what was to come? Even his mother had stopped begging Kellen not to speak, and her trembling hands clenched her skirt.

He hadn't thought much about what the first day of being the commander would bring, but this outdid any expectation.

A battle at dawn, an engagement, and now a secret that threatened bloodshed. What next, Veles knocking on the door of the Tower for a visit?

Shit, he better not wish that into existence.

Kellen sat up a little. "Once I tell you, if you command me to step out of the hunting team and into another role, I will understand. Or even if you have to exile me—"

"Exile you?" Torin was in disbelief at his words. "I can assure you, I will never exile you unless you are a threat to me, Emara, or the clan."

"Well, it is for you to decide if I am a threat to the clan or not." Kellen swallowed, and bravery took up residence in his eyes. "But I cannot keep this secret to myself any longer, not when we are all in danger." His gaze scanned the room before it found Torin again. "I am a True Dreamer, Commander."

"A what?" Torin asked, not sure if his hearing was playing up. He had been punched in the head a *few* times today, and hearing someone address him as commander was still overwhelming.

"I am a True Dreamer, Commander Blacksteel." Kellen's words lay like concrete in the room.

Emara's shoes could be heard on the wooden floorboards as she walked forward and stood by his youngest brother. It was clear she was in support of his secret. Somehow, she already knew.

A True Dreamer.

He had always admired that about Emara; she was unafraid to stand in adversity or on a side that felt right to her. And it seemed like her action gave his brother the courage to continue.

"I see things," he said tiredly. "I dream of events that come true.

Well, most of them, anyway. And I normally see my visions in my sleep—until now."

A True Dreamer.

Torin had thought them to be nothing more than an old folktale or something that had disappeared with time. But as long as magical factions produced children, their enchanted blood would create all sorts of wonders. The problem came from the fact that the clans saw them as an abomination, a curse.

Torin sucked in a breath. He had no idea how to comprehend what his brother had just declared.

"A True Dreamer? As in a seer?" Gideon asked, and his voice sounded a little strangled.

"Yes." Naya defended him quickly, pushing her shoulders back. "I have tried to protect him from your father for as long as we have known. You know what kind of reaction he would have had knowing one of his sons had more of my blood than his, more blood of Rhiannon than of Thorin. He would never accept it." Naya shot a look at Torin.

But Torin was still trying to process it all. It felt like minutes ago he was just fighting for his life, battling his father's fists.

This day was...unthinkable.

"What happened to you in the entertainment room was a *vision?*" Torin asked. "You looked...tortured."

"Yes. It was a dream." Kellen panted slightly.

"Why were you screaming?" Gideon asked. "Do they hurt?"

Kellen moved up in the bed so that he was sitting upright, his mother's hand still intertwined with his own. "They don't always hurt. Sometimes I can feel, smell, or taste things, but that is only if it's really strong. When I was younger, they started off as dreams, but then the despicable things that started to creep into my head would come true. I would hear of it happening somewhere in the city or whispers would come from other parts of the kingdom. I tried for so long to write them off as mere coincidences, terrible accidents. I started to write them in a journal and draw what had happened, and the details were too accurate for them to be a coincidence." He took a breath, looking at his mother's pained face as he did. Kellen's eyes then flickered to Torin.

"When I was little, I used to sit outside your briefings before the Selection," he said, "so that I could hear of the tragedies that I had dreamt of just to confirm that I was some sort of freak. I was different, and I knew it. There would be nights where I would try to stay awake so that my dreams couldn't happen just in case I was the reason bad things were happening to people. I would beg Thorin to stop them, plead with the Three-Faced God to listen, but they never did. My dreams only increased with time. It was like they wanted me to suffer. I believed the Gods hated me. They turned a blind eye on me like my own clan eventually would." He looked down at his mother's hand as she stroked a thumb over his own. Tears streamed down his mother's face, and Torin choked down the buildup of emotion in his throat.

"Mother found out about my abilities after my eighth birthday. One night when I screamed and screamed and I couldn't stop, I had to tell her my secret. I told her that the Dark Army had washed up on Tolsah Bay and slaughtered witches who belonged to the House Water. I tasted the sulphur and I felt their blood on my skin. I described every detail to her and she was convinced that I was just having a bad dream." Emara wiped a tear from her cheek, her lip trembling. Torin found himself struggling to hold back his own tears. His baby brother had suffered all these years and he had never known a thing. Guilt ripped through him and he distributed his weight to shake it off, still trying to focus on what Kellen was saying. There would be time later for the guilt to eat him alive.

"The next day, word came from the east that what I had dreamt was no nightmare, but reality. Witches had been butchered on the beach during a summer solstice ritual; demons had killed them for sport." Kellen shook his head. "I couldn't tell anyone about it. Mother didn't want anyone knowing, especially Father." He looked at Gideon and then Torin. "She didn't know how you would react. You might deem me unworthy of the Blacksteel name and shun me even now. My blood caused me this affliction; I did not ask for it."

"It is not an affliction" Naya's tears streamed from her eyes as she held her youngest son's hand, and the lump in Torin's throat only magnified. He shoved it down.

"It's an incredible gift," Emara said from beside him. "The power of Rhiannon runs in your veins, and that is not by accident." Emara brushed back a strand of long black hair from her face. "I have been looking for someone to mentor you, but it's hard to find someone who knows anything about seer's magic because it is so unspoken of. But I will not give up on you. I will keep looking. We will find someone."

"It doesn't feel like a gift. Not when your own blood will not recognise it as a skill. True Dreamers are shamed in the hunting community and you all know it." He looked at every hunter in the room, even Artem, who had barely moved an inch. Breighly said nothing as her eyes began to glow with a sadness he had not seen in a while. "We are deemed as cursed, bringers of bad fortune. They see it as a demobilisation of the hunting spirit, a bad omen, a weakness."

"I do not see how you are anything but an advantage for hunters," Emara said. "You could change how the clans hunt." Her beautiful eyes found Torin's face, and like always, his heart quickened. "It could change how hunters plan. If they knew where and when the darkness would strike, they could always be ahead. They could always be in a position to win against the underworld."

She has a point, Torin thought. Her strategy for deconstructing archaic views was rather refreshing. She had an eye for change.

Torin loved her rebellious streak. His smart little empress could help his clan be utterly brilliant under his watch.

"You saw what became of me when I had a vision," Kellen cut in. "I am disoriented, I sometimes cannot see or wake myself up. I often cannot hear the world around me until the vision is through with me and I am released from its claws. And I certainly wouldn't be able to fight should I have one whilst hunting. I would be the perfect target, the weakest of the clan."

"And you do not know when these visions will occur?" Torin asked after pulling a hand through his hair and taking a deep breath. He had to gather himself together and think like a leader, but his mind was a whirling vortex, every emotion smashing against the inside of his head.

He was dizzy, and the thoughts of his brother hiding who he was under Viktir's reign was even more maddening than he could have ever thought.

"I don't." Kellen's head shook and he looked down at his hands. "They are normally stronger when the moon is coming into her new phase or when she is full, but I cannot know when I will see for certain."

"Can they be controlled?" Gideon asked.

"Not really," Naya said, giving Kellen a reprieve. "But we have been giving him an elixir that slows them since he was a child, hoping that only one or two would sneak past the enchantment every so often. We knew it was possible for him to have a Dream when awake, we just didn't know if it would ever happen."

"Mother's elixirs are how I made it through the Selection," Kellen admitted.

"You did the best you could to control them," Arlo agreed, offering him a small smile.

A thought struck Torin hard. "What did you see in your vision that had you on your knees?"

Silence filled the room again.

Kellen took a long breath. "It's hard to explain. It sometimes comes clearly to me and other times it's murkier. Like when I had the vision of the darkness taking Emara at the Amethyst Palace, I was compelled to tell her about it, but we couldn't work out what the darkness actually was. I just knew something had a plan for her to be taken. And then she *was* taken by our own kind—"

"Wait, hold on." Torin threw up a hand, squeezing his eyes shut. He reopened them slowly, already seeing red. "You knew that Emara was going to be taken, that her life was in danger, and didn't tell anyone?"

He must be mistaken.

"I warned her—"

"You warned her?" Violence stirred in his soul.

"It was my idea not to tell anyone. Do not blame him," Emara interjected. "I couldn't tell anyone without exposing Kellen's secret and I refused to do that. I should be the one that gets your wrath, Torin. Not him."

Sweet fucking underworld. Was today going to kick his dick in any more? "Well, I suppose that makes it okay then, since it was *your* idea." Torin could feel the vein bulging in his neck. He turned and walked to the mantle, placing a hand on it and feeling like his world was exploding. "Fuck," he hissed before swinging back to face them all. "You were almost transported to the fucking underworld, Emara. Kellen, she could have died. People did die. Fuck!" He kicked over the wooden chair that sat close to the fireplace, splintering it. "And you are telling me we could have prevented that? You're telling me that I could have prevented you from being tortured and almost dying? Are you kidding?"

"Hey!" Emara yelled, her eyes scarily dark. "You do not get to raise your voice and shout about something that I decided was best for me." Emara pointed at him. "You can't be angry at us for something that didn't even happen. What's done is done. I made the choice to keep it from you. Let it go."

Torin grunted, his eyes widening in rage. "Oh, I can be angry if I want, angel. But I am not just angry, I am pissed. I am furious. You should not be hiding things like that from me. Things that endanger your life—any one of you. What you two did was utterly reckless and absolutely senseless."

"Senseless?" A spark of fire burned in her dark irises. "Don't you talk to me about senseless, Torin Blacksteel. Not when you have been fighting in the pits of the underground for no reason."

Naya gasped. "You haven't." Her eyes lit with concern and rage.

Torin ignored her, his eyes still locked with Emara's.

Artem Stryker cleared his throat, reminding everyone he was in the room. "I must agree with Torin on this one. You cannot expect us to think that we shouldn't have known that information, Emara. I am your guard. We were placed in our positions to avoid that happening to you. Our job is to protect you."

"Well, it wasn't your decision to make." Emara's jaw locked. "It was mine."

Torin let out a breath and took a step back as anger and fear coursed through every muscle. Shaking his head, he had the urge to wreck something. When his eyes met hers, he saw her on the floor in that room in the Amethyst Palace with a chain around her neck, screaming. Tears on her face. No hope left. Fear and blood.

Anger turned his bones into steel that melted as he took in the beauty of her face. "I almost lost you. I could have done something to protect you, to stop how they—" His voice broke off as flashes of what they did to her pushed past the barriers in his mind.

Silas had slammed her head into a mirror and beaten her. She had fought, but she had struggled. He remembered the blood on the floor, the ring he was supposed to have given to her lying with

Magin as his soul left this world. It could have been her. It could have been Emara who had died that night.

Torin felt that beast that often awoke when memories of her screams invaded his mind. It burst out of his cage, and he let out a roar.

Everyone flinched.

Emara's eyes softened after hearing his voice break, and she moved towards him. A cool breeze skated over his face, cheeks, and chest as she walked closer. "I know that night was hard for you too, and I am sorry, but you didn't lose me. Can you focus on that? Focus on the fact that I made the right call."

"That was not the right call and I don't care what kind of glitter you sprinkle over it to shine it up," Torin seethed, but the cool air soothed him again. "You were taken, Emara! Taken! Almost killed—or worse, sent to the underworld. I wouldn't...I couldn't even—"

Breath escaped him, his words lost to the hurt and rage that swirled into one huge mess in his mind.

"Brother," Gideon's voice pulled him out of his mind, "we are digressing from the true matter at hand here. I know you are pissed, but we can work that out later in the training room, yeah? Right now, if Kellen saw something that was worse than the vision before, I think we ought to listen to it. Don't you?"

He was always so level headed. That was why he needed Gideon to be his second-in-command—when he could get a minute to fucking ask him. His brother was calm, reasonable, and not a fucking hothead with murderous tendencies. He was probably the better man for commandership, but the Gods just had to go ahead and make Torin the first born.

He blew out a breath and relaxed his clenched fists.

Torin nodded at Gideon and then turned his gaze to his youngest brother. "What have you seen, Kellen? It's important that we know."

He hesitated for a few seconds, his eyes fluttering closed. "It was dark at first, but then I saw water, a gorgeous blue lake. I am certain it was the Lake of Rhiannon. But that's where it gets murky."

"What does?" Torin encouraged him.

"My visions. They don't always come in order; it's more like frames of what will happen. That's why I have trouble communicating or connecting them. Can you always make sense of your dreams?"

"Not always," Torin agreed.

Kellen's gaze flickered over everyone. "In the vision, I saw the Dark Army obtain the knowledge on where an ancient relic of the Gods is—a stone—and they are going to go after it. They are ready. I saw them break through a portal near a huge temple. I think it could be the Temple of the Gods. But blood ran through the rivers and the sky darkened like the magic of the underworld had swallowed us whole. There was screaming and death..."

Emara walked towards the window where moonlight glimmered in her hair. "Which stone is it?" She turned, looking over her shoulder, and the fear in her eyes sent Torin's blood into a quickened thrum.

"I am unsure, but it was smoother than the Resurrection Stone, almost whimsical."

Emara's gaze swept to Torin. "It has to be the Protection Stone."

He nodded. "That's what my bets would be on."

"How would you know that?" Gideon asked.

Artem said, "Think about it, if you have the Resurrection Stone here and Veles has the Immortality Stone, that leaves the Dark Crystal and the Protection Stone." His eyebrows rose. "And everyone knows the Dark Crystal is lost to the Broken Sea of Thorin."

"Unless the Dark Crystal has been plucked from the seabed, it has to be the Protection Stone," Emara agreed. "Its whereabouts are unknown, but it makes sense for it to still be on land. And it makes even more sense for the stone to be at the Temple of the Gods."

Kellen leaned forward. "If you are going to get there before the Dark Army, if you want to stop them retrieving Light Gods' Stones, you must leave tomorrow."

"Tomorrow?" Torin repeated.

"Tomorrow?" Emara exclaimed.

"If Kellen has no way to know when the Dark Army worked out where the Protection Stone is, it means that they could have a head start." Naya finally stood; her face stony. "And whatever we do, we cannot let them get another stone. They already have one; Gods know what they could do with two."

"When is the next full moon?" Torin asked, unable to think clearly.

"A few days from now," Naya said. "It's the Wolf Moon and she is a supermoon. She is so extremely powerful. It would make sense for the Dark Army to travel then."

"Great," Artem huffed.

"Demons always strike when the moon is at her fullest," Breighly added, her voice soft but wise. "But we have been tricked before. It is not their armies that are weaker when the moon isn't at her fullest, just their portals. It might not be as obvious as it seems for when they will move; they could be on their way there now."

"For a mission like this, it is too dangerous for them to do anything otherwise," Gideon argued. "They will be readying to portal when the moon is at its fullest. They have too much at stake if they are going to the Temple of the Gods. They need full power to get as many of them through the portal as possible to find the stone. The grounds are massive and the temple is protected. There's no way they would risk that."

"What if they are already there?" Arlo asked.

Torin let out a huge breath, and everyone looked at him.

This was what it was going to be like for the rest of his life, wasn't it? Everyone watching him, analysing how well he was coping and looking to see if he could make the decisions. "Gideon." He finally glanced up, his head still fuzzy with information and his blood still thrumming at the thought of a hunt. Damn Thorin's blood. "Round up the clan and let them know that the celebrations are over. They have to be ready at dawn for a mission. Artem, Arlo, if you are staying under my roof, you are abiding by my orders. I am giving you the choice to be in or out of this mission."

"I'm in." Artem grinned. "I am your soon-to-be wife's guard, after all."

Torin walked a little closer. "If you ask to be the best man *at all* during this mission, I will remove you from that position." He gave Artem his showtime grin. "Do I make myself clear?"

"Crystal." Artem's smirk was so feral it reminded Torin of who his next point of call was.

He switched his gaze to the other Stryker. "Are you in or out, Stryker Number Two?"

Arlo nodded once. "You know I am in. Any chance to beat the Dark Army is a chance I will take."

Torin stepped to the side. "Breighly, can you take the information of the mission back to the pack? I want the alpha to know about this development and decide if they will join the hunt or not. We have always had an unofficial alliance with the Baxgrolls; let's hope it continues."

She nodded. "Of course."

Torin looked down at his littlest brother and said, "You better get these infirmary blankets off of you. If you have Blacksteel blood in your veins, you will be there. You are a key part in all of this, and I won't leave a brother behind."

Delight and relief shone in Kellen's eyes, and Torin wasn't sure which outweighed heaviness in his heart.

A seer. A True Dreamer.

Emara's words drifted through his head.

It's an incredible gift.

I do not see how that is anything but an advantage when you are a hunter.

Thorin only knew how this evening would have gone if it had been his father who had found out the truth. But Torin had vowed that he would be better than his father ever was. If he could do that, it would mean more to him than winning any fight or hunt.

"Wait," Kellen said, jolting up as everyone moved. "I have one more detail to share."

Everyone turned to him.

"It wasn't all horror that I saw in my vision. When I mentioned the Lake of Rhiannon before, it was because that's where I saw the both of you bind your souls to each other." He looked at Torin and then the empress. "That's the place where Torin and Emara will get married. That part is set in stone."

CHAPTER TWENTY-SEVEN
EMARA

Emara took to her chambers to ready herself for dawn. How much sleep did the people of the magic community actually need? She was part of it now and still her body knew damn well that it needed rest. Her back ached, her head pounded, and her eyes were stinging like she had opened her eyes under sea water. Emara's legs felt heavy as she made her way around her own room to pack for her mission. She had no idea what to pack, her brain unable to function. What would she need?

As she folded some fighting gear into a satchel that she had brought with her from Mossgrave, her heart started to thump in her chest. When Kellen had mentioned everything about the vision, he had waited until the very end to confirm that she and Torin would marry. Instead of feeling it was too soon, something in her chest told her that it was right. It was like the ancestors of the Otherside had been there, setting that part of their story in stone, like the Gods had acknowledged their path by sending him that vision. And even though they travelled for something greater, she knew in her heart that that was where they were supposed to join each other in oath.

She would marry Torin Blacksteel at Lake Rhiannon.

Her next inhale of breath was hot and thick as it swelled in her throat. Although it felt right, that didn't take away the nerves. In the human world, a wedding took place on a part of land that was governed by the elite, and the bride and groom had to request a treaty of marriage vows from the Minister of Coin. It was over and done within an hour. However, it wasn't like that in the hunting world. Some unions went on for days.

This was more than a wedding; it was an alliance. It was strength and harmony. It was two powerful houses of the magical factions coming together.

She needed a minute to breathe. Before she added anything else to her satchel, she quickly made her way to her bathing chamber. It was too hot for a bath in the summer heat, but the coolest thing in the room was the floor. As she folded down onto the floor, the temperature of the cream and white tiles found her skin, stealing her breath. Basking in the coolness, she lay for a few moments, processing every part of what had happened over the last few days.

If Lorta or Kaydence found her like this, they would be worried, so she threw a gust of air at the door, enclosing her in her bathing chamber alone.

Her thoughts were loud and so was the pulse in her ears.

Torin had challenged his father, the duel, the new commander, the treaty, the ring, the proposal...

Marry me, here. Marry me now. Marry me tomorrow. Marry me any time you want. But just be mine forever.

She had sat on the commander's desk, taking in the details of Torin's bruised face, his eyes, his mouth. The corners of his lips had turned up as she had uttered the word "yes." Yes, she would marry him. What they had was eternal. Emara would never forget how his crystal eyes had explored her face like she had said something unbelievable, how he had picked her up by her thighs and embraced her until she couldn't breathe. They had both laughed as they had kissed. He had cupped her face in his hands and just looked at her in awe before kissing her breath away again.

And what had come next was even more beautiful. He'd lifted

her up onto the desk and whispered promises to her whilst he kissed every part of her skin. He left no parts of her flesh untouched by his mouth or his hands. Her body had arched into his mouth as he had devoured between her thighs.

Her pulse raced now even thinking of it.

Bringing her hand above her flushed face, she wiggled her fingers, and the stunning diamond that sat on a gold band twinkled. Torin had kept his mother's ring for his wife, and it felt like the stone had been cut especially for her. It was timeless yet fierce. And in a few days' time, another band would sit on that same finger, signifying their marriage.

She turned from her side to her back, feeling the cool tiles press relief into her spine. She let out a massive exhale. Emara had no idea what awaited them on this journey, or if they would even be successful in finding the ancient relic, but she was certain she had found her own path. It felt right, regardless of how terrifying it might be and how much it had broken her. It was making her stronger, giving her the grit and determination it took not only to be an empress, but a warrior too. Should the Dark Army find them in the race for the Protection Stone, she would be prepared. Emara would fight them until her arms could not swing anymore. She might not have the blood of Thorin running through her veins, but she did have Rhiannon's, and she knew that the God of the Moon and Dreams would never give up on her. If Rhiannon could fight the Dark Army, she would too. If Rhiannon had found a way to stop an almighty war, so would Emara—no matter what it took.

She would find a way.

As she looked down at her hand, the black diamond winked at her. Rhiannon must have heard her thoughts and granted her the grace to dream as her eyelids fluttered shut and exhaustion took over.

CHAPTER TWENTY-EIGHT
BREIGHLY

The Empress of Earth had suggested to Breighly that she could portal her back to the Ashdale Forest, but she had politely declined. Sybil was kind to offer, but she fucking hated portals, and she was already dreading using one tomorrow to get to the Crismon Dock at dawn. She didn't want to puke up her guts in front of everyone in the clan. Breighly had no idea how she could drink a tavern dry and never hurl up her guts, but the minute she stepped through a portal, the Gods decided to give her a jittery stomach.

Her belly churned at the thought of it. The lights. The spinning sensation. The feeling like your lungs were collapsing in your chest and that stars were burning through your body.

She shuddered.

Taking the time to run from the Tower to the Ashdale Forest had been a blessing in disguise. The moon was almost in her fullest phase, and its beams shimmered on her fur as the cool night breeze stroked its soothing fingers through her coat. She was warm in wolf form, and it didn't help that she didn't know how to approach her next conversation.

Apart from Roman, she hadn't seen her family since the prime meeting, and she knew that leaving her pack behind to guard an empress would have all sorts of unknown consequences. Still, she hoped her pack would be willing to join the mission for the Gods' Stones.

Shifting fully, Breighly ran up the cottage steps in human form, landing on the front porch. She reached the straw basket that always held extra clothing and found a flannel shirt and a loose pair of bottoms. They were old clothes her brothers no longer wore, so they were huge on her frame, but she hardly cared about what she looked like right now.

Opening the door to her cottage, she could hear her brothers and father in the living room. Their loud voices always tried to compete with each other in the humble room. The living room had been the same since Breighly was little. Comfy sofas cornered all areas of the room, and a large dining table crowded the front of the room. A fire always burned bright against the furthest wall, no matter the weather. Paintings of moon phases rested on the wood-panelled walls, and a warm rug took centre stage in the middle of the room. She had lain on that rug many times with whatever brother was her favourite that day. But the best times were when her father had joined her, telling her stories in front of the fire about a fierce princess wolf who lived in a faraway land and feared nothing.

But those eras were gone now, buried by time, grief, and unresolved trauma. So much had happened since those innocent moments.

As she rounded the corner, Breighly noted Waylen's large body spread along the biggest sofa and her father playing cards with Roman at the dining table. They all still managed to have whiskey in their hands. She smiled quickly. Eli would have been playing cards too if he were still here, probably sitting at the table opposite Roman. She wondered if the miserable look on Waylen's face was because he had been put out of the game first.

An overwhelming wave rocked through her body, unsettling her nerves. No wonder she didn't like to come back here. Everywhere she looked, she could see a memory of someone who no longer existed.

"Princess." Murk's dark eyes lit up like they always did when he saw her. He placed his cards down on the table and stood instantly.

"Bry," Waylen announced, sitting up from his relaxed position, his eyes wide with surprise.

"Well, if it isn't the Empresses of Air's favourite guard." Roman winked her way as he sat his whiskey on the table.

"Hi, Papa." She flashed her father a smile, who looked grateful to see her safely back in this house. "Shit heads." Her chin lifted to each of her brothers.

They both flashed her a toothy grin, and in that moment, she could see why too many people commented on how alike they all were.

"What brings you back here?" her father asked, shock lingering in the air. "Are you coming back home?" Hope sprang into his deep voice, and it gutted her.

Breighly's throat threatened to close as she looked at him, but she was relieved when Roman gave a dramatic sigh.

"Fuck," her twin cursed as he eyed his father's deck lying flush on the table. "Not again. How can you beat me every time?"

Murk pulled his hand across the coins lying on the solid oak table, a wise glint in his eye. "You can't beat the alpha." He smiled at Breighly. "Isn't that right, Princess?" He flicked her a coin, and she caught it with lightning speed. She tucked the gold coin into her pocket.

"That's right!" She grinned back at one of her favourite people in the whole world.

"Are you going to answer your alpha?" Waylen stood, resting his drink in the crevasse of his folded arms. "What are you doing back here? Don't you have a rather *official* role to be doing now?"

"I am here on official business, actually," she said, ignoring the burning in her cheeks.

"Oh, official business for the hunters?" Waylen probed again.

"Official business for my empress," she snapped back.

"God, that sounds awful. What, are you just her little bitch now?"

"Shut your mouth, Waylen." She eyed him. Breighly had hoped she would be inside more than a few seconds before his whining began. "You are the one that sounds like a little bitch."

A laugh burst from Roman, and a growl rumbled from Waylen's chest.

"I am back here on behalf of Emara," she announced. "Not for you to question anything about my role."

"So *official.*" Waylen's hazel gaze narrowed on her face, and she imagined smashing the glass he was holding in his stupid, smirking face.

"Enough," Murk said calmly. "Your sister is right. We don't need to question why she is here, but welcome her with open arms. You are starting to sound like a wife of the elite with your jealous mouth." Her father's dark gaze fell on Waylen, earning a scowl in return, then he turned back to her. "If you have something of importance to say, I want to hear it."

Breighly took a small breath and hoped that none of them noticed her falter. She really hoped this would go the way she wanted it to. "Father, the Blacksteel Clan believes that they know where to search for the Protection Stone. If they find it, it will mean they would be the first clan in history to have two of the Gods' Stones at once. It would put them in an extremely powerful position."

Murk's brow pulled down into a scowl, but she couldn't tell if he wanted to dismiss her or if she had piqued his interest. He always was a hard man to read. He could go from calm to terrifying in seconds. But never with her.

"And what trouble has Torin Blacksteel found himself in this time?" Waylen questioned with a laugh as his father mulled over the possibilities. "How has he, of all people, found a second stone?"

She shot him a warning glare. "Torin didn't figure it out; it was actually Kellen."

Murk's eyebrows rose again, a shimmer of concern in his eyes. "How? How did this happen?"

The alpha's tone was commanding in its own way, and his authority made the words in her mouth want to work their way out.

Breighly gave her alpha all the information that Torin had asked her to pass on, from their strategy to their reasons behind their new embarkment. And she couldn't leave out the fact that the information had come from Kellen's dreams. The Blacksteels trusted the pack with their secret.

"A seer? Kellen Blacksteel is a *seer*?" Roman let out a low whistle and ran a hand over the back of his neck. "I did not for the life of Vanadey see that one coming."

"Fuck, Viktir won't like that." Waylen took a sip of his whiskey.

"No, he won't," Murk agreed.

"Well, it's a good thing that Viktir has no authority in the clan anymore," Breighly reminded them. "He's the only Blacksteel who won't be joining the mission. He is in the Tower cells until Torin decides otherwise."

Murk let out a slow sigh as he moved to acquire another drink.

"And Torin wants our help?" Waylen asked as the flames of the roaring fire flickered up his cheeks, making him look flinty and menacing. "He wants to put the Baxgroll pack at risk and help to find this stone? Doesn't he have enough clan members to sacrifice? If the Dark Army knows of the stone's whereabouts, this is ludicrous. Madness."

Breighly didn't like the tone of her brother's questions. "He isn't asking for your help. The Commander of the Blacksteel Hunting Clan," she reminded him, "is giving you the information so that you can decide as a pack what you want to do. If you are in or out. It's a Gods' relic, Waylen. Do you want Veles' disciples to obtain it first?"

"So that *you* can decide as a *pack*? Why did you say that like you are not a member of said pack?"

Breighly ground her back teeth together and ignored him. For once in her life, she needed to take the higher ground. "I have come here on behalf of the Empress of Air to ask you if you would like to join us on the mission. As her guard, I will be joining them, and she knows how powerful we are as a pack." She looked at her father and then Roman. "If the pack does not want to be involved in securing another of the Gods' Stones, then that is fine. But I would highly recommend that the wolves come with us. There is strength in numbers."

"Oh, you would highly recommend that the *wolves* come with you?" Waylen took a few steps forward. Being the beta of the pack, he was the mouth until the alpha spoke. "Do you think because you are a guard to the Empress of Air that you are allowed to forget about your pack and saunter into our home spouting off about hunter and witch business like you are one of them? You haven't so much as looked at your pack since the summit and now you want us on board? You want our help for your crazy missions?"

Her jaw almost locked in anger, but she looked over to her father, who looked contemplative. "I do not demand anything of the pack or anyone. I am only asking if you would want to be a part of history."

"A part of history," Waylen sniffed. "You should hear yourself, Bry. You have been staying in the Tower two fucking minutes and you already have a god complex. You should really take a look at yourself."

"Waylen," Murk growled, his eyes glowing a fiery gold.

She moved towards Waylen, ignoring her father. "Maybe you should ask yourself why the pack must be in each other's arseholes every two minutes to feel validated. I don't need that, so I don't need to take a look at myself. I can be my own person. You have made it extremely clear that I am a female in this pack and always love to remind me where my place is, princess or not." She shot a look at her father and then back to Waylen. "When I choose to run alone in the woods it is because I am tired of all your male bullshit suffocating me. Bullshit that I need to suffer alone."

"And what bullshit would that be, Bry? Is it because we expect you to attend our *bullshit* traditions?" Waylen said through his teeth. "Is it because under the Wolven Moon, you are supposed to mate at your age? Are you running away from that as well as your responsibilities within this pack?"

"I owe nothing to the mating moon, just as much as I owe nothing to you," she growled.

A glint in his eye told her that he knew he had hit a soft spot in her armour. "You know it reaches its peak in a few days and we honour Vanadey by running through her woods to celebrate the mating bond, and now you want to fuck off to a mission? You have been there every other mating moon and you have seen what it can do, how powerful it can be. So there is no doubt in my mind that you are just trying to avoid your heart by going off and gallivanting with the hunters to find a stone just to avoid your fate. It's pathetic."

Her fate.

A mate.

A wolf.

She lifted her eyes, catching his hazel gaze that burned in the firelight. "Maybe you should focus on your own mating bond this Wolven Moon since you clearly think it's so much more important than—oh, I don't know, saving the fucking kingdom from the Dark

God. I do not see you standing in front of me with a mate, *brother dearest*. Oh no, wait, that's right. It's only women who are seen as charred goods if they don't marry before a certain age and have a litter of cubs." She could feel the anger spiking in her blood. She pointed a clawed finger at him. "But you fuckers with dicks think its fine if you mess around until you are full of fucking wrinkles. But no, not us. We are to submit to the mating moon. That is the bullshit I am talking about. It's one rule for you and another for me. Your traditions are misogynistic, and I am over them."

"Okay, Bry, you've quite clearly made your point." Her father glared at her, his chiselled face lined with hurt. "I don't need you to give me another lecture on how shit it is for women in society. I see it every day working with the prime." He moved closer to her, and he had a softness across his face. "You know how much I have tried to give you everything a little girl should have." He swallowed, and it was evident that he had a lump in his throat. "Ever since your mother left, I tried to work out how to raise you, and, by Vanadey, I had no clue what to do. How to make sure you had everything you could ever want. And I know that sometimes the pack isn't enough for you. And you are not a little girl anymore. I must let you choose your own life. But I still wanted you to be a proud wolf, Princess."

A lump fisted its way into Breighly's mouth. "I know, Papa. I know you did. And I am. But I just want to be able to help change the kingdom. This mission could really change everything."

His eyes flickered to the glass in his hand before he looked up. "Tell me, did I do something wrong that makes you want to be with the hunters? Is it because they are letting girls fight? I know I have made a lot of mistakes; it's just you are my only girl—"

She went to him then, and her hands found his wrists. "Gods, no. You did everything you were supposed to, Papa. You gave us everything." She heard her voice break a little, and her soul did the same. "I just feel...free when I get to choose. I would never reject the pack. They are my family, my blood. You all are my family, but I need to walk under my own moon sometimes. I just need to be me."

Murk nodded, something bubbling on his face that made Breighly feel a sting in her eyes. "Okay, Bry. Just always come back to us, promise me that."

"I promise," she whispered as she squeezed his hands. "Does that mean you are not coming?"

Murk hesitated.

"Father, it's the Wolven Moon."

"Leave it, Waylen," Roman finally waded in. "There will be other mating moons. Your ego is just hurt that Emara picked Bry over you to be her guard."

Breighly looked over to Waylen, who was shaking his head. His glare finally landed on her. "If you walk out that door, you are choosing the witches and hunters over your own pack's ancient traditions, no matter what moon you walk under. It's the super-moon, a fucking wolven supermoon. It's not like the witches are going to run with you when it's full in respect to your Light God. It's an honour to Vanadey."

She let go of her father's hands. "I know what moon it is, Waylen. I am not stupid. I just didn't realise we were all divided." Breighly shot him a violent look that she was rather proud of. "Do we not support all Light factions? Is it not everyone's goal to keep the Dark Army at bay?"

Waylen bared his teeth. "You know you can't be both a guard and a wolf. It doesn't work that way. Eventually, you will need to choose."

She turned away from her father, leaving him at her back. "I will be whatever I choose to be. If I want to run with the wolves, I will run with the wolves. If I want to hunt with the hunters, I will damned well carve out the hearts of the Dark Army. If I want to use my skills to guard an empress of our magic community, I will guard her with my life. And as a *beta* of the pack, you are not going to tell me otherwise. Stay in your place, Waylen."

His face screwed up horribly. "You know, you are just like her."

"Waylen," their father warned, "do not go there. You both need to let me think without wittering on."

Breighly froze, her skin crawling.

"She always left too." Waylen's chest heaved, and his clenched fists tightened the muscles in his forearm. It took her back to when he was angry as a child, the foul mood ruining entire days.

Breighly's hands began shaking at his declaration. She forced them steady. "I am nothing like her."

"You are exactly like her," Waylen spat. "She ran from the pack too, always searching for something more, something better than us. We weren't enough for her and we are not enough for you. I thought you would turn out different, but you must forget that you and Roman both sat on the porch for days waiting for her to come back. She couldn't care about traditions either, eh?"

Pain drove through Breighly's heart, punching her in the gut, slamming her into an oblivion of trauma.

Even though it hurt to hear them, Waylen's words were the truth. They hadn't been enough for their mother. They'd tried to be everything she could have wanted, but they couldn't make her enough flower bracelets, couldn't clean their rooms enough, couldn't give enough hugs or words to make her stay.

"Waylen, that's enough," Murk warned again, and Breighly couldn't ignore the upset in his voice. "I mean it."

Their mother had been his mate, his wife, and he had never met another since her.

Waylen pointed his finger at Breighly. "No. She needs to hear this, Father; you have protected your little princess enough. You let her do whatever the fuck she wants with no consequences, running around Huntswood like a fucking party girl and now fighting with the hunters like she doesn't have the blood of wolves in her heart. But she does, and so do you. And you are selfish, just like *her*. You do not deserve the pack."

"I am not like her." Anger, shame, and heartache broke through Breighly's body. "I am nothing like her."

"And when you scowl like that"—Waylen pointed at Breighly again, sharp and aggressive,—"you even look like her."

Breighly shook her head, feeling her legs tremble. "I look like her as much as you do. As much as Roman. As much as Eli. I am no more her than you are."

They all had her fair hair and skin. But only Breighly and Waylen had gotten the badness her traits offered; Roman was good through and through. And Eli...well, he was an angel. But Breighly and Waylen had that hardness that had only penetrated their souls deeper when their mother never returned. They had their father's kindness, but, by the Gods, when cornered, they were every part the brutal, selfish wolf their mother was.

"You have gone too far, Waylen," Murk growled in a calm, scary way that left everyone wondering what he would do next. "I think you better take a run to cool off and tire out that mouth of yours."

Waylen finished his whiskey in one swig and began to move towards the door. "Well, if there is one blessing that graced this family, it is that I am glad Eli isn't here to watch you turn into a woman that he resented so much. He would be ashamed to call you sister."

"Shit," Roman whispered under his breath. "You always need to go for the jugular. It's so uncalled for, brother."

Waylen only glanced at him before dragging his eyes back to Breighly.

For all Breighly knew, her heart had been gouged out, pulled through her spine, and was now lying on the floor.

Murk let out a roar. "You were told to leave it alone. Go for a run and don't come home until your poisoned tongue is clean of insults." He moved towards the beta intimidatingly.

A lump worked its way into her chest and up her throat as a sharp pain stabbed her heart. She looked at her papa. "I am not doing what she did. I am not rejecting my pack because I want to pave my own path. I am just—"

Waylen cut her off as he moved towards the door. "It's only a matter of time before you leave and don't come back. You have responsibilities here and you choose to ignore them. We even gave you La Luna to keep you tied to the pack, but you decided to play at being a warrior of Thorin. You gave up running with wolves to stab with steel, and you will probably end up fucking one of them and having one of their bastard children right before they marry their witching wife." Waylen's words wrapped around Breighly's throat and choked her. "In my eyes, Bry, you are a lost cause. Just like mother."

Murk dove for Waylen, and the two of them somehow ended up out the door before Breighly could even register it. The fire crackled, and there were a few hissing sounds, but nothing compared to the roar in her head. She steadied her legs, trying to stop herself from crumbing to the ground. When her eyes shifted to Roman, he opened his mouth to speak, but she couldn't hear another word of what anyone had to say.

She turned, running through the hallway to her bedroom and slamming the door shut. Her back fell against the wood of the door and her breathing hitched as she tried her best to hold in the crushing emotion swelling in her chest.

She heard footsteps travel the length of the hall, and they paused outside her room before going to the adjacent room next door, Roman's room. He knew she needed time alone. Taking shaky breaths, Breighly covered her mouth. She couldn't let her father or brothers hear her cry. She wouldn't dare. One single tear broke free and cascaded down her cheek as she swallowed every other feeling she had, forcing them down to the darkest parts of her soul until her lungs felt like they could burst.

She wiped the tear away quickly, destroying all evidence that it had ever been there in the first place. She'd gotten too good at hiding her emotions, crying in secret when her father came home with cuts and wounds. She could count all of the birthdays she'd spent in her room, muffling her cries for her mother who would never celebrate the occasion with them. Eli, watching her from the Otherside, was the only one who knew how many tears she had shed for him. She wiped away any trace of emotion because that was how she got through every day. She couldn't let anything in because if she did, she would feel everything.

She would feel every love she was never meant to have and every loss that had torn apart her family. So instead of feeling, she took a breath, counted to ten, and packed her satchel for the mission.

"It's only a matter of time before you leave and don't come back. Just like her."

Jumping from her window to avoid walking through the cottage, Breighly headed towards the rising sun. Hooking her satchel to her arm, she shifted and ran in wolf form to the Blacksteel Hunting Tower until her brother's words melted away.

CHAPTER
TWENTY-NINE
EMARA

E mara had hazy memories of falling asleep on the floor of her bathroom, but she could no longer feel the cool tiles underneath her. All she could feel was skin and muscle with the rising and falling of a warm chest. She instantly took in the scent of pine and frozen berries and fluttered her eyes open. Sheets wove around them subtly, exposing a few parts of skin. One of her arms lay over his chest, and he had fallen asleep with his hand tangled in her hair.

She hid a lazy smile at that.

The beating of his heart was soft and steady, and she loved it when she knew he was relaxed with her.

Soft rays of light filtered through the fluffy clouds that drifted outside her massive window, and as they found Torin Blacksteel's chest, they illuminated old scars. Her hand travelled up his torso, feeling his soft skin contrasting with the ridges of his carved body. Inky black hair lay against the white pillow, and his skin practically glowed against the crisp sheets. He was a masterpiece. Waking up to him was like a dream.

Is this what *married* life could be like for them, or would they end up in separate quarters like Naya and Viktir?

They hadn't even talked about this kind of thing.

Suddenly, the room was too hot and the light sheets were suffocating. She flung her legs out of the bed and sat up. She had been getting used to the idea of sharing a bed with Torin, sharing her life with him... What if that was not what the Commander of the Blacksteel Hunting Clan had in mind?

"Emara?" Torin's hoarse voice struggled to wake from its slumber.

She looked over her shoulder, and the glory of him lying in her bed like a god hit her heart. The sheets that covered him had been pulled down his torso, dipped low enough for her to see that little trail of hair that led south. The sunbeams softened his angled features, but his ocean eyes weren't soft. Concern and desire swirled in his irises like a constellation of blue stars.

Her breath caught in her throat.

He was the most magnificent thing in the whole kingdom, and in that moment, her world rocked.

"Is something wrong?" he asked as his hand raked through his unruly hair.

When she saw him like this, it was like magic coursed through her veins and spilled into her heart, filling it so full it could burst. There was something so raw and beautiful about him when his eyes were just awake and his hair wasn't swept tidy. When his muscles were relaxed and the day's troubles were not on his mind yet.

He was breathtaking.

Her teeth caught her cheek so that the truth would stay locked behind her lips. She shook her head, spilling hair all around her like a black satin curtain—probably just as messy as his.

"You do know," he said, lips twitching upward, "you more often than not chew your cheek when you are lying or hiding something."

She stopped her bad habit instantly. How could he read her so well?

He placed his hands behind his head, displaying his bulging

biceps; he lay there like the subject of an oil painting, unaware of how the light was capturing every muscle and every shine in the strands of his hair. "Want to tell me what's going on in that pretty little head of yours? Or maybe we can start by you telling me why I found you sleeping on the bathroom floor last night?"

A heat rushed up her neck to her cheeks. "I just have a lot going through my head."

He moved, and one of his hands came over to the small of her back as a gesture of comfort. "We are in this together now. Your dark thoughts are my dark thoughts. Let me ease them."

But she wasn't sure if she could show him every piece of darkness that she kept deep down. She could feel that it was bubbling up, and the more she suppressed it, the more it felt like it was screaming. She swallowed as a thick tendril of darkness threatened to curl up her spine. "It was honestly just an uneasy thought. Silly, really, especially with everything going on."

There were a few moments of silence before Torin spoke again. He drew a little circle on her spine, pushing away the darkness building under her skin. "Do you want to postpone our union?"

She turned to look at him, and her chest tightened when she did. His face was full of apprehension. "No," she said quickly. "Not at all. Do you?"

The sparkle came back like a tidal wave in his crystal eyes. "Not even my nightmares will dare to dream of it."

She laughed as his fingertips made their way up her spine, sending shivers across her skin. Before she could lean in and feel the warmth of his lips, embers broke in the fireplace. Emara looked up to see that there was a fireletter hovering above the flames. She leaped from the bed and opened it.

"Who is it from?" Torin asked, relaxing back into the same position as before.

Emara rolled her eyes. "Artem."

"What is he saying now?" Torin sighed.

Emara tried to hide a small smile that was sneaking onto her lips as she read it. "He has advised that they have readied the supplies, and Gideon has organised the weaponry and the men. And he's afraid of you gutting him alive if he knocks to wake us."

"Dramatic prick."

"You love him really."

Emara saw a shy smile tuck into Torin's lips, and his dark lashes swept down as he said, "I wouldn't go that far."

A rattle came from the door, causing Emara to leap from her skin.

"Did you get my letter?" a loud voice broke through the door.

"Are you not supposed to wait until we respond to the letter to knock on the door, Stryker?" Torin called. He stood, revealing that he was entirely naked under the sheets.

Emara's face must have revealed her surprise because he gave her a quick wink and one of his most wicked grins. "It's not like you haven't seen it before, angel."

By the Gods, why did this man make her feel like her heart had never been alive until him?

He paraded across the room and pressed his mouth to hers, claiming her lips. It stole her breath, and her stomach flipped as she melted against him. His hands caressed her face once and then he pulled back reluctantly.

"I couldn't have started my day without doing that." He rubbed his thumb on her chin and then passed her, leaving her robbed of more kisses, breath, and the heat of his body.

She swallowed, collecting herself as Torin opened the door, still entirely naked. "Good morning, Stryker."

"Well hello, sailor." Artem whistled and made his way into the room uninvited. "What a way to greet your best friend, Tori-boy."

Torin blinked. "You're not my best friend."

Artem's booming laugh could have been the alarm clock for the full Tower. "You have no other friends, Torin, which makes me your best one."

Emara sniggered, and Artem threw a wink her way as he tucked his inked hands into the groove of his weapon belt.

Torin turned and mouthed, "*Traitor.*" The look in his eyes told her that he would get her back for betraying him. But why did that look make her toes curl?

"What made you so chipper this early?" Torin asked as he strode across the room to find bottoms to pull on.

"I am ready to seize the day, Commander Blacksteel." His golden eyes glittered as he announced Torin's new title. "And by the looks of things, so are you two." His eyebrows wobbled suggestively. "Did you manage to get any sleep at all, you little love tigers?" He made a pawing action that almost sent Emara over the edge.

"We have a long journey ahead of us, Artem." Emara sighed. "Let's not make it painful."

"We have a long journey *and* a wedding." Artem grinned.

"Okay, Artem. I am fine with you just barging into our space, unannounced—"

"I did announce myself—by fireletter and by door. What more could you want from me?"

Emara's eyebrows rose. "Maybe a little privacy?"

"I don't think Stryker could spell privacy if he tried." Torin laughed.

"You guys are just...delicious." Artem beamed as he looked between Emara and Torin. "Aren't you glad the three best friends are back together again, the ultimate trio?"

"Fuck me." Torin sighed. "If I need to listen to this the full way to the Temple of the Gods, I will place you in the cells next to my father and leave you there until we return. And I will accept the wrath of the chief commander happily."

"Why do you pretend to have such a cruel heart, my beautiful, brooding friend?" Artem's lips turned up as he batted his eyelashes.

Torin looked at Emara as if to say, "*You take care of this before I do.*"

She stepped in. "You actually interrupted an important conversation between Commander Blacksteel and I."

The minute she announced the title, she could feel the burn of Torin's gaze on her, and it set her alight internally. He clearly liked hearing that from her lips, he had made that clear in the commander's office. "Artem, I need you to go and check in on Breighly. Get the news of what happened with her pack and then report it back to Commander Blacksteel and I," Emara commanded on Torin's behalf, and as she stole another look at his face, it seemed that her authority had set him on fire. She pushed out her hand, and Artem's huge mass started sliding backwards towards the door.

"I hate when you do this," Artem called as the wind pulled at his cheeks, his hair, his clothes.

"See you in the foyer, *friend.*" She smiled callously, slamming the door in his face.

"I am still keeping my hopes up that I am going to be your ring bearer at the wedding," Artem shouted from behind the door. "I am still your favourite guard, even if you don't want to admit it in front of Blacksteel. I know the truth."

She flipped him a rude gesture that she wished to the Gods he could have seen as she laughed her way to the bathing chamber to get ready for their journey.

Torin moved so quickly he was like a flash of lightning, and his hard body pressed against her spine. "Where do you think you're going?" he asked as his hands found her waist and then her hips. He tugged her against him so that she could feel his hard length at her rear.

Heat instantly pooled between her thighs at how he sounded, how he was ready for her.

"Do we not need to get ready to leave?" Emara tried her hardest to keep her tone unwavering. "We have a mission, remember?"

A squeal left her lips as he spun her to face him. His forehead bowed to hers. "I have never had an interest in being called Commander Blacksteel." One of his sinful dimples appeared. "Not until it left your lips." He walked her backwards, his hands still firmly flexed around her hips. "And now I am just wondering what it would sound like coming from your mouth as you moaned."

She panted in delight at what he was offering. "And how are you going to do that, Commander Blacksteel?" She smiled up at him.

"I am about to show you."

Torin pounced on her, and Emara's back hit the mattress before she could even blink.

CHAPTER THIRTY
GIDEON

The Blacksteel Hunting Clan stood in the foyer, awaiting the arrival of the commander and the Empress of Air. No one knew what was in store for them, as they still needed to have a briefing, but Gideon knew to expect the unexpected. Going on the whim of a vision wasn't going to be easy, and he had no idea how Torin was going to explain why they were heading to Skyelir. There were a lot of parts that were missing, and his mother had said that visions can change depending on the hand of fate.

He wasn't going to lie to himself and say that Kellen's visions hadn't kept him up all night. Knowing that his brother was a seer and that he had envisioned the Dark Army obtaining the Protection Stone was a scary thought alone, but the fact that it was a race against time to change the fate of the kingdom was terrifying.

What if time wasn't on their side?

I do not feel fear. I do not feel fear. I do not feel fear.

His childish chants had a funny way of always coming forth to calm his mind, even in adulthood.

His thoughts were interrupted when a ray of sunshine followed Sybil Lockhart through the threshold of the foyer as she arrived from the gardens. The early morning sun shone through her hair, illuminating the fiery red strands that curled all around her wildly. She flattened out her modest olive-coloured skirt before clearing her throat. The earth witch had a softness to her voice, and when she tried to get the attention of the chattering hunters, she failed.

Her creamy cheeks gave a hint of embarrassment as she tried again. "Excuse me, everyone, the portal is ready."

Still the men spoke over her.

Annoyance ran through Gideon's veins. It boiled his blood to see her shrink into herself, nervously holding on to the material of her dress. He'd seen her crawl out of her shell over the last few months; it would be a crime to send her hiding away again. Gideon watched as Sybil rose to her tiptoes and tried to yell over the loud men, but again, she failed.

Before he knew it, he had sprung from the wall to stand by her side.

"Silence," he roared over the din of the crowd, and it cut through every conversation like a dagger. Every person in the foyer looked his way. "The Empress of Earth has important news. Show the Empress of Earth some respect and listen to what she has to say."

Fuck, he had never sounded more like Torin. As he looked at the men's faces, he thought they were shocked to see that it was he who stood there and not his older brother.

Gideon glanced at Sybil, who had a bashful blush on her cheeks. She bowed her head as a thank you to him, her huge moss-green eyes glittering with gratitude.

She cast her gaze out to the watching crowd. "The portal is ready to take us to Tolsah Bay. Gather your things and meet me in the gardens; I will wait for you all by the rose arch," she announced, her voice still sounding a little shaky. She wasn't a speaker like Emara could be, but when she produced magic, she was a force to be reckoned with. Her portals were probably the strongest in the witching world now that they had no supreme. "Oh, but please do not step through it until I say."

Gideon's chin lifted. "You heard what the empress said; not a person steps through it until she says. Let's get moving!"

As the hunters moved, she reached out and caught Gideon's arm. He met her stare. "Thank you for that," she said, "truly. I never have the nerve to shout in front of hunters. I feel like I am doing something wrong."

"You are not doing anything wrong." Gideon tried his best not to smile. He lowered his head so that he could whisper, "Maybe next time you should just shake the ground. They would listen then."

A genuine smile lit up her face, and Gideon did all he could to stop his heart from feeling like it could tumble from his chest as he drew away from her.

"I think I might try that next time." She found a corner of her lip with her teeth. "Thanks for reminding me that I am an empress who could part the ground from underneath their feet."

Gideon laughed and then his eyes met hers again. "I am more than happy to remind you of that every day."

It looked like her breath caught in her chest, and her eyes diverted to her hands as a rosy blush stained underneath her freckles.

"I mean, I am your guard, and I get to watch you create magic all day, every day," Gideon said, flustered, trying to hold on to any professionalism he had left.

"Right." She finally looked up from her hands. "Shall we get to the portal, then?"

"Yes, let's." He gestured for her to go first.

BREIGHLY

When Breighly's hands hit the white sandy shore of Tolsah Bay, so did her vomit.

"Fucking portals," she cursed as she wiped her mouth with the back of her hand.

She knew the portals did not agree with Shifter blood. her bones already shifted, her magic already running through her blood so that she could transform; she didn't need to add another dimension onto that.

The summer sun was scorching down on the bay, so much warmer than in Huntswood, burning into her scalp. She had vomit tracking down her tunic that suffocated her neck and barricaded her chest. Hunting gear was not made for women, and it was noticeable. Her feet were in heavy boots, and it made it hard to even walk in the sand. Her stomach was still unsettled, swishing and splashing like the waves behind her.

And the words of her brother carried to her ears even in the sea breeze.

You know, you are just like her.

She always left too.

She ran from the pack too, always looking and searching for something more. We weren't enough for her.

Her day was already a shitshow; she'd fought with her brother, her pack hadn't joined the hunters, and the memories of her mother's abandonment were all too fresh in her mind.

Just as she thought she had stabilised the nausea, a wave of it overtook her again and Breighly hurled over in the sand, emptying the contents of her stomach. She retched and she heaved until there was nothing left in her belly.

A shadow in the sand notified her that someone was coming towards her, but she couldn't hear anything from the pounding in her head, nor could she see anything, blinded by tears brought on by the retching. The large figure stood over her, shielding her from the sun's heat long enough to feel shade kiss her skin.

It was glorious.

"You need to drink more water," a deep, strident voice said from behind her.

She didn't have to look up to know who stood in front of the sun for her; she could already smell his scent. It wasn't enough to keep the liquid from filling her mouth.

She spewed again.

Great! Maybe the day could get worse.

"I didn't bring any water." She tried to swallow the relentless surges of queasiness. "I was going to refill on the ship."

The shadow moved to crouch beside her. "Drink this."

When she finally had the courage to look up, Artem Stryker was holding out his metal flask of water. The hand that offered it to her had a rose inked into it.

"You need that," she refused, tearing her eyes away from a hand that knew her body well. "I will be fine."

"I will find another source when we get to Skyelir; the place is brimming with fresh water." He urged her to take it again. "I want you to drink it."

His handsome face, strong and fierce, looked down on her with eyes golden like the sun.

With a trembling hand, she cursed inwardly and reached out to take it from him. Placing the cool steel to her lips, she drank, and the freezing liquid finally seemed to settle her raging stomach and burning throat. Taking a few breaths as she sagged against the sand, she uttered, "Thank you."

Artem grinned. "Can the princess wolf not handle a portal?"

One of the warrior's inked hands came down—the one that bore a skull—as he offered to help pull her up. Fighting against her pride, she slapped her hand into his, and he hoisted her off the ground.

His infuriatingly perfect eyebrow ventured upwards. "You good?"

She nodded, but when she closed her eyes, all she could see was Waylen's face as he scorned her last night.

In my eyes, you are a lost cause. Just like her.

Her brother's words carved another slash in her heart.

Artem's brow pulled down. "No evil glare? No snide remark? No threat to chop off my balls for calling you princess?"

When she looked up at him, the glow of the sun burned around his back and illuminated the colours of his tattoos. It filled his skin with a thousand pictures of lives that had been before him and traditions he believed in. His russet hair was lighter in the sun, and it sat neatly atop his head, short and tidy. His tunic hugged his ridiculous body, and the steel littering his belt was a sign of how dangerous he could be. He was the chief commander's son, and the crest of his clan sat on his chest.

Her heart's wounds bled out a little more as she took him in.

He was...otherworldly.

His expression soon morphed into a concerned one. There was hardly ever silence between them, and the broken part of her hungered for that normality. Her turmoil was obvious on her face for him to see, and in this moment, as the sea breeze pulled at her hair and the sun shone on him, she didn't care if her sorrow was laid bare.

She couldn't hide it, not when she felt the snake of vulnerability coil around her throat and choke her.

"What's wrong?" he whispered.

He somehow knew.

She inhaled to speak but no words came out, Only the tears that she wanted to hold back so desperately. She would never in her wildest dreams have wanted Artem to see this side of her. She took two steps back. Her legs shook and she wobbled in the sand.

No, she would not feel this.

She would not feel anything.

She couldn't do this.

And you will probably end up fucking one of them and having one of their bastard children right before they marry their witching wife.

"Breighly..." Artem caught her wrist and searched for answers across her face. "What is wrong? What happened? I can feel...something."

"Stop!" she cut in.

Roman was the only one who knew when she was on a downward spiral into the pit of self-hate. Everyone else saw her as someone who was so confident and fearless, but she had her moments of weakness. And Artem Stryker had just witnessed one of them.

Fuck!

Breighly managed to shake her head and tried to pull back her wrist from his warm grip.

"Something has." He pulled her closer, and one of his hands found her shoulder. "I have never seen you like this. You're shaking."

She managed to shove him off. Eyes would be on them for sure, and she was just as much a warrior as him. "It is not a special honour to see me this way. You have never seen me this way because no one ever does."

His eyes narrowed as he stumbled back, caught off guard at her sudden movement. But then his full lips parted and his soft golden eyes warmed. "Just talk to me. Let me see if there is anything that I can do—"

"There is nothing you can do," she hissed.

He flinched.

Oh fuck, she could feel her claws sharpening under her skin.

Waylen's words hardened around her heart.

You're a lost cause.

She was a mess, but Artem was good, warm, and stable. He was a Hunter of Thorin.

What the fuck was she doing? She wasn't going to drag him into her mess. She was a wolf and he was a hunter from one of the wealthiest and most powerful clans in Caledorna. What did she think was going to happen? As much as she knew he liked her and couldn't get enough of her, he would marry a high-ranking witch and Breighly would find a mate.

She was a girl who found it hard to run a tavern in the city. She struggled to feel anything but rebellion and a thirst for trouble. She liked to bite off more than she could chew and said horrible things when she was hurting. She was a girl who liked to challenge the world, yet couldn't handle it when her heart challenged her head.

Artem reached for her again, but she withdrew like a viper that felt threatened. And like her, when vipers felt threatened, they spat poison. She couldn't let Artem Stryker into her heart anymore. Somehow, he had managed to wiggle in a little, and it was time she shut it down and lived up to her reputation.

"Stay the fuck away from me," she said, feeling the poison of her self-hatred turning her heart dark. "I mean it, Artem Stryker. Get away from me. And do not lay another hand on me."

His face was a mix of hurt, anger, and confusion as he looked at her, a little gulp tracking down his throat.

"You need to stay away from me."

She turned from him, the memory of his face burning in her mind, and didn't look back as she walked along the beach of Tolsah to find a moment alone.

CHAPTER THIRTY-ONE
TORIN

Artem made his way along the white sand of Tolsah Bay looking like he just had his heart ripped out. Torin had watched as his brother had tried to speak to Breighly, but it had not gone down well. Something had happened back in Ashdale, but Torin didn't have the time right now to figure it out.

Maybe she was having second thoughts about being a guard. If she was, Torin would need to know; it was Emara's life that was at stake should she falter. Emara had taken a risk asking for Breighly to be a part of her cluster; the wolf wasn't a trained hunter or guard, but she had great potential.

He would have to watch the wolf closely.

Emara had also watched the altercation between them from a sand dune. Men were still coming through Sybil's portal, and he could see Gideon herding everyone towards the dock.

Torin hid a smile from his brother as he moved towards Emara. "What do you think that was about?" he asked as he approached, nodding at Breighly.

Emara's shapely eyebrows pulled together, and she rolled her lips. "What they have...it's complicated."

"Like 'us' complicated, or like 'ancient magic of Caledorna Gods' complicated?"

"'Ancient magic' complicated." She stared out at the glistening sea that met the blue sky in a profound embrace. "I didn't know what they had was quite so deep until...well, I caught them in my bed a few nights ago."

"You what? You caught them in your bed? They should both be punished for that, Emara."

"They are already punishing themselves by feeling the way they do for each other." She finally looked up at him. "Why would I add anything else on top of that?"

Torin hummed. "So you think there are feelings involved from both sides?" He took a seat beside her in the sand.

"Mmm." She hummed.

He could see that something was lingering below the surface, waiting to get out. He wondered if her darkness was scratching under her skin for release.

Torin leaned in. "Why is it that when people stare at the sea they always seem to be contemplating something serious?"

She let out a small laugh and looked down at her hands buried in the sand. "The first night you agreed to stay in my bed in the Fairlands, I had a dream about this place. But the dream that I had was about Cally and I." She paused as she let grains of the soft sand filter through her fingers. "She always wanted to come here. She said she would start up a business dressing the merchants' wives and that she would be rolling in the coin before she reached cronehood. Callyn claimed no one would look better in a bathing suit than her and that she would make a line of swimsuits so scandalous the women of Tolsah Bay would beam bright red when they saw them. But now I understand why she wanted to come here." Emara looked out to the calm waves once more. "It wasn't because of all the things she had said, but because of the water element in her witching blood. I think the ocean would always call to her. She would have been a vision on this beach with her smile and her golden hair. And she would have lived in every moment, sparkling like the sun herself."

Torin smiled as he remembered the spirit of her best friend.

"Callyn saved me that night at the Amethyst Palace." Emara's gaze finally found Torin. "As I lay choking on the element of my bloodline, Callyn saved me with hers. She came when I needed her and she held my hand when I thought it was the end." Her voice broke, and it made Torin's throat bob. He had thought it was the end too, and he had done everything he could to take the Supreme's magic upon himself instead of Emara. He would have done anything in that moment to stop her from suffocating.

"She would have been so up for this mission just for the simple fact that she would absolutely refuse to go any further than this point and stay here to frolic instead of joining the hunt."

Torin reached out for her hand. She let him take it, and he kissed it gently. "You miss her."

"With every part of my heart." She looked down at her knees as they pushed together. "It never occurred to me that I would have to go through life without her, so it sometimes hits me hard, especially in moments when I need her."

He rubbed his thumb over her skin. "You never know, she might be sitting with you right now on this very beach, admiring how strong you have become and how wonderful you look with the sea wind in your hair. She would be so utterly proud of you, Emara." He squeezed her hand. "And when I tie my soul to yours, I know she will be looking down on you then too. As will your grandmother. Everyone you ever wanted will be there, even if it is in spirit."

Emara nodded as tears washed down her cheeks. "I know." She gripped his hand tighter. "And that is why we are going to find this relic before the Dark Army. I will not have another person taken from this kingdom by their ruthless hands. I will not allow another person to look at this world from the Otherside because of the Dark God. I will not allow another person to feel the sorrow that I do."

Torin guided her to look at him as he promised, "In the darkness of this kingdom, *we* will rise. In the light, the Dark Army will fall. I will not stop hunting them until this world is safe for you and rid of them—and that includes your father."

CHAPTER
THIRTY-TWO
EMARA

Emara was thankful when the Broken Sea decided she wouldn't be too rough with their ship. Every hunter from the Blacksteel clan (with the exception of Viktir and those who stayed behind to guard the Tower) were crowded on the ship's forecastle, going over their first briefing. Torin stood in the middle, letting everyone know that this was their first mission under him and why it had come around. He spoke of its importance and why he needed every man from the clan involved. Emara was shocked when Kellen stood up and told the clan of his seeing abilities, and what was even more remarkable was that no one seemed to think that he would be a curse to the unit. Kellen was one of them. And Torin let them know that if anyone *did* have a problem with his youngest brother, they would have a problem with him too.

"So we're going to the Temple of the Gods, then?" an older clan member asked as he took a sip from his flask.

"That's right," Torin said. "We will rest a few times, especially at the Lake of Rhiannon, but ideally, I would like to get there before the Dark Army, so we can't mess around. If the Protection Stone is there, then we need to make sure we get it first."

The Lake of Rhiannon.

"And if they are already there?" another asked.

Torin's crystal gaze turned a little icier. "If they are already there, then you will do what you were born to do—hunt."

The clan agreed in unison. Emara noted a wolf at the rear of the ship, her golden hair wild in the aquatic breeze. She excused herself and left the clan discussing a strategy for when they got to the temple.

As Emara neared her, Breighly ran a hand under her eye and plastered on a false smile. "Empress."

Emara tutted, finding her sea legs as she staggered closer to the Shifter. "Come on, Breighly, you know better than to call me that when we are alone."

She let out a small snort. "I know. But I like the flash of shock in your eyes every time someone says it."

Emara laughed at the accuracy in her truth as she made her way to sit on a wooden bench. "I can never really hide my emotions well, can I?"

"Not for as long as I have known you." Breighly smiled, but it faded quickly as she looked out at the vast ocean. Its swells moved underneath them like a thousand small whales all coming up for air at once. "But I wouldn't say it's always a bad thing."

"Mmm," Emara hummed. "I think a lot of people would disagree with that."

"Fuck those people," Breighly said softly.

"You don't seem like yourself today." Emara held on to the cedar taffrail that ran all the way along the ship's edges.

"Why does everyone keep saying that?" Breighly's light brows pulled in.

"Maybe because you are alone at the back of the ship instead of bossing around all the hunters at the front. It has them all rather worried."

Emara had also noted that none of the Baxgroll pack had shown up at dawn. Maybe that was the reason for her distance.

Breighly's chocolate eyes narrowed, and she drew in a breath. "I can't be *her* all the time." She glanced at Emara. "I can't be the woman who fights my way to the top every single day of life. It's exhausting. Sometimes my *actual* life gets in the way, you know? Sometimes my mind just needs a break. I don't know how you do it."

Emara had never seen Breighly's features so soft. "I know what you mean," she agreed. "The weight that is put on a woman's shoulders to equal a man in Caledorna is preposterous. But we get the job done. I know the clan likes having you around, as much as they tease you." That earned a small smile from the wolf. "And I do too, Breighly. I wanted you as my guard because I think you are the most capable woman I have ever met."

Breighly's eyes widened at that. The sound of the ship parting the waves filled in their silence for a moment.

"Is there something back home that requires your attention? You know I wouldn't mind you skipping this mission and returning to the Ashdale Forest until you sort out whatever you need to," Emara offered.

There's nothing for me back home, not really." The wolf's forefinger tapped the railing. "Sometimes I just...overthink."

What Emara loved about Breighly was that she appeared to never second-guess anything she did, but apparently, there were more layers to her front than Emara knew.

Emara pinned an untamed strand of hair behind her ear, wishing she had worn it in a braid. "I don't want you to feel pressure to live up to the male guards of the trio. Breighly, I put you forward for the position of protecting my life because of who you are, not for you to prove yourself to anyone. I see who you are, I see the fearless stars that sparkle in your eyes when a challenge is put your way. I see the way that men look at you, not just because you are beautiful, but because they are intimidated by your strength and skill. Women like you are going to change the kingdom. But that doesn't mean you can't be soft, kind, and have emotions. Being my guard doesn't mean you can't have bad days or days you have a good cry. You don't need to be strong all the time. You can just be you."

A little colour made its way back to Breighly's cheeks as she tried to bite back a smile.

"You are a warrior, regardless of your faction of birth. I don't want you to be anything other than yourself. You are not a hunter, you are Breighly Baxgroll."

"It takes a strong woman to understand that she can stand with other strong women and not be threatened." Breighly straightened up from her sulk against the edge of the ship. "That's what my father used to say anyway."

"Murk said that?" Emara was surprised.

"You would be surprised if I told you all the beautiful things my father has said to me."

She smiled. "You're a strong, beautiful, fierce, loyal, and insanely witty wolf. Lean into that."

Breighly finally gave her a smile that lit up her eyes, warming them from that cold stone to honey brown. "You forgot intelligent."

Emara chuckled. "I want you in my trio because I trust you. When I was attacked at the Amethyst Palace, it was by hunters—the people who are supposed to be protecting me and my coven. I knew from the moment that I recovered that I needed something different. I didn't want to see another hunter in my guardship. I wanted someone who looked at the world like I do. I needed a woman who could relate to me. I needed balance. You're the perfect fit. But I understand that you're adjusting to this world. Being around hunters is not easy. You must find it hard to not be free to run with your pack or shift. I understand what you have given up to be here. But I don't always need you to guard me with a weapon, Bry. You are more than capable, in human form and in wolf form." Emara reached over and took Breighly's hand, sending a soothing current of magic into her. "And when you get in your head and tell yourself you are not good enough, you start to believe it. You are enough. Don't let the darkness in, Breighly Baxgroll."

Her voice was meek as she uttered, "I didn't say I wasn't good enough." The wolf wiped away another tear.

"No, you didn't. But I can see that glimmer in your eye that tells me that you are thinking it. I know what it feels like to question everything about yourself, question what your life's purpose is, question if you are on the right path or if you are even in the right skin. But trust me when I say this"—Emara squeezed Breighly's hand—"the moon and stars shine down on you brightly; they know how special you are. I can feel it. I know it."

Breighly gave a thankful smile as she choked back her tears. "Don't tell me you are claiming to be an Empress of House Spirit now too?"

She laughed. "I am getting stronger with spirit, and I can always see and feel things around me. I can even see them around you too. But I wouldn't quite call myself an empress in the element."

"Eli?" she whispered.

Emara nodded, trying to swallow a huge lump in her throat.

The wolf's teary gaze found Emara's face. "I have a feeling that I could be guarding the Supreme soon."

Her airways slammed shut.

Supreme.

"I don't think I will ever be powerful enough to be the Supreme."

"We'll see." Breighly side-eyed her.

A soft wave of silence fell over them as they listened to the merging water slap against the ship's wood. There was a stunning tranquillity about sailing, and for just a second, Emara pictured Cally laughing with Breighly about how society viewed the length of their dresses and their casual attitude to relationships. She imagined Cally bringing out a bottle of sparkling wine from her satchel of tricks and Breighly's eyes lighting up.

They would have been some pair.

Abruptly, Breighly stood and gave a sharp exhale. She shook her head twice and squared her shoulders before looking over to the briefing that was still taking place. She combed her fingers through her beautiful blonde hair. "Please excuse me, Empress."

"Where are you going?" Emara stood too.

"To disconnect a hunter's dick from his body. He commented on my mood earlier in the foyer." That wildly sunning look was back in her eye. "With the moon being full soon, it will only spiral from there. He's in for a treat."

Emara couldn't stop herself from smiling. "Welcome back, Guard Baxgroll."

CHAPTER
THIRTY-THREE
EMARA

Crimson Dock was guarded by Fae officials, and Emara hadn't realised how long it would take to get through their inspections. The Fae king didn't own the land of Skyelir, just the dock, but he was commissioned by the prime to control who went in and out. Not just anyone could enter Skyelir without permission, and portals were banned.

Some people still portalled in, but it was treasonous to not declare yourself at the border. Torin stood at the top of the line as each hunter passed controls. A Fae guard stamped a large black sign next to their names on a scroll that was longer than Emara's leg, granting access to be here on business. Torin had firelettered the king to fill him in on their mission.

Before they made their way to the Temple of the Gods, they would reach the Lake of Rhiannon. The lake was a sacred place below the mountains of Skyelir, shielded by a monstrous forest. It was said to be a spectacular sight. As Emara took in the Skyelir breeze, she could feel her magic tingle in her blood.

Once they had passed the dock authorities, the real journey began. After a full day, they still hadn't reached the lake yet. The Wolf Moon was mere days away, and her beating energy radiated down on them powerfully. Breighly had informed her that it was considered a mating moon in the wolf community, and it gave birth to new and intense connections.

Or, in her own words, "*It made everyone raunchy as shit.*"

Emara could have sworn she saw a hint of jade in the glow of the moon, but that could have just been the forest. The area was rich in berries and beautiful flowers that fragranced the air. Trees as tall as the Tower sheltered them as they moved between them and to Emara, it looked like most parts of Skyelir lay untouched.

Artem had informed Torin of a place he and his clan camped out on their many trips here, just on the outskirts of Lake Rhiannon.

"Here where the ground is flatter should be good," Artem advised, pointing to a small clearing. Gideon dumped a few of his things on the mossy ground; it appeared that he had been carrying Sybil's supplies too.

Sybil made her way across the clearing and grabbed Emara's hand. "I wouldn't mind sleeping under the stars tonight, would you?"

Emara toyed with the idea of sleeping under the stars without a tent. "That sounds beautiful."

"I don't think so," Marcus Coldwell said as he walked past, carrying a massive log. "The women will sleep in the tents; us clan members can handle the wild."

"Speak for yourself." A more upbeat Breighly Baxgroll sauntered into the conversion holding an axe. "I think the *ladies* will choose where they will want to rest their heads tonight and have no questions asked."

Marcus leaned in, full of mischief. "It's a good thing you are a wolf and not an empress, Miss Baxgroll. You can rest your little wolfy head wherever you like."

She flung out her axe, smacking the log from Marcus' hands. It plummeted onto the toes of his boots.

He let out a shriek and bent down to grip his toe.

"Oops. My *little wolfy* hands just don't know how to control themselves these days."

The group let out a few laughs as several curses left Marcus.

Breighly severed the space between them. "Now who is howling like a *little wolf,* Coldwell?"

The clan around them broke out into laughter, and Marcus shouted a few curses at them, waving his hands for them to stop. Breighly winked at Emara before leaving to help set up a tent with Gideon.

"Don't injure my men, Baxgroll," barked Torin. "And no laughter until this camp looks ready for this evening. I want tents and stations set up quickly." He glanced over to Emara, who had let out a small chuckle too. His hair looked like spilled ink over his forehead under the silver of the moonbeams, but it was his ocean eyes that caught her attention. They twinkled with sin. "I said no laughter, Clearwater."

Emara bit down on her lip as she moved a little closer. "Do I need to remind you that you may be *their* commander but you are not mine, Torin Blacksteel?"

She could feel every ounce of heat that radiated from him as he towered above her. He leaned in to whisper to her, "Do I need to remind you of what you said whilst I had you sprawled over my desk only one night ago?"

A hitch in her breath gave away the fact that she did remember, and that familiar tingle in her core rose up her spine. Nevertheless, she shut it down, knowing that she had to fight for a little bit of control around here. "Commander Blacksteel," she whispered back, and she could feel her voice lure him closer, "if you don't keep your voice down and stop barking orders at me, you will never see me sprawled across that desk again."

All she could see was his dazzling grin. "I better be careful, then, because not seeing you over that desk as I taste every part of you would be an utter travesty."

She swallowed hard at the thought of him working his mouth all the way down to between her thighs. "Yes, Commander. It would be a travesty, so you better work on that indoor voice before you have a very disappointed empress."

He brought a hand up to track his fingertips along her collar bone and tuck a wild strand of hair behind her ear. "A commander does not have an indoor voice, angel. So I must beg for your forgiveness." He leaned in to claim her lips.

She stuck up one finger, and his mouth hit against it. "Well, he better find one soon if he is going to be welcomed by me in my tent tonight. I am sure you'll figure it out." She gave him a wink and patted his chest before leaving to make herself useful in the setup of the camp. She heard him whistle softly, but she didn't dare look back.

CHAPTER
THIRTY-FOUR
GIDEON

An array of cheeses was being passed around, and there were different liquors depending on who you sat next to. The smells of bourbon, whiskey, rum, and wine all lingered in the sweet night air. They'd roasted meat on a fire Emara had started with her own hands. It was good to see her laughing with the clan, accepting them as much as they accepted her. The men didn't get overly involved with the wives of clan, but she was no ordinary wife-to-be.

Sybil was buttering bread as she sat on a log next to the fire. Lorta and Kaydence sat beside her, a woven blanket around their laps, each taking turns to dish out the food. His mother had come along too—she would never miss Torin's union—but she was already in her tent for the night. Gideon's eyes fell back on Sybil. The trees around them seemed to develop more colour as she sat next to them. More flowers started to bloom, even at nightfall, and the sweet smell of cut grass and honey drifted over from where she perched.

Sybil was also an empress, yet here she sat, cutting bread. Something hitched in his chest.

Although Gideon had had a fair amount of food, he wasn't sure if Sybil had eaten anything yet. She was probably too busy helping the men to take anything for herself. Using his small steel tray, he gathered a few cubes of cheese, a selection of whatever meat was left, and wine before sitting down on her log. The heat from her body touched his arm as he nestled beside her.

Kaydence and Lorta gave one look at each other and then moved quickly away, mumbling about helping Emara.

"Bread?" Sybil asked him.

Gideon shook his head, offering her a polite smile. "Sybil, have you eaten anything yet?"

"I will." She nodded. "Just after I make sure everyone else has had something."

Typical earth witch, always putting everyone else's well-being before her own.

"Here." He handed her the small tray of food. "Eat this; I will take over the bread. I think us hunters are capable enough to cut through a loaf and butter it." He smiled at her as he removed the knife from her small hand. "They've probably all had more than enough anyway."

She took the tray of food from him. "I just like to make sure everyone has something to nourish them."

"Well, how are you going to nourish everyone when you are not nourishing yourself?"

Her nose wrinkled and the freckles across her cheeks danced. A small breeze blew embers up into the air, and she combed a hand through her hair, leaving a curl bouncing across her face. "You shouldn't worry about me, Gideon."

He placed down the knife and bread that he hadn't even attempted to cut yet. "What kind of guard would I be if I didn't worry about your well-being?"

A moment passed between them, and Gideon was sure there was a little flush in her cheeks. It was probably just the warmth of the fire.

"I was going to ask..." Sybil's voice brought his gaze away from the enchanting flames. "Instead of sleeping in my tent tonight, I thought maybe we could sleep out underneath the stars."

We.

His heart pounded.

The way her skin caught the attention of the moon was staggering, soft and creamy, like it had been blessed by the Goddess Rhiannon herself. For a brief moment, he envisioned them lying together under the stars. "You mean like sleeping out close to the fire for more heat?"

Her blush-coloured lips pulled into a curve. "No, I mean like wild camp, Gideon. Sleep under the stars with some rugs." Her stunning mossy eyes lit up, and Gideon found himself wanting to agree immediately. "We never got the chance when we were travelling to the Amethyst Palace because of the icy conditions, but since it is close to summer solstice, I thought we could."

We.

Again.

Gideon looked across to where her other guards sat talking, Arlo with Kellen and Marcus with a kid who had newly passed his Selection.

Gideon didn't want to burst her bubble. "Arlo would probably say yes, but I don't know if Marcus would be happy with that."

She leaned in close, causing Gideon's heart to stammer. "We don't need to tell him. Besides, you would be with me. No risk, right?"

Gideon's pulse hammered in his neck, and he found his tunic almost too tight. *No risk.*

Her smile was brighter than the moon herself, and he found himself grinning back at her. "Tell me, Empress of Earth, what other mischief do you get up to behind the backs of your guards?"

She let out a small giggle and she took a cube of cheese in her hand. "Maybe I could show you tonight, beneath the stars."

The knife tumbled from Gideon's tray and hit the ground. The shy flush on Sybil's cheeks told Gideon that she knew what had come out her mouth was not how she had meant for it to sound. He leaned down to pick up the knife and placed it back on the tray, a little more flustered than he would have liked.

He cleared his throat.

The Wolf Moon had a lot to answer for. Even he could feel its effects. He was her guard, for Gods' sakes.

He leaned closer. "I won't tell Marcus if you won't," he said, stealing a piece of meat that she hadn't touched.

"I love when you get that glint in your eye."

Her words took his breath away.

"What glint?" he asked, his voice rough.

Her lashes swept up, and the look that burned from underneath was pure, unintentional seduction. "The one that appears when you feel like living for something other than the hunt."

Her words smacked his chest again.

"It doesn't happen often, Mr Serious." She nudged him, and a tender laugh escaped her. "But when it does, your eyes glitter and your features relax into something...wonderful."

Again, no air could make its way in or out his lungs, and he could feel an energy running through his spine that was sparking all sorts of forbidden feelings.

"Anyway, thanks for the assortment of foods." She stood, placing the tray down on the log. "I am going to head over to my tent now, but I trust you will come and find me when everyone else is asleep." Delight crossed her face and something prosperous danced in his heart. "See you soon, Gideon Blacksteel."

He watched her as she veered over to Arlo, who rose to follow her to the tent. The younger Stryker took up post, and he could hear Sybil telling him that Gideon would relieve him soon before she disappeared behind the fabric of the tent. With a large exhale,

Gideon's gaze was back on the fire that reminded him so much of her hair.

As the night drew on, hunters trickled off to find their bed beneath the stars or stand guard. Gideon had watched the embers burn down as the camp turned silent. Hushed breathing could be heard over the hooting owl in the distance.

Kellen still hadn't turned in yet. His younger brother sat on a faraway log, nursing a glass of wine. His eyes were heavy, and it was clear he was doing anything he could to stay awake.

Gideon made his way across the clearing.

"What a wild few days, huh?" He sat next to his youngest brother on the soft forest floor, and even as the stars burned bright in the sky, Gideon could still feel the summer heat clinging to his skin.

"I don't think wild even cuts it," Kellen whispered as he took a sip of his wine, spinning a dagger through the fingers in his other hand.

"No, it doesn't." Gideon pulled his knees up and clasped his hands around them. "I prayed to the Three-Faced God for you this morning, especially when Torin told me that you were telling everyone today about your Dreams."

Kellen's lips pulled down and arched an eyebrow. "And how did that go? Did she listen?" He stabbed the dagger into the ground.

"Who knows?" Gideon drove a hand through his hair that was messy from the salty Tolsah Bay air. "I suppose everyone took your news well."

"Careful, brother. Every time we think we are getting on our feet, something else happens." Kellen's eyes lingered on the blade too long before a yawn broke through. "I can't remember a time when things have changed so much."

Gideon nodded as he glanced over at Kellen.

The baby of the Blacksteels was a baby no more.

His jaw was more defined, his arms were bulkier, and his eyebrows pulled down into a scowl. The paleness of the moon's glow highlighted the lilac circles under Kellen's haunted eyes that told Gideon he hadn't had a proper rest in days. Kellen had always been different, gentler and more refined.

Gideon's voice was soft and gentle as he said, "I am proud of you for letting us know what you are. It was brave of you." He cast his gaze up to see Kellen's nostrils flare in apprehension. "You are a member of this family, our blood. The old legend of the seer is not going to change your course in the clan. It doesn't change anything."

"Doesn't it?" Kellen finally looked up. "Because we both know that is not true. If I were not Torin's brother, I would have been dismissed from my post, treated like I had some sort of plague for hunters. Don't pretend. I am safe—for now—because of who our commander is. It doesn't mean I am safe anywhere else. Hunters hate seers. They think they are weak. A curse. A disgrace of Thorin's blood."

Something burned deep inside of Gideon. "I have not heard one man mention your gift since we had our briefing."

Kellen's glare met Gideon's, a heavy intensity lingering there. "That's because my big brother commanded them not to."

Gideon knew what it was like to have Torin's legacy cloud his own. He was the first-born son, and in his own way, he was everything a warrior of Thorin should be. No man or beast dared to mess with Gideon or Kellen because they knew they had Torin to answer to. And he had cut down men for less harsh words than what Kellen had mentioned.

"Torin may have commanded that the clan accept you, but we are under new times. Our men are good men. Maybe Torin will bring forth a change in mentality with his commandership. Thorin knows he encourages Emara to do things that the old traditions say she shouldn't. He allows women to fight with the clan. He allows wolves to fight with the clan. He won't allow anyone to have a prejudiced outlook on them, so why would he let them do that to you?"

His brother released his bottom lip. "It's not as easy as that for me. It's not like everything is right with who I am because I told the clan of my abilities," Kellen argued. "I know there are going to be men who do not agree that I should fight. I know that men will hold their tongues on what I am because of Torin and because of my name. But it doesn't mean they will proudly fight next to me like they do with you."

Gideon's heart fractured a little. "Well, you know that your brothers will always have your back. We will always support you; that's what blood does. Fuck anything or anyone else." He moved in a little closer and lowered his voice. "But until you are sure of who you are and until you own that, you will always find yourself unhappy Kellen, regardless of what others think."

Gideon knew that to be true because he had felt it, especially after what he did to Emara. When he had stolen the Resurrection Stone and seen the look on her face when she realised what he had done, it had forced him to think about his morals. It had forced him to question who he was as a person and if he was truly happy with what he saw in the mirror. The truth was, he had hated himself.

"I will work on it," Kellen said unconvincingly as he drained the last of his glass of wine.

"Good." He patted Kellen on the shoulder and rested his hand there. "I am proud of you. You gave strength a new meaning today."

"Thanks, big brother," he choked out.

Just as Gideon moved to stand, midnight black hair caught his eye. It made its way out from an empress tent and into the forest.

"Excuse me," Gideon said as he made his way towards Emara. She should not be wandering out here alone, and he wondered if her guards were asleep.

He didn't have to walk long to catch up with her. She stood at the clearing's opening against a huge fir tree, gazing up at the almost-full moon that had an emerald glow around it.

"Hey," he said softly.

She turned around to face him, and Gideon wondered why no one had ever painted her. She held such exquisite beauty and grace, yet there was an edge to her too. She reminded him of a siren's call, as dangerous as she was beautiful.

"Gideon." She gasped like he'd scared her despite his gentle approach.

"I didn't mean to startle you," he said. "I just wondered where you were going without your guards."

Her curved eyebrow raised, and a smirk broke her lips apart. "An empress can walk without her guards, you know."

He smiled back. "I know."

He knew better than to challenge her these days. The power that was beginning to radiate from her was magnificent, and even now as he stood a few feet from her, he could feel the elements of her magic on his skin. It was inspiring and terrifying.

Her gaze turned back up to the moon, and as Gideon came to stand beside her, he noticed that her face seemed troubled.

"Can't sleep?"

Emara chewed on her cheek and shook her head. There was a comfortable moment between them before she spoke again. "No matter how many times I look at the moon and am in awe of her beauty, a little part of me wonders why she merely watches from her castle in the sky as darkness rushes in on us. It's rather cruel, is it not?"

Her profound words hit him like a knee to the gut, and it was like he had never seen her in this light before. The air around her had changed; she commanded it now. She carried herself differently from when he had first met her, and she sounded like someone who had been on a throne for years.

"That is because the moon is waiting for you to follow her light into battle and do everything on these lands that she cannot. You are her vessel on earth like I am Thorin's."

Emara turned to Gideon, and a gentle wind swept over both of their faces, ruffling their hair. He was sure it was her element because it was stronger than a summer breeze. A staggering pride broke through him for the girl he had found welcoming death at the hands of a knight of the underworld. Back then, she had no idea who was. She had been no one. Anyone.

But now she knew exactly who she was.

She had magic in her veins and darkness in her blood. She was Emara of House Air. She was Fire and Earth. She was Wind and Water, Spirits and Enchantments. And he could feel that her ancestors were watching her from above.

"Gideon?" A small voice came from the woodland behind him, and he turned to see Sybil standing with a few fur rugs slung over her arm.

"Sybil," he choked out. Guilt instantly raked through him.

Sybil's eyes strained with something unspoken, and her cheeks flushed with something that was neither delight nor desire.

It was embarrassment, he was sure of it. But he couldn't understand why.

"I had no idea you were still up, Emara. I am sorry if I am interrupting something between you." Sybil nodded towards the Empress of Air.

Emara looked to her friend and then to Gideon. "You are not interrupting anything. I was just heading back to bed. I only needed a moment with the moon." She smiled at them. "Goodnight, you two."

Emara took her leave between the trees, and it left only the silence between them, lingering thicker than the darkness. Sybil glared at him, waiting until Emara had gone before saying, "When you didn't come and find me, I thought I would come and find you."

"I was just about to come—"

Sybil looked down at the folds of her blankets as she cut him off. "Are you still in love with her, Gideon?"

He wasn't sure if he could take any more blows to his chest tonight, but Sybil's words punched him hard. His words bubbled in his throat, and the truth that he so desperately wanted to say tied his tongue in knots. He was so caught off guard by the look on Sybil's face that his mind dissolved into a blank nothingness. Why did that pain in his chest tighten?

"It's a simple question, Gideon," Sybil said, frustration flashing in her eyes. "Do you still love her?"

Sybil knew of his heartache, of his past with Emara, as he had opened up to her about it during their travels and time at the palace together. But that seemed like so far in the past, and so much had happened in between the Blood Moon and the one he stood under now.

His lips parted to say that she didn't own his heart, but nothing came from his mouth.

Sybil looked at him in a way that made Gideon's heart thump in his chest. "Understood," she whispered.

"I didn't say anything." He stepped forward, reaching for her.

"You didn't have to." She stepped back, placing a hand up for him to keep his distance.

"Sybil..." He hesitated about telling her the truth. It wasn't the Empress of Air who he dreamt of, who he couldn't wait to see in the morning. He didn't dream of kissing the Empress of Air. But he didn't know if it was professional of him to overstep the line between them. His heart had somehow shifted, and he didn't know how to handle it.

Sybil Lockhart had snuck into his broken heart and mended it.

Sybil turned and was out of sight before his stupid feet would work to go after her. "Sybil, no. Wait!" But she was gone, and his voice rang through the trees—and possibly the camp. He placed his hands atop his head. "Shit!"

CHAPTER
THIRTY-FIVE
TORIN

They reached the outskirts of Lake Rhiannon a few hours before sunset the next day. The forest's canopy was the only reprieve from the summer's sun during the day, and they had tried to keep in the shade during their vigorous hike. Weapons and tents were carried between the men, and the women had taken the food and medical supplies. But even at dusk the air was so thick and moist with heat; he had perspiration in places he didn't even sweat after a full day of Viktir's training.

Viktir Blacksteel.

His father's name rang through him like a temple bell, buzzing and vibrating in his heart. He didn't want to give his father much thought, especially not on this day, but the time would come when he would need to face him and deliver his punishment fully. He was still considering what role he would have him play in the clan.

Boot scrubber.

Weapon polisher.

Personal ass-kisser to the commander.

Maybe mucking out the stables was a kind role to give a man who had ruined a big part of the goodness you had held as a child.

He was supposed to punish the men who chose his father over him too. Torin did not blame them for choosing Viktir. He understood that no one liked change, and some struggled more than others to accept it.

However, there were other pressing matters at hand. Like the fact that he would be wed to Emara Clearwater at dusk.

The pulse in his neck was hammering as he thought of her being his wife. Hope swelled in his chest where he always tried to balance it with reality. But today, he couldn't. She was going to be his *wife*. Emara Clearwater, the girl from Mossgrave who had turned out to mean more to the kingdom than anyone would have ever thought, was to be intertwined with his soul, his and hers combined for eternity.

He would forever be grateful that his path had led him to her.

He knew the nuptials wouldn't last as long as they normally did —usually taking days—as they had to make their way to the Temple of the Gods. But he could make that up to her in other ways. He could spend the rest of their lives making it up to her. He wasn't going to think of a single thing that involved demon hunting or the Dark Army tonight.

He would be present, absorbing every moment. He would enjoy all of her and cherish this night, and no one or no *thing* would change that. Even Thorin knew not to interfere with his life today. For so many long, torturous years, he couldn't even imagine having what he had now. Emara Clearwater had given him hope, a chance at a future that was full of things that were real and raw, things that made his heart full. They could spend long nights exploring each other until dawn split the trees. They could exchange gifts at winter solstice. Thorin's tradition dictated he gift her weapons, but he would give her so much more; he wanted to spoil her with everything she ever wanted. On clan birthdays and weddings, they would stand together. They would have dinners with everyone that would bring joy and quiet evenings alone that would bring solace. He could watch her read, dream, and practice magic. They would have so many moments together that no one else would share.

Torin had a future with her, a true partnership.

But Torin knew he would never be Emara's equal; she was superior in every way. But she had chosen him back anyway.

Something jumped in his heart at the thought of it all.

He turned around, looking behind himself to see a weary clan with the same sticky skin he had. Emara walked just behind him with Breighly and Sybil on either side; they were chatting about a book Sybil had read. All of them had perspiration in their hairlines and a flush on their cheeks. But they were keeping pace, and he was proud of them for it. Gideon was scouting the area with his bow in his hand. Kellen, to his surprise, was just behind Emara and engaged in conversation with Arlo, his eyes shining bright. His mother and Emara's maids walked in the middle of the formation, and all the remaining hunters surrounded them as a coat of protection.

But he could see the exhaustion in their eyes, the heat of the sun draining their energy.

"Halt," he yelled, loud enough to scare birds from their perches overhead "This is the spot. We will stop here. Get yourselves hydrated and cooled down."

Just around the treeline to the left was Lake Rhiannon, and Torin could see the glimmer of her waters through the gaps in the branches. Already, his magical blood sang Rhiannon's song, her mystical aura calling to him. The magic of the grounds was already whisking through the clan in a summer breeze, refreshing them.

Torin remembered the last time he had been at a God's hallowed place, the Waterfall of Uttara, where he first kissed Emara. The stars had truly exploded above them to form other galaxies as he claimed her mouth. He would remember that first kiss for the rest of his existence.

He shook the memory out of his mind and the excitement out of his leathers as he realised all eyes were on him, his clan still waiting on a command. "Rest up after the camp is set." He glanced over at Emara. "And I will see you before sundown."

How could someone look so fucking sensual in plain training gear? The material hugged the curves of her breasts and hips. And praise Thorin that he couldn't see her from behind; her ass was perfection, especially in tight black leggings.

He needed to banish these thoughts before the ceremony.

"Stryker, Coldwell, Limebode, Wellholme! Scout out the perimeter before helping the rest set up. I will take the north with Stryker, and I want the rest of you to comb the east and west regions."

"Baxgroll," he called over to the wolf, "and Gideon, can you take the south?"

"On it," she said, and he quickly wondered if she would shift to cover more ground in less time.

They had come in from the south, but he wanted to make sure no one had been trailing them.

"Leave no stone unturned before the ceremony." His powerful voice reached out to them all, and he was surprised at how official he sounded.

He gave Emara a quick wink and she shot him a smile back. Everything had moved very fast since Kellen's vision, but she had assured him back at the Tower that she wanted this.

Artem jogged beside him as Torin turned to secure the north perimeter.

It was a few minutes before Artem spoke. "I was thinking—"

"Actually, I wanted to catch you on your own," Torin said. He turned to see his friend slowing down, interested in what he had to say. "I know we have joked around about this more times than I can count, but—"

Artem ground to a halt. "Torin, my man, are you about to ask me to be your best man?"

Torin let out a sigh, trying to pull back any amusement that had already leaked through. "Not my best man, Artem. I have two brothers I would consider for that position before you."

Artem's face fell. "The deceit."

"However, we do need someone who is versed in hunting marital vows."

Artem's eyes lit up. "You want me to be your officiant?"

Torin placed a hand on Artem's sturdy shoulder. "You're as good as anyone here, Stryker. We have been through a lot together, you and I." Torin cleared his throat before any real emotion worked its way out from his heart. "Plus, you looked after Emara when I didn't. And though she would never admit it, I know she loves you. I appreciate what you have done for her more than you will ever know. I owe you."

"Don't mention it." Artem coughed down his own emotion, but it lingered longer on his face than the Stryker Clan normally allowed. "You know I would do anything for you both."

He liked that Artem had a secret depth to him. He was less fond of how he'd let Emara do as she pleased, like going to the pits, but that was a conversation for another day.

Torin cleared his throat. "So how do you feel about it?"

"Is this why you paired yourself with me, so we could have this wonderful moment together in the woods?" The most Artem-Stryker grin pulled across his face.

Torin didn't hide his eye roll. "Stryker, you have three more seconds to answer me before I change my mind and ask Marcus. We all know he is the better choice."

"Of course I will, brother." He leaned over to pat his shoulder. "I would be honoured. And over my favourite tattoos is Marcus the better choice; I have more star qualities than him."

"Good." Torin cleared his throat, keeping his eyes on the greenery ahead as he stalked through the forest. "I am glad you can finally put your star qualities to good use."

"I brought a clean tunic just in case you asked me." He sniggered.

Torin laughed as they powered through the trees. "You really are a dick."

"Aw, stop fighting the fact that you love me."

Torin huffed a laugh as his eyes roamed the land around them. There was a silence between them as they settled into a jog, his legs already heavy from how much they had walked today.

"Tell me something, Blacksteel," Artem said, sounding surprisingly serious. "What does it feel like when you meet the one you want to spend the rest of your life with?"

"What a fucking question, brother." Torin shook his head.

"I know it's a big one, but how will I know if I have found something special?"

Torin thought about how much Artem had been losing his shit over Breighly. "You just know. You can feel it somewhere deeper than your heart. It's not your heart that is ruling your emotions, but your soul." Torin swallowed. "It's not as fickle as your heart's feelings; it's more like your soul wrapping around someone else's. It's something that the stars will know before you do."

Artem hummed before letting out a sigh. "That's beautiful, Tori-boy. I always knew you had a poet's heart."

Torin scoffed. "Fuck off, Stryker. My heart is pure warrior through and through."

"I am serious." Artem pushed away a huge branch that was in their way. "I think we hunters struggle with being emotional. Eventually, I want to have what you and Emara have. And I can't see how it's possible if I think about marriage being for nothing more than power. I want it to be about feeling, you know?"

Torin's dark heart wavered, and he risked a side glance to see Artem's brows pulled down over his golden eyes. "You will get there, brother."

"I know." He sighed. Torin could see Artem contemplating something serious before he noticed him watching. "Okay, I don't know about you, but I am itching to get back so that I can wind up Emara about how I will be conducting the vows at the ceremony."

Torin's brow lifted. "You do realise that she could emerge as the Supreme of this kingdom at any time but you still want to go back and fuck with her before one of the biggest moments of her life?"

"Of course I do." His gilded eyes sparkled. "We are best friends. She won't harm me."

"You're a braver man than me, Stryker."

CHAPTER
THIRTY-SIX
EMARA

The sky above Lake Rhiannon was utterly breathtaking in its pink and gold glory. The broken wisps of clouds had parted, giving the overall backdrop a stunning softness as the subtle pastels from the sun's rays glinted off the still waters. Bristlecone pines edged around the far end of the lake, and from what Emara could see from behind the tent flap, it looked like little white candles outlined a walkway on the grass.

Her throat closed shut.

She had washed up the minute everyone had begun setting up camp and then the rituals of the coven had begun. Lorta had brushed her hair, cleaned her feet with moonwater infused in lilacs, and painted her lips red. Emara barely heard the chatter outside her tent through the drumming of her pulse in her ears. Kaydence hummed a sweet melody as she weaved wild roses and gypsophila into Emara's intricate braid.

Naya Blacksteel's head popped in the opening of the tent. Almost immediately, her eyes filled with pride as she looked at Emara in a white slip dress. "Oh, my love, you are just beautiful."

Emara looked towards Kaydence and Lorta, and they bowed out, leaving her alone with Naya. She inhaled a huge breath and then blew it out.

Naya nodded as if knowing the nerves that were fluttering

around in her heart. "Are you all right? I feel like we haven't had a moment to catch our breath lately. I wanted to check in on you."

Emara swallowed, nodding again. "Yes, I–I...Weirdly..." She tried again, her eyes sweeping over the tent, "This feels exactly where I should be."

Naya's smile was so warm and inviting. "I don't think that's weird at all. I saw this moment for you." She walked towards her, her tiny fingers linking with Emara's. "I knew you would become family some day. And I know that I promised you that my boys would look after you, but I am just so happy it's you."

The lump in Emara's throat thickened. "And they have looked after me. They have saved me more than they will ever know."

"And now Torin gets to do that for the rest of his life." Naya squeezed her hands as an excited yet emotional smile reached her eyes. "He will always save you."

Emara squeezed back. "And I promise to look after him. I will always fight for him, Naya."

Naya's smile softened. "I know you will look after my son. You are made for each other."

Emara's breathing hitched as she heard the truth.

"You are all he has ever wanted, and I truly wish you the best life together." Naya pulled back, wiping a finger under her eye. "I hope you don't mind, but I have a little something for you."

Emara's eyebrows pulled down. "You do? You didn't need to get me anything."

"Yes I did, my girl." Naya walked over to the opening of the tent and appeared a second later with a huge box. Emara didn't remember seeing it at all whilst travelling here. "I wrote to King Oberon about your union here and he arranged for this to be brought to you." She sat the box on the ground. "It's a good thing the king understands the importance of one's attire on such a special occasion."

Emara gasped at the thought. Had Naya arranged for a dress to come from the Faerie court? Emara had made her peace with the simple dress she wore now; she'd had to travel lightly.

"Open it when I am gone," she encouraged. "Take your time and feel the magic of this gown. It is breathtaking." Her stunning blue eyes twinkled. "You will be a vision, Emara Clearwater. I am so proud of you, just like your mother and grandmother would be if they could see you at this moment. I know they will be here today, standing with us all as we watch you build a future."

Tears fought to pour from her eyes, but Emara didn't let them fall. Her lip trembled, but she couldn't ruin the effort that Lorta and Kaydence had put into her face. She sucked in a tremor. "Thank you, Naya. For everything."

Breighly popped her head in through the opening of the tent. "It's almost time. The sun is setting. Kellen was certain it happened at sundown, right?"

"Yes." Emara nodded, feeling a few nerves snake in her belly. "That's what the Gods showed him in the vision."

Naya bowed slowly and then her fierce crystal gaze was back on her face. "As the new Commanding Wife of the Blacksteel Clan, I know you will change this world. One step at a time. There is no one else I would rather take my place."

CHAPTER THIRTY-SEVEN
EMARA

The gown had stolen her breath and her heart from the minute she had opened the box. It had soft bell sleeves and the structured bodice was covered in embroidery of tiny star-beaded crystals. Coming down from the corset, the sparkling gold embroidery flowed into a full skirt with a beautiful blush underskirt. She was honoured that King Oberon had allowed her to have this. It was already gorgeous in the dull light; she couldn't wait to see it in the glow of the setting sun. It was the most beautiful gown she had ever laid eyes on, and she wondered for a moment if the Queen of the Fae had worn such a grand gown. She felt like a queen—an empress. Pulling up her hand, the black diamond in her ring twinkled at her like it was supposed to be with her at this moment.

It felt so right.

Breighly Baxgroll's blonde head popped back into the tent. Kaydence and Lorta had entered moments ago to make sure every detail was attended to. Her beautiful brown eyes flickered with emotion. "Everyone is gathered by the lake. They are ready to begin when you are." She smiled gently, and it was very unlike her.

Emara's heart stammered in her chest, causing both heat and coolness to travel along her skin. She was woozy like she had had a glass of wine.

She wished she had.

She nodded at the wolf, who smiled and said, "What a vision you are, Emara. Torin is going to die—but in the best way, of course."

Kaydence let out a small giggle and Lorta snorted. "I do say, Kaydence, we make a good team. The empress looks utterly beautiful."

"It isn't hard with a face like hers and a heart that shines through for everyone to see. We are so honoured to have this moment with you."

Emara took a breath and smiled back at the girls who had made her more comfortable in the world of magic than she could ever say. "Can I have one moment to myself, please?" They nodded, understanding her requirement to take a few beats to herself.

She presumed the women had moved to the ceremonial space without her because she heard no chatter from outside the tent as she stood taking a few deep breaths.

In the silence of her tent, with her heart fluttering, she knew one thing was missing. She reached for her satchel and dug around until her hand hit something velvet. She pulled out an emerald pouch, and her heart sank. Pulling its drawstrings, she slid out the weighty crescent moon. The different diamonds and stones in it dazzled as she slid it into her braid.

Her own moonlight.

It had been Cally's last gift to her.

When she'd given it to her, Emara had sworn to never forget the look in her eyes. Emara's eyes fluttered shut, and she heard Callyn's voice drift through the tent.

If there is anything in the world that represents who you are, it's the moon. She shines in times of darkness, and everyone looks at her to lead us into a better day.

With her pin in her hair, she was ready to walk to where Torin

stood waiting for her. She hadn't had time to study how the ceremony would work, but he would guide her through it. She trusted
him to see her right. She could depend on him to always have her
back.

Her stomach flipped as she slipped outside. She closed her eyes
again as the warm summer breeze tickled her skin, and she wished
Cally was here to walk with her down the aisle.

A trail of colourful petals wove a path to the top of the altar. The
flames burned brighter as she approached, acknowledging her presence. Budding flowers bloomed as she passed them, spilling out
colours of powder blue, rose, buttery yellow, and bright orange. She
could feel her element building at her back with each step she took.
She barely took in the smiles of the clan gathered around as she
moved through the grass. Her train gushed out behind her, gathering all sorts of pine needles, petals, and grass. Her bare feet left
footprints in the grass as its soft blades caressed her skin.

When she finally glanced up to the cusp of the waters, she saw
him.

He was wearing a tight black tunic tucked into his leathers. Atop
his muscular shoulders sat silver armour, what he wore for fighting
on special occasions. The emblem of her coven now sat in unison
with his Commander's crest on his armour, a bigger version of the
one he had worn previously.

The lowering sun crowned him with a glow of fire. His sinful,
wonderful eyes were on her, and his full lips were parted in a grin
that took the air from her lungs. One dimple was on show, deco-
rating his left cheek. His confidence was astounding as he stood at
the top of the aisle, and Emara wondered if she was even putting
one foot in front of the other because she didn't seem to be getting
any nearer to him. It was like there was no one else around them,
not even the gentle breeze or the birds in the sky.

Just them.

And as they locked eyes, something in her heart locked too. Something overwhelming. Something remarkable. Something stormy and powerful yet calming and right.

It was him.

He was the one who made her blood boil with his cockiness, yet he could calm her fire down within seconds. He shared her bed and her secrets. He was the one who guarded her life and saw it as something more valuable than his own.

He was her soulmate.

Their collision was written in the stars.

A single tear fell from her eye as she reached where he stood, overwhelmed by the rush of emotions that hit her heart. Torin swallowed a lump in his throat as his gaze shifted from her face to the mossy grass below her feet. His beautiful skin was glowing, and the striking angles of his face had softened into something so staggeringly handsome she couldn't breathe.

"You look," he whispered, "spellbinding."

"So handsome, Commander," she whispered back, and he gave her a devious wink.

He looked dangerously attractive in full battle regalia, and she was thankful that one of the earth witches had taken a short time to heal some of the wounds on his face. They were now subtle bruises and cuts, but still there as a reminder of what he had earned in the duel. But her favourite scar was still there between his brows, and she had an urge to reach up and touch it.

"Today marks a new beginning for you both." A familiar voice sent a shock wave through her, and she turned her head to see Artem Stryker standing before them also in a black tunic. He sent her a boyish grin, and she had to stop herself from rolling her eyes.

By the Gods above, how had she not spied him at all?

She turned to face Torin again.

Artem Stryker, really?

Her thoughts must have somehow travelled into Torin's mind as he raised his eyebrows, his hands clasping in front of him innocently. *Let him have this moment, angel.*

She rolled her eyes a little, and as Torin fought a smile, his right dimple finally appeared in his cheek.

"Surprised to see me?" Artem whispered to her, and she wanted to send a spout of fire up to burn off his eyelashes. But she didn't, she just flashed him a smile bigger than usual, telling him that she would get him back later. "The Warriors of Thorin, Covens of Rhiannon, and everyone from factions in between are gathered here to witness a treaty of marriage between Torin Blacksteel, first of his name, Commander of Clan Blacksteel, and Emara Clearwater, Empress of House Air, heir to the elemental crown. They will join together in matrimony under the Gods of Light and bind themselves as one today."

Emara glanced at Gideon as he moved from behind Torin and handed him a small dagger. Emara's heart quickened again.

"Repeat after me," Artem said. "With this weapon that Thorin granted us, I will bleed."

"With this weapon that Thorin granted us, I will bleed," Torin repeated as he carved a small cut into his palm. He didn't even wince.

Emara's heart skipped a beat as his bleeding hand reached out for hers. She carefully placed her hand in his. Torin looked at her in a way that promised he would try not to hurt her. He nodded for her to recite the vow.

"With this weapon that Thorin granted us, I will bleed," she whispered. She gasped as Torin quickly sliced her palm. It was strange to see another wound where her ascension scar was so slightly faded.

Artem raised his chin. "With this blood, I give to you my life and mix your soul with mine."

Torin repeated his brother's words and clasped his hand over Emara's, his piercing eyes on her face. He nodded to let her know that it was her turn, but as she said the words, she got lost in his stare.

Kellen moved from Torin's side and handed Artem a strip of cloth and then Lorta did the same. Artem placed the fabrics over their connected hands and wrapped their grip like a parcel, binding their hands together.

"With this Blacksteel cloth, your hands are now bound together. With the cloth from House Air, your lives are now joined and your knot of marriage is now infinite."

Emara took a breath, and something low in her stomach shifted as she watched Torin. He tightened his grip on her hand, and the little slash in her skin stung as his blood mixed with hers.

Artem's deep, velvet voice broke through the silence once more. "Like the stars, your love is eternal, and like the earth, your bond is the foundation for your union to grow. May your union be as strong as the mountains of the north. And may the ancestors that went before us bless this marriage in the Light Gods' names. May this knot hold tightly through the storms of life, and may the hands that hold each other now be blessed by the Mother God."

"Blessed be," the crowd around her vowed, including Torin. And he gave her a gentle nod.

"Blessed be," she repeated.

Gideon stepped forward with a quaich engraved with the clan's ancient crest. He poured an auburn liquid into the quaich from a flask, and Emara knew straight away from the scent that it was whiskey. Gideon passed the quaich to Artem and he said, "From this drinking vessel, you will both share your first toast as husband and wife and seal the bond between your two factions."

Emara watched Torin as he unbound the cloth from their hands, and a cool breeze swept in around her wrists, kissing her cut palm. Torin reached up and took the quaich from his brother. Turning to look at Emara, he said, "To Emara Blacksteel, Commanding Wife of the Blacksteel Clan and Empress of House Air." He drank from the quaich, and the clan roared around them.

Emara Blacksteel.

Her heart almost burst at the sound of her new name on his lips. She took the quaich in two shaky hands as Artem said, "As you pass this drinking vessel with both hands, each of you know that trust is present in the marriage as neither of you can reach for your weapon."

That earned a laugh from the clan and even a smirk from Emara.

Torin raised an eyebrow. "Is your spear strapped around your beautiful thigh?"

She didn't answer him, not in front of so many people. He was disturbed and overly confident, but so very utterly handsome.

He gave a snippet of a laugh. "Are you just going to stare at me, or are you going to sip the whiskey, angel?" Torin's brows danced in amusement as his sharp features pulled into an exceptional smile.

She tipped the quaich to her lips with both hands as she heard Artem say, "Careful, Empress, it's strong."

That spurred her on to drink the full vessel dry. Another cheer erupted from the clan. She handed the vessel back to Artem with a cocky smile. "I know what it is. But I am a Blacksteel now."

A flare of pride flashed in Torin's eyes, and he took a step closer to her. "In this body, I will die, but what my heart feels for you will be eternal, Emara. Even when my bones are dust and my soul twinkles amongst the stars, what I feel for you will not change." His fingers coasted down her arm and he took her hands in his. "I am forever yours. And you are forever mine."

Emara's breath caught in her chest, and before she could say anything back to him, his mouth was on hers. His hand slid around her waist, pulling her into him, and she melted into the kiss, falling against his chest. The cheering of the crowd faded and it was just the two of them in the universe. Just Torin Blacksteel kissing her, floating between the pink and golden clouds. She wrapped her arms around his neck and gave in to his demanding mouth as it sent flames down her spine. He pushed a large hand into her hair, and tingles spread all over her body. Her spine curved so that her body arched into him, and he greedily took everything he could get from her.

A cough came from their officiant. "That's enough, you two."

"It's never enough," Torin whispered, only to her, not breaking away from their kiss entirely.

A little bashful, she pulled back to see Artem Stryker grinning from ear to ear.

"It is my utter pleasure to say that I now pronounce you husband and wife," he announced.

Her lashes fluttered shut as white rose petals rained down on them. She turned to face the crowd and saw Sybil's hands in the air, controlling the flow of petals that fell from above them. Her eyes were brilliant with delight, and a giant smile breached her lips. Emara mouthed, "Thank you," and the Empress of Earth grinned wider, tears shimmering in her eyes.

Artem leaned in again, catching her attention. "I would say it's time to kiss your bride, but you took that liberty yourself, Tori-boy."

"I couldn't wait a moment longer." Torin's gaze didn't leave Emara's face.

"Well, on that note, let's get pissed." Artem called out, and laughter bellowed all around them. "I am starving, though. Let's eat first, shall we?"

Emara let out a choked laugh, relief spilling from her heart. "Yes, let's."

As Emara walked through the congratulating crowd, holding her husband's hand, she wondered how she could make this happiness last forever.

CHAPTER
THIRTY-EIGHT
BREIGHLY

The stars of Caledorna watched them dance, sing, and rejoice, but Breighly was sure that the night creatures prayed to the Gods they would stop soon. Emara had disappeared with Torin just moments ago, taking time to themselves, and as Breighly watched them leave hand in hand, an envious streak pulled apart her heart.

She wasn't envious of them—the Gods knew they deserved whatever happiness they had left—but when she looked at them, she wanted what they had. Emara had looked so beautiful as she walked to where Torin had stood at the edge of Lake Rhiannon. Her hair had been braided with flowers and her beautiful dress had trailed behind her like a sparkling snowdrop. She had looked at peace as she walked towards the man she would spend the rest of her life with. And she had never seen Torin Blacksteel so smitten in her whole life. His eyes had burned brighter than the sun as she had walked towards him.

She had witnessed the Empress of Air marry the Commander of the Blacksteel Clan, and that was epic as fuck.

The Wolf Moon was just one night away, and it was clear the clan was feeling her effects. The men were either blindingly drunk or edging towards a witch, drawn to feel the touch of someone under the mating moon. Even though the alcohol had started to make her bones a little soft, she knew that what she really needed was a decent run under the moonlight. She always felt the need to shift into wolven form when the moon was swollen; it made the Shifter magic tingle through her veins and her feral heart thump louder in her chest.

Moving silently into the forest, Breighly removed all of her clothing and let the moon soak in her bareness. It felt incredible to take off her tunic and drop her weapon belt from her hips to the grass. A gentle breeze washed over her skin, and she sighed in relief. Her eyes closed and she blocked out all the distant chatter in the background. She was finally alone. She was comfortable being naked, but what she really longed for right now was to be running on all fours as fast as she could until the beams of the moon's magic couldn't keep up with her. Finally, she shrugged off her boots and felt the light touch of air swarm around her ankles and toes. The pads of her feet found the mossy earth, and she took in a huge breath, releasing it with a smile.

Shifting, she made off as swift as an arrow.

There was no target, no goal, only trees, moss, and the feeling of the earth beneath her paws. Even the other wildlife cleared a path for her. She veered to the left and then to the right as the branches of the trees combed her face.

To feel the summer air carrying the starlight through her fur was exactly the medicine she needed. She could smell the pine trees and the swirling smoke from the campfire. Breighly could taste the summer berries growing around her, their sweetness on the wind as it hit her lips. And the sound of her paws bounding on the slightly damp moss was ritualistic as it matched the rhythm of her heart.

But it would have felt more wholesome had Roman been with her, snapping at her ankles to be quicker. She wished Eli were running alongside her, racing Waylen to be at the head of their pack.

She ceased as a tight pain went through her heart, her paws skidding on the ground. She dug her claws into the earth and finally halted.

They wouldn't be together again, not all of them. Eli was gone.

Forever.

And it was unbearable.

A broken howl shattered through her throat, and her neck craned back as she called up to the moon or Vanadey or anyone that would listen to the pain in her cry.

Why would the Gods let the Dark Army take Eli? He had been one of the good ones. He was an integral member of the pack, a great wolf through and through. He was the most mellow and charming of her brothers, kind and affectionate, always protecting her.

And he had met with such a violent end.

He had been shredded. She would never forget the way his legs lay on the foyer floor or the amount of blood that soaked his clothes.

A howl broke from her throat again, one that was married with the agony in her heart.

She would always be grateful to Emara for what she had done for Eli. Word had come from Melione—a trusted spirit witch in the markets—that he had gone over to the spirit world without the pain of his trauma. Emara had failed to heal him, but she had taken his pain, allowing him to pass over peacefully.

A whimper left her and her head bowed as the pain in her heart stabbed through again.

She had prayed to the Gods to take their mother instead of Eli. Why had they not taken someone who abandoned her four pups and stole from a family that she had brought into this world?

Her heart cracked open at the truth she smothered with so many distractions.

Breighly shifted back to human form and let out a scream,

unable to bear that her pack would feel her hurt even miles away from where she stood. She let out a sob as her fist hit the bark of the tree trunk in front of her. Pain seared up her hand and her bones hummed with a biting pain that brought more tears to her eyes. But it was better than the pain in her heart, so she punched again. She punched until the salty tears ran down her chin, soaking her bare neck.

A snapping branch had her whirling around.

She wasn't stupid. She knew that a full moon often brought out more demons from the underworld, their portals being stronger than normal. Her heart started thumping as much as the pain in her hand.

A shadow appeared from behind a tree. Instantly crouching, she readied herself to shift into the monster she could be. An inked warrior walked into a beam of light that had found a gap between two trees. She snarled and he placed his hands up.

His golden eyes were filled with caution. "It's me."

She snarled at Artem Stryker again. "Don't you know it's total stupidity to sneak up on a wolf?"

Especially one filled with pain. One with an injured heart.

His face was taut, pale. "I heard you howl and scream. I—"

"I am fine." She tucked a loose strand of hair behind her ear. His eyes tracked the blood on her hand, examining her open flesh that surrounded her knuckles.

"Breighly," Artem whispered, "are you hurt?"

"I said I am fine," she snapped. "You can see that I am absolutely *fine.*"

"Clearly." Artem's shoulders squared, and his strong chest puffed a little. "The minute I heard a howl in the woods, I knew it was you. And I was worried you had..." His voice trailed into nothing as he stood watching her.

He had known her howl, and he had gotten here faster than she

thought a hunter could run. She wanted to question it, but the
intensity of his gaze had her whole body on lockdown. A tingle of
panic ran through her heart when she couldn't find a single part of
the comical mask he usually wore. Maybe she watched him more
than she would care to admit. But right now, there was something
different about the air that lingered between them.

He reached down to the hem of his tunic and pulled it over his
head, revealing every part of his torso and arms. Amongst the
muscles were inked pictures all over his skin, telling stories of who
he was and mattered to him. Her lips parted to ask about them, but
she stopped herself, knowing that she shouldn't go there. She had
always been curious as to why he would mark his full body with ink.
Did he want to hide the skin underneath?

But it was beautiful.

Breighly didn't need to know any more about him. He was a
hunter, a guard, and the son of the chief commander, and that was
all she needed to know. That was all that mattered. He was her
companion in guardianship, nothing more.

"Here," he said, "put this on. I know you left your clothes back
near the camp." He tossed her his tunic. "I passed them on my way
here, along with your weapon belt." He shot her an unimpressed
look that stirred up desire in her heart. He was so attractive even
when he was frustrated with her, and that was a whole lot of
trouble.

A. Whole. Lot. Of. Trouble.

As she caught his tunic, she was graced with his warm scent of
baked oranges and soft summer rain. The tunic was still warm when
she pulled it over her naked skin, and it was around three or four
sizes bigger than her own. She had worn dresses with a shorter hem.

He crossed the space between them when she was dressed, and
his russet hair looked darker in the moonlight. He stopped just
before her and lifted her hand so that he could inspect it.

"It's just a little blood." Her heart thumped against her ribs, and she was grateful that he didn't have wolf hearing.

He looked down at her through knowing eyes. "I know what blood looks like." Again, there was no grin, no jest. She had been so horrendous to him lately. And she knew she had hurt him even though she didn't want to.

"I think we should get back to camp and get Sybil to take a look at this." He looked over her knuckles again, and instead of pain being the dominant feeling in her heart, it was longing. Longing for his hands to move from her wrist to her back. She wanted his hands on her hips, on her thighs, pushing through her hair.

She shut down those thoughts because it was the right thing to do.

For both of them.

He dropped her hand, and it was like he had been holding her heart. His dark lashes swept up. "You will heal quickly anyway. You Shifters always do."

He had almost turned away from her when her hand shot out and grabbed his thick wrist. He twisted back around to see her, his huge frame drowning out anything else in her vision.

"I am sorry for how I treated you on the beach." She glanced up at him and immediately noted the surprise on his face. She took a deep breath. "I told you to stay away from me and I shouldn't have. That is not what I want," she admitted. "I shouldn't have been so horrible to you. You didn't deserve it."

If he had wanted to keep his emotions a secret, then he had failed, because his face sold him down the River of Vanadey. His eyes widened and his lips parted. Shock lifted his brows.

She hesitated as his silence lasted longer than she hoped. "I was in a foul mood and I shouldn't have taken that out on you." She looked him over. "I have...I have a lot going on in my head and at home, and I just snapped." She shook her head and looked at the ground. "I don't want you to not speak to me." She curled her toes as his gaze saw right through her soul. "I don't want you to stay away from me. It wouldn't feel natural."

She didn't know why she was putting this out into the open when moments ago her heart had decided that this couldn't be anything. Why was her heart betraying her head already?

Finally, he looked down at her hand on his arm and then he met her glare. "All I wanted was for you to speak to me and tell me what was going on. I wanted to help."

Artem was short in his delivery, and she had never heard him take that tone with anyone.

Shame engulfed her. "I know. I know. I am a mess." She offered him a broken smile. "I am a total fucking mess and I don't know how to be so...together like all of you."

"You think I have my life together?" A dry laugh left his chest. "You think hunters have any say in how their lives go?"

There was so much she wanted to say, and it looked like he did too, but if she did, she knew she would just dig herself a deeper hole.

"I don't want to stay away from you either," he finally made an admission of his own, and Breighly's heart kicked against her chest. "I can't explain what I feel. I just know that when you are in the room, I can't stop myself from finding you."

His words were like a battering ram that forced open the closed doors to her heart.

Fuck. Why was that the truth? Why did she feel the same?

The truth of her heart was not to be explored.

"We can't do this, Artem," she whispered, knowing full well that because she had denied herself something, she wanted it all the more. "We are not supposed to. You are a hunter and I am a wolf."

He moved further into the thick air between them and his hand wove its way in behind her ear. She fought off a shiver, her body bending to him too easily. She hated that she was so quick to welcome his touch.

"I know," he said, his brow pinching together. "But I can't stop thinking about you, and that is the truth. So fuck our stupid traditions. It's like we are drawn together, different factions or not. What does it matter?"

Her hand found his strong chest and she swallowed at how good it felt below her. "It's the moon. It makes us do crazy shit. It's not real."

It wouldn't matter when the sun came up, she told herself.

His face brightened as a chuckle escaped. "I have never met a girl who blames everything on the moon quite like you do."

She bit back a smile. "It's the truth. This is her kingdom and we are all just her puppets. And when she goes to sleep during the day, we have to live with the consequences of that. It's selfish, really."

He smiled at her words like he didn't quite believe them, but instead of challenging her, he said, "I don't believe that anyone or anything in this world could tell you what to do, Breighly Baxgroll. And that includes the powers of the moon." His voice was so low and charming that it reached out for her like a lure and pulled her in.

She was sinking, and fast.

"I think that's the most intelligent thing I have ever heard you say, Hunter." She flashed him a daring smile, and she could see how much it affected him. She wasn't sinking alone; she heard his breathing hitch as he rubbed a thumb over her cheek.

He lowered his chin, and she could feel his warmth rush towards her. "There are a few more things I would rather be saying now, Breighly. But I don't want to confuse anything. You have made yourself very clear."

The way he said her name sent stars shooting through her veins and fire up her spine. How was he still getting under her skin? She had shut this down in more ways than one and more times than she could count. How was she so quick to find herself in murky waters again?

"Especially when I see you standing there with my tunic on and the Wolf Moon's beams glittering through your hair. I know you didn't mean what you said to me on Tolsah Beach, but somehow, it still struck me like an arrow in my gut."

Fuck.

"But here I am, still so lost in trying to understand you, like a man who has never understood a woman before." His tongue rolled over his lips slowly.

Why did his words always send her frantic? She couldn't let them. She had to shut this down, right?

The Wolf Moon's energy was pounding through her heart. As much as she should fight it, she knew it was a lost cause tonight.

"If the tunic is ruining your better judgement, I am sure I can take it off," she replied. The invitation to start this forbidden dance between them had just been delivered, and she wondered if Artem would choose to feed the same longing that she felt right now.

It was definitely the moon. Once she had passed, her mind would be clear again, free of him. Free of her head telling her heart that she was stronger than this and not to give in.

Artem finally grinned, and it almost stopped her Gods-damned heart altogether.

Why could Emara's guard not be a fucking troll instead of a colossal tattooed warrior?

His smirk was full of cheek. "If you took it off, my judgement wouldn't even be rational, Princess." His eyes glittered with feral promise, and her core tightened.

Princess.

She knew he only called her that to mock her position in the pack, but why did her body react to him even when he did? Why did she want to see that feral side of him again? Fuck it. She was playing with fire now, and the only way to stop the burning in her heart was to feel something else entirely, to share that burning with him.

She swallowed, keeping her eyes on his, and drew a clawed nail down the front of her tunic. It parted like water to reveal half of her nakedness. "What does your judgement think now?"

His large hand that still lay at the back of her neck slid up and fisted in her hair, his hips rocking towards hers. He hovered just over them. "I think my rational judgement is completely irrelevant when all I can think about is fucking you hard against that tree behind you."

She dug her nails into his torso, dragging all the way down to his waistband like she knew he liked. A groan left his lips like a growl, and that encouraged her into pushing past the band of his leathers to find his want for her, solid and ready. She stroked his length once, and he shuddered under her touch, his head tipping back. This time, she didn't fight the smile, she let it spread across her face. Breighly looked up to find his glare penetrating through her, and it called to all the darkest parts of herself. It silenced all the voices that told her she shouldn't be doing this.

She stroked him again, and she could feel his impressive length grow harder for her. His grip tightened on her hair, and she hissed in delight as he yanked her head back and leaned into her arched body.

She smiled at him as she said, "You know this needs to be the last time, right?"

"I know it won't be the last and so do you," he vowed, his eyes hungry and wild for her. "So stop fucking pretending."

Seeing him in a dominant light only encouraged her wickedness to tease him.

"This is just the moon and her energy." She nodded, trying to convince herself. "This is nothing more."

"Nothing more than me giving you what you need," Artem agreed on a rumble of need. "What you deserve."

"And what do I deserve?" she asked smartly.

"Absolute fucking feralness."

"Is *feralness* even a word?"

"It is now."

His lips came down like a comet and smashed against hers as if he had been waiting a millennium to crash into earth. Before she knew she had moved, her back hit a tree, and it knocked the air from her lungs. The bark spiked into her skin beneath the tunic, but Artem gave her no time to recover as his tongue claimed the inside of her mouth. His hand was still yanking her hair back, tilting her head the way he wanted, and she leaned back and exposed her neck to him. He took it with his teeth, his lips, and his tongue, feasting on her. She moaned in ecstasy, and he wasted no time as his hand found her peaked nipple underneath the tunic.

She writhed against him. She needed his fingers, his cock, his anything.

Still gripping her hair, Artem slid his mouth up to her jaw. "You have been the one in control many times." He coaxed her nipple between two fingers, and already she wanted to scream. "But this time it's my turn."

A thrill ran through her, and the magic in her blood pounded at his dominance. She could see that he had been willingly letting her do whatever the fuck she wanted before, but the tables had turned. Breighly was out of control under his touch, her hips driving into him, desperate for that sweet friction, the climax already beginning to build.

The hand that had teased her flesh dove down and parted her legs. He growled again as his fingers found how ready she was for him. "I fucking love how wet you get for me, how you moan for me, how you feel when I am inside of you. You can't pretend this is going to be the last time when you want this just as badly as I do. Do you want me to stop?"

He teased two fingers across the bundle of nerves and she saw stars. How was he leading this? She had always been in control of what they did together.

"No," she breathed, pulling him closer to her. She was a slave to his touch. When he only continued to tease her, she dragged her nails down his arms. "I want it. I want it now. Give me what I want."

"Don't tell me what to do." He moved his hand from her hair to the front of her neck, pinning her against the tree. "Because I am going to make you come harder than I have ever before. You good with that, Princess?"

Delight ran through her like lava, filtering into every nerve in her body. "Good with it," she repeated as she felt his fingers flex around her throat. She tilted her chin, relishing in the challenge. "I hope you don't disappoint, *big boy.*"

The mockery made Artem's smile all the wider. His large hands gripped her hips and turned her. Her ass slammed against his cock and she almost moaned at the touch of it against her heat.

"Put your hands on the trunk," he demanded.

She craned her neck so that she could look back at him. She raised her eyebrow in true Breighly fashion. "Yours or the tree?"

A barking laugh left his lips before the feral energy of their lust took over and he thrust himself inside her.

CHAPTER THIRTY-NINE
TORIN

Torin was starving for her, and he was insatiable.

It had nothing to do with the fucking moon and everything to do with her.

His wife.

And his mouth was already on hers even though they had just made it into the tent. Everyone had stopped to talk to them, and Emara had been accommodating while he had wanted to shove through them all to get his wife alone.

Someone had set up lanterns and arranged flower petals in the marital tent. Torin didn't think Emara had even seen them yet, her eyes closed as he kissed her. He pulled the ribbons apart at the back of her dress, and she let out a moan against his mouth that he was not ready for. He needed to be inside of her, to feel her skin beneath his lips. He kissed down the back of her neck and she melted into him, her hands running over his shoulders and into his hair as he loosened every hook on the glorious dress she was wearing. He considered keeping it on, but there was too much material.

As beautiful as she was in the dress, he needed it off.

Because of its weight, it was already falling to the floor, revealing what was underneath. He took a moment to watch her, reluctantly pulling back from her mouth to see the dress slide over her curves and hit the floor. Her breasts were full and shapely, and he immediately wanted to glide his tongue over them to earn a moan from his wife. He could tell she was ready for him—she always was—and he was more than ready for her.

He was hard, and he couldn't wait to feel her softness. Unable to wait, she pulled at his tunic, and he worked to get every weapon off him as quickly as he could. Thank fuck he had taken off his armour earlier. The leather hit the floor at the same time as his belt and weapons scattered.

"I have waited all night to have you like this," he admitted as he breathed into her mouth.

"I have waited all night for you to take off this tunic." She pulled, and a gust of air aided her in making sure the clothing was off quicker, the breeze blowing against his skin.

She was getting better at those little tricks, and Torin had all sorts of ideas he wanted to try with her, all sorts of *magic* they could do together.

Torin kissed from her neck down to her perfectly hard nipple. A loud moan escaped her as he took her flesh in his mouth, and she fired a hand across her lips, sealing it in.

He removed her hand. "Don't." He almost had to stop himself from growling. She should never shut down those beautiful, breathy moans that meant she was getting as lost in this as he was.

"What are you doing?" she exclaimed through panted breaths. "They will hear me."

"Well, let them fucking hear."

"Torin!" She laughed, and her head fell back as he turned his attention to her other breast. She gasped, and he liked that.

His fingers danced around the hem of her underwear, and she arched into him, giving him permission to take it further. A smile graced his lips. "You are so bossy even when you don't speak."

"Get used to it, husband," she whispered, her eyes shut in anticipation of the pleasure he was about to give to her. She called out as he slid his fingers between her thighs, heated and wet, and her nails scored into his back. He teased the bundle of nerves. "I need you inside me." She rolled her hips impatiently, encouraging him.

For one second more, he enjoyed looking at her like this, her cheeks blushed pink with pleasure, her features relaxed, and her hair already messy.

"No, angel," he breathed. "This is our wedding night, and as your husband, I am going to take my time to pleasure my wife." As he kissed her collarbone, Torin brushed down one stroke of his thumb over her swollen apex.

"Oh Gods," she almost screamed. "Torin, please, as your *wife,* I need you to be inside me. I need it. I command it."

He withdrew his fingers and her eyes flew open.

"What are you doing?" she breathed.

"You command me?" he said, his voice low. "You *command* me?"

A dangerous smile of her own met with his.

His *angel* believed that she could command him, that she could demand anything she wanted and he would give in. It was normally true, but if she wanted to be in command, she would need to fight for it tonight.

Emara stood, breathless and needy in front of him, and the most beautiful part of it was that she finally didn't shy away. He fucking loved it when she was feisty. Confident. *Commanding.*

"Yes," she said with a little more resistance this time. "I command you to stop teasing me and just give me what I want."

He gave her the showtime smile. "Oh, angel," he said in a sultry voice that he knew only multiplied her desire. As he walked around her, he placed a hand on her navel, and it travelled with him as he walked around her, pulling a shiver from her spine. Torin was happy to see her skin prickle at his touch, to see his effect spread across her body.

He pressed a kiss into her spine and Emara shuddered. He

nibbled on her earlobe before he said, "Do I need to remind you that I am the commander, Emara *Blacksteel?*"

He loved her old name, Emara Clearwater, but her new name on his lips made his dick harden even more. He had to gather his willpower—and fast—to not give in to her.

"You know I will never fall in line, Torin Blacksteel." She glared up at him, and the magic in his veins screamed at her power matching his. The lanterns that lit the tent sent shadows into her eyes, making them darker, and those same shadows hugged her beautiful body. Her mouth, full and swollen from their kisses, was ready for him to take. "But only in these moments, where it is just me and you, will I surrender to you, Commander."

She sent him a look of pure defiance, and his heart almost combusted in his chest.

Torin closed the distance between them, his frame towering over her. "You're mine and only mine. And in these moments just between us, I am going to remind you why you should never surrender to anything but what we have, what we share together."

Torin edged her backwards so that her back hit one of the poles that kept the tent standing, and a gasp escaped her mouth. Torin took advantage of it, swooping in and crashing his lips to hers. He ripped the lacey bridal underwear from her body and discarded them with one hand.

She gasped again. "Will you ever stop doing that?"

"Never," he said. "Only if you stop wearing them will I stop ripping them off of you."

A giggle escaped her, and her hand pushed against his chest to halt his movements. "Take note, Commander Blacksteel," she said in between kisses, "the next briefing that I have with you, I will not be wearing any underwear."

A scandalous smile breached his lips. "As your commander, I agree to this."

Reaching up, she grabbed his hair, but he took both of her wrists in one hand. She wasn't going to talk about wearing no underwear so that she could get what she wanted. He was still in charge here.

He hoped.

He prayed.

"No, angel," he said. "You're going to keep your hands on the pole and you are not going to remove them until I say otherwise." He let go of her wrists and grinned as he said, "That is my first command as your husband. I am in charge tonight."

He could see the stars of glorious dominance dance in her eyes, but for the first time ever, she bit down on her lips and did as she was told.

Maybe this surrender was a wedding gift.

He swallowed down the need to be in her as his eyes raked over every part of her. Her eyes were like flames as she watched him drink her in. Her beautiful thighs pressed together, and he so desperately wanted to be between them. Torin wanted to feel every bit of her as he buried himself inside her.

Emara's head fell back against the pole, surrendering to him, and Torin dropped to his knees. "Put one leg over my shoulder," he commanded her. She looked down through dark lashes and lifted her leg, exposing herself to him.

With a grin on his face, Torin leaned forward and drove his tongue right up her core. She couldn't hold in a cry of his name, and he wasted no time in sliding his fingers deep into her. His tongue found the bundle of nerves that had been waiting for his touch. Her back arched, pushing herself even further into his mouth and she yelled at the Gods. He withdrew his fingers and put his hand to her hip, stopping her swaying.

"Keep your hands on the pole," he reminded her as he stood. "Do not remove them no matter how intense this gets."

She whimpered as her crash of release came to an end. Hooking his arms around her thighs, he hoisted her up. She wrapped her legs around his waist. He gripped her ass, holding her in place as his mouth found hers and the tip of his cock found her entrance. A high moan left her throat as he thrust every inch of himself inside of her.

Fuck she felt so good.

He rolled his hips again, and all the tension and desire bundled together and threatened to explode already. He thrust forward again, causing another cry to spill from her lips, and before he knew it, he was lost to her. He thrust again, picking up the pace, and pleasure ripped through his entire body. Her hands tightened on the pole as her hips met his endless demand, the pounding together of their skin a melody that he craved so much.

Her thighs tightened around him, and his hands firmly gripped her ass.

He was wild and unrelenting as he worked himself inside her, holding her in place so that he could meet her in a euphoric rhythm as she ground against him.

"I love you," he breathed against her cheek as he gave her everything that he had. "I loved you before you would even look at me that way, before I knew this was possible."

Every breath, every moan, was sending her closer to the edge of that spiralling bliss, and he loved it.

"I love you too," she managed. "I've loved you from the minute you challenged me to use my magic to the minute I took your name. I love you, Torin Blacksteel. Endlessly."

The sound of his name on her lips sent him crazy. Her climax exploded and he tumbled over with her as he called her name. With his last thrust, they collapsed into each other, snapping the pole and taking the tent down with them as they hit the ground. Heavy fabric surrounded them, and Emara quickly snuffed out any flame with her magic.

Torin couldn't even register what had happened fully, but all he knew was that he had somehow twisted and Emara was now on top of him. A tremor shook through him, and he blinked away the stars from a mind-blowing release.

Emara laughed and batted away the tent's fabric. "Did we just break the martial tent?"

He bit into his lip to hide how much he enjoyed it. "I think we did."

CHAPTER FORTY
BREIGHLY

S o..." Artem and Breighly melted against the mossy forest floor, spent of everything. "You really still have no feelings for me? Even after that?"

He had fucked her hard against the tree, and she had greedily taken everything he had to offer—every stroke, every thrust, every bite. It had been wild, untamed, euphoric.

Why must he be so talented with his body? Why couldn't she get enough of it?

Breighly considered the question and blinked. "Nope."

Her head rested on Artem's bulky arm, and as they lay together, she noticed the ink on his body as he stroked his fingers down to her navel, enticing goosebumps from her skin. He was relentless. His endurance was impressive. And he was totally distracting her from the sword of Thorin that marked the skin on his stomach.

He gave her a grin. "I thought you females released a hormone that meant you had attachments after sex."

Breighly rolled onto her side away from him and snatched up Artem's ripped tunic that lay an arm's length away. She flung it over her shoulders. "I can see that your cocky arrogance continues to fill your head with utter nonsense. You really should stop listening to all that male drivel they teach you in the Selection." She flung him a daring scowl over her shoulder.

He rolled onto his side with a grin plastered over his face. His hand landed in the space she had been, and she noted the beautiful black and red rose on it. "Really? No feelings whatsoever?"

Breighly hesitated for a second longer than she would have liked. "Absolutely not," she said, getting to her feet. Her fingers acted like a comb as she dragged them through the front of her hair, brushing out a few small twigs and moss.

"Nothing?" His voice was a little higher than normal, like he didn't believe her. She heard him pulling on his leathers behind her.

"Zero feelings," she said, her heart thundering as she lied.

"Then why does this need to stop?" Artem caught her off guard, and she turned to look up at him. "You said it yourself that you like no strings attached. Why are you so insistent in pushing away something that works? If this is what you say it is and you don't have feelings for me, why end it? This doesn't need to be the last time."

She took a step towards him. "Why are you so insistent in getting your heart broken?"

He scoffed. "You think that you can break my heart?"

She bit down on her tongue; she had learned from her mistakes on Tolsah Bay and she needed to keep her inner wolf in check. "I know I can."

"Look..." All six feet and five inches of statuesque warrior moved towards her. "I like you. You make me laugh and you keep me on my toes. Plus, I can't stop thinking about how you make love." He knew those two words would rile her heart, and he waited for a beat to see what reaction he had provoked. All Breighly did was roll her eyes and scowl.

Rein in your inner wolf! she screamed in her head.

He chuckled like he'd heard it. "Why do we need to end something that works for both of us?"

"Because the world doesn't look at you like you are whore for enjoying sex." She was quicker and snappier than she had wanted to be, and she had to pull back the fierceness in her tone. "I am a guard now."

His brows pulled down and his lashes fluttered a little. "Emara didn't care about you having sex, Breighly. I don't even think she cared about *us* having sex. I think it was just because it was in her bed."

She let out a dramatic sigh. "The fact that you think it's Emara that I am worried about says it all about your male privilege." Her gaze bore through his soul, and he shifted his weight to his other leg. "It's not about the sex or the bed or even you. It's about the fact that I am a guard and I need to be—"

"Respected?" He cut in.

"Not sexualised because I am a woman. Can you imagine if the men in the clan found out about us? They would think I got this post as Emara's guard because I fucked the chief commander's son. When I worked in the tavern, it was normal for a guy to look at me and notice my body. I was fine with that because it was what earned me money there. Fuck, I am not even ashamed to say that I played into it. I am not embarrassed about my sexuality. But you have no idea what it is like to be a woman in this position, trying to earn the respect of men who see you as an object of either pleasure or child-bearing." She only came up to his chest, but she looked him in the eye as she continued. "They see me as the weaker sex and nothing more. Someone who should get married and have kids. I should stay at home and bend to the will of my husband. They don't see my teeth or my claws or my speed. They don't see how easily I can kill. They don't see my clever decision-making. They see a girl who wants to prove a point, and they want to see me fail because that's how they built the world for people like me."

Artem shook his head. "Then that is foolish of them to not see all the things that you are. You are a powerful wolf and an even more powerful woman." His thumb ran across her jaw just as the heat of his body caressed around her. She wanted to pull away, she knew she should, but something rooted her to where she stood. "Doesn't that make you our greatest weapon? If the men in the clans cannot see what you are, doesn't that make you even more dangerous?"

Her bones froze at his words, and her heart sped up.

"Because that's what I see when I look at you—power," he continued. "Breighly, I don't see you as a girl who is chasing a dream to fight for a cause. I see a woman who is earning respect for every little girl who even dares to dream big in the first place. A woman who isn't scared to get her hands dirty or curse or throw a punch. By the Gods, you put all of us fucking hunters in our places daily." His hand waved around them. "But we can still have...this. Us being together doesn't change anything for you. I am drawn to you regardless of what the factions say. And I can't ignore that. I have been unable to ignore you since that first moment in La Luna—or maybe it was when you threw an axe at my head. Who knows?" He grinned, a little less confident than usual.

It took her a long moment to digest his words, and the tingle in her heart shocked her. Maybe he was right; maybe she was pushing him away not because of what everyone else thought, but because of who she was. But that was just it. She wasn't a witch from a respectable family who could give his clan elemental magic or stability. He would be married to someone like Sybil or Emara. Gods, he could have anyone he wanted because he was the chief commander's son. And she was the alpha's daughter; no doubt the Gods had her mate already chosen for her.

Her blood boiled at the thought of not being able to make the decision for herself. Her heart rebelled against it all, and her stomach lurched.

She shook her head and looked at her fingernails, trying to appear as unrattled as she could even though her heart was pumping so fast she was dizzy. "It doesn't matter." She finally met his gaze, and it was strong and unfaltering on her face. "It can't happen between us. Even if Emara said she was okay with both her guards...you know. We can be nothing more. You are a hunter and I, a wolf. Our paths are different—too different. I will find a mate, and that wouldn't be fair to you. So what is the point in all of this?"

Something lingered on his face for a moment before a little emptiness echoed in his eyes. He opened his mouth to speak, but he frowned in contemplation before he let the words float through the air between them. "Okay, I respect that." He paused, and a heavy sigh came from his chest. "My heart may be wounded, but I respect that."

A magnetic pull tugged at her heart like she had just done something wrong. It was like the tides of fate threatened to wash away what she had laid out in the world to replace it with something else. Her breath caught, and a staggering light flashed above the trees. Was it a shooting star?

When she brought her gaze back down to him, the energy changed between them. Breighly stumbled back, almost choking on what consumed her heart. It was unspoken and rare. Was it pain? Was it her way of acknowledging that this thing between them was over? She had never felt like this before. It was consuming her full being.

A swirling wind brought in his last words. *My heart may be wounded, but I respect that.*

She swallowed down the emotion in her throat as she clutched the tunic together tightly. "Hunters are not supposed to have hearts."

The look on his face was peculiar, as if he had felt a shift in their energy too. He took a step back, his eyes wide and his jaw strained. She could see the muscles in his shoulders tense, and his hands clenched into fists, but she wasn't sure if it was hurt or if he was restraining himself from doing something he shouldn't. Did he want to battle her? Kiss her? Shout at her? Hate her?

The inability to read him caused her heart to stammer, and it was getting harder for her to breathe.

He glanced at the stars before he spoke. "You and I both know that's not true. Hunters do have hearts."

Her stomach churned as she looked at him. Something wasn't right. Something between them—

He dropped his shoulders, and his body finally relaxed. "What I do know is that wolves have the biggest hearts in any of the factions even though they try to hide them. So I know that when you do find the mate that you choose for yourself, they are going to be so extremely lucky."

That you choose for yourself.

Every particle of air was sucked from Breighly's chest to form a barrier around her own heart, protecting her from the pain that rattled her soul. Why did her heart feel like it was being ripped from her chest? Only moments ago, she had told this warrior that she had no feelings for him whatsoever, and now they were swirling in her heart.

"Good night, Bry," he said in a soft whisper.

As Artem turned to leave, Breighly opened her mouth to call his name, to stop him from leaving, but she could make no sound. The moonlight hit his back, causing her legs to almost buckle beneath her.

No.

It couldn't be.

Why hadn't she never noticed it before?

There, tattooed in black, was a wolf, an alpha of the pack. It faded into the darkness of the forest with Artem Stryker as he left her.

CHAPTER FORTY-ONE
GIDEON

Gideon was glad that his mother had stayed behind at the campsite with Lorta and Kaydence. It wasn't the most comfortable journey to the Temple of the Gods when the newest joke of the clan was that his brother and Emara had destroyed a tent consummating their marriage. And to top off his splendid situation, Sybil was ignoring him now too.

He had witnessed the disappointment in her eyes as she stood in the clearing with her rugs, ready to go stargazing. It had shifted something in him that was confusing and brutal. How Sybil had been so far off about his relationship with the Empress of Air had frustrated him a bit too, but he knew it was his fault for not being clear.

Yes, it was complicated, and he couldn't just switch off how he once felt. He still cared for Emara. But his heart had eased up on the pain he had once felt at the sight of her and his passion for her. He knew it wasn't right; Emara was not his to love. And he was okay with that, because somewhere down the line, his heart had taken a beat for another, one with hair that could rival a sunset and eyes of the truest green.

But for whatever Gods-awful reason, he couldn't convey that to her last night.

The Gods really did hate him.

It was more complicated than just having fun with her. It was more than just kissing her and letting the temptation of their chemistry unravel. He was her guard. Had he not been burned in a situation like this before? He had jumped in with two feet and sunk straight to the bottom like a broken ship in a storm. He had made so many mistakes before and he had sworn to himself that he would find the better man within himself before he gave his heart to another.

He sighed and ran a forearm over his brow as the Skyelir sun reached his skin. Gideon had set a pace faster than anyone else to get to the Temple of the Gods. By Thorin, he wanted to get this mission done and be granted some alone time.

That was what he needed.

It had been on nonstop training sessions, guardianship, and hunts, fatality after fatality, blow after blow. His soul was being pulled in all different directions between his family's unrest to the new birth of his brother in the commandership. Gideon's body wasn't as exhausted as his mind, but every hunter knew it was your mind that kept the body going. And if his mind had to conjure up any more thoughts of his brother's marriage consummation or the memory of Sybil's disappointment, he was likely to drown himself in Rhiannon's Lake.

They had been trekking for hours, and he had taken a few breaks to refuel. Torin hadn't questioned it when Gideon had kept walking without them.

Hopefully, with the rate that he was travelling, he would reach the temple before sundown.

Gideon saw the peaks of the Skyelir mountain range, and he knew that he was closing in on the temple. He let himself find a slower pace, and shortly, the clan caught up from behind him. He felt a large hand on the back of his neck, and he turned to find his elder brother walking beside him. "Everything okay, Gid?" Torin checked in.

Gideon kept his hands tight on the straps around his haversack. "I'm good."

"Are you sure? I normally set the pace for the clan and you scout from our tail for danger. But our tail has lost its best stinger today, and you are marching on like a man possessed—"

"I am fine, brother."

Torin nodded, acknowledging that he would push him no further. "I have put Marcus at the tail of the formation; he is the second best with a bow."

Gideon said nothing as he marched on for a few moments, trying to pretend that there wasn't an unnecessary awkwardness between them.

Torin's jaw clenched as he strode toward, placing himself in front. He held out a hand, and it hit his brother's chest gently. "It was never my intention for any of this to hurt you."

Gideon's hands fell from the straps of his cargo. "Let's not talk about this now, especially when we have so much to do. The clan is right behind us."

Torin's eyes narrowed. "I don't give a fuck if the clan is up my ass, I think you should air your frustrations with me. Go on, punch me."

He sneered. "I am not going to punch you."

"Then talk to me. I can command you to, you know."

Gideon pulled in a breath through his teeth. "You don't want to hear what's happening in my mind."

"Believe me when I tell you that I do." Torin shifted his weight and folded his arms across his chest ready to listen. "I need you to vent. It's not healthy to bottle up all your thoughts. I know you."

Distant chatter from the clan could be heard as they moved through the trees a few throws back.

"Honestly? I don't really need to talk right now. I just need a break. But warriors of Thorin aren't granted that grace, are we?" Gideon asked his brother.

"No, we are not." Torin's mouth slanted as if he knew the feeling well. "You know I am here when you want that chat, Gid."

"I know," Gideon assured him, and he was grateful for the effort. "Maybe someday but let me focus on the mission. My head's a mess and I need it not to be."

"Okay, then. Let's talk business. When we get to the temple, I am going to need you to lead some of the clan in a different direction. I need someone I can trust to be my second-in-command, and I choose you to lead them. I know you are tired, and your head might be a mess, but you are my brother, and persistence runs in your veins. You are the one I trust."

A little shock sprung in his heart. Gideon and Torin had not always seen eye to eye, but they were brothers, and no matter how many fights they had, no matter how many punches or harsh words they threw at each other, they had a bond like no other.

"I would be honoured to be your second-in-command," he said as he looked to Torin's icy eyes. "What do you need me to do?"

Torin grinned back. "You were always going to be my second, Gid." He slapped his upper arm. "I need you to lead a split in the clan and work your way from the furthest entrance of the temple to the front, combing over what you can. If we split up, we'll cover more of the grounds. You can take the higher sections of the temple and I will take the lower. Do you remember the number of times we studied the Temple of the Gods in the Selection and thought that it was just pointless nonsense? Now it's a test for us to remember it."

"I just wanted to leave those lessons and shoot something."

"See"—Torin's mouth curved up at one side—"I knew we had something in common. Maybe you will even grow as handsome as me too."

Gideon finally found it in his heart to laugh. "Fuck you. Everyone knows I am the best-looking Blacksteel."

Torin chuckled. "Who are we kidding? We both know the best-looking Blacksteel is Kellen."

Gideon had to agree. "That is very true. Have you seen the size of him lately? Baby Blacksteel is more like Bulky Blacksteel."

Torin's laugh broke through the trees, and his piercing eyes found themselves back on Gideon's face. "The kid is massive these days."

"That he is," Gideon agreed before he cleared his throat. "Do you think the Fae guards will grant us access to the temple?"

Torin's gaze flickered with something that looked like uncertainty. "I am not going to take no for an answer."

"Of course not," he scoffed. "But they aren't just going to let us walk right in and search for an ancient relic."

"I know. But we can tell them that we are looking for something from an old clan. We don't always need to tell the truth, brother." Torin turned to finally begin walking again, and Gideon followed. "Besides, I have already had a conversation with the clan about where I want them stationed with whom. I just wanted to run it past you to be my second-in-command for this mission; and when we get back to Huntswood, I want it to remain that way."

Gideon nodded. "I am on board, brother. When I stood at your side days ago, that wasn't just because I wanted you to be my leader, but because I would follow you into any battle and be any station you want. Just tell me everything you want me to do."

Torin slapped Gideon's back in a show of gratitude. "I need you to find the Library of the Gods within the temple. That's where I want your team to find something for me."

Gideon kept his eyes on the ground as his boots crushed whatever was underneath them. "And does it have anything to do with where the Dark Stone might be?"

"You know my mind so well." His brother's hand fell from his back. "I am not only looking to see if the Protection Stone is within the walls of the temple, but if there is any information on the Dark Stone too. There must be something in the library that gives us an indication of where its resting place is or how we can retrieve it. That's what I need you to find. Use Sybil; surely, she can get a feel for the old manuscripts, draw it out somehow."

Gideon nodded. "When I gave her the old grimoire, she said she could feel its magic, its ancientness, from being in its presence. So maybe I can get her to pull on some of that magic and see if we can find what we are after."

Torin grinned. "Sounds like a plan to me."

As the Blacksteel brothers walked on, the clan inevitably caught up. The dense forestry began to thin out, and the moss-covered banks turned into gravel. They were so close to the temple now, and Gideon could see the huge limestone walls.

Torin held up a fist, and every member of the clan froze.

There were no birds singing their usual nighttime song, no animals grazing through the trees, and no marching boots on the stones.

Something was off.

Gideon could see beyond the long gravel path that led up to gilded gates, and where guards normally stood surrounding the temple, it was bare.

The gates should be heavily guarded; it was the most protected temple in the kingdom. Emara made her way to the front of the formation, standing between the brothers.

"What's wrong?" She looked between them both.

Torin didn't answer her as he looked above the trees and searched the grounds.

"Something is not right," Gideon whispered to her.

"What do you mean?"

"Do you see those gates up ahead?"

She nodded, gulping down trepidation.

"Those gates should be crawling with guards."

"And they're not." Her shoulders tensed like she could feel the strange atmosphere slide in and around her bones.

Torin looked at Emara with concern heavy on his brow as he reached up to unsheathe one of his swords. "Stay here. Gideon, cover me."

Gideon nodded, pulling an arrow from his quiver and setting it into the notch of his bow.

He was ready for anything to unfold. Anything *could* unfold. The sun was setting on the temple and soon it would be dark. Anything that lurked in the dark was always stronger when the moon was in the sky, and she would be full tonight.

Emara shifted on her feet beside him. "Tell me what I can do."

"When your commander tells you to stay put, that is what you should do," Gideon whispered.

He could hear the clan pulling steel from their scabbards and weapons from their belts. It was familiar, but it sent the shivers up his spine all the same.

Torin stopped moving, his knees bent, ready to spring. The clan stilled. A bead of sweat trailed down Gideon's forehead and into his eye, but he wouldn't dare blink it out of the way in case he missed something. "Do you smell that?" Torin whispered, still not turning his head to engage in the conversation.

Gideon pulled a demonic scent into his nostrils in one inhale. "Sulphur."

Torin cursed. "Fuck."

"We're too late," Gideon whispered, still aiming his arrow at anything that had the potential to move.

Torin pulled a second sword from his back. "They might already be here, but that doesn't mean they have found what they are looking for. They could be gone."

Torin made a good point.

"This is where we part, brother." Torin looked back for a second to meet Gideon's stare. "If you find anything—and I mean anything—that could be of use to them or us, I want you to bring it back to the front of these gates. If you hear the sound of a horn, I want you to retreat. I need you out of there regardless of what you have found. And we will do the same. Understood?"

"Yes, sir," Gideon acknowledged. "Heard loud and clear, Commander Blacksteel."

Torin nodded in respect for Gideon.

"From this point on, our unit will split." Torin's eyes gazed over the clan that was at Gideon's back, but he didn't move to look at them. He kept his eyes on the walls of the temple. Who knew what lurked behind them, waiting to devour? "Coldwell, Kellen, Sybil, I need you with Gideon to search the library. The men from the back half of the formation, you will cover Gideon and his unit. The others, you are with me. This might be my first mission as your clan commander, but it is not my first mission, and you know how our unit operates. There are no differences. We are relentless, unyielding, and uncompromising." His eyes glittered with danger. "We didn't come here to spare the lives of the Dark Gods' army, so should they get in our way, remove them from this earth. That is my command."

An agreement of brutality circulated from the clan, and Gideon saw Emara take in a huge inhale.

"See you on the other side, brother," Torin said to Gideon.

Emara smiled politely at Gideon before moving with the men and Breighly towards the gates.

Gideon turned. "Marcus, cover me. We need to move in a different direction and enter from the back." He glowered over his clan for the first time as second-in-command. "We head north of the temple and we do so under the instruction of the commander. And how do we do that?" he asked.

"Relentless, unyielding, and uncompromising," the men said in unison.

Gideon's eyes slid to Sybil's, the first time she had looked at him all day. Something rushed through him, an energy untouched by this moment. But there was no time for matters of the heart.

"Let's move," he commanded as he began his journey to the back of the temple. "Stay vigilant."

He could hear their feet behind him, but his men were silent. Gideon looked up to the walls that protected the temple and assessed them as he led his unit away from Torin's.

The wards that had protected the temple had clearly been severed, and it would be quite easy to get over them if they could find a part they could climb.

"Sybil, whose magic normally wards this temple?"

In a second, she was by his side. "I believe it to be a combination of both Fae and witch magic to ensure that it never fails." She huffed a little as she held out a hand to touch the wall. "It must be someone whose magic is so old that it would surpass any of the new empresses and the Supreme. We know it's not Deleine; her magic would have died with her. This person would need to be powerful enough to build the wards for this temple without being one of the coven heirs." Sybil's bright green eyes lingered long enough on Gideon's face for his heart to quicken. "I have been reading a lot and studying the old grimoires, including the one that you gave me. There are only a few other witches out there that it could be. One is the Black Widow Witch; she lives in the mountains alone, unwilling to succumb to any coven. Although she did not vow herself to a coven, she still lives from the magic of our world, said to be born of both Fae and Witchling blood. The Fae respect her enough to grant her solitude here in the Skyelir Mountains. Your grandmother's grimoire seems to reference her a few times. She is alleged to be extremely powerful and maybe even an oracle, but she hasn't been seen in years."

"But she could have died in the mountains and no one would have known," Marcus Coldwell said from behind. "Would the Dark Army know of her and possibly try to kill her?"

"I would know if she had died," Sybil claimed as she brushed a curl from her petite face. "If a powerful witch like that had entered the Otherside, the whole witching kingdom would be talking, spirits and all. There have been no whispers of her death."

"It can't be her, then," countered Marcus. "Or the wards would still be up."

"She's definitely a person of interest," Gideon muttered. "Leave the wards for now. Torin wants us to look for anything that could shine a light on the Dark Stone."

"Of course he does," Marcus said with a spring of jest. "Because the commander can't just look for one thing at a time. The guy needs to go all in for everything."

Gideon gave one look at him and said, "He's a Blacksteel, what do you expect?"

CHAPTER FORTY-TWO
EMARA

Dead.

The Fae guards that had been protecting the gates of the temple were dead, slaughtered and pushed behind brick and iron. Their bodies lay in a heap in front of Emara, their gaping wounds still spilling crimson blood into the sacred soil.

Torin was now in full hunter mode, as was the rest of the clan. She had no doubt they were ready to fight. Her element was curling around her, ready to attack. The goosebumps that littered her skin when something awful was about to happen rose with a vengeance, coursing all over her body. Her stomach churned and her heart couldn't decide if it wanted to listen to her and slow down or batter against her ribs in defiance. The magic under her skin thrummed in her blood, sending a spark into every bone that she had, fuelling adrenaline through her body.

Emara wasn't sure if it was a warning for her to run or if her magic was responding to the darkness that had been here.

Steady, she warned her magic as they took a few steps past the gates. Maybe she shouldn't use too much magic in case the swirling shadows arose from her palms once more.

Shoving a hand into the strap around her leg, she unsheathed her spear, gripping it tight. The red ruby begged to be pushed, but Emara kept *Agnes* contained for now.

"The wolf in my blood is telling me to shift," Breighly said lowly, looking like she was fighting with her urges to transform. Her breathing was heavy. "That's never a good sign."

"My magic is sizzling too," she told Breighly. "It's pulsing under my skin. The Dark Army is here."

"Yes, they are." Torin nodded as they made their way along the path through the temple gardens.

Tall hibiscus plants bloomed in oranges and reds on their left, and as Emara turned to the right, she was faced with tidy bushes covered in white and violet petals. Behind her, two archers pulled their bows tight.

Torin threw a look her way. "Just don't look, angel. He's gone. There is nothing you can do."

But she did look. A guard dressed in the Fae cobalt robes of his court lay in the bushes. Emara noted that his throat had been ripped out, and the flesh of his neck was hanging to one side on the path. Crimson blood spilled into the flower beds, and a little vomit tracked up her chest.

Just as the nausea rose to her throat, they took a left and the Temple of the Gods came into view. Its jagged rooftop was coated in gold, and the lowering sun reflected a glare off its spires. White columns that stood momentously at the front of the temple held up other layers of the ridged roofs. The entire building was covered in a hand-crafted mosaic design made of small, mirror-like tiles that glinted like diamonds. Emara had to move her arm up to shield her eyes. Borders of red defined the edges of the roof, and the architecture seemed to curl and wave like a beautiful spell to finish off the composition. Four smaller columns stood behind the larger, and the mosaic tiles on them seemed to form faces. Emara quickly realised they were the Light Gods.

As Emara stood in front of it, a thousand tiny tingles made their way across her skin. The magic that radiated from this place of worship was so powerful. The brush of wind against her skin was a sign that she was always supposed to have made it here to this landmark, to this moment.

Centuries ago, this would have been the place that many thousands would have come to pay their respects to the Gods when faith was not dying or lost to a new world. They would have come here to be closer to their spirituality, each God representing something different but good.

Emara explored the depths of its power as she pushed her magic out to feel it, and as it came back, it whispered to her. Feeling the magic enchant her skin and thrum against her heart, she took a breath. It was captivating. The colossal size of what she could see from the front of the temple was jaw dropping, never mind what lay inside.

"If you think she's beautiful in the light of dusk, you should have seen the way you looked walking towards me on the day we got married."

The comment caught her off guard and took the air from her lungs.

She flickered her gaze over Torin. "You cannot compare me to the beauty of the Temple of the Gods."

Torin grinned. "You're right." He closed the distance between them, turning his back on the sacred place of worship. "My wife is more exquisite."

A cough came from behind them.

"Being in such close proximity to the temple makes me feel like the Gods will send me into flames any minute," Breighly muttered. "Only if the sickness of listening to your marital bliss doesn't kill me first."

A chuckle left Emara's lips as Breighly's remark earned a few sniggers from the clan.

"If you're going up in flames, Baxgroll, then I certainly am," Torin said.

"I guess I am the only one deemed worthy to enter the temple, then." Artem grinned like a cat.

"Doubt that," Emara said.

He threw her a scowl. "You take that back, Mrs Blacksteel."

Gods, would she ever get used to that name?

"That's Commanding Wife Blacksteel to you. And need I remind you that I am also still your empress?" She gave him a wink.

Torin's face was feral with desire. She could feel that he loved when she used her authority and even more so when it involved her new name.

He rolled his lips, and she thought she caught sight of a dimple, but then it was gone and now he wore his commander's mask. "We need to get past the grand doors and make it inside to an area that sits in the heart of the grounds. That's where the room that honours the Three-Faced God is. If my assumptions are right, I would bet my life that we would find something in there regarding the Stones, if not one of them. It is dedicated to their creator, to their mother."

"How do you guys not know this stuff for sure? Aren't you sent off to hunter school for this shit?" Breighly scowled. "Are we really going off assumptions? This place is huge."

Torin's gaze flickered over her. "I learned more about this temple in the fighting pits, than I did in the Selection, put it that way."

"What do you mean?" Emara coaxed, unable to hide the surprise in her voice.

"I wasn't only in the fighting pits to let off some steam and avoid my father's decisions." Torin finally halted and looked over his men. "I had caught wind in the markets that some temple raiders were betting stolen goods instead of coin on the winners in the pits. Some were said to be invaluable. I was hoping there was someone crooked enough to have stolen one of the God Stones or something that would help us find one. I was hoping that they would have been stupid enough to talk. Or, if I won enough fights, that I could negotiate some information." The lowering sun blessed Torin's hair with a golden shimmer amongst the black. "I was hoping that someone down there was working on behalf of Veles or Balan, something that I could go on."

"But nothing?" Breighly asked.

"Not nothing," Torin replied as his eyebrows pinched. "I didn't come across any Stones with my wins, but the traders did like to talk, especially after I got them shit-faced. One night, one of the fixers told me that he had once tried to raid the Temple and had gotten as far as the room of the Three-Faced God. The man said he had almost gotten down the steps."

"Steps?" Artem butted in, surveying their surroundings. "There is no downstairs in the room of the Three-Faced God; it is at the lowest part of the temple. That's impossible. So your fixer wasn't just drinking rat piss, he was talking rat piss too."

"That's what had me intrigued, Stryker." Torin grinned wickedly. "Get a temple raider drunk enough and they begin to trip over their words; they lose their secrets to the liquor." His ocean eyes glowed like he was part of something more mysterious. "There must be a secret floor. There must be *something* that holds a secret passage to a tomb underneath, because the man who told me the story lost his own eyes and hand as the Fae guards seized him. They didn't want him seeing what was in that room or where the passage was, so the blinded him and cut off one of his hands for even having been near the tomb. That leads me to think that there is something there. And we are going to find it."

"Well, as the saying goes, there is no smoke without fire." Artem twirled an axe in his hand.

"Exactly," Torin agreed. "These temples are bound to have hidden passages—look at how many the Tower has."

"The Tower has secret passages?" Emara exclaimed.

"Maybe I can show you them when we get back." Torin's tone was so low and suggestive, heat flushed through Emara's cheeks. Did he have no shame?

Gods, it was warm outside.

Breighly held out a hand. "Are we going to pretend that there are not dead guards lying everywhere? Like the *something* that wanted to get inside got inside and—oh, I don't know—maybe hasn't come out yet?"

"It sounds like the princess wolf might finally feel fear," Artem teased, his eyebrows dancing up.

"It's not fear that I feel, you idiot, it's intelligence. You should try it sometime," she hissed. "Seriously, what if the knights of the underworld are in there and it isn't just a band of lower demons? We are fucked."

If the Knights of the Underworld were here, it would be more than slaying one demon and moving on to the next. They were faster, more powerful. They could use their voices to manipulate your mind into pain. They could transform into Rhiannon only knew what. They would be much harder to kill, and everyone standing here knew that.

Arlo came to stand with his brother. "The wolf has a point. We have no idea how many demons are here."

"Well, we are here now, so you need to make the decision if you are in or out." Breighly swallowed, and her gaze turned steely as her shoulders pressed back. Torin glanced at Arlo, who squared his shoulders. The clan behind them also agreed that they should continue the hunt. Torin nodded. "I have already killed a few of the higher demons in the Dark Army, so these won't be my first or my last. If there are any knights of the underworld here, take no chances. Aim for the heart and the head. Do not miss." Torin began his climb up the temple steps. "I mean it, do *not* miss. They are hard to kill, not impossible. Hunt smart."

"Let's hunt." Artem grinned.

Emara could feel the power radiating from the temple. It leaked magic, and some of it brushed against her skin like an ancient hand caressing her magic.

The steps to the entrance were steep, and Emara was terrified that if she looked down, she would lose her balance and crash into the stone. The gilded doors were open, suggesting that whatever had come before them had pried them apart. Torin's movement slowed in front of her. Her heart almost bruised her ribs as she took in the blood on the floor. Yet there were no bodies.

Aromas swirled from multiple hanging copper incense balls at the front of the temple; they seemed to levitate in the air above them like huge planets, spiralling under some sort of air witchcraft. Candles burned, flickering as they walked past each one, and Emara wondered if the person who had lit them still lived.

The space was eerily quiet as they tiptoed through the huge room with high ceilings and floors like water, the blue marble detailed with swirling gold. Silver and gold tiles continued up the walls inside, casting broken reflections of the unit as they walked through the home of the Gods.

Following Torin's lead through the temple, they finally reached a mural-covered door. Fire licked up from the bottom, painted in russet and bronze, and water spilled from clouds, droplets of rain trickling down onto gardens of metallic green. Emara's eyes slid to the silver whooshes of air that blew in tiny orbs of spirits that glowed in a delicate lilac.

All five elements, working together.

Above the colourful beauty was a golden rune, the old symbol for the maiden, the mother, and the crone.

Torin reached out like the door called for him to open it, but there was no handle. It was locked.

Artem hissed a curse. "Great, a door with no handle! Is there anything else you want to throw at us, Gods?"

Emara shuddered as that question went unanswered.

"Are you sure this is the one?" Breighly asked, moving closer to the door to study it. "This is the Three-Faced God's door?"

"It has to be; look at the rune," Torin whispered. "It was said that after her mother was slaughtered by Veles, Rhiannon enchanted this door with magic from every element. Only those worthy of entering the tomb of the Mother God would be allowed to open it."

"And you think I am going to be worthy of opening this thing?" Artem snorted.

"No, but I think Emara could be worthy of opening it." Torin's sapphire gaze landed on hers, stealing a few beats of her heart.

He thought she was worthy.

Without wasting any more sacred time in this temple, Emara closed her eyes and gathered all the strength in her heart. Her magic prickled as she called to it, spreading shivers all over her body. Summoning air, she pulled her hands back and threw them forward, casting a spell towards the door. Fire of vibrant red intertwined with the green of her earth magic and the silver of her air. The double doors flew open, and she stumbled back. A few gasps and whispers came from the men behind her, but she didn't look around as a flush moved up her neck to her cheeks.

She had opened it.

"Damn." Artem whistled. "I reckon we should have witches with us on every mission."

"You're welcome." She grinned at him, a little breathless from how much her magic had pulled air from her lungs.

An impressed smile cut across Torin's lips. "Don't even think about trying to lure my wife into every dangerous mission you can think of, Stryker. I will have your balls on a stick."

Emara cleared her throat. "Excuse me, your wife can speak for herself. I think we have established that."

"I am telling you, Blacksteel"—Artem patted Torin's shoulder, and a breathy chuckle escaped him—"you married the right girl."

"You are all too distracted." Breighly barged past them and into the room that was a little darker than where they stood now. Arlo followed close behind.

Emara hid a half smile as she followed them.

The only light in the room came from a few large lanterns in the far corner. However, her eyes went directly to a beam of light that shone from the floor to the left of her. A rug had been rolled back, exposing a secret hatch. Someone clearly hadn't had the time to cover it back up.

"Well, I am not going to lie, I expected that to be a lot harder," she heard the oldest Stryker say. "That looks like our secret passageway." Artem pulled his favourite axe from his weapon belt.

"It does," Emara agreed, taking a few more steps inside so that she was in front of everyone else as some of the clan spread out in the room. "But who could have been in here?"

She felt Breighly's shoulder brush hers, and the wolf's warm presence was a reminder that she always had her back. "Maybe the temple priests who look after the grounds lit the beacons. They could have access."

"Or maybe the Dark Army did," Artem countered.

"Only one way to find out," Torin said casually, moving towards the trap door.

"Wait," Emara called out, the words spilling from her mouth and echoing around the room. "Breighly and I should go down."

"We should?" Breighly's head turned so quickly it almost snapped.

Artem's shapely eyebrow angled up.

"You should stand guard here." Emara lifted her chin, and a breeze blew against the back of her hair, spilling it around her shoulders. Her element was awake and present with her in this decision. "The Dark Army couldn't have gotten in here. Surely, Rhiannon wouldn't have deemed them worthy? You should wait for any signals from the other men outside."

"No," Torin said.

Artem hit his elbow against Torin's arm. "You were right. She is slightly crazy."

Emara glared at him. "If I am wrong and there is something down there, if it is something dark, then I can match it," Emara said. "Think about it. The Dark Army doesn't want me dead; I am the best person to go down." She looked between the few hunters she could see in the dim light. "I need you hunters to be able to protect me from up here. I don't believe that this room has been infiltrated with demons, so I need you to keep them out. The Dark Army doesn't stand a chance with you all protecting the entrance."

Arlo glanced from Torin to Artem. "She has a point."

"You can go down," Torin agreed reluctantly. He knew when to bow out from an argument to save time. "But I am going with you. Breighly and Artem will stand guard up here at the foot of the passage. I know how well they work together. Arlo, I need you stationed outside the doors with the rest of the clan. Nothing comes in here."

The youngest Stryker nodded, and the rest of the clan did as instructed.

Emara noted a glance from Breighly to Artem, and she couldn't decide if the wolf liked the idea of them being left alone or not.

It didn't matter. Artem kneeled on the ground beside the door to the underground tomb and lifted the hatch. Everyone took a step back, and Emara was thrilled when nothing popped out. Torches threw out some light, and it cast shadows on their faces. Artem found their gaze again. "Be careful, you two. You just so happen to be my favourite people. I need you both back alive."

Torin said nothing as he stepped onto the first step. Emara rested a hand on Artem's shoulder as an acknowledgment of his kind words, and he gave out a sigh. Before Emara and Torin disappeared down the stairway, she threw a glance over her shoulder at her remaining two guards to let them know that she would be safe with Torin—her husband. She needed them to protect one another, no matter what. She had no idea what awaited her at the bottom of the stairs.

CHAPTER
FORTY-THREE
GIDEON

I t was eerily quiet at the back entrance to the temple's library, and there were still no guards in sight. They had been so very careful as they moved through the temple, waiting for something terrible to finally show itself.

He wasn't just going to assume that it was the work of the Dark Army, because in times past, it had been his own faction or the witches that had meddled with the darkness. Regardless of who was behind this, good blood had been spilled here. Years of service to this place by the people who maintained these grounds had ended in horrible deaths.

The Dark God had seemed to work his influence through every faction lately. It had been the humans at the uplift, then his corruption had spread through the witches, and then the son of a bitch had turned Gideon's own faction into traitors. They had sided with the Dark God so that their hearts would never stop beating. It had cut his soul into pieces as he took them down, one after another, in the Amethyst Palace to show that the Dark God had lied.

Veles was never going to protect them.

Torin had taken care of most of them, shattering their disloyal dreams of immorality with the swords that were always strapped across his back. They had folded like a stack of cards under his wrath, and they had not risen despite the deals they had made.

Death had been the only thing they had been promised that day. Gideon had both envied and admired Torin as he watched him brutalise his brethren without blinking an eye. He made it look so easy. He made it look like he didn't even think about what he was doing as he ended their lives to protect Emara. And Gideon often wondered if Torin suffered from the same night terrors he did. The screams, the swirling black portal that led to the abyss of the under-world, the destruction, the blood, Emara's choking, his brother begging the Supreme not to kill her but to take him...

"Over here," shouted Sybil, pulling Gideon away from the night-mare of his memories. She was in a corner of the tremendous library.

His team had split up around the library, and as he heard the fear in Sybil's voice, he knew it had been a mistake to leave her with someone else.

Gideon, Kellen, and Marcus ran over, meeting from all different sections of the space to find the tiny earth witch leaning over a body. Her hands were on his chest, and she was already pressing healing magic into his heart. But he was grey and frozen in a time before now. He was certainly not alive. She whispered something to the Gods, and her eyes closed. Her small hands shook, already covered in blood. Sybil couldn't mend what lay bleeding under his robes, and that would shatter her.

Gideon wrapped his arms around her waist and pulled her up, leaving the man on the floor. It was then he saw a crest on his chest. He was a retired hunter. He had to have been a credible warrior of Thorin to have been granted retirement here.

"Do you recognise the crest?" Kellen asked.

"I do. He is of Clan Brownclad, a clan almost gone with time." Marcus leaned over him, brushing his hand over the old hunter's eyes, and whispered, "May all the stars in the Gods' sky guide you back home."

Marcus turned to head back in the direction of the stairs to the second floor.

"No, wait," Sybil called out and moved from Gideon's embrace. "Look what he is holding."

She glided forward, her gown smeared in blood. As she kneeled again, she pulled out a crumpled ball of paper that was tucked into his sleeve, the corner of it sticking out.

"It's a drawing," she announced, and then turned to face him. Her vast green eyes flashed with something unfamiliar to him, and he took a step towards her, as did Marcus. Kellen remained rooted close to a large bookcase, watching the grounds around them. "It's from the Book of Light," Sybil choked out.

Marcus blew out a whistle. "Shit the bed."

Gideon could feel his brow pull down. Although he was versed in the books of his teachings, he was ashamed to say that he'd thought the Book of Light had been a myth. A journal kept from the beginning of time, handwritten by the Gods themselves, couldn't be read.

"Gideon..." She turned to him, her voice breathless. "This piece of scripture is so old; I can feel my magic calling to it and it's calling back. I can feel the ancient magic lingering in the ink. This wasn't written by an empress or a Supreme. A God has written this." She turned the single page over to reveal a scripted passage. "It's even marked down the bottom as a passage from the Book of Light."

"It can't be a coincidence that he is holding it." Marcus looked at Gideon, and a rake of goosebumps littered his skin. "But surely if that scripture is from the Book of Light, it wouldn't still be in his possession."

Marcus's head tilted. "Not if the thing that killed him overlooked what it was, too thirsty for death and too stupid to see what was in front of him.

Kellen left his post and moved closer. Gideon moved to stand directly beside Sybil, so close he could feel the heat from her skin touch his. He looked down at the ancient page in her hand. "What does it mean?

"I can't work it out here." Sybil's hands ran over the wrinkled paper again.

"It has clearly been ripped from a manuscript," Kellen waded in. "So where is the full book?"

"Why would there be pages of an ancient manuscript shoved up a dead man's tunic sleeve?" Gideon asked.

"Because he was trying to protect what he could," Sybil whispered.

Concern pushed through Marcus's dark features, and he moved uneasily. "Do you think he was trying to hide the Book of Light when the Dark Army found him? Could it still be here?"

A tear ran a track down Sybil's face. "He most certainly died trying to protect something." Her moss green gaze gently lifted to Kellen before asking, "Can you do something for me?"

Kellen hesitated for a second. "Yes?"

"You have magic, right?" Sybil asked outright, and Kellen's eyes widened at her being so direct. "Maybe the magic that runs in your veins will be old enough to feel this kind of power. Seers are of such ancient magic that they can bring forth things my elemental magic can't. I think you could help." Her stare burned through Kellen. "Can you place your hand over this page and tell us if anything comes to you?"

Kellen's lips parted like he was going to protest, but he ran a hand through his dark brown hair and then held out his hand. "I don't know what I am doing."

Sybil placed her hand over his, and his unusual eyes locked on to hers. "I am not versed in the magic of a True Dreamer, but I will help guide you anyway I can."

A few of the other men looked on, intrigued by what was

happening. Sybil's lips parted as she closed her eyes, Kellen copying her. They were vulnerable in this state, and Gods knew what still lurked here.

Gideon looked up to where the other clan members stood watch, and he nodded to them to keep their posts. Sybil began to chant something in a language that was unknown to Gideon. The lanterns of the room began to flicker, and he looked all round them as an easy breeze blew whispers through where they stood—spirit magic

"Breathe," Sybil coached Kellen. "Let your magic come to you in a daydream and push it forward into my mind."

Kellen's chest began rising and falling more quickly and his eyes scrunched shut, pulling lines onto his face that were not there before. His body jolted slightly and his head threw back.

"Be careful, Sybil," Gideon said. "He doesn't know how to harness anything yet. He has never practised."

Her gaze met his and she nodded, confident in her ability to keep Kellen safe. Kellen's head turned to the side and his hands began a shake that led all the way up his arms. He noticed Sybil's grip tighten around his brother's.

"I can...I can feel...something," Kellen panted, his eyes scrunching up.

"Good. Now explore that feeling. What does it show you? Call it forth, like a spirit."

He craned his neck at an uncomfortable angle. "I can't see anything; it's dark. It's more of a feeling."

"Ask your vision to come forward into the light. Speak to it like I speak to my earth magic. Encourage it forth. Hold its hand."

Gideon hadn't considered Kellen's magic to be as simple as that or as similar to elemental magic. This could be a dead end, but it was better that they tried everything that they could whilst they were here than nothing at all.

Kellen's grip tightened on the paper, and a transparent glow peeled from his body like a ghost of the Otherside. Gideon stumbled back, and Marcus swore under his breath. He had never seen anything like it before.

"Kellen," Gideon breathed, "you are glowing."

A few of the men around them muttered.

"Yeah, I tend to do that," he quipped, his eyes still shut.

"By the Gods," Marcus whispered.

"Don't panic," Sybil coached. "That's a good sign. Your magic has been ignited."

Suddenly, Kellen took a breath and stepped away from Sybil, breaking their magical bond. Sybil stumbled back a little, but she caught herself as the jolt of magic left her body.

Kellen turned to face Gideon, his face too pale. "What is it, Kellen?"

"What did you see?" Sybil asked.

Kellen's eyes met Gideon's. "I saw Balan. I saw the King of the Underworld."

"Balan is here?" Sybil squawked.

A cold shiver ran over the whole of Gideon's body.

"But how can that be?"

"Get them out of the Mother God's tomb." Kellen gulped, trembling. "Get them out."

"What?" Marcus stepped forward to comfort him.

"The others—get them out of that fucking tomb!" Kellen screamed. "It's a trap. They need to leave the Stone. Balan has been waiting for the Protection Stone, and they used Emara to open the door to the tomb. This mission has been a trick." Gideon's blood ran cold. "Marcus, sound the horn."

CHAPTER FORTY-FOUR
EMARA

Heading down the passageway to the tomb of the Three-Faced God was worse than heading into the pits. At least there you could hear the life above you or the shouts and screaming from the fights. Down here, it was just cold, stark silence. Even the condensation did not dare drip from the stone.

The magic that slipped out of the darkness was calm but unmistakably alive. The ancient stones that built the passage even seemed to give off a vibration that she felt all over her skin. The beacons of light had trailed off, leaving them in utter blackness. She had tried to ignite a flame at her fingertips, but it seemed like the walls of this place had been spelled so that no elemental magic could be used down here. A stroke of fear pushed through her.

"Can you see at all?" Torin whispered.

"No, nothing," she breathed, placing her hand out to feel his back. It was a comfort when it reached him.

"I can see for us both," he promised her.

After what felt like forever, a flickering light could be seen at the base of the staircase. Emara blinked to adjust to the lighting.

"Be careful, the steps are beginning to crumble at the bottom," Torin warned her. He placed his arm out to catch her in case she took an unexpected tumble.

Once at the bottom of the steps, he took down a torch of swirling moonlight preserved in a glass ball. Inside the rune-covered glass, the light rotated like a crashing wave. He took a few more steps until he was standing in a threshold between the stairs and darkness. Emara stepped to the side of him, and they entered the poorly lit tomb together.

The air was dense. She couldn't feel the magic stirring in her blood anymore, and it was like one of her limbs had been cut off.

Torin cast the moonlight into every nook of the room that he could, inspecting it for demons. But nothing came forth as the light shone into the crevasses.

"Over here," Torin guided her, and she followed him over to an altar. It was lined with white cloth, covered in the same runes that lit the moonlit beacon.

Black and white candles littered the shrine of the Mother God, and a bed of black roses lay amongst them, untouched by death. The altar was covered in citrine, jasper, and a few shades of quartz. Weapons of all kinds had been offered to Mother God, including gilded arrows and even a sword.

But there, on a pedestal draped in obsidian silk, was a stone so vibrant and bold that it out shone everything else.

Emara's lungs filled up with awe and she struggled to breathe as the magic from its aura stole all the air that was left in the room. She shuffled forward like it called to her, luring her in to touch its rough and rugged shape. Unlike the smoothness of the Resurrection Stone, the glowing stone was all sharp, irregular edges. It looked like water circled around inside, hitting off all its valleys.

"Can you feel the power coming from that thing, or is it just me?" Torin's voice was husky and vacant, and she wondered if he hadn't pulled his eyes from the stone either.

But, oh Gods, could she feel it. It had to be the Protection Stone. The pull of its power invited her to take it, feel it, bathe in its glory.

"Why do I not believe that it should be here?" she asked Torin, extending a hand toward the glow.

"You took the words out of my mouth," he said, his voice laced with pessimism. He grabbed a hold of her hand. Her hand fought to reach out for it and pluck it from where it sat.

She turned to him. "How can this still be here? Even after the amount of people who died to protect it, it can't be. Is it the right one?"

A muscle in his jaw tightened. His hand gripped her tighter, dragging her closer to him. "Maybe the Stone is protected somehow, guarded with magic like the room above us."

Maybe a demon couldn't touch it. Perhaps the darkness in her blood would stop her from touching it. But then why would the elemental door deem her worthy enough to open it?

"Something doesn't feel right in my gut," she told Torin. "But I have no doubt that it is one of the Stones of the Gods. Should we take it and get out of here?"

Torin held a hand out like he was testing how close he could get to the stone. Instead of touching it directly, he swept up the fabric beneath it and bundled the relic inside. He handed the silk to Emara. "If this is the Protection Stone, I want you to hold it. It is the Protection Stone for a reason, right?"

Before Emara could protest, she heard Artem cry out, his loud voice carrying all the way to them.

"Go!" Torin lunged at Emara and pulled her along with him as he hurled up the steep stone steps.

By the time they reached the top, her legs burned just as much as her lungs. Her magic was awake again, frantic beneath her skin. She could see blades stabbing and killing at unknown evils. Breighly, in her wolf form, was entangled with a huge creature with crimson eyes.

Emara sent out a blast of air in her friend's direction. It rushed through the room and collided with them, giving Breighly enough time to scramble away, whining.

Torin set to work, driving his swords through the first thing that moved in their direction. From what Emara could see in the dark, there weren't that many demons, but they were huge winged beasts like the ones that devastated the uplift. Emara ripped the fire from her veins and threw it across the room. It hit one demon, burning it alive, and its screech sent a sharp dizziness through Emara's skull.

She fought to keep herself upright, its dying screams still ringing in her ear.

"We need to get out of this room," Artem called. He threw a knife into the back of a demon that had been trying to work its claws into Breighly's vital organs. Breighly took that opportunity to sink her teeth into its neck and rip it open.

Emara flinched.

"Get Emara to the door," Torin yelled as another bat-like demon dropped to the floor. Torin wasted no time hacking at limbs and wings until he could get a clear shot at its heart.

Its gaze found Emara as it died, and she could have sworn it smiled at her, revealing rows of sharp teeth. A chill crawled all over her body, pushing fear from her stomach into her throat.

"Everyone, retreat. Now! This room has us all caged like sitting ducks," Torin roared as he neared the door. Artem pulled Emara away from the dead creature. "We have the relic, now we need to get back out of here."

A sudden sound stilled everyone, even the beasts behind them. Torin looked at Artem as Emara glanced at Breighly.

Arlo Stryker's face appeared in the threshold of the door, his cheeks flushed. "Gideon's unit have just sounded their horn."

CHAPTER FORTY-FIVE
GIDEON

Gideon raced through the temple with his team at his heels. Every few strides he would look back to see if Sybil was keeping pace with the hunters. And she was. Gideon had to get to the other team. He was the quickest, so he would reach them first. He just hoped it wouldn't be too late.

He sprinted ahead, trying to conjure up the temple map in his mind. He took a sharp left down a hallway, his hunting boots pounding the stunning blue marble floor. Taking another quick turn, he landed in a huge congregational room. A chill hit him, bringing him to a stop. He pulled an arrow from his quiver and nocked it, ready for something to jump out at him.

Pews sat low to the ground and multi-coloured cushions littered the space. This was where the greats of the kingdom would have kneeled to worship centuries ago. There was a strangeness about how they were scattered across the room. Although he couldn't see any bodies, there was certainly a sign of a struggle.

Walking through the middle section of the messy prayer pillows, Gideon released a breath. It swirled into the air, reminding him of training in the winter months. It shouldn't have been so cold. Something dark was close. Every hunting instinct he ever had sprung to attention, and the deep-rooted itch to fight stirred in his blood.

Footsteps and panting breaths told Gideon without looking

around that the others had caught up. He turned for a moment, knowing Marcus would cover him, and his eyes found her. Her cheeks were flushed from running and her hair had managed to form its own pattern on her head, loose curls dangling everywhere. Her beautiful big eyes looked at him with fear. Sybil's magic would be ringing through her bones. She still clutched the paper they had found, her knuckles strained white. A moment passed between the two of them, so many things unsaid. They might have run out of time to say everything that lingered between them.

"Whatever happens, if I tell you to run, you run," Gideon whispered to Sybil, and his voice was raspier than he could control. She nodded back at him. Reluctantly, he looked to Marcus. "Marcus, when we get out of the temple, I need you to take her out of here. Find a place and stay low for a few days."

"Gideon—" Marcus tried to reason.

"Being second-in-command, it's all I ask of you," Gideon intercepted. "She comes first."

Gideon realised he would do anything to keep her safe, and it went above and beyond just the guardianship. His heart felt things for Sybil that a guard's heart shouldn't feel.

Movement behind a pillar caught his eye, and Gideon aimed his arrow toward it. Before he could see a face, he saw two familiar swords. With a sharp exhale, he lowered his bow.

"Torin," he breathed, relief filling his lungs.

His brother strolled out from behind the column and stood in front of an altar. He looked untouched by battle, and that was a good sign. His icy blue gaze found Gideon. "I need you to take your men and leave."

Gideon's brow pulled down as his brother stood in front of him, unmoving. "Why would you have me leave? Did you get what we came for? We sounded the horn because—"

"You must take my command and leave."

"Torin, you know I am not going anywhere. I am your second-in-command; I am with you until the end."

"You must leave," Torin roared, and his body was so rigid that he almost looked in pain.

Was he hurt?

Gideon stilled.

Torin's gaze pierced him like a dagger. "You do as your commander asks, Warrior."

Gideon shifted on his feet. "Where is Emara?" he asked. Why was Torin alone?

Torin stepped closer, his large body travelling with sleek ableness. "She is outside in the temple gardens."

"And did you obtain the Stone?" he asked again.

"I have left the relic with her."

A crawling feeling spread over Gideon's spine, and his fingers twitched around his bow. "Torin, what colour is the stone in Emara's engagement ring?"

His brother's head tilted and a cruel smile spread across his lips. "Red."

"Wrong."

Sybil screamed as the arrow penetrated the arm of the knight pretending to be his brother. Gideon released another arrow, but the demon veered to the side.

It was the highest kind of demon if he could take the form of his commander. It had been so convincing in its image of Torin, but everything else had been...off.

A knife flew past Gideon, but it didn't make it into its flesh. Instead, the knight caught it.

Marcus hissed a curse.

"Warriors of Thorin are my favourite kind of flesh to devour," the demon hissed, sending pain into Gideon's head. He tried to fight it. "It's always a pleasure to rip your bones apart."

"Get Sybil out of here, Marcus," Gideon demanded. The demon began to shed Torin's skin, changing into something more horrific. Gideon took a step into the challenge. "Now. Go!"

He aimed for the demon's head, but it dove to the side and the arrow hit its shoulder instead. The beast roared as it ripped out the arrow from its flesh, and the dark smoke of its power morphed into something bigger and more terrifying. Its face ripped open, spilling dark gore down the tunic it wore. As Gideon released another arrow, a dagger flew past his face. Kellen threw a small axe, but the demon was too quick. The axe hit off the altar and fell to the ground, the sound ringing through the place of worship.

The only way to kill this repugnant beast would be if he got closer. Kellen was behind him, and another throwing knife flew past Gideon's head to reach the demon before they did. The blade landed, wounding the nightmare creature in the leg. The creature reached down as it transformed human hands into claws and pulled the blade from its thick thigh. The demon threw it back, a cruel grin slashing across its face.

Gideon slammed into it, taking it to the ground. The disciple of Veles rolled, its strength unbelievable, and slammed a fist into Gideon's jaw. His skull cracked off the marble floor, and the creature shrieked above him as Gideon's mouth filled with blood. His mind rang, and the magic in his blood screamed to beat the thing that had just bested him. The knight pulled out a dagger from "Torin's" belt and slashed out, aiming for Gideon's throat. Before the steel touched his skin, a huge boot struck the knight in the side, kicking it off of Gideon. The knight tried to get back to his feet, but Kellen ducked and rolled before slamming a short spear through its foot, nailing it to the ground. A roar erupted from the beast, and its claws and fangs elongated in agony. One massive wing batted Kellen backwards and out of Gideon's sight.

Fear ran through him as the roar from the demon called in a few others. As he scrambled back, he realised they were surrounded. His men fought them viciously down the aisles, spilling blood on books meant for prayer.

I will not feel fear. I will not feel fear. I have war in my veins and battle in my blood. I will protect the Light.

The underworld knight looked to where he lay before plucking the small spear from his knee-high boot. Gideon reached for a small sword on his weapon belt, but the demon moved too rapidly. It knocked the weapon from his hand and curled its claws around Gideon's throat.

"A Blacksteel crest on your tunic," the demon hissed. The pungent scent of sulphur caused bile to rise in Gideon's stomach. "I came across a Blacksteel once." Its otherworldly voice sent waves of pain through his mind, but he tried to block it out. His years of training were for these moments. "A Warrior of Thorin called Viktir Blacksteel. They said he was the best of his kind, yet he couldn't best me when I killed his father before him." Its crimson eyes lit full of dreadful delight. "I bet if you told him my name, the fire of fear would ignite in his weak eyes."

"Fuck you," Gideon spat as the creature smiled down at him with blades and blades of teeth.

Its serpent-like tongue slithered from its mouth, and its huge wings cocooned around him. "Once I am done feasting on the blood of a Blacksteel, I am going to drink from the heart of the pretty little redhead you were so keen on protecting—if my brothers of the dark haven't finished her off already."

"If you touch her, I will fucking kill you." Gideon thrashed under him, "I will rip the wings from your back and feed you them as you beg for mercy."

"That will be hard, little warrior"—the creature lowered itself onto Gideon so that its mouth was in his eyeline—"if you're dead."

The creature lunged, mouth wide, rows and rows of needle-sharp teeth ready to devour—

A sword sliced through the higher demon's mouth and almost touched Gideon's nose.

Gore sprayed onto his face, and a strangled sound cut the demon's vocal cords.

Torin stood above him and somehow managed to throw the demon's body across the room like it was a sheet of paper instead of a massive beast. "Don't ever try to impersonate me again, you vile fuck."

Torin dragged his focus back to his brother and held out a hand for Gideon to take. Gideon stood on trembling legs. "Do you have any idea how close you were to my face with that fucking sword? You almost cut my nose clean off."

Torin rolled his eyes, blood covering his face and sword. "Why does everyone question my impeccable accuracy? You should know better, brother. I am very disappointed that you would even doubt me."

Even though Gideon couldn't believe that Torin always had time to jest in a full-scale battle, he needed to see his brother's real smile. Gideon lunged at him and wrapped his arms around Torin. "You are right. He was never handsome enough to be a Blacksteel. I should have known."

Torin slapped his brother's back. "Too right. You can't mimic our genes no matter how powerful you are."

They pulled back as Emara blasted two smaller winged creatures with air and Breighly jumped at them, ripping them apart with her teeth. Fire blasted across the room in scorching white heat as Emara whirled around to cremate the final few demons in the room.

"I can see your wife has arrived." Gideon smiled at his commander.

"Brilliant, isn't she?" Torin's gaze softened for a fraction of a second as he watched Emara's magic devour the last of the demons.

"This place is crawling with demons. We need to go," Artem said, a lower demon still hanging from his axe. He shook it off. "We don't need to win this battle when we have won the Stone."

Emara smiled at him with black gore spattered across her face and darkness in her eyes, looking like a true warrior. "That's the smartest thing I have ever heard you say."

"I have my moments." Artem grinned, and even Breighly snuffed a laugh in her wolf form. She shook blood off her coat and sauntered up beside them.

The Empress of Air looked towards Torin. "Let's quit whilst we are ahead, *Commander*. We got what we came here for. Let's not risk anything else if we don't need to. Take me home."

Torin took her hand and dragged her off to find their way out.

But Gideon was left feeling like this couldn't be the end, especially not after Kellen's vision.

"Wait," Gideon yelled. "Kellen has something he needs to tell you."

CHAPTER
FORTY-SIX
TORIN

With Emara's hand in his, Torin stood at the top of the temple steps looking down at a bloodthirsty army. Kellen's words ran through his mind over and over again. *"I saw Balan. Here. The King of the Underworld is here."*

But the King of the Underworld was locked in a cage. The vision had to be wrong.

Emara's hand tightened on his own as his gaze finally fell upon the giant portal that hovered like a dying star between the gates of the temple and their exit. It swirled like a maddened galaxy, blowing apart the garden's shrubbery, sending leaves and twigs into the air. His heart fell still and fear for his wife spread thick in his veins. He had never seen a portal from the underworld, only the disgusting creatures that crawled from it. They were unusual to catch, normally only open for a few moments to let demons rush into his world. But this one was huge, pulling the air around them, commanding it into chaos.

No elemental magic surrounded the portal, only dark energy that looked like it could be the soul of Veles himself. Bubbles of blackness festered as sparks of power burst from within it. It oozed death and destruction. Torin raised his chin, showing no fear to the army whose crimson gazes were hungry for blood.

He could hear daggers being pulled from their sheaths, the promise of a battle in the silence of the space.

He could feel Breighly's magic urging her to devour them. He could feel Artem itching to sink his axe into the demons' skulls. He could hear the stretching of Gideon's bow beside him, ready for release. He could feel Emara's magic radiating from her like a beacon. But they all waited for his instruction. He let go of Emara's hand and unsheathed his second sword and swaggered down a few steps. He picked out the biggest bastard he could find in the crowd of demons. He wanted his swords to bathe in the blood of the biggest fucker there.

"Are you going to let us through the gardens peacefully, or are you going to feel my steel corrupt your pathetic skulls?"

The madness that he knew glittered in his eyes began working its way through his veins, brewing a storm of violence in his heart. They were outnumbered, like always, but that didn't mean it was a losing battle. Gods only knew how many Emara could wipe out with her power, and the normally peaceful witch standing beside her had a glint in her eyes that promised death. He knew how capable his clan was; he wasn't worried.

"Since none of you answered my question, I guess death is on your spirit cards today." He winked at Emara before he jumped off the steps and planted his sword in the skull of a lower demon. In the same breath, he swung his right arm and decapitated another one.

Before its head hit the ground, the promised chaos erupted around him. As he sliced through another two demons, arrows and steel began flying through the air, taking out the army around him.

His clan was on the move.

Battle cries ruptured the air, and the smell of death and blood was no longer on the horizon, but in front of him. Soldiering forward, he took down four demons with brute strength, stabbing his swords through their hearts. Spinning to stand, he saw a demon running at him. Before he could pin it and make the kill, flames engulfed the demon.

Torin had never felt heat like it before. Emara's power was undeniable, a rage of wind whipping around her as her palm glowed with fire. Still safe on the stairs, she sent out another blast of flames and wiped out a full line of demons in Torin's path.

He was so utterly proud of her. She was making her title her own. She was anything she wanted to be, and he loved that about her.

She gave him a look that sprinkled shivers all over his spine.

She was so dangerous, an ultimate weapon.

Her mystical eyes left his face and she pulled on her magic once more, sending fire across the gardens to a new target.

Torin reluctantly turned away from her and noted a wolf diving and ducking, slicing through the army with her fangs. Artem Stryker was just behind her, ending anyone who came close to her. Gideon fired arrows from beside the earth witch, who was still on the steps, pulling on her magic to create vines from the ground. The vines wormed their way around the demons' legs, rooting them to the spot, making them easy targets, or pulling them to the ground. Arlo was fighting closely with Kellen, and Torin could see how united they had been in the Selection with how synchronised their movements were. A single heartbeat later, he felt a thrumming power radiating behind him. He turned to face a demon. He was ancient, clad in battle regalia. This creature was no minion. He had the features of a human man and the build of a warrior. Torin recognised the pointed features and crimson eyes immediately.

He had come face to face with him before.

He was the same knight that had put a demon blade in Gideon's arm, almost killing him in the Blood Moon battle. The bastard was born and bred in darkness, and its power reeked from its core.

"It's a shame that you have lived so long only to die in a battle such as this one," Torin taunted. The knight's vile lips parted to show rows of black teeth that had been sharpened into lethal points, and his tongue swished over his lips like he could already taste Torin's blood.

"You are blind, Warrior of Thorin," the demon sneered. "The Light Gods have given you such a false purpose."

Torin twirled the sword in his right hand. "Oh, and what would that be?"

"To think that you could find happiness with the daughter of Balan." Torin's heart stilled in his chest. "She does not belong to the Light, but to the Darkness." The demon's words were a blow to Torin's heart. "She will not be with you long, son of Clan Blacksteel." The knight's crimson eyes were unfaltering on Torin's face. "She will return with us to where she belongs."

"That's where you're wrong." Torin raised his swords again. "And I am just about to show *you* how blind you are if you think that I am going to let anyone or anything come between us." He shot the creature a dangerous smirk of his own. "I will tell your fucking Dark God that myself."

Torin moved quickly, but he knew a demon of that calibre would be able to anticipate his move, so he didn't strike him yet.

He had a secret weapon.

Kellen Blacksteel thrust out from behind the demon, severing an arm.

So much satisfaction thrilled through Torin's bones when shock lit up the creature's blood-red eyes. It was then that Torin moved, severing the arm that held the weapon intended to end his life. As Torin swung for the head, Kellen stabbed through the heart. The surprise was still lingering on the knight's face as its head rolled from its body and hit the ground.

"Well done, Baby Blacksteel." Torin nodded.

"Now that I have helped kill a knight of the underworld twice in one battle, does that mean I have earned the right to never be called that again?"

Torin felt his lip turn up at the corner. "Never. You will always be the baby." But Torin could see the satisfaction of the kill in Kellen's eyes, and it was beautiful to see him happy even if it was just for a moment.

A rumble vibrated through the grounds. Shrubbery was uprooted, and a scream came from Sybil as her vines were tugged out and broken. Lightning flashed and thunder broke from the portal. Even the demons stood still as a vicious wind pulled through the trees, making them tremble. It was not the air of the empress that was tearing through the kingdom, but the wrath of the underworld. Dark tendrils of smoke poured from the underworld's portal, reaching for Emara. Torin pushed her back from the grip of the underworld's claws. He heard Gideon roar, but he couldn't make it out as the winds whipped his ears numb and a piercing sound breached the night sky.

Emara tried to pull at Torin's back, but he rooted his feet into the ground and watched as the darkness filtered out into his world like poisonous snakes that were ready to strike.

He would not let them take her.

One of the dark tendrils struck for Emara and Torin jumped in front of her, cutting through the mist with his sword. A terrible, insufferable shriek split the air, pushing Torin to his knees. His vision was cut off and then the world went black.

CHAPTER
FORTY-SEVEN
EMARA

Batting her eyelids open, the pain that pushed through Emara's head was unnatural. It was a dangerous song that sang only to her.

It was the portal and she knew it. The dark magic of the underworld was calling to her, yet she couldn't concentrate long enough to pull herself together and deny it. The brutal wind tugged at her lungs and shredded at her hair. The pain of its song called to her, and the power of the portal suffocated her.

Yet it was intoxicating.

"Emara!" Sybil screamed over the deafening noise that clashed with the wind. "Emara, you need to drown it out. You need to use your magic and drown it out. Listen for the Light of your magic."

A whisper as cold as frost and as cruel as Veles broke through the shrieks and called to her, *"Emaraaaaaa."*

It whistled her name again and again until a scream ripped through her throat and she clutched her head, pushing herself away from the portal.

"You need to tune it out, Emara." Sybil made it to her side, drowning in an agony of her own. Her healing magic hit Emara, trying to subdue the pain. "Shield yourself from the portal's darkness. Cast the Light elements around yourself, use your earth magic, heal the pain."

But she couldn't. It was too strong. The darkness of the portal was a magnet to her soul, a song to her ears, and it was calling her forward, pulling her in. The more she fought it, the more painful it became.

Sybil hit her with a wave of healing power again, and for a moment, Emara could breathe, a sweet reprieve from the dark power and pain in her head. The earth witch's small hand wound around hers, and her mass of red curls almost strangled her as the wind whipped at them.

"Keep calling to the element of earth, Emara," Sybil called. "I can feel it trying to help you."

She wobbled to her feet and watched the warriors who had set their lives on the line for this mission struggle to do the same, most of them holding their heads and screaming.

She turned back to the Empress of Earth. "You need to help them, Sybil. Use your earth magic to help them block out the darkness taking their minds. You don't need to help me anymore, now save them."

Sybil's vast green eyes blinked away a few tears of her own and then threw out her hands to send a blast of healing powers over the men.

Emara's eyes flew to Torin, who was writhing in agony on the ground a good bit away from her, a silent scream on his lips.

He was in so much pain, but she could stop it. All she had to do was listen to the earth call to her.

A crack of thunder from above startled her still. Another rumble crashed through the air, and before Emara could get to Torin, a figure appeared at the portal's entrance.

Emara collapsed to the ground again.

It was not one but three knights of the underworld, the most ancient beings she had ever seen.

She froze as more tendrils of darkness followed the momentous figures out of the portal to stand just before Torin's prone body.

Emara heard a roar from Gideon that sent a coldness into her spine. "Come for me," he begged. "Me. Leave him. Leave my brother." Emara's heart cracked as she witnessed Gideon desperately trying to get to his feet. He roared again and again. "Leave my brother." He staggered, finally standing.

But the knights didn't falter in their stride towards her husband.

As her trembling legs finally allowed her to stand, an arrow flew towards the three knights. A scream left Gideon's throat as he tried to run towards them. Dark mist swirled into a huge vine, mimicking Sybil's, and tied itself around his throat and torso.

Fear turned into rage as Emara watched the most powerful creatures she had ever laid eyes on stalk towards the man she loved. The man who had saved her time and time again. The man who had put her before any oath, before his own life.

She blasted every ounce of fire she could towards them. Her hand shook as the strength of her magic poured from her soul out of her body. One of the knights cast up a hand that seemed to block every element she threw at them. They were getting closer to Torin, and Gideon's roars had turned into cries. The tendrils of darkness swirled up, pushing around the necks of everyone she loved.

"Stop!" she roared. "Stop. Stop hurting them. Stop. I have something you want. I will give you anything."

As she roared, it seemed the screeching of the dark portal listened to her and the pain ceased. Grunts and groans of relief spread through the clan and the darkness eased up a little. She was dizzy with relief and she had to stop herself from swaying.

A knight with long dark hair looked up to Emara and let a dreadful grin play on his face.

I will give you anything.

She shuddered and tried to square her shoulders. "I am the one you want, not him."

His dark red eyes moved from her face and found his target —Torin.

"No!" she roared again, and it echoed through the kingdom— through the universe.

They didn't look her way again.

The fighting started again, but she blocked out all the roars from the demons as she ran towards Torin. He had gotten to his feet and readied himself to take on all three knights.

He would never survive that.

Fear ran too close to her heart and she batted it down. There was no place for fear here, only bravery and skill.

A shadow reached for her, and she stabbed at it with her spear. Two breaths later, she ignited it in flames. It sent up screams to the stars, but she didn't care.

Two lesser demons caught her attention as they jumped to attack Kellen, who was still struggling with the dark vines. Before the demons could land a blow, she blasted them with her element, knocking them on their asses.

She had to ration the magic in her and keep it for what she was about to come up against. Reaching the knights of the underworld, she threw out both hands and let her fire burn. One of them ducked into a roll and recovered on the other side of her flames, and another landed on top of Torin, toppling them both to the ground. The third one had evaporated into nothing.

"Behind you," Torin managed to yell as he fought off the demon.

Emara swivelled, but she was too late.

The demon's fist crashed into her head. The sharpest pain she'd ever felt knocked the air from her lungs and she fell into darkness.

CHAPTER
FORTY-EIGHT
TORIN

A visceral rage stabbed through Torin's heart.

That evil prick had just punched Emara so hard she had fallen, her body lying in the hands of his greatest enemy. A carnal snarl ripped from his throat, a promise that he was going to kill every last fucking one of them.

He punched the knight that he was still wrestling with, striking its face. He stunned it long enough to reach for a dagger, and as he withdrew it from his belt, he threw his head forward to stun the knight again, breaking its nose. Torin stabbed his knife into the dark heart of his enemy, but that wouldn't do.

He needed more.

Torin straddled the knight, holding him in place as gore spilled onto his arms and hands. Before he could even register the satisfaction of its death, he reached out and grabbed the sword he had lost during the scuffle. Spinning on his knees again, he sliced his blade through the legs of the second knight. Torin stood and took its head clean off its shoulders.

As his attention turned to Emara, he realised that she hadn't been knocked out for long. The knight's huge hand had wound around her throat and his other gripped her waist. The wicked shine in its eyes said that the monster loved every single second it could force Torin to witness someone else touching her.

"Remove your hands from her neck and I will let you live long enough to go through the portal to tell your king that he is a fucking coward."

A slight grin appeared on the knight's face as its grip tightened around Emara's throat. She didn't have the air in her lungs to even scream, but her eyes went wide with panic.

Torin raised his sword.

"*Dooon't,*" its ancient voice poured like poison from its mouth, stabbing into his head. "*Don't take another steeeep.*"

The sounds of the battle ending around him meant that his men were either victorious or dead, but. he couldn't take his eyes from Emara's long enough to see which it was. She was terrified, her irises almost black.

"It's going to be okay, angel," he whispered to her. "It's okay. I am here. I won't let anything happen to you."

"*She is no angel.*" The otherworldly voice of the demon pierced into his skull, making it hard to remain standing. "*She has demon blood. She is one of usssss.*"

Seeing his fingers dig into Emara's hip and drag her into his chest further sent a flare of absolute undiluted fury through every part of him. Torin struggled to remain calm, to even see clearly through his blistering rage. "Look at me when I say this, you worthless demon fuck. I am going to be your end. Take. Your. Fucking. Hands. Off. Of. Her."

The knight did not react to his threat. Instead, he said, "*Take the ssstone from your binding and put it through the portal.*" He placed his mouth to Emara's skin, kissing her neck. "*Or I take herrrr with me to the underworld.*"

His blood boiled, threatening to erupt. A silver wolf had stalked to his side, her teeth gnashing, ready to rip the demon's throat out. Blood dripped from her mouth, and the fierceness of her face was something terrifying.

"*If anyone attackssss, you will kill her too, for she shields my vessellll.*" The knight's eyes slid from Torin to the wolf and then to anyone who had gathered behind him. "*You know you can't get to me without going through her firsssst, Torin Blacksteellllll.*"

He hated the sharp pain his voice caused. He hated his hands on her body, his mouth at her neck. He hated that the demon was right. He couldn't get to her with the way he had shielded his own body with hers.

Scum.

Coward.

Bastard.

"Stand down," was the only warning shot he sent to his clan.

The demon seemed to smile at that, knowing that he had gotten an advantage. "*Drop the pretty sssstone in the portal.*"

"Don't do it, Torin," Emara rasped, the fear in her eyes making him want to ruin the world. "They won't kill me. I will find my way back to you."

A growl left Breighly and a cry could be heard from Sybil.

"Over my fucking dead body will I let you go to the underworld."

"Trust me," Emara rasped again.

She would sacrifice herself for everyone here. She couldn't trust them, regardless of her bloodline.

He wasn't going to lose her. They had just begun their life together; they were just finding happiness.

"That...is not an option." A rumble broke through the sky again, and a flash of lightning struck over Torin as he spoke.

"You are not going to the underworld." His brother's voice sounded strangled, but Torin was relieved when he agreed with him. "We would rather die than watch that happen."

"*That could be arranged, Hunter,*" the knight cooed, his hand tightening around Emara's neck enough to make her choke.

"I will fucking end you and everything you stand for." Torin went to move toward him, but someone caught his arm. He guessed it was Sybil, as a calming energy wrapped around his blinding rage.

"Drop the Stone in the portal, Torin," Kellen said. "Give them the stone. There are others, and we are on track to find them. But there are no other witches like her in the kingdom. She will be the new Supreme, I am certain of it. I can see her power in my visions. You can all feel it now. If they only came here for the Stone, then let them prove it. Give them the Protection Stone."

Kellen's words shook Torin to the core, and he could feel everyone's eyes on him.

She will be the new Supreme, I am certain of it.

Emara had never confirmed if she felt anything superior emerge. She had probably never wanted to acknowledge it, especially with everything that had been going on in her life. She had fought too hard to be here and she had led with more bravery than he ever had. There was no doubt in his mind that he would drop the fucking Stone straight into the portal to save her life, but he just didn't trust the deal. He had made deals before that hadn't turned out well for Emara. Flashes of Callyn Greymore's heart being ripped from her body flashed through his memory.

"If I place this in the portal," Torin started, "I need you to swear on Veles that you will not harm her." He pointed his sword at the demon as a promise of death should he break his word.

The knight smiled so cruelly. "Place the Stone in the portal and I promise not to harm the Daughter of Balan."

"No, Torin, don't trust him." Emara struggled against the hold of the demon.

But he couldn't keep looking at the demon gripping his wife while she bled from the blow to her face. He would do anything to have her in his arms, to know that she was safe and would live another day.

He stepped towards the portal that swirled like galaxies of

cruelty. A few gasps from his clan travelled through the air as he cut the silk cloth that held the stone. Torin took one look at his wife in the arms of a demon knight and threw the Protection Stone into the portal.

CHAPTER
FORTY-NINE
EMARA

The portal crackled sounds of imminent death. Torin's inky hair was blown away from his face by the sheer power. Emara watched him with tears spilling onto her cheeks as he took a few steps back, a hand shielding his eyes as the greedy portal swallowed the Stone whole.

No, no, no! What had he done?

Torin turned, his gaze on the demon. "Now let her go." The scar on his forehead was now under a full scowl, and his cheekbones were sharper than the blade in his hand. "Now!" he roared, taking a step in Emara's direction.

The clan on the other side of the gardens readied themselves once more, moving into a battle stance.

"Release the Empress of Air," Artem Stryker said, stepping forward and removing a second axe from his belt, "and we will let you live."

Just as the knight of the underworld loosened his grip on her neck, a boom travelled from somewhere deep in the portal. A flash broke through the gardens, and everyone shielded their eyes. Vibrations rocked the earth, and everyone stumbled.

As Emara regained her vision, she saw a colossal man standing face to face with Torin. Her legs gave out, and the only thing that kept her from hitting the ground was the hand that was still around her neck. She would recognise that face anywhere. She had slept with the portrait of it under her pillow since she had found it as a child.

Emara had never understood why her grandmother protected her from the truth of who her father was. Now she did.

Theodora had been protecting her from this moment, from this fate, from seeing in the flesh the man who had fathered her. She had been protecting her from seeing the cruel creature that her mother had given up her life to banish to the underworld.

The King of the Underworld had obtained the Stones he needed to escape his cage, and destiny had brought darkness and air together again.

Her mother had died for nothing. Her mother only used two of the relics to bind him in the underworld, but Emara was never sure which ones.

Dizziness consumed her.

Balan, King of the Nine Hells, looked down at the Commander of the Blacksteel Hunting Clan.

But Torin, as bold as the temple that stood behind her in the darkness of this storm, did not recoil. The wind pulled at his clothing and ripped at his hair, and the blood of the beasts that he had slayed dripped down his face, arms, and tunic.

He lifted his chin and squared his shoulders as the most dangerous creature in the whole of the universe looked through him. "Too long have you sat watching from the darkness. Too long have you had your dark underlings destroy on your behalf. It's good to finally see the coward that calls himself the king come out from behind the veil."

Everyone was so deathly still and so violently silent.

Emara's heart was screaming and battering against her ribcage.

Torin pushed out his chest with that Blacksteel confidence as he warmed up the swords in his hands. "If you defile our lands to seek out relics you are not worthy of taking, you better bring your worst, *Dark King.*"

The Dark King's smile made Emara's skin want to slither inside of her bones just to avoid being present. The knight that still held her began laughing as the earth began to shake again.

In the shadows of the portal was a serpent's head, larger than any demon she had ever laid eyes on. It slithered onto the hallowed grounds, and Emara heard the screams of the ancestors that lived in the veil between worlds.

CHAPTER FIFTY
EMARA

Arrows from Gideon's bow sank into the serpent's flesh, and an array of knives hurled towards the beast from the remaining clan members.

But Emara was still, unable to move as she witnessed such a creature enter her world. It was easily the most terrifying thing she had ever been in proximity to, something from her darkest nightmares and deepest fears mixed together. The things that came from that portal just kept getting worse.

And as Balan smiled again, he spoke in a tongue so ancient that Emara didn't understand it. The serpent snapped forward just as Torin took a swing at Balan. Emara's heart almost stopped entirely. She kicked back and made contact with the knight's shin, and he finally let go of her throat. Emara spied a ruby that twinkled at her on the ground just below her. She flicked her hand and the earth where the Agnes lay exploded, tossing the weapon into the air. With her arms still bound by the shadows, she caught the spear horizontally in her mouth and bit down hard on the ruby. The blade fired out, and she whipped her head to the side. The blade penetrated the knight's heart, finally freeing her of its grip. Without taking a moment to breathe, she turned on the demon, palms already blazing with fire, and scorched it alive.

But that wasn't enough. She hurled air at it and swung Agnes at its neck, taking its head off through the flames.

Finally, she took a second to breathe and gather herself.

She had just killed a knight of the underworld.

"That was utterly breathtaking, Empress," Kellen Blacksteel said as her gaze met with his unusual eyes. "What a kill."

She bowed her head to him. "I hope to do this clan proud."

Kellen darted off, hurling another knife. It landed between the serpent's eyes, but a small hunting knife wasn't going to make a dent in such a huge beast. Emara had used a lot of her fire and the majority of her air magic, but she felt another element bubbling under her skin.

Earth thrummed in her veins, and as the beast hurtled towards Breighly, Emara brought forth everything she could feel and slammed her hand into the ground. The earth beneath everyone's feet rattled and groaned, and the serpent paused, rocking with everyone else. Emara's eyes met Sybil's, and for a short moment, the earth witch smiled a grin that Emara had never seen before. Together, they were an unbelievable strength. Together, they could use earth to win.

Sybil conjured four massive vines that rose into the air like serpents of her own. Torin and Artem continued to battle with Balan, but everyone else stilled as the redheaded witch slammed her magic into the serpent. Her vines snatched around it and it growled, its teeth snapping at the indestructible vines. It let out a roar that could have deafened everyone around it.

The Empress of Earth closed her eyes and Emara followed her lead. They gathered their magic together, pulling from the gardens around them. As earth called to her, stealing the breath from her lungs, Emara slammed her hand into the ground.

The world shook.

Cracks began to form, and Breighly was the quickest to jump out of the way, followed by the surviving hunters. The ground opened in a huge fissure that was travelling directly to the serpent still struggling against Sybil's vines, which had only multiplied. Emara bellowed, feeling the magic in her blood take over and push through her boundaries. The ground wedged open wider, and the serpent struggled to stay above the earth. The land began to tumble into the open ground, falling into an abyss below the surface. The monster clung to the broken gravel, and Emara smiled as she stood. Sybil's hand moved in a command to the vines to drag the beast into the abyss, and the demon screeched as it fell into the blackness forever.

In a rage, Balan threw out a hand at Artem Stryker, and a tendril of darkness threw him through the air and pinned him to the ground. A whine left Breighly as she ran to his side. Emara couldn't look away as three more tendrils of dark magic broke from Balan's hands and made their way to Torin. It worked its way around Torin's sword like a snake and disarmed him. Torin tried to punch out, but before he could hit the mist, the dark tendril dove through Torin's chest.

The whole kingdom spun.

Gasps and screams whirled around in the wind. Silence filled Emara's ears as she witnessed Torin choke and spit blood from his mouth. His eyes found hers, and horror took over all sense as she screamed. Air exploded through the gardens and fire soared from her palms, but Balan dodged every unruly flame. The vines followed her as she walked towards him.

This wasn't happening. This couldn't happen.

The earth trembled and trees began to topple. Little orbs floated around in the winds of terror that Emara had created, and murmurs from the ancestors sang through the temple grounds.

Torin roared and fell to the ground in agony. "Get her out of here, Gideon! I won't let her watch me die. Don't let her see me die."

Another dark tendril struck through Torin's torso, and his eyes bulged from his skull in pain. A third picked him up by the tunic and held him so that he was dangling in front of his clan.

Emara blasted the king with the last bit of magic that she could summon before her legs gave out. Gideon caught her and spat, "You fucking let my brother go. Take me. Have me."

Horror filled Emara's lungs, her veins, her heart. Her lips parted, but nothing formed. Her magic was trembling, her darkness building.

"Get...h-her out of here," Torin begged Gideon as blood dripped from his mouth.

A horrible cry left her mouth as she began running towards him.

Balan, with the most callous look she had ever seen, dropped him to the ground. She wondered how her mother could ever love such a creature. She slid to a halt and her knees hit the ground. She tried to see where Torin's blood was coming from, but her bones were shaking and her vision was blurry. She quickly wiped her tears, knowing this wasn't the end. She could heal him, couldn't she?

"Torin," she called as her blood-stained hands found his face. "Stay with me. Sybil!" she screeched, her voice ripping her throat apart.

He was pale, so pale.

No, no, no.

This wasn't happening again.

"Go, angel. L-leave," he said as his hands tried to find hers. He was struggling to keep his ocean eyes open, and his lashes were wet with tears.

Dying. He was dying. Torin was dying.

She grabbed a hold of his tunic, and with strength that she had no idea she had, she ripped it open to find two huge wounds.

Oh Gods, oh Gods.

Vomit was crawling up her throat and the cold feeling of death was skating across her skin.

She could feel the spirits of the Otherside watching her as she struggled to breathe. "Torin, please, please," she called to him—or maybe to the Gods. "Please. I need you. You won't die. You can't. I need you."

"Angel." He tried to place a hand to her face, but he was too weak. He was beginning to shake. "Save yourself."

A roar erupted from her, and the whole temple grounds quaked again. Even Balan took a step back. Sybil arrived and gripped Emara's hand. "Emara, listen to me. You need to focus if you want to heal him. Block everything else out."

She tried, but her blistering rage sought revenge and carnage. It consumed everything, even her pain.

"Emara, there is darkness coming from your hands," Sybil announced. "That will not save him. You need to focus on the Light of your healing magic."

A small scoff came from the king. Emara glared at him, ready to end his life, the darkness building in her veins.

"Do you want to know the beauty of this moment?" Balan asked so calmly it made her want to burst into flames.

She let a fierce growl rip from her throat.

"I have the Immortality Stone. The Stone that I stole from your mother as she tried to end me can save his life."

Her mother had used the Immortality Stone and the Protection Stone to ensnare Balan in the underworld. Then why had she had the Resurrection Stone?

"No," Torin choked, gargling on a substance that Emara couldn't bear to name. "You—you w-will be fine without me."

She heard a cry from Gideon and a roar from Marcus.

Tears blinded her, but she placed her hands over his wounds, trying to pull back on the darkness and let the light in. "I am not letting you die. No. I am not letting you die."

Sybil chanted something under her breath, but Emara couldn't focus on what it was.

Torin somehow found the strength to pull her to his lips. She knew it was his way of saying goodbye. "Warriors never die, Emara. Their soul...their soul will always be a warrior. I will always look over you from the Otherside."

She cradled Torin's head in her arms. "You are going to be okay. You are not leaving me. You are not leaving me." She stroked the damp, dark hair from his eyes as her tears fell onto his face.

A bloody cough made its way up his throat, but he still tried his best to show her his dimples. "If I die protecting y-you, it was all worth it. You were worth everything." The glittering of his eyes faded slightly, the same way Callyn's did before she passed over. "Every sassy remark, every...elbow." He forced a smile. "Every kiss, every laugh. All of it. I would die over and over again just to see you smile one last time."

"Stop talking like that." Her tears splashed onto his bloody face and panic absolutely drenched her soul. "I am not going to lose you. You are the best thing to ever happen to me, and I need you alive. Even if you hate me for what I am about to do, I need you alive, Torin Blacksteel. I can't—I won't lose you." She turned to face Balan. The faces of her clan were pale and taut, and Kellen was weeping as Arlo Stryker tried to hold his hand through the tendrils of darkness that rooted them where they stood. "I will do it," she choked. "I will do what you want. Anything. But I need the Immortality Stone to save him and I need your word that you will give me it."

"No, Emara," Torin coughed out, and she gripped him tighter. Balan smiled. "No. Emara, no," Torin spat out, trying to move. "Please a-angel, live. Live...without me."

Choking on a cry of her own, she gathered enough strength to ignore the man that she loved more than herself. "I am not stupid," she cried. "I know he's dying and I know that is what you want." She gripped into the ripped pieces of Torin's tunic.

"Artem, if Gideon can't c-convince her, you need to," Torin hissed, his breathing laboured. "Do not let her make...any...deals."

"Brother." Artem's voice was soft and pleading.

Moments. She had moments left. Seconds.

"Name your price, *Balan,* and I will pay it," she roared. "I will do anything."

Artem Stryker cursed.

Balan moved towards her, and she lifted a bloody palm into the air and ignited her darkness. It swirled around her fingertips, waiting to be released.

The King of the Underworld halted causally, knowing he had won. "Your payment will be that you will become the Princess of the Underworld, the Empress of Darkness, and follow me into the nine realms. You are the key to it all. You will be the queen of it all one day."

You are the key to it all.

Cally had said the same thing, but in a completely different way. The way Balan said it sent the most vile shivers through her.

She could see it now, her two worlds unfolding in front of her. If she stayed in the Light, she might lose Torin forever and still face the Dark Army anyway. But if she went with Balan now, maybe she could find a way to kill him herself.

She gritted her teeth. "Give me the Stone to ensure he lives and you have a deal."

"No," Torin begged. "Stop. Emara, s-stop. Let me go. I will always be with you."

She turned to look down at the only man that she ever loved as his blood spilled out around her knees. "I love you, Torin Black-steel. I love you more than the moon loves the stars," she whispered as she lowered her mouth to his and placed a delicate kiss to his lips. It wasn't enough, but his life was so fragile that he couldn't take any more. "And I will find my way back to you, back home. I promise."

Emara could hear Gideon and Artem screaming in the background, restrained again by Balan's darkness. She could hear a howling wolf. As Balan, King of the Underworld, ordered her to rise, she did, blocking out everything else in the kingdom. She would do anything to save Torin. If Balan wanted her to play at being the Empress of Darkness, she would.

Before Torin could try and pull her back down, she filtered a light healing spell over him to put him into a sleep. His lids shut, and she hoped to the Gods that they would open once more when she was gone.

Balan smiled as she walked towards him and he pulled a silvery stone from his armour. She could feel the pull of its power calling to her like the others had, and as he held it up, she could see little souls swimming underneath the rock's surface.

"Place this over his heart and it will beat again. He will awake at dawn as an immortal solider, living as old as the trees if your Gods allow him." He threw the Stone at Sybil. "I will be back for that Stone, little Empress of Earth, and soon." He looked towards Emara. "Come with me, Empress of Darkness."

"Wait," she called out, her heart pounding. "When you return for the Stone, I need you to promise me that you will not harm a person standing here."

"Emara, Torin's not breathing," Sybil wept.

Emara's heart shattered. Her gaze flicked to her father, but before she could say anything to him about not keeping his end of the bargain, he said, "Give it a moment."

Emara's eyes darted back to Sybil, who had her hand over Torin's chest and the Stone on his heart. Even one second was too long to wait, and the pain that drove through her heart was enough to bring her to the ground.

Sybil lifted her gaze and found Emara. "His pulse is faint, but it is there."

A sigh of relief not only swept through her, but the crowd too.

"Keep that Stone over the warrior's heart," Balan instructed. "You wouldn't want all of these deals to not be worth it."

Rage built up in Emara, but he had a point. All of this couldn't have been for nothing. Balan turned, and a tendril of darkness pulled Emara with him.

Like her air, it wrapped around her entire body and swept her towards the portal. Taking one look back at her clan—her family—she whispered, "Look after him and tell him I am sorry." She looked to Gideon, who was as pale as snow, and Arlo with Kellen now in his embrace. Breighly stood alone, her eyes teary. "Look after each other. I will find my way back to you all, I promise."

Then she turned her back on them and vanished into the portal. Balan's tendrils clutched her hand as she travelled into a world of brutality and darkness to become empress.

EPILOGUE
TORIN

Torin felt a coolness wash over him. It was calming and relaxing. It was beautiful. But it was clearly magic; only magic could lure him into a false sense of security like this.

"I love you, Torin Blacksteel. And I will find my way back to you, back home."

Torin sat bolt upright. A scream left Sybil's lips as she jumped back. Gideon shouted too, but then he moved in towards him.

Gideon threw his arms over him. "Brother..." And his body sagged against his own.

"Torin..." Kellen kneeled beside him, and both of his brothers embraced him.

His body hurt, as did his head, but it was nowhere near how much his heart hurt.

But why?

"Where is she?" he breathed, replaying the last memory of her crying face. Torin looked at his brothers, who had pulled back from their embrace. "Where is Emara?" he asked them again. He placed a hand where the shadows of the Dark King had penetrated his soul.

He was healed.

Kellen fell back on his ass and ran a hand down his dirty face.

Gideon's lips were taut and his face pale. His unruly hair had been swept to one side, and there was a strain in his voice. "She's gone, brother."

Torin got to his feet so fucking quickly, dragging Gideon with him. "Gone?" He fisted his tunic, bringing Gideon up with him. "What do you mean gone?"

Flashes of remembrance flickered in his mind.

Him begging her, Emara's tears, the deal she wanted to make...

Gideon's eyes were lined with worry, and it looked like his lashes were sticky with tears. Torin's hand tightened around the tunic, scrunching it up to Gideon's neck. Artem placed a hand on his shoulder. "Hey, Tor? Why don't you come and sit down a minute?"

Torin dove towards him. "Sit down?" He grabbed Artem's tunic. "Sit down? You want me to sit the fuck down? Where is she?" he bellowed, feeling the tidal wave of rage about to breach the shore. It wasn't just a tidal wave, it was a fucking tsunami.

He had an overwhelmingly horrendous feeling that he knew where she was.

Gideon pulled him back and stood between them. "There was nothing we could do." His brother's green eyes were full of sorrow and rage. "But we will get her back. I promise you that."

"Get her back?" He almost wheezed as panic flooded into his bones, his knees too weak to keep him standing. "Please don't tell me..."

Unfiltered fear overtook his rage.

"No," he whispered as his world spun on its axis. "No, she hasn't...she isn't..."

It wasn't long before rage boiled the fear and served a plate of flaming-hot fury. He grabbed his brother again. "You let my wife, my whole fucking heart, go into the underworld alone?"

Gideon sucked in a breath.

"Fucking answer me."

"We had no choice," he breathed. "She wanted to save you. She would have done anything to save you and there was no stopping her without you both dying. I would have done anything—"

Torin broke away from Gideon and raced to where the gates had been clouded by a huge portal to the underworld. It was gone.

"No, no, no!" He halted as he realised that nothing was there but traces of blood that dripped into nothingness. "No!" he roared, and he swore the sky shuddered as it looked down on him. He spun, whirling on dizziness. "You two"—he pointed at his brothers—"you should have fucking let me die." He pushed Gideon and then Artem before heading to Kellen. He grabbed his littlest brother. "You should have fucking let me die. You know my life is worth nothing without her. You know she is everything, fucking everything." Torin's legs gave out, and Kellen tumbled to the ground with him. His youngest brother put his arms around him, holding him tight. "It should have been me. You should have let me die and saved her. I told you to always save her, always fucking save her. " A sob broke from his chest. "She is my wife, my soulmate. I will tear this fucking world apart to find her. My whole—my—"

Torin Blacksteel broke apart. Kellen said nothing as he held Torin in his arms, struggling to hold him up. Sybil sat down beside them, still covered in his blood, and placed a hand on Torin's cheek as he sobbed and sobbed.

"What do we do now?" Artem said.

Gideon ran a hand over his face. "It looks like we need to find a way into the underworld before my brother burns this kingdom to the ground."

ACKNOWLEDGMENTS

Firstly, I want to acknowledge anyone who has ever created a book pregnant. You are incredible. I found out I was pregnant during the curation of this book and WOW has it been the biggest test and struggle of my life. Not only was my motivation nowhere to be found, but by mind didn't feel like my own and it was a constant strain. But there got there! And that is the main thing. I tried really hard not to delay this book and get it into the hands of my readers. You are what matter.

Secondly, my readers...how have we got here together? Thank you for following my journey and continuing to invest in the world that I have built with you—for you. You amaze me every day. I thank you from the bottom of my heart.

To my Alpha Reader—Chanley—thank you for always being the first to pick up my world and throw yourself into fantasy. I know it's not completely your thing, but you have made it so. Your feedback is so appreciated.

To the AEOEAD Beta Reading Team, your comments have made me laugh, cry, and buzz all at once. Thank you for picking up on so many things that an author just can't. You absolutely rock!

TO HOUSE RAYNE, your efforts are untouched. I honestly wouldn't have anything without you. You are a bunch of unbelievable humans, and I am so proud to have you on my team. I love you guys.

To my mum, you are my Naya Blacksteel and Satan all wrapped into a 5ft 2 bow. I couldn't get through life without you.

To my husband—when I say I couldn't do this without you, I mean I couldn't do this without you. You pick up so much so that I can follow my insane characters into an oblivion. You are my soul-mate and best friend. I love you.

Jorja—my unpaid PA, and mini me, thank you for all the work you do from the unofficial photoshoots to the admin. It's always good to train you up hehe.

To the amazing indie authors, I have met along the way...

A.P Walston—you are a formatting life savour. Melissa Hawkes, I would have thrown in the towel at book one if you hadn't found me. RaeAnne, (Lavendersprose.editing) I would ramble in Scottish lingo without you. Thank you so much!

And with that being said, I am probably rambling, so again to my readers, keep talking about Emara, Torin, Giddy-boy and the team.

You are the best!

Stay tuned for book 4.

ABOUT THE AUTHOR

Noelle Rayne is the debut author of An Empress of Air and Chaos. An Empress of Fire & Steel is book two in her debut fantasy series, and An Empress of Earth and Darkness is book 3. She has an Honours Degree in Drama and lives in Ayrshire, Scotland. When she is not writing, she is binge watching supernatural TV shows, cuddling her fur baby or curling up with a good fantasy book under fairy-lights. *Or possibly doing all three at once.* She is obsessed with storms, glitter and all things witchy. If you like any of these things, I have a feeling you might like her books...

Printed in the USA
CPSIA information can be obtained
at www.ICGtesting.com
LVHW040419090923
757629LV00030B/498/J